Praise for *Under Your Skin*

"Durrant skillfully keeps the twisty story on track through convincing characters and domestic detail—right up to the shocking conclusion."

—*Publishers Weekly* (starred review)

"Meticulous and detail-laden, with plenty of red herrings. . . . Gaby proves an interesting central character. . . . Probably Durrant's best to date."

—*Kirkus Reviews*

"Recommended for fans of *Gone Girl* and of Lisa Unger's *Fragile*."

—*Booklist*

"A cunning murder mystery with some clever twists and turns that lead to a stunning ending."

—*Fresh Fiction*

"The book doesn't leave one moment for the reader to be bored and I couldn't put it down. Psychological thriller? That's putting it mildly. . . . Get yourself a copy, lock the door, and settle in for a ride you won't forget."

—*Night Owl Reviews*

"Gripping and utterly absorbing."

—*Curled Up with a Good Book*

UNDER YOUR SKIN

SKIN

A NOVEL

SABINE DURRANT

EMILY BESTLER BOOKS
—
WASHINGTON SQUARE PRESS

New York   London   Toronto   Sydney   New Delhi

WASHINGTON SQUARE PRESS
An Imprint of Simon & Schuster, Inc.
1230 Avenue of the Americas
New York, NY 10020

First Emily Bestler Books/Washington Square Press trade paperback edition April 2015

EMILY BESTLER BOOKS / WASHINGTON SQUARE PRESS and colophons are trademarks of Simon & Schuster, Inc.

For information about special discounts for bulk purchases, please contact Simon & Schuster Special Sales at 1-866-506-1949 or business@simonandschuster.com.

The Simon & Schuster Speakers Bureau can bring authors to your live event. For more information or to book an event, contact the Simon & Schuster Speakers Bureau at 1-866-248-3049 or visit our website at www.simonspeakers.com.

Designed by Kyle Kabel

Manufactured in the United States of America

10 9 8 7 6 5 4 3 2 1

ISBN 978-1-4767-1623-7
ISBN 978-1-4767-1628-2 (pbk)
ISBN 978-1-4767-1631-2 (ebook)

For G. S.

FRIDAY

I left the house earlier than usual this morning and, though it isn't exactly dark, it isn't yet light. The common is full of ghosts and shadows; the trees still ironclad, unyielding figures to the early gauze of spring; the bushes and brambles along the railway line knotted and clumped: a mugger's paradise, though I try not to think about that.

I take my usual route—over the bridge and round the soccer fields, pitches, churned into clods like a choppy sea. It's darkest where the path hits the corner, and there is an uncomfortable moment where you are hemmed in, rail cutting on one side, the adventure playground on the other. A blue anorak, sodden and draped, gives a creepily human form to a post, and my pace quickens until the path channels across the open grass toward the main road. The headlights of cars—commuters who need to be at work earlier than me, if such a thing were possible—rake the pavement. A shape comes toward me almost silently, another runner, a flash of headphone and Lycra, gone in a breath, a whiff of warmth and sweat. You are never alone in London, not in the dead of night, or even in the bone-cold chill of a predawn March morning. There is always the possibility of someone watching, following, seeing what you're up to. I'm not sure I like it.

It helps to run. The pace, the rhythm, the sensation of regular movement in my limbs help give order to my thoughts. I didn't sleep well last night. Even in the short snatches of unconsciousness I dreamed I was awake and anxious. In the end, I had to get up. I focus on my breath. In and out. In and out. I will run, try and sort things in my mind, and then once home, I will shower. Steve will be there to drive me to the studio at 7:00 AM. Kiss good-bye to Millie—Marta will give her breakfast. (Try to like Marta more.) Will I see Philip? Probably not. Already now it is—what, 5:15 AM?— he is showering, shaving, shaking off Nobu and the Dorchester (I smelled the cigars when he stumbled in at 3:00 AM), elbowing into all that spandex and peddling off on his brand-new carbon bike for Mayfair, Tokyo, Bloomberg. We used to run together. (Matching running tops, his and hers Asics. Is it pitiable to say I loved that?) But we haven't since last summer. With the city as it is, he says, he needs serious muscle feedback. He needs powerful resistance. Running, he says, doesn't come near reducing *his* stress.

My breath is ragged. I can feel it, hot, in my chest. It's all wrong; I'm not doing it right. I'm hopeless; I'm a person who can't even run properly. I turn up the central path, past the heartrending bench where someone ties a wreath ("MUM") at Christmas. It might help to filter out the facts first. Philip's parents: want an answer about Sunday lunch. Millie's pretend birthday: beg Philip not to miss this one. (How could he have not turned up on Tuesday?) The weekend in Brighton . . . Something horrible happens in my stomach when I think about this. He says he's too busy. "No biggie," I said, but I didn't mean it. It's not even the kind of phrase I use. It was as if I were pretending to be someone younger, sassier: India, that girl at work with the orthodontically perfected smile, Stan Kennedy's protégée, pretty and clever enough to have her eye on my job. No biggie? Did Philip look at me oddly when I said that? Did I sound as if I was trying to be cool? *No biggie.* All this little stuff is big; that's the problem. What's trivial? What's serious? Sunday lunch with Philip's parents, fancy undies in a suite in Brighton, a younger woman's pearly teeth, an eight-year-old blowing out her candles. It's what life is made of. It's all about love in the end.

Up to the bridge and over. It's busier out here now. I spot two other runners across the grass, a large dog nosing toward the pond. Three geese fly up, flapping, cackling. Somewhere behind lowering gunmetal clouds, a sun is rising, creating blank trickles of light that seem to flatten the common, leach it of contrast and color. By the children's playground, a toddler's red shoe is stuck upside down on one of the gray railings. A wet, spotted ladybug hat hangs from a silvery branch. All these abandoned possessions, these bits of people left behind. Once, out running, I saw a pair of men's pants in the undergrowth. *How?* It's not like Clapham Common. It's Wandsworth. We're all Labradoodles and Rusty Racquets here, not cabinet ministers in compromising positions.

At the café, I make a split-second decision and turn off, keen on a quick jog round the bowling green. But when I reach the hut by the tennis courts, something draws me into the wilderness of the wooded copse beyond. I don't usually run there. It's only a small triangle of denser trees, tall and narrow, that edge the soccer field, but you're out of sight of the main drag. It feels too dodgy, too risky. Why did I do it? The gathering light? A desire to outrun the day? The manicure of the bowling green, and the sedateness of my pace? My hopeless failure to *sort*? I don't know. Afterward, I might say it was a sudden yearning to feel fresh vegetation beneath my feet, to push the pathetic and tame boundaries of the common, to be, for a few seconds, on my own.

I can't tell you.

I'm not scared—because I'm running quite quickly, maybe—but it's harder going than I expected. The ground is uneven, shifts to trip you up. Tree limbs poke at eye level; tangles of grass lunge at ankle. And then, through a crisscross of branches, I see it.

At first, I think of blow-up dolls. Or fish. Once, on holiday in the Isle of Wight, we came across a dead porpoise high up on the sands—unsettlingly pale and fleshy, a disturbing incongruity. Then, walking along the canal at Oxford years ago, when I was a student, I stumbled on a dead swan, stretched out across the embankment. It was shocking, not so much because it was dead—though there was a sense of savagery in the wasted beauty, all that whiteness—but because it was just there, because no one had cleared it up, I suppose, before me.

I push a little farther into the undergrowth, pressing back the pale limbs of the silver birch saplings, to a place where someone or something has worn the foliage flat, to where the muddle of object is.

She is lying on her side, her bare white arms outstretched above her head, her back arched. Hair the color of mahogany is away from her face, as though someone had pulled it. Her eyes are open, but they are glazed, as if covered in plastic wrap. She has long, thick eyelashes—I wonder if they might be fake—and a thin face. Her teeth are small and her tongue swollen. It looks to be pushing out of her mouth against her bottom lip. She is wearing tight khaki-colored trousers—Topshop perhaps—with pockets on the thighs and little zips on the ankles. Her feet are bare. Her toenails are polished, almost black. Her fingernails, in contrast, are ragged and torn. A triangle of black thong shows where her pink cap-sleeved T-shirt has ridden up in back. The skin on her face, neck, and some of her chest is bluish white, but there are marks, blood, cuts and scratches, tiny dots and dark horizontal lines, all over. I can hardly bear to look at her neck.

I haven't screamed. I haven't made any sound at all. Isn't that odd? But I'm suddenly aware of my own breathing; it sounds like sobs, or retches. I'm sort of panting. There are lots of things I don't expect—the Topshop thought, for example. Why do I care where she bought her trousers, or whether her eyelashes are fake? I list the details that I notice in my head. I don't process them, for now I'm just ordering them. I'm thinking about telling other people. I'm already thinking about later.

My hand is at my mouth and for a moment I think I am going to be sick. Bile has risen at the back of my throat, but I force it down and stagger toward the path. I fumble for my phone, zipped in that thing round my neck, and it takes me several tries to unlock it. I keep pressing the buttons too fast. My hands are shaking so hard I almost drop it even as I get through.

The voice at the other end is calm and quiet, so quiet I find myself repeating, "Can you hear me? Can you hear me?"

She says she can and I stumble out the details. I can't remember the name of the road—the one that comes closest to this bit of the common, really near where I live, one of the roads parallel to mine, with the same big, solid houses, a road I know well—but I say, "Trinity Road, the prison, the Toast Rack. You know those roads in a grid? The café there. Common Ground. Just beyond. In that triangular bit of woodland." She must have it up on a satnav screen or something, because she seems to know more than I do. She asks if I am okay, whether I feel in danger. She tells me to wait where I am.

When the connection is cut, I suddenly *don't* feel okay, not at all. I don't know what to do with myself. I run back toward the tennis courts so I can see the police coming, show them where to go. No one is in sight—just the cars moving steadily backward and forward on Trinity Road across the cricket pitch, the distant roofs of Wandsworth Prison, the light changing above the big houses on that road whose name—Dorlcote—I now remember. A creak from the tennis hut; darkness behind the windows of the little cabin on the bowling green where years ago a skanky black and white cat used to live. I'm on the other side of the railway line now. The banks on either side of me are steep but mostly obsured by bushes and trees that drop their wet leaves in autumn and hold up the trains, shadows and dark corners where one could hide. A rustle—it could be a fox, or a squirrel, or just a bird, but for the first time I think I feel fear. I think someone is here. I think I am being watched.

I find myself heading toward the road, then changing my mind and skitting back again. I'm what a rat might look like in laboratory conditions of stress. I'm out of sight of the girl and suddenly I have a feeling that she is gone, that someone has taken her, or that she was never there in the first place, and I'm running back down the path, tripping, stumbling, my arms out to protect my face from the reaching twigs and branches, and I'm pushing through the hawthorn and gorse and silver birch—I don't care about the scratches—until I reach that awful place. And I know even before I get there that she hasn't gone, that she is lying there, in that terrible contorted position, and she is still dead.

It's quiet for a moment. Birdsong, that's all. A train squeals. It's daylight now, properly daylight. Green tips blunt the ends of branches near me. They must be buds. I'm going to be late for work—I'll have to go straight to the studio, put my face on in the car—but I mustn't think about that now. I crouch down, above the damp grass, and it's just her and me. She looks so vulnerable. I notice a sharp, stale smell of hospital corridors or swimming-pool changing rooms. I try not to look at her eyes. Tiny pixilated spots freckle her eyelids, up to the thin plucked brows. I touch her hair. It feels dead, but then hair is, isn't it? Something about her top— cap sleeved, buttons down the front—nags at me. It's pulled tight under one armpit and her bra is showing. The strap, a loose string of black lace, is dangling out at the front, like it unpinged from its fastening. I don't know why I do what I do next. I do it without thinking. I take the loose string of black lace and slot its hook into the loop on the cup of the bra. My knuckles graze the fabric. It's a cold, hard, wet surface. I begin to cry quietly.

It feels like forever, but it is only a few minutes before a siren sounds. I knew something was going to happen from the moment I left the house. I had a feeling: a sinking, slightly cloying sensation in the pit of my stomach—an eerie premonition, if you like. Does that sound unconvincing, too far-fetched? Mea culpa if so.

Two of them come. The woman recognizes me; I can tell from the quick flush in her cheeks and the glance she gives her colleague, slightly widening her eyes as if to say, "It's her—you know, her off the telly." If the man knows who I am, he's not going to show it. He's in street clothes—jeans and a polo shirt—which is a sign of his importance in the police hierarchy. I've watched enough *Morse* to know that. He introduces himself, running the fingers of one hand through slightly greasy, thick dark hair. He's DI Perivale, and "this here is PC Morrow."

We're at the tennis hut. I ran back when the siren stopped, when the blue light spun through the trees. I shake their hands, suddenly overcome with a strong desire for physical contact. I can't think about crying; I'm not the one who's dead. PC Morrow, who looks about twelve, holds my arm as we walk. She is small and freckly, with light brown hair pulled back in a ponytail; she is almost pretty, though her eyes are a bit too close together, and one of her front teeth is badly capped. She tells me she was just going off her shift when the call came in. "Already had my mind set on a bacon sarnie. Ketchup. Bit of brown sauce." She's putting me at ease. DI Perivale doesn't care about that. He's stalking ahead—shoulders hunched, his jeans hung low at the back. He puts each foot in the ground like a skier places a ski pole, determined, as if to give balance.

I don't have to tell them where she is. It's obvious. Once we're close, DI Perivale tells me to wait on the path—or rather he shows me to wait by putting out his arm like a barrier.

"CID. He's just come on," PC Morrow whispers apologetically. "We've called for the dogs. The soccer team will be along in a sec—eight minutes if they're on a blue light, that's my guess."

"The soccer team?" I ask, thinking of the soccer field only a few feet away.

"SOCO—Scene of Crime Officers. They'll seal off the area and conduct a fingertip search for evidence."

I ask her what sort of evidence, and she says, "Anything. Footprints, the weapon, of course, fibers, blood, hair, paint, glass. It's amazing what they pick up. So we can't have you contaminating the scene."

"I hope I haven't already contaminated it," I say.

She gazes into the undergrowth and tuts, wonderingly, "You really would think people would pick up after themselves."

For a bizarre moment, I think she means the body and I half laugh in shock, but then with her chin she gestures to a scrunched-up McDonald's bag, spilling squashed polystyrene and bits of lettuce.

"Do you think that might be evidence?" I say, studying it.

"More like bloody litter. Not to mention what all that fat and salt does to their arteries. Kids probably."

"Kids," I repeat, thinking, Who else has been out here?

DI Perivale is still crouched over the girl. He isn't touching her; just looking, and then he's on his phone. He calls something out to PC Morrow—sounds like a stream of numbers—and she makes a call herself. Exhaustion seeps into my neck and head. When she hangs up, I ask if I can go, but she says she has to take down a few details first.

I explain that I am needed at work and she nods. "I. Can. Understand. That," she says. Drawing out the words, distinguishing between the pace of my life and the priorities of hers. After she confers with DI Perivale, the two of us walk back to the café to find a bench. She says, "You look a bit different. I'm not being funny or anything, but you look younger than you do on the telly."

I laugh. "It's the hair. Big hair. Big, red, daytime-telly hair. It's quite fine naturally, but for the show it's got so much lacquer in, it's like a helmet."

"Do you have a hairdresser to do it?" she says, and when I nod, she asks, "What, every day?"

"It's very surreal, this," I say, "talking normally when . . ."

"I know. Your first body is always a bit of a shock. Someone said to me there are two smells a police officer gets an instinct for in the first year. One: dope. The other: death."

"There *was* a smell . . ." I say.

She wrinkles her nose. "Like an old people's home—sour."

"Something else," I say.

As she reaches for her notebook, she lists, in the manner of someone cataloguing books they have recently enjoyed, the dead bodies she has seen in two years on the beat—a suicide (hanging), a traffic accident, and a couple of heart attacks.

"A suicide?" I say.

"Yes, golly," she says. "You get a lot of them in this job." She tells me how women and men do it differently, overdoses and slit wrists, hangings and shootings. And I know I could stop to think about this, but it is all too much. I want to get home now, have a quick gulp of coffee if I have time, drink it in the car if not. I'm aware, guiltily, of being irritated by her chattiness. Maybe she's not being kind and intentionally putting me at ease; maybe she's just *like* this. So I interrupt and start telling her what happened ("Ooh, slow down," she says): how I had been running and I don't know what led me down that path, but something had, and how at first I had thought the pale, elongated shape was a swan or a porpoise . . . She writes down what I say, asks if I saw anything, or anybody. I mention the runners, the dog by the pond. No one else, no.

"Nothing else out of the ordinary?"

"Just . . . the girl."

She is reading back what she has written down. I decide to ask her about the dotting on the girl's face. "Little spots," I say, "the sort of rash you look out for when you have a baby in case it's meningitis."

"Ah, that one I know," she says, putting down her notebook. "Petichiae—sign of asphyxiation."

"And she had these marks round her neck—like she had been cut with a cheese wire—but also bruises, abrasions, like fingerprints. Do you think her neck was cut, or she was strangled?"

"We'll have to wait for the pathologist on that one," she says. "I'm no expert, but finger marks in a case like this often don't belong to the assailant but to the victim. You know, when they're fighting to get the ligature off?"

I shiver involuntarily, and then do it again because it makes me feel better. A gray hoodie is knotted round my waist. I untie it and put it on over my T-shirt. I can feel the shock settling, becoming something more normal, *explainable*.

PC Morrow says, "Can I have your autograph?" and I turn, instinctively smiling, hand obligingly raised, before I realize she just wants me to sign my statement.

When I look up, DI Perivale is trudging back down the path and I can hear new sirens in the distance, coming up the Wandsworth one-way system, getting louder. Dogs and SOCO, people with cameras and things—what, sticks?—to prod through grass, to find evidence, to find out who did this.

It's a peculiar feeling, and I don't know if you'll understand, but it's like letting go. It's no longer my body. It belongs to them now.

Snarled in traffic from Stockwell to Waterloo, incrementally delayed, forty-five minutes telescoping out into ninety, I miss the morning production meeting, which puts me on the back foot all day. If—as a person who has found a dead body—I'm not already on it.

Stan Kennedy, my cohost, is in the green room when I walk past, chatting up a couple of the guests—a midwife who has won the Pampers Award for Excellence, here to talk about childbirth in relation to a new sitcom, and a woman about my age whose teenage child killed himself a year ago after a period of Facebook bullying. Snuffling about under the table for dropped Danish-pastry crumbs is a lurcher, who, Dawn the assistant producer tells me, has "stolen the nation's hearts" as the result of a YouTube clip in which he plays football with a chicken. Life, death, and a dog, it's all in a day's work here on *Mornin' All*.

If Stan sees me, he doesn't look up. Life would be easier if he and I got on. He is laughing loudly as I head for makeup, the throaty trademark guffaw that makes him so natural and likeable, in which his whole being seems concentrated on the person before him. Even the bereaved mother will be charmed, smiling down at her feet, smoothing invisible creases from her skirt. He does it to everyone except me. It's war by omission. My friend Clara, who has met him a couple of times, says it's the jaggedness of his eyeteeth that make him so attractive—the sharpness of his canines offset the slightly feminine features. His lower lip is much thicker than his upper lip—as if he's been punched. Clara, the minx, says it makes you want to bite it.

I can still hear it, his affable cigarette-and-booze bellow, when I get down the corridor to my dressing room. Something about his laughter always makes me feel left out. Annie is waiting, edgy at my lateness, tubes lined up, BaByliss Big Hair Rotating Styler at the ready. I come in on an apology; I hate making her job more difficult than it already is. I don't know if she's been told why I'm late or not—from the car, I gave the producer a rundown of what had happened, and she might have passed the message on.

"You look like death," she says when I sit down. Not, then.

I wish I had time to confess. She's lovely to talk to: I'm always telling her that, trying to make her feel better about her job. Actually, though, I am probably just trying to make *myself* feel better about all this looking after I don't deserve. It's not the right time, though. It's almost 10:00 a.m. Annie is too tense to chatter, and I've already put my head through a crimson Diane von Fürstenberg and now I'm ready for Bobbi Brown. I hold open my lips for Sangria or Old Hollywood, close my eyes for Wheat and Sable, Toast and Taupe. She's probably right, though. I bet I do look like death— violet patches under my eyes, the lids creeping more every day. My hair isn't as thick as it was; the Titian is fading into—what, salmon? I think about Mother's hair, so bright, so rudely vibrant when I was a child, and yet by the end a sort of dirty orangey pink. The dead girl's hair was red, too. It can't have been natural. Is it mad to say she looked familiar?

"There—" Annie says, standing back, "you look more alive."

"You're brilliant," I say, though actually I'm the one who's brilliant—all that shimmering pigment, all those light-reflecting microparticles. I'll look decent enough out there. No one will be able to see the tiny muscle that's twitching in my eye. It's not me, though, this look, this big hair. To be honest—which I never would be to Annie—I think in the magnifying mirror I look like a tranny. Women turn into men when they get older, men into women. I can't remember who told me that. Aging is a bugger. Still, as Clara says, the alternative's worse.

Could I have taken today off? Was it enough? Even when my mother was sick, I hardly missed a show. There were nights when I didn't go to bed; I just dealt with the horrors of her illness and hammered back down the M4 in the early hours. I stood in front of the cameras smiling, the whiff of vomit on my fingers. Do a lot of women feel this? That it's only luck that has got us where we are? One slip, one lapse, and we're out. But this morning, perhaps I shouldn't have come in. When you get close to tragedy, sometimes, at first, it can be hard to see it. We had a couple on the show once who had been packing up at the end of a skiing holiday when their toddler was killed by a snowplow, suffocated by the displacement of snow. One unbearable detail: after they had taken the body of their tiny child to hospital, they drove across the Alps and took the ferry they had already booked. You can't even begin to compare my experience with theirs, I know, but I suppose what I mean is, people do odd things under stress.

Annie wants my fingers so she can paint my nails scarlet to match the carnations in the vase on the coffee table in the studio. She has her instructions. These details matter. If she notices the shaking in my hands, she doesn't say. I press my palms into the towel on the dressing table, feel the tremors up my arm.

The red nails. The red flowers. The long-sleeved red dress. I think about blood and death, bloodless death—those marks across the girl's neck. I wave my red-tipped hands at Annie. "Am I not too red?"

"You're jolly," Annie says. "Uplifting on a gray old March morning like this. God knows we need it."

I never intended to become a daytime television presenter. I was a researcher and a reporter and then the offer came up and Philip was keen and I said yes before I thought of saying no. It's a funny old job. It's not acting and it's not journalism. You can't really imagine it being high on anyone's list of ambitions. No one respects a daytime television presenter. We're assumed to be "vacuous," even farther down the food chain than our colleagues on news—"Cute faces and cute bottoms and nothing else in between," to quote Kate Adie. "When Mr. Blair starts to bomb Baghdad," Richard Ingrams said, "we shall be informed of the fact by a smiling bimbo with a perfect set of teeth."

When I see contemporaries from Oxford, serious players in publishing and academia, or bump into any of those bods I trained with on the BBC Trainee Scheme—now producers on *Panorama* or behind the scenes in policy—I am hardened to affront. "How's the world of rudely bent bananas?" shouted some bloke across the floor at the National Television Awards the other night. I was a researcher with him on *Newsnight*. God knows what he does now, but he seemed to be wearing the same shirt. I smiled and said, "Pull down your trousers and I'll let you know." Everyone else on his table laughed.

I feel shifty remembering it. It wasn't funny. They only laughed because I am (a bit) famous, a household name. Their chortles were worse than his jibe, really, because of that. Thing is, I know daytime TV is associated with the long-term unemployed, and the terminally depressed, and only marginally preferable to silence as an accompaniment to the ironing. "Household" is the right adjective here. But I also know there is a lot to be said for what I do and that not everybody could do it. It's not about a set of perfect teeth, or the ins and outs of EU vegetable regulations; it's about speaking to the viewer directly, one at a time, the common touch. We're real life in your living room, Stan and me, and there is a skill to that.

Despite everything, I'm on the sofa today before him. Annie says he likes to get there first so he can josh about my tardiness, "my busy, juggled life," as he calls it. I've told her it's all just joking, lighthearted banter, feeding into the faux-rude repartee between us that makes the show the hit it is; that he doesn't "mean" a word of it. But behind the smiles, the claps on the shoulder, I fear he does, that it is a tiny little element in the one-upmanship, his campaign to replace me. He doesn't know for sure that I earn more than he does, but he can't bear the doubt.

I'm having my microphone fitted. Hal, the floor manager, is clipping it underneath the dress to my balconette, nestling it in my cleavage—and I'm thinking of the girl and her bra, that it must have been a style they call "multiway," which adjusts to fit whatever type of shirt you're wearing, or it wouldn't have come undone at the front. I'm thinking about this, but it seems too intimate, so I'm trying not to think about it when Stan saunters in, chatting to Terri, the producer.

He sees me and holds up his hands in mock surprise. "Miss Marple. Solving a murder, helping the police with their enquiries, and still at work on time. Or do we find Miss Marple as a role model a little aging?" He twiddles an invisible mustache and adopts a Belgian accent. "Perhaps Hercule Poirot?"

I wonder if he planned to come in after me all along. It is always better to be standing up when putting someone down. In this context, the context in which my life has been taken out of the ordinary and the domestic, perhaps it's important to him to look busier and jollier and more in control and more alive than me.

"Not solving a murder, Stan the Man." I grin. I'd never let Terri see me crack. She's tough and has no time for slackers, but as long as I stay dignified, she'll stand up for me. "Just finding one."

When he plonks himself down, the cushions beneath me swell with displaced air.

"Remind me never to run with you," he says, to the room in general.

The *Mornin' All* studio takes up the entire fifth floor of a tower on the South Bank. Out of the window behind me is a view of London and the Thames—as magnificent, as picture-perfect as an artificial backdrop. Our section, with its mock-up "warehouse-style" wall, its swirly carpet, its nestle of lounge, is in the middle of the studio. The lighting is rigged. We're a glossy, brightly lit spot of loveliness, a ray of sunshine, but I'm sitting here and all I can think is how ugly Stan is. The music is playing, they're running the intro, and he's wisecracking away across the room—to the lighting and the sound guys, to the researchers, to pretty India in her corner, waiting for her Twitter and email and Facebook slot. He's an uncouth rugby player on tour: "What do necrophiliacs call morticians? Pimps . . . What's the difference between pedophilia and necrophilia? Eighty years." He's trying to unnerve me. I'm wondering if his words aren't slightly slurred.

Then we are on air. I say my good mornings, give my own spiel, and he turns to the camera, engages it with his eyes, and stares into the viewer's soul, like he is the only one who understands. His expression is somber, the corners of his mouth turning down, when he announces the sadness to come later in the show. "A year ago," he says simply, "Maggie Leonard's fourteen-year-old son, Saul, lost his life as a result of Internet bullying." He gives me a look heavy with shared sorrow. I nod sympathetically, allow a doleful half smile. We're in this together, him and me.

He rubs his hand across his jaw; I alone can hear the rasp of skin on bristle.

"A raw day," Stan concludes.

A few weeks ago, when a cabinet minister was caught lying on *Question Time,* we invited a psychologist into the studio to talk about body language and the art of mendacity. Children, she said, often cover their mouths after telling fibs; grown-ups touch their chins with their hands or fiddle with their cuffs—an unconscious desire to cross their arms.

I work hard to control my body language during today's show, because I feel as if I am lying all the way through. Today, the trivialities feel particularly shallow and vapid. I'm late with my prompt for India, have to apologize on air, make a "pratfall" face for the viewer. "No biggie," India says in return. I coo over the lurcher—Billy, he's called—tease Stan, wish I had checked the burglar alarm before I left home, told Marta not to walk across the common, but to take the long way round to school. I hadn't been thinking straight. There are precautions that have to be taken.

During the interview with Maggie Leonard, I sit with my head cocked to one side. We know what vocabulary is permissible this side of midday and what isn't. We say "passed on," "lost his life," "no longer with us," "left you." It's insane, the efforts we make to stop ourselves from saying the word *dead*.

In the car on the way home, I lie my face against the window. It's a relief to let my guard down. I think about that poor girl. The car stops and starts, jerks and accelerates. I bash my chin, knock my forehead. My neck has come loose. Steve, my driver, is chatting away about last night's darts and the roadworks at Elephant and Castle. "Fed up with this weather," he says. "It's not cold; it's not wet; it's not hot. It's just nothing, isn't it? This year March is just a load of nothing."

Shopfronts, corrugated iron, roundabouts, Tube entrances, building works—cranes and drills and graffitied awnings—it's all still there. Horrible things happen to good people. Buses crash and children die. Women are raped and mutilated in the Congo—there was a program about it the other night. Friends tell you about tragedies—a young husband's unexpected heart attacks, brave six-year-old with leukaemia. They touch your life, these terrible happenings. You wish they weren't real, and your heart lurches in the dead of night, but then they slant away, and you carry on with your own little existence. But this, this death knocked everything sideways. It is too close. No one is safe. It's a world in which people kill other people. Death isn't just slow, stretched over months, years, like my mother's. It happened in an instant. In a few seconds. A rope round the neck, a tug; it's all it takes. Thinking this, I feel dizzy, as if I'm about to fall.

The car vibrates at the lights. My perfect life. What is it next to this? Nothing. I think of the girl's mother. Father. School days. Summer holidays. Jobs. Family. Friends. *Boyfriend*. Have they been told? Have the police found out who she is? *Was*. Did she like her life, or did she long for it to be different? I've started shivering, even though it's warm back here.

The BBC News app on my iPhone has no mention of anything "breaking." Is this news? I don't know. A torso bobbing to the surface at Limehouse, that bin bag of limbs found floating in the Regent's Canal, that was news. But perhaps whole bodies are found, in patches of common ground, in other suburbs—Bexleyheath, Southall Green, Crouch End—every day.

The traffic cranks to a stop. A skip lorry, ratcheting into the junction from the Walworth Road, is blocking everything in all directions. Horns screech. Exhaust fumes bloom.

"Driven by morons, skips," Steve says. "No respect. They're all the same. Ex-cons, I reckon. The way they take speed bumps down my road—make a sound like a bomb going off. They have to be doing it on purpose. They need anger management," he says.

Congestion eases. We slide unfettered down Kennington Park Road, the tarmac smooth beneath the wheels, and Steve, who had opened his window to release an angry elbow, is talking into the wind now as it whistles past his ears, past Oval Tube and St. Mark's Church. I should ask him about his wife—she had her ob-gyn appointment today—find out if his daughter, Sammy, got her interview. I'll do it in a bit, when the window's shut. Now's a good moment to ring Clara, she will be in the staffroom, as peaceful as her life gets.

"Hello, Gaby Mortimer," Clara says, as she always does.

I can hear clattering behind her voice, like a slow train on a track, or a canteen worker clearing trays.

"You there?" she says.

I clear my throat and say, "Hello, Clara Macdonald."

"God. Friday. Couldn't come soon enough as far as I'm concerned. Just want to get home, run a hot bath, sort out the kids—Pete's cooking—and put my feet up in front of *Mad Men*. I've got a mountain of lesson planning, but I won't feel guilty, because Sky Plus is getting so full I need to clear the list or it'll start deleting itself, or is that just a myth? Anyway, if I watch a bit of telly, it'll be like tidying up."

Just hearing her voice is encouraging. We've been friends since grade school, and for me, Clara Macdonald is about as bloody close to perfect as you can get.

"What's up?" she continues, reading my silence. "Who's upset you? Is it Philip? Is he still in plonker mode? Or is it that handsome twat at work?"

"Both," I say, half laughing. "The plonker's being a plonker, and the twat's being a twat, but also . . ."

I've been wondering how to say it, what order to put the words in, whether to begin with "You will never believe what happened to me today" in an upbeat, imparting-of-*top*-gossip sort of way, or whether to be earnest: "Listen, it will be on the news soon and I wanted you to hear it from me first." I still don't know. Neither seems right. The first, too blatantly callous. The second, well, there's that tone, isn't there, that slips into people's voices when they are telling you awful things? A bit what my favorite aunt would have called "churchy," a bit marbles-in-the-mouth self-righteous. I know, too, that Clara will be tear-prickingly sympathetic about my trauma, and I don't deserve that. It isn't fair. Not at all.

I visualize her in the staff room, colleagues bustling around her, a reading bag, slung across her shoulder, her Tube pass—quick pat to check—padding out her back pocket. She may already have her coat on—that tweed thing from Primark ("Primarni," she calls it), her stripy scarf round her neck. I imagine the door about to open, a splash of thronging corridor, some nice fellow teacher offering a lift to the Tube.

Steve has wound up the window. I change my mind. I will speak to her later, when she is not in a hurry. I am probably overreacting anyway. In as upbeat a tone as I can manage, I say, "Just checking in before the weekend."

She sounds blithe, not a care in the world. "Before all hell breaks loose," she says.

Marta is in the kitchen, not eating, but sitting at the table fingering through *Grazia*. She never seems to eat. It worries me. Last summer, everything happened in such a hurry—Robin, our old nanny was pregnant, my mother was dying. I didn't take as much care as I should have in hiring a replacement. Perhaps I didn't ask the right questions. I panic-bought a nanny. Now she concerns me. I don't blame her for not eating my food—I'm not exactly Michel Roux. But I wonder when she does eat and what, and whether somehow it should be my responsibility. She's only twenty-four. Perhaps she is homesick, or has an eating disorder of some kind that I should know about.

Millie is at gym club, being dropped back. Marta has finished the laundry. Square piles of folded jumpers and T-shirts—including my running gear from earlier, are washed and pressed—awaiting redistribution. Kitchen surfaces, pale polished granite, stretch uncluttered; the floor gleams. Click open a shiny cupboard and the boxes of cereal, the pots of jam will be neatly lined up. That's the other thing: she is so tidy. When she first arrived, her one request was special cleaning gloves—latex, like a second skin. I know I should be grateful. Philip is in his element, at last in surroundings that match his brain. But it makes me uncomfortable. Robin, who came from New Zealand and lived with us for seven years until she got pregnant and married her East Anglian farmer—the audacity of the girl!—was unbelievably messy and that was just fine. She was part of the family. We all—or she and I—mucked in together. Marta is different. Marta feels like an employee, and I know this is a high-class sort of problem, and I know I should probably get over myself, but I'd like it if she felt like a friend.

Quietly, I make some tea—a lemon-and-ginger infusion, good for the nerves—and sit down on the bench. Marta looks up, resigned. She's thinking I'm about to make a stab at conversation. She's dreading it. But I have to tell her what happened. I don't want to alarm her, I say, but she needs to be cautious. She should make sure the doors and windows are locked. She is not to walk across the common, not with Millie, not alone. She should be on her guard. We don't know who is out there, I say, searching for *alarm* on her face, seeing only impassivity.

She stares at me from behind two drapes of black hair. When I have finished, she looks away, bites at a piece of skin at the corner of a nail, and then picks at it with her thumb. She tells me she is always careful when she is looking after Millie and is always sure to put on the burglar alarm. It's probably just my imagination, but she sounds a bit defensive, as if I have made up the whole story just to get at her. I must have said it all wrong.

I stare at the magazine open in front of her. It's a photo spread of Pippa Middleton, and Marta has doodled on the page in pen, though they are not really doodles, more like score marks. She seems to have scratched out Pippa Middleton's face.

I ask her how her course is going—she is learning English at a school in Tooting. I mention some bar I've heard about where young people go that "sounds quite jolly." I can't believe I've just said that. *Quite jolly?* Bloody hell. No wonder she hates me. But I worry for her. When the doorbell rings, I flee, grateful for the reason to shut up.

A tall, dark-haired man in baggy jeans and a dirty-green waxed jacket is standing there, slightly bent over, his back to me. He is looking closely at a leaf on a branch of the olive tree nearest to the path. He turns before I get a word out and says, "Press your own oil, do you?"

It's DI Perivale.

"Only dug the olive trees in a month ago," I say. "We had the whole garden done, back and front, a complete redesign. A company called Muddy Wellies. We hope to but I don't know yet. There are only three trees, so even with a hot summer, probably not."

He steps forward, puts his hands out, as if measuring distance. "Nice gaff. Big for just the three of you."

To cover my surprise that he knows anything about me at all (*the three of you*), I lean back and survey the repointed red brickwork, the three floors of window, the elegantly tapered Victorian gable, the thick entwined ropes of newly planted wisteria, as if seeing my house for the first time.

"My colleague," he adds casually, "tells me the one next door went for five million."

I flush. He's just making conversation, but I feel uneasy. I don't know why he'd say that. We stand there, looking at the house, looking at each other, and I'm not sure what to think. And then he says something I've been dreading, because I was hoping my part was done. I was thinking it might be over.

"Have you got a minute?"

Marta must have escaped upstairs, though I didn't hear her go. The ironing has gone and so has my unfinished mug of herbal tea. She must have put it in the dishwasher.

I tell DI Perivale to please sit down, but he doesn't. I fill the kettle from the tap, for something to do, and I can hear the faint noises of his shoes, the little creaks in the leather, as he shifts his weight. He is wearing brown brogues, the ones with perforated holes on the toe caps that you associate with Jermyn Street, posh cobblers who whittle things by hand.

"Do you live nearby?" I ask.

"Battersea." He has his back to me. "The other side of Clapham Junction."

"On the up," I say, and then hate myself for it.

"Nice picture. Your daughter do it?"

I'm flustered. Of course he only had to Google—I did "A Life in the Day" in the Sunday *Times* just the other week—but it is unnerving when people you've never met know things about you. That's what I tried to explain to the constable I spoke to last summer when those odd stalker-y things started happening. (In show business, you're no one until you've been stalked.)

"Craigie Aitchison," I say, moving to stand next to him. The picture is of a dog against a simple background, Play-Doh-blue sky and jelly-green grass. There is one tree, a dark tapered streak, like the head of a paintbrush. Deceptively simple, of course: there is something isolated and meditative about the dog. I think you are supposed to think about Christ. "It's a Bedlington terrier," I say.

"A *Bedlington* terrier, not just any old terrier. And another olive tree. Obviously a bit of a theme around here."

"I think it's a cypress. You know, death and all that. My husband bought it years ago, but when Aitchison died, prices rocketed. Quite a clever buy."

"Quite a clever buy," he repeats, as if he has never heard anything so stupid in his life.

The note I am hoping for next is playful. I probably just sound prickly. "There are four hanging at the Tate. Elton John has one."

He shrugs. He is younger than I thought he was. I had imagined him in his fifties, but he's about my age, I think—early forties. His mannerisms, the stoop, intended perhaps to hide his height, the droopy jowls, which he accentuates by pulling on the side of his mouth, as if removing crumbs, make him seem older. No gray in that brown hair—Philip's temples are sprinkled with silver. There are hollows below this man's cheekbones, an elongated chisel: more weight on him and he would almost be attractive. With his long hair, his bone structure, he is like a dandy gone wrong.

Enough of this. "Right, tea. Builders okay, or do you fancy something more left wing?" I could shoot myself.

"As it comes," he says.

He has sat down at the table at last, having shrugged off his Barbour and hung it neatly on the back of his chair. He looks out at the back garden now—at our lovely green lawn and landscaping, the raised beds, the trampoline, the clever "tree house" contraption that runs on struts along the back wall, behind the row of hornbeams. Philip decided we had to have the garden redone when we dug out the basement: the builders made such a mess.

Something out there in the shrubs, thrashing in the March wind, seems to interest him. Maybe that's what happens when you are a policeman: your eyes hook on every small detail because you never know what is important, what isn't.

"Did you touch the body?"

I almost drop his cup of tea. I am carrying it to the table, and the hot water slops on that delicate triangle of skin between thumb and index finger.

"Ow."

I run my hand under the tap, watch the water spool over my skin. For a moment my brain focuses on this, the water and my skin. And then all I can think about is the woman's hair, the lank, stringy texture of it.

"Her body?" I say. "No. I didn't touch her *body*."

When I turn round, he is looking at me.

"Did you know the woman?"

"No." I take a deep breath, shake my hand dry. The moment has passed. "As I told your PC, I've never seen her before. Have you found out who she is?"

"Not as yet. No."

I sit down opposite him, on the bench that runs down one side of the table, with my back to the garden. He has launched into his interview now—small talk over. He asks me to run through what happened. He doesn't take any notes. It is a seemingly informal chat, but as I talk, every gesture feels self-conscious, like I'm on display. It's a generally understood social norm that the person listening looks at the person speaking, who is allowed to look away. DI Perivale doesn't look at me at all, though—I'm the one who's watching him—until the moment I pause, and then his eyes swivel back, skewer into mine. It's disconcerting. I tip my head, gather my hair into a ponytail, and twist it round to make it stay like that, a habit of mine that suddenly feels unnatural, like someone pretending to be relaxed. Same sensation when I burrow my hands up the sleeves of my sweater. Best to try and stay still: it's what we tell guests on the show. Sit on your hands if you need to. My neck is hot. When I have finished my narrative—the identical story PC Morrow wrote down earlier—I tell DI Perivale that he is making me feel guilty and defensive, like I'm walking through security or past bouncers at the doors of expensive shops.

"Do that often, do you?"

"What?"

"Walk through doors of expensive shops?"

I give his arm a frisky slap. It's not a comfortable moment. His skin, below the short sleeves of his polo, is pale with dark, spidery hairs. He looks down at my hand, at my crimson nails. "I had to have it on for work," I say, taking it back.

He gives a half smile.

"You'd better drink your tea," I say. "Sorry I can't be of more help. I wish I had seen something, anything. I'm sorry it's been a bit of a wasted journey. That poor woman, though."

"No journey is ever wasted for me."

He is perhaps one of those men who feels less inadequate when making other people feel small. He reminds me of my boss on *Panorama* when I was a trainee—Colin Sinclair, with his big black leathers and his little red Suzuki 125. "You might say that; I couldn't possibly comment," he would venture at any observation even remotely controversial. Or when my train was late: "I believe you; millions wouldn't." His brain was lost unless he could find a little worn groove to slot into, until he found a preconceived idea to latch on to. And this policeman seems to be doing the same. And a body out there . . . if it is still out there.

"Is she still there?" I ask. "In the middle of the common? Or have you moved her? I've no idea what happens in these situations." I tap the table, touching wood. "Luckily."

He rubs his face. "We've taken the body away. She's with postmortem."

"Did you, they, SOCO find anything? Anything at all that might tell you what happened? Was it a mugging, do you think? Or a rape? A random killing? Is there some maniac out there we should all know about? Sorry to ask these questions, but it would be nice . . . to know." To my surprise, I think I might be about to cry.

"We need to wait," he says, not unkindly. "We'll know more later. My motto: ABC. Assume nothing. Believe no one. Check everything. I will be in touch. I promise."

"I suppose auto-asphyxiation is out of the question?"

"Even assuming nothing," he says, "I think we can rule out auto-asphyxiation."

"It's funny how no one had ever even heard of it before Michael Hutchence, and now it's the first thing we all think of. 'Oh. Auto-asphyxiation,' we all say, people of the world now, unshockable. But it's still such a weird thought, to find strangulation sexually exciting." I'm gabbling, being facetious, a habit when I'm nervous. He's just staring at me, half bored, half interested, as you might stare at a brightly striped fish in an aquarium. "You don't know who she is? No mobile phone . . . or wallet?"

"No." He gives an almost theatrically heavy sigh. Perhaps he is not so insufferable. "At the moment, we know nothing."

I feel suddenly very sad. "I suppose you are used to this sort of thing."

"Not really."

"Well, I am sure you'll do a good job," I say inadequately.

"There's nothing else at all you can remember?"

A memory washes over me, the shock of a cold wave. "An odd smell. Almost . . . it sounds stupid, but almost like bleach."

He nods. "I noticed that. The pathologist will confirm."

"And her eyes? I meant to ask? They looked like they were covered in wax."

"Conjunctiva. Nothing to do with how she died, more about when. It happens when the pressure drops behind the eyes—the eyeballs soften. It gives them a thin, cloudy, filmy appearance."

"The light goes out."

"Indeed."

I look at my watch. Millie will be back any minute, and I wouldn't mind him gone before she gets here. I need to think about what to tell her, and how to tell it. And I must ring Philip. It's terrible that I haven't. During my mother's final illness, I was on the phone to him every day. It's peculiar, disturbing, that I haven't spoken to him yet. Another sign, if I needed one, of the distance between us. I get to my feet and collect the DI's mug, rolling up my sleeves as an indication that I am about to wash up. I see him looking at my arms. I follow his eyes. My inner forearms are scratched and grazed, seed pearls of dried blood at the crease, and my bracelet's gone, the bracelet Philip gave me for my birthday. I must have dropped it. That isn't what the policeman is interested in, though. I give my wrists a rub.

"Undergrowth," I say. "When I was pushing through. I didn't even notice. Good thing I was wearing a long-sleeved dress for the show or viewers would have been sending me literature on self-harm. Be nice to me," I add, in an American accent (why?): "I am literally scarred by the experience."

Luckily, he doesn't seem to hear. He is putting his jacket back on. It is greasy around the cuffs and at the hem where his fingers have held on to tug at the zip.

"I just need to take a DNA swab for elimination purposes," he says, "and I tell you what would be really helpful: the trainers you were wearing this morning. For the tread."

"Of course."

He rummages in his inside pocket for a plastic bag and cotton bud and, in a sudden, almost hilariously humiliating sequence, I have opened my mouth, emitting a little haze of lemon and ginger, and he has stabbed the cotton bud in, pulled it out, and sealed it in his little bag. I leave the kitchen in a hurry and run upstairs. I pound the stairs more noisily than I need to. I let out a laugh. He had that plastic bag there, waiting. I think of boys I knew in the past, in my Yeovil teenage years, and the ever-ready foil-creased Durex in their back pockets. In the bedroom, I make a silent scream at my own face in the dressing-table mirror, just to release some tension. I grab the trainers from the cupboard and run back down. When I pass Marta's room on the half-landing, I hear music from behind the door—a thumping electronic sound, too much bass for my liking.

DI Perivale is in the room that opens to the right of the front door—he has just wandered in there by himself, as if he owned the place. It is two rooms knocked through, a pale, creamy, sumptu-ous display of a room, glass coffee tables and sink-in-able sofas and puffed-up cushions, a room, of course, we never use, and DI Perivale is standing by one of the fireplaces, looking at the framed photographs.

He picks one up. I know what it is from here. It is of Philip and me on our wedding day. I am laughing into the camera, and Philip has one arm round my waist, pulling me to him. Philip, wild dark hair, wide-eyed, ridiculously boyish, is in a baggy charity-shop suit. I'm wearing a wrinkly white dress—in that clingy polyester that was the edge of cool back then; it shrunk up when you washed it; you had to pull it into shape with the iron. In the awkward sideways pose you strike when you think you have to squeeze to fit into the frame, I look as if I am about to topple down the steps of Chelsea Town Hall. I remember thinking, I can't believe he's chosen me! He's married me! We had a party in the pub, and the rest of the weekend we spent in our flat with no clothes on, because we were newlyweds, newly-*mets*—we'd known each other six months—and those were the days when we couldn't get enough of each other.

DI Perivale holds the photograph out and to my surprise I have to resist the temptation to dash it from his hands. I make some comment about how young we look, but he has an odd expression on his face, as if there is something I am not getting.

"Is it just me?" he says.

"Is what just you?"

He shakes his head, getting rid of a thought. "Sorry. Nothing. It's just . . ."

I take the photo and pretend to study it, and then I put it back on the mantelpiece. It makes me feel sad, the picture. I take a while lining it up so it is symmetrical with a picture of Millie doing gym.

"So," he says, "I expect you will be hearing from us."

"Really?" I say. "Oh, victim support. Of course."

"Victim support?"

"We had a visit from an officer concerned about my mental health when my mobile phone was nicked out of my handbag during a trip to Cineworld. She was really quite persistent. So I imagine you're offered counseling when you find a dead body. Or maybe I'm wrong about that."

"I suppose the real victim of this crime isn't in a perfect position to receive counseling in this particular case, however persistent." It's a reproof, and he is probably right, but I do wonder whether he realizes how awful it is to be an ordinary person and find a body.

"A lot of alliteration in that sentence," I say.

"Plosives. A *p* is a plosive."

We study each other, as if neither of us is quite sure about the other anymore.

"Anyway, I don't need counseling. I'm stronger than I look," I say.

He is still standing by the mantelpiece and in this moment he seems to make up his mind about something. I can hear doors slamming in the street outside, the high-pitched squeals of exuberant girls. It's too late. I didn't get him out in time.

"You know I'm just really struck," he says, "by the physical similarities between you—or the way you look in this photograph—and the girl out there."

He gestures to the window with his chin, and I know he doesn't mean my daughter, who is already clattering up the steps.

"Just because we've both got red hair," I say, flicking it over my shoulder to hide how unsettled I feel. "She looked much younger than me. And . . . and shorter."

He is zipping up his jacket, pulling on that greasy spot of fabric at the bottom, then stuffs his hands in the pockets. As he crosses the room, I notice the soles of his brogues leave the shape of themselves in the nap of the cream rug.

At the front door, he says an odd thing: "'Unnatural deeds do breed unnatural troubles.' William Shakespeare."

"Poetry now. You're not just a pretty face."

"What I mean is, be careful. That's all. Be careful."

SATURDAY

Philip is next to me when I come to. He is down for the count, a still, quiet heaviness, a steadiness to his breathing. A fragment of feather on the pillow by his mouth flutters when he exhales—the only sign he is still alive. I have never known anyone to sleep as deeply, or wake as abruptly, as Philip. It's a knack, I suppose, or a gift. It was about 2:00 AM when last night's call came. He sat bolt upright and talked for ten minutes about convertible bonds, calculations spilling from his mouth like coins from a fruit machine, and then he hung up and lay back down and was dead asleep again before you could say "Diversified return." He hardly noticed me; I kept my eyes closed.

He had promised he wouldn't be late when I rang him, said he would forgo dinner at Zuma, but in the end, *I* let *him* down. Exhaustion, the same head-crashing, world-blotting fatigue I remember from the day I buried my mother, caught up with me. I had fallen asleep before he came in; in fact, I *kept* falling asleep. First, while reading to Millie. We're reading *Swallows and Amazons,* which we both love, but there is more sailing in it than you remember, and to a landlubber, it can have its longueurs. And later, after extracting myself from the entanglement of stuffed pink rabbit and duvet and small warm body, in my bath: Deep Relax oil, which Clara gave me after my mother died. She told me it would do the job of a sleeping pill or a big glass of wine. (Well, I had had one or two of those as well.) In the end, I rolled into bed, legs snarled in a towel, still damp.

I wake with the same headache, the same clunking bowling ball of a migraine that I fell asleep with. After a short while, I bury my cheek in the pillow, concentrate on keeping the ball in one place, and watch Philip. He is two years older than me, but he looks younger now—life's unfair that way. A fine head of hair helps, though the silver strands at his temples have become plentiful. This close, you can see the pinpointed pores on the side of his nose, the tiny threads in his nostrils that have evaded the tweezers. After plucking them, he sneezes: a big whoosh of a sneeze, which, if I am in the bathroom, he orchestrates with a conductor's invisible baton. He's always been good at self-lampoon—the exaggerated physical gesture, self-mocking and endearing at the same time—though, now I think of it, I haven't seen him do anything like that for a while. He is browner than a person deserves to be in March—wind-burn, apparently, from that twenty-four-hour golf trip to Turn-berry. Funny how a tan can make you seem distant.

I have barely seen him since our "date night" on Wednesday. I got the idea from a magazine in the green room—"make a thing of it," "talk things through." I know everyone has busy times—that days and weeks and sometimes months trot by and suddenly you realize you haven't spoken properly for a while. My birthday, last June, that's a happy point to latch on to. He gave me the bracelet—a twist of fine gray, threaded with silver balls—which I've lost. He'd bent his head, the heat of his breath on the inside of my wrist, as he fastened it. A pizza with Millie, a laugh, a bottle of wine, good God, even sex. Turning it over in my mind, though, I can't find a moment after that to fix on. August . . . September . . . he withdrew, clammed up, grew distant. His work, the market, my mother's disease . . . I can find excuses if I try hard enough.

I had put Wednesday in the household diary—in red capitals, underlined! We went to Chez Bruce. Philip once said it's handy to have a local bistro with a Michelin star—oh, how I laughed (when I was growing up, I told him, a Vesta chow mein was a treat). But what a waste of a Cornish pollock and a pea tortellini. They could have kept their *trompette* garnish and their *lardo di* Colonnata and given extra portions to someone else: Philip was too busy on his BlackBerry to eat, and I just toyed self-consciously, feeling sorry for the waiters, wishing I had brought a book.

I shouldn't have mentioned Brighton. His mood was wrong. "It's just a wedding anniversary," he said. "Take a rain check, Gabs. We'll go another time, when things let up." Things never let up. That's the problem. It's all work; even teeing off on the shores of the outer Firth of Clyde is work. Lying next to him now in bed, I launch into a satisfying internal monologue: I'm going to go mad waiting for things to *let up*. They will be ushering me into my nursing home, and I'll still be muttering about things *letting up*.

I must release a heavy sigh because Philip opens his eyes. There's a fraction of a second when his eyes hook into mine and then, his brain registering the fact he is awake, slide away. He props himself on one elbow. "Gaby," he says to the top of my head. "Gabs, what a thing to happen. I can't believe it." He throws his spare arm round my shoulders. His chin rests on my scalp and I bury my face into his neck. I have that sneakily self-righteous feeling you get when a person close to you hasn't been around when you needed them. His top smells of basil and lime. I try and remember when he started dressing for bed. A present from his parents (whom, Lord, I still haven't rung), crisp cotton in innocuous dark checks from Savile Row, but still—the wild, unfettered Philip I married in cozy, comfy, conventional *pajamas*?

I give the soft crease between his collarbone and his neck a

nuzzle—not quite a kiss, but a tug of lip on skin, nothing too humiliating if turned down. His body is firm under his shirt. The
second button has come undone and I resist the temptation to run
my hand beneath it over his naked chest. He pulls away and leans
across to smile at me. "Tea, that's what you need, and a lie-in. I'll
bring up the papers."

"I expect Millie is already up," I say after a beat, "watching telly."

"I'll pop a Weetabix into her and I'll be back. I want you to tell
me everything."

He kisses the top of my head and levers himself off the mattress. He won't be as quick as he promises, because he never resists
a lunge at the punching bag, a pound of the treadmill. Philip's
brain is extraordinary—he can commute a line of figures in mil-
liseconds, can construct a complicated investment multistrategy
from an array of quantitative variables without breaking a sweat.
(Do I sound as if I know what I am talking about? I don't.) To
his individual investors, to the American owners, he *is* the hedge
fund; that, I do know. I've always known his mind was wired
differently from mine. He is pathologically calm, meticulously
thoughtful. I have never seen him make a rash decision, appear
flustered, see red, but he can also be obsessive. Pete Anderson, a
guy he worked with at Nomura, once told me, "Philip lives and
breathes other people's money." I was appalled at the time—a
life reduced to pounds and pence, not even his own!—but I've
thought about it since and it's not quite right. The synapses in his
brain may thrill to the vagaries of the market, but his body has
its own obsessions, its own all-consuming love affairs. It used to
be larking on hilltops, swimming in the sea, *me* that did it, but
recently his physical preoccupations have become more refined.
At the moment, he is in thrall to his custom-made bike, a Parlee
Z2, complete with level top tube and wishbone rear end (I heard
quite a lot of this during the planning stages, as you can imagine),

and the bespoke fitness arena that occupies half of our basement. Two-timing bastard.

"Here we go, my darling—cup of tea and the *Times*."

I must have drifted off. Philip is standing in the doorway, wrapped in a towel from the waist down. The hairs on his chest fan out in the shape of a feather. He hands me a white mug, the china not as hot as it should be. He will have poured boiling water onto the tea bag on the way down to the gym, taken the tea bag out on the way up. *My darling*. It's so grown-up. Where did it come from? How can an endearment jar? How can a sweet nothing sound detached?

"Thank you," I say, taking a loud gulp. "Did you see Marta?"

He wrinkles his nose. "I ran past her room, just in case. I wouldn't want to risk catching a sight of her naked. Might do me in for the rest of the day."

"Don't be mean!"

"The lights in the gym have gone again," he says. "Can you get on to the electrician?"

"Yes, of course." (I do everything like that in the house. I'm your go-to snagging girl.)

He perches on the side of the bed. "You look tired. Done in. I can't believe you went to work afterward. And your poor arms . . ." He turns them over, runs his fingers over the cuts.

"Undergrowth. Brambles and stuff."

"Was it just awful?"

"It was a shock."

I tell him what happened again. Talking through it does help. Words have their own character, their own momentum. I realize I am not actually remembering the impact of finding her. I'm concentrating on how to order events and on what I've said before, of where I diverge from the original story. I don't talk much about the body, but I tell him about almost dropping my mobile, fumbling for the number—because I think he will find that funny. I ham up the comedy: PC Morrow and her bacon sarnie. It's the sort of thing we've always done—seen the humor in terrible things, sought out the ludicrous. I tell him about ringing 999 and how humiliating it is that I directed them to the Toast Rack, like an estate agent. He chortles, a sort of chortle anyway, a distracted staccato gulp at the back of his mouth. He does it again when I confess I thought Morrow wanted my actual autograph. I thought he would laugh more, though. "God!" he says. He shakes his head. "Bloody hell. It's a nightmare."

He asks a few questions. Who was she? What do the police think? He says, "Her poor parents. Presumably she's not local?" I've described a "girl," not a "woman," and so he is imagining a teenager, or someone not much older. He probably has a runaway in mind. I could clear it up, but I've bored him now. He's moved on to "our area," safety issues, the recent surge in crime. Four muggings have taken place since Christmas. The PTA at Millie's school keep us informed by e-mail of every unpleasant incident, every scare: jewelery wrested from women's wrists and fingers in broad daylight; side doors bashed in by crowbars; babysitters accosted; the lurking of hooded men in alleyways. Every time I hear a story, sneakily, I hope Philip notes it, adds it to a mental file. I so want to move to our weekend cottage in Peasenhall as soon as possible—we would send Millie to the village school, keep chickens and bees, ride horses, make jam. He's promised me a "five-year plan." So really, he can't start expressing doubts or anxieties or fears about London crime without knowing what I'm thinking. And really, *really*, isn't this as good a reason as any to move, and *soon*?

As lightly as I can, so lightly it's as if fairy moonbeams were falling from my lips, I say, "Peasenhall has a very low homicide rate per capita."

Philip smiles fondly but doesn't say anything. He has started getting dressed, chinos and button-down cambric shirt, and after a moment, I kick off the duvet and throw open the doors to my walk-in wardrobe. It was built by a special company that sorts out your storage. Our house is full of things built by special companies. There is probably a special company that would sort out our sex life if we could find it. I dread to think what they would build.

"All this stuff," I call over my shoulder. "I don't need all this stuff."

It is a subterranean continuation of the Peasenhall conversation we are not having.

"How many pairs of shoes?" Philip says, wrestling on a charcoal cashmere V-neck. "And how many of them still have their price tags?"

"It's not my fault. It's all work stuff." I am wriggling into the same pair of jeans I always wear. When Philip doesn't answer, I add, "If I didn't have to wear it, I'd chuck it all out."

When we met—at a wedding of friends from college, now divorced—I was wearing a dress I had borrowed from Clara. In our first flat, we didn't have a wardrobe. We shared a rail from Ikea. I was just a researcher then, Philip a trainee accountant, but I was happy. We lay in bed most weekends eating toast. We never shopped. We read books. Talked. Went to the cinema when we could be bothered. Then Philip got a new job and started earning money. And the money turned into Proper money and then into Big money. And then something I don't quite understand happened, which is that for Philip, not the money but the *earning* of it became a trap, a vice, a drug.

Now he is tilting open the serried row of cedarwood plantation shutters with the remote control he used to call his "new toy." Not much light steals into the room. It's another dirty gray morning. I watch him sit on the corner of the bed and lace up the pair of plain dark blue suede and leather loafers he bought himself in Prada.

I try to conjure an image of us old, but I can't.

We spend the rest of Saturday attempting normal family life. Or *I* do. I read all the papers, but I file information, or ideas, in a part of my mind labeled LATER. I try not to think about work—even when I notice in the *Times*'s "Saturday Review" that Stan is on *Top Gear*. I compartmentalize. My brain is like a cow's stomach. If I try hard enough, I can shut bits of it down. It's a trick from when I was little. I could do anything, by the end, whatever chaos was unwinding around me. Even now in moments of tension, I find myself visualizing pages of a school textbook—*Revised Nuffield Biology* or a Longman *20th Century History*—burned on to my retina by the force of childhood concentration.

It is overcast but not raining, and when Millie gets back from her ballet class, we persuade Philip away from his computer screens—the spreadsheets, the Bloomberg market news site—and into his waterproofs. He protests ineffectually, says, "Mills, my poppet, Samsung is tanking—don't you care?" but she levers her little arm through his and yanks him away, and today, for some reason, his resistance is low.

Our house is on a corner, across the road diagonally from a narrow alley that leads to the common. Millie, linking the two of us, in her leg warmers and stripy wellies, skips along like the parody of an eight-year-old girl. My daughter is everything I could have dreamed of. A tight ball of energy and cheerfulness, she adores school and gym and ballet and hockey and swimming. She is in minichoir and drama club. She loves her friends, her family. She is the platonic ideal of a child, the best of both of us. Philip's mother says she is a credit to us, that we've "done something right," but she's also a credit to Robin, our old nanny, who combined enviable reserves of patience with amiable antipodean energy. As we reach the other side of the road, Millie trips, and while some children might darken, turn to glower at the curb, Millie giggles. "Oops," she says, her hazel eyes widening in comic amazement at the face-forward tumble that might have happened. My heart clenches. I tighten my grip on hers. All the clichés are true: I would kill for my daughter, I really would.

It feels odd venturing on to the common, unnatural somehow. I hadn't thought it would come back, but it does. No sign of anything untoward at first—just wobbling tots falling over their own feet in minifootball, a Pilates class on mats by the monkey bars, ambling groups of adults in coats, bare-armed kids on bikes.

We set off toward the playground, not directly across the grass but round the path. I keep my eyes on the ground, scanning it in case my bracelet fell off my wrist when I was running. I give Philip his messages. His best mates from university—specifically Rog—have rung about a lads ski weekend. I recite the dates and he mutters something under his breath that I will have to decode later or Rog will think I haven't passed the dispatch on. I cup my hands ostentatiously over Millie's ears and remind him about her birthday rerun the following day. "No calls," I say. I've made another cake. His parents, who are coming to eat it, want to drive up early and take us out for lunch. They are going away next week, on a Swan Hellenic cruise of the Ancient World. It's been nagging at me all week to check if that's okay—sometimes he just wants space on Sundays—but now he says, "Fine," shrugging, as if it doesn't matter either way.

I've been trying to distract myself, but we have reached the part of the common the police have roped off with their red-and-white plastic tape; it drapes from tree to post to railing, fluttering and twisting like grotesque bunting. The café owners, facing a weekend of lost takings, have set up a mobile coffee-serving stall this side, on the grass. It's stupid, but I've started trembling, breathing in an odd way. I feel claustrophobic—and fight off the urge to force through the police cordon, to run over to where the body lay. Millie has seen a friend and is swinging open the gates of the play area. Unsteadily, I move toward Philip, but he has taken a phone call. His head is bowed; he is looking at the ground, scuffing a clump of grass back and forth with his Prada-encased toe.

The playground is full of people I recognize—parents from school, neighbors I've seen around. Most of them notice me and glance away. I'm not very good at making friends. I'm busy, not there at the right times, and even when I am—those hanging around moments, like school pickup, I'm self-conscious. More to the point, Philip isn't keen on meeting new people. He doesn't have time, he says, to put in the effort—the getting-to-know-you conversations, the dinner parties . . . . We have enough friends already he says. He may well be right, but such intractability has its drawbacks at moments like this. I wish Millie still needed pushing on a swing, or guiding up the steps of the slide, so I would have something to do with my hands, an object to lean on, but she is horsing about in the bushes with a gaggle of others. Climbing frames pall by the time you are eight. I can understand that. Who needs modular outdoor play when there's a real tree to dangle from? I sit on a bench, leaning forward on my knees, trying to look perky.

I catch others' eyes and smile. I do up a little girl's shoelaces. A toddler tumbles into a puddle next to me and I scoop him up and put him back on his feet.

"Gaby!"

Phew. It's like being picked last in school games. It's Jude Morris, mother of a child in Millie's class. I don't know her well, but I like the look of her. When we first met a few months ago, she told me she used to be a corporate lawyer. "And now I channel all that energy and education into powder paints and playdates and PTA events. I'm that woman. I'm that sad." She is the first person I've met in ages who hasn't immediately told me how moved they were by some interview I've just done—possibly because she's had the sense never to watch one—or make me think, by being a bit stand-offish themselves, that I need putting in my place.

She plonks herself down next to me. "So," she launches, in a semiwhisper, "what a thing to happen. Here! I expect you've heard. Have you seen the police tape? I mean, horrendous. I'm so shaken up."

It hasn't occurred to me that anyone else might be shaken up.

"I know," I say, smiling. "Extraordinary."

A couple of other women sidle over. I remember both their names—Margot, who has a sporty boy in Millie's class, and Su-zanne, whose daughter is a natural actress—I've seen her in drama club. They probably know who I am, too, but they do this thing of addressing Jude, not me. They know her better, I suppose, but I find myself trying hard to make them talk to me. I like the look of them, too. I realize I want them to be my friends.

Margot, a neat German woman with wonderful cheekbones, tells Jude she's heard it was a man walking his dog who found the body, on Friday afternoon. She screws up her face. "I think the dog was rolling in it."

"No!" I say.

"It's true," Suzanne tells Jude. Round her neck is a series of colorful Tibetan scarves, which she adjusts, disentangling an av-alanche of hair. "My dog rolls in awful things—dead rats and fox poo. Anything disgusting he can find."

"Ughhh!" I say.

They talk about dogs and their habits for a bit. Then Jude men-tions auto-asphyxiation, and someone else ventures prostitution. Margot, pursing her lips, says she heard the corpse was naked.

"Oh!" I say. The word *corpse* is not one that has entered my mind.

It is so absolute, so removed from life and humanity. Dead flesh. Dryness. Finality. A naked corpse, disengaged from my experience, my moments with her.

"I know," they both say, acknowledging me for the first time.

"I can't believe she was naked," I say. "What do you think happened? God, it is almost unbearable, isn't it? And so close to us."

Margot looks at me. "You never think it, do you? You always think this stuff happens somewhere else."

Suzanne says, "Perhaps it's good for us to be shaken up once in a while—we can all be so smug. We don't live in the real world."

"It's true," I say. "It's like a wake-up call."

And Jude says, "Second that."

And Margot says, "Third it."

And we all laugh.

Is it terrible that I don't mention my part in the discovery of the body? The more they chatter, the harder it becomes. I should have said something at the get-go, but now it's too late. I didn't because . . . why? In my line of business, one whiff of the wrong kind of publicity and a career can implode. Just look at the presenter John Leslie. The accusations of sexual assault may have been unsubstantiated, but he never worked in TV again. Stan the Man has an agent, his own media machine. I've always tried to avoid that sort of thing. It seems so grand and self-important. Philip handles the legal side of my contracts, and the production company has a perfectly good publicity department. But now, well, I can see how useful another person would be. It occurs to me with panic that I should have contacted Alison Brett, who deals with *Mornin' All*'s PR. I should have asked DI Perivale to keep quiet about my involvement, secured a seal of confidentiality. It seems more urgent now that I have sat here and listened and not said anything. I care less about my career, I realize, than about what these nice women think.

I look across at Philip, who is standing by the gate, hopeless and stiff. He is wondering, Why do I have to stand by this gate? What is my purpose here? Why can't I be back at my computer, watching Samsung tank? I take a moment to watch him. I see him notice Millie, high in some branches, and his face brightens. I feel a swell of hope. I get to my feet and help her down, clinging on to her legs, catching her wellies as she scrambles. Jude reminds me about the charity auction I have promised to host at the school quiz in April, and I say good-bye to everyone as if they were my proper friends, trying hard not to mind too much that they aren't, and the three of us set about our family day as if nothing were out of the ordinary at all.

At dusk, I see a man outside our window. He is on the other side of the road, behind a car, so I can't catch the whole of him—just a snippet of his head, an arm, the change in light and texture as he moves behind glass, a tarnish of the silver, a mottle of the steel. I'm not imagining it. I stand and watch from the drawing room, wait for him to move. I am hyperaware these days, my nerve endings alert to every encroachment.

They haven't caught "my stalker"—it sounds a bit showy-offy to call him that, I know, but I don't know what other word to use. It could be a ghost, really, a figment of my overactive imagination, a sense of a person. Once, I told PC Evans, the policeman assigned to the case, I thought someone had been in the house. I smelled a sickly aftershave. Other times, I tried to explain, I feel watched, or shadowed. But it's true I've never seen an actual person. Enquiries after Millie on Twitter: "How's the little one's nasty cold?" Presents—a pair of slippers from Toast, a CD of random songs (Ben Folds: "You Don't Know Me"; Joe Jackson: "Another World"), a book (*Dear G-Spot: Straight Talk About Sex and Love*) from Amazon. "Maybe someone is being kind," the policeman said, "looking out for you." I asked him if he had ever dreaded the post, the clatter of the letter box? Since I withdrew from Twitter, the gifts have become sporadic.

I'm standing just to the right of the bay, concealed by the shutters. I can tell it's a man from his height. It could be a smoker, banished from a nearby house. An estate agent waiting for a client. A neighbor locked out. Or what? What am I dreading?

Millie yells from the kitchen. She's *starving*. When's supper? Can she have a snack?

I sort her out—make a sandwich and a hot chocolate. I look for Philip, though I can't find him. I'm not long, but by the time I get back to the window, the figure has gone.

MONDAY

It began yesterday. I was woken by the phone. It was a journalist called Jack Hayward asking for an interview.

"What's your peg?" I asked warily, as politely as I could manage, considering I was still half-asleep.

"You know, this unfortunate incident with the dead woman: two worlds collide sort of thing."

"That's a very complicated concept for this early in the morning," I said, my mind working fast. So it *was* too late. My involvement was out there. Had the police held a press conference? Or alerted "their sources"? Either way, the information had been released. There was nothing I could do. "Surely you just want the dirt on my marriage, my infidelities, my teenage bulimia?"

He laughed, and it was a nice laugh, a laugh that had seen a few cigarettes in its time but was trying to cut down. "Give us a break," he said pathetically.

I apologized gently, said I was sure he understood.

"Can I leave my number in case you reconsider?" he said.

"I won't," I said, but I took it all the same.

I rang Alison Brett, the press officer, at home. I hope I didn't wake her. She was immediately efficient if so. "Avoid talking," she said. "But if any of the paps turn up, give them what they want. They'll go away then. Pose a bit. I know it's a pain, but this sort of off-duty shot can be good for ratings. You know the drill. Casual, stylish, approachable. Cool but not *too* cool."

Well, I could certainly manage the last bit. I had opened the door yesterday to pick up the Sunday papers in "natural-look" makeup, i.e., quick dab of lippy, and jeans, i.e., what I was wearing already. Two photographers, straight from central casting—short, stocky, red of face—were already out there. They stubbed out their fags when they saw me. "Give us a pic, Gaby," "Come on, Gaby," and "Smile, Gaby."

I waited for a bit, holding the papers under my arm. Afterward, I thanked the photographers—which always surprises them—and closed the door.

That was that, I thought. But the papers were full of it. In the car, on the way to work, I learn about "TV Gaby's Secret Horror" and "Gaby's Mournin' Pall." Most of the details are there, plus new information about the woman. Not her name, but the fact that she was Polish and apparently lived "nearby." An employer is quoted, her sadness squeezed into tabloid platitude: "She was a lovely person who will be much missed by everyone she touched." None of the articles included pictures of her. She's an absence. I'm the presence, mournful but plucky, on my doorstep. It's so wrong, that.

In one of the photographs, a shadowy figure hovers behind me, in the hallway. It takes me a moment to work out it's Marta.

Steve looks at me in the rearview mirror. "You all right?"

"I'm fine," I say. I drop the newspapers to the floor, beneath my feet. "How's your wife? Any ob-gyn news?"

"Nothing serious," he says. "Polyps."

"A polyp?"

"No, polyps."

For some reason we both laugh.

• • •

Terri accosts me at the door to the production meeting. Boris Johnson, booked to come and talk about his "estuary airport," has begged off with a gippy tummy. She needs something serious, something "current affairs-y" to plug the hole.

I head her off. "What else have we got?" I say, sitting down. It's quiet in the room, tense with a feeling of anticipation.

Dawn, the assistant producer, consults her clipboard and reads out what I remember from Friday: a flirting master class from the presenter of a new dating show; Simon Cowell in the kitchen, doing his signature lamb brochettes; India's 'Appening Apps; Kate Bush, recently back from the dead ("It's me. I'm Cathy. I've come home") with a new album; three pretty actresses from *Downton* in to talk about . . . well, *Downton*.

I am racking my brains. I made a mental list on the weekend and I run through a couple of my ideas—they're not brilliant: the rise in flash mobs (a rock choir in Berkshire is taking over a shopping mall in Basingstoke); a blind high-street coffee test (Starbucks, facing dire quarterly figures, has gone for double shots).

A silence descends. No one looks at me, apart from Terri and Stan, who has his feet up on the other end of the table.

"It's just . . ." Terri begins. She pushes the bridge of her black thick-framed glasses—fashionably unfashionable—farther up her nose. "I was thinking . . . you know, the big story from this weekend is . . ."

"You." Stan has taken his feet down off the table. "You, sweet pea, are the story." He doesn't sound as confident as he might. I wonder if he is working out what's in it for him, whether he's weighing up the pros and cons, whether his publicity consultant has suggested *he* get caught up in a police investigation.

"I was thinking," Terri says again, "an item about what it felt like to have gone through your terrible experience. You talking directly to the camera, telling your side of the story. We could get a psychologist in, sit them next to you on the sofa, to explain what sort of aftershocks to expect. 'My trauma,' that sort of thing."

Alice, the new researcher, looks up. "Adam Phillips says he can get here by ten a.m."

"It's not my trauma," I say. "I just found the body. It's not my tragedy. It's not about me."

"I don't know much about the dead woman," Terri continues. "What was she—some Polish cleaner turning tricks on the side?"

I wince. "I'm not sure . . ." I begin.

"Whatever. I just imagine that her life wasn't that close to yours, that she moved in"—she shrugs, as if even she is aware of dangerous assumptions—"different circles."

"Two worlds collide," I say, "that sort of thing."

"Exactly." She rubs her fingers quickly back and forth at the top of her head, as if making pastry up there. She has short hair, bleached at the tips. She often does it. It's not an itch, but an impatient gesture, conveying a desire to get things going, to hurry things along.

"The outrage you feel," Dawn suggests. "You among many."

"I'm not outraged," I say.

"Maybe we don't know enough, but it has definitely shaken up the middle-class enclaves of . . ." Terri, who is Hackney born and bred, tries to remember where I live, "New Malden or wherever."

"I don't think so," I say, thinking protectively of Jude, Margot, and Suzanne.

"Come on," she urges, like someone coaxing a child into a coat. "It's good. We need you. It's fascinating."

"I don't care," I say, trying to stay calm and focused, trying to block out swathes of panic by visualizing Longman's timeline of the Second World War. "I don't feel comfortable with it. I'd rather not do the program at all rather than exploit her."

"My horror." Stan has put on a deep, gravel-scraping dramatic voice. "My heartbreak."

I probably wouldn't have reacted, except that I see him court a look from India. She's curled up in her chair, twisting her hair, trying to keep out of it. He winks. And perhaps it's priggish of me, perhaps in different circumstances I'd be finding it funny, too, but I feel something snap.

"I don't feel horror," I say. "I don't feel heartbreak. A poor woman has *died*."

I've raised my voice. Embarrassed, no one looks at me. Stan smirks.

Luckily Dawn, who has been tapping away on a laptop while this has been going on, saves me. With a satisfied click of her fingers, she says she's checked and we can bring forward Britain's fattest woman, on a video link from her home in Tyne and Wear. (She hasn't left the house in four years.)

"The live *feed*," Stan interrupts, in another movie-trailer voice. Later, of course, he will be the model of anguished sympathy.

Alice suggests we get Adam Phillips in regardless—cue him up for psychological insights into obesity—and Terri, panic suppressed, seems at least placated. I've got away with it for today, and with any luck, tomorrow my story will be stale.

I have five missed calls after the meeting, and a heap of texts, including one from Jude Morris. "You dark horse! Why didn't you say? You must think Margot, Suzanne, and I are idiots!" Clara has phoned twice, and Margaret, Philip's mother, once. Our dearly beloved, dearly departed ex-nanny, Robin, has left a voicemail: "Hi, hon. Blimey, what's going on? Can't leave you guys alone for a minute!"

I ring Clara on the way to makeup, but she must be teaching because it goes to voicemail. So then I try Jude instead. "Do you hate me for not telling you?" I say when she answers. "It's complicated. I will explain."

She says of course she doesn't hate me. I tell her I'm sorry, that I am the sorriest of sorry things—a construction Millie and her contemporaries use all the time—and she laughs. "But no more lying."

I'm just about to put the phone back in my pocket when Stan catches me. "Yeah," he says. "Well done. Right decision, bro, I think." His breath is an unpleasant cocktail of garlic and mints.

"Thanks, bro," I say.

"But you're mad not to take a couple of days off to recover. Don't feel you can't, or that you would be letting the side down. It might go against the grain. I know you soldiered on when your mother . . . whatever . . . and only took two weeks off when you had your kid all those years ago."

"Back in the distant mists of time," I say.

"But we would all entirely understand. I was saying to Terri, India's desperate for the experience on the main sofa. Be interesting to see what kind of chemistry we whip up. I know you're an old pro, but you'd be doing her a favor."

"That is so kind, Stan," I say, saving the "old pro" up for later. "I really appreciate it."

I ring Robin from the car on the way home. She wants to know what's happened—Ian's mum brought the *Mail* up this morning "and we were all, like, *what*?" But a day is a long time in the life of a new mother. My shenanigans have been swept off the agenda by the bewildering complexities of a four-month-old body clock. Robin is trying to get the baby's nap "home and hosed" before Ian's "rellies" arrive for supper.

"Sometimes," I tell her, "I can't believe you've lived here eight years. You sound like you've just lugged your backpack off the Tube from Heathrow."

"I lucked out, didn't I, finding you waiting for me at the top of the escalator."

"Robin, we're the ones who lucked out."

I can hear Charlie fussing, hiccup-worrying in the way babies do when they want to go to sleep and don't know how.

"Come on, hop to it," Robin says. The cries become more insistent. "Oh, come on. I need you to sleep. I've got to get blimmin' cooking."

"Do you remember that brilliant advice you gave me—that you should rock a baby really quite forcefully? It's counterintuitive, but it works. Eventually you reach that moment when the crying becomes rhythmic and then their eyes slowly close."

"You should have more," she says.

I almost sing my answer. "Too late now."

We talk a bit longer—about the baby and his erratic sleeping patterns, how Ian's mum thinks a bottle would help. I keep talking, telling her what a great job she is doing, what a wonderful mother she is, because I can tell Robin needs the cheering and the distraction, but after a few minutes, her voice gets quieter. "So, are you all right?" she whispers.

"I'm fine," I say.

Robin yawns. "I might grab forty winks."

"That's my girl," I say.

A man is sitting in a car outside my house when Steve pulls up. I think of ringing the police, but it turns out they're here already.

DI Perivale has brought PC Morrow with him this time. She grins when I stop in the doorway of the kitchen, a wide-mouthed "me again" Wallace and Gromit grin. Marta has let them in, though she has gone out to collect Millie, "leaving them to it," in DI Perivale's words. My cleaner is in the house, PC Morrow adds, as if I might be worried about security. I can hear Nora shunt the Hoover back and forth in Marta's room, the gurgle of water in the pipes as she Mr. Muscles the guest bath.

I lean against the doorframe for a moment, not sure I have the strength to move. My legs feel wobbly. "Haven't I answered all your questions already?"

PC Morrow, who is sitting on the bench, wrinkles her freckled nose. Her forehead is without lines. She is wearing tiny gold hearts in her ears. "I know it's a real pain," she says, "but . . ." DI Perivale, at the head of the table, is studying a piece of paper in his lap, and because he's not watching, she rolls her eyes and shrugs.

"If you wouldn't mind sitting down for a few minutes," he says, looking up, as if I have just been ushered into his office. "It won't take long, but it is important."

I unpeel myself from the doorjamb and sit. I think about offering a cup of tea, but something in his tone tells me I shouldn't.

"Have you seen this woman before?" DI Perivale asks. He has a slither of lettuce caught between two incisors, and a blob of what might be dried ketchup on the upper breast of his zip-up Adidas top. If I were a forensic pathologist, I'd say he had had a Big Mac on the way over.

He spins a photograph toward me.

I dread looking at it.

It was taken in a garden, by a climbing frame. Two children are stretching from the lower bars. One of those red plastic climb-in toddler cars has been abandoned at her ankles, and she is leaning back to grab the smaller child's legs, smiling broadly. She has those front teeth that lean in a bit, as if they have been pushed, and her dark red hair is pulled back in two bunches. She is slight, with a thin, narrow face, and thick fake eyelashes. One of her earlobes has about six rings in it.

The picture makes me unbearably sad.

"Are those her kids?" I ask.

"Do you recognize the woman?"

"Yes, of course . . . Who is she? Are they her kids?" I ask again.

"We know she was Ania Dudek, aged thirty, of Fitzhugh Grove, SW18." *Was,* he said, not is. "The family she worked for in Putney reported her missing when she didn't show up on Saturday. It's their children in the photo. She was working for them in the capacity of weekend nanny."

"Ania Dudek," I repeat. A nanny. At least they weren't *her* children. A nice job with a nice family in Putney, that congenial safe suburb where Nick Clegg lives. Not really two lives colliding at all.

"Does the name mean anything to you?"

"No." I shake my head. "Nothing."

"You ever been to Fitzhugh Grove?"

"No. I know where it is, of course." It's a group of high-rise buildings on the edge of the common, formerly owned by the local authority. "But I've never been in."

"Are you sure?"

I nod.

"And Ania Dudek has never been here?"

"No." I look across at PC Morrow, who has put on a sort of "rather not be here, but I have to" face, a stab at female solidarity. I smile at her. "Never."

"Interesting." He produces another sheet of paper. It's a torn-out page from a magazine—a cutting—in a thin plastic folder. It's an advert from the *Lady* for a live-in nanny in the Wandsworth area. The moment I see it—from the shape of the words, the layout—I know it is the ad I placed last summer after Robin gave in her notice.

"Any notion why this might have been stuck with a magnet to Ania Dudek's fridge?"

I had sinusitis last winter and the infection went to my inner ear, causing sudden lurches of imbalance—unilateral vestibular dysfunction, the doctor called it. It wasn't so much vertigo as a precipitous spinning; the room would shift on its axis. I have this sensation now. I'm staring at the table, at the plastic folder; I can see the sky and the clouds reflected in its transparent surface, and for an instant or two, I don't know if I am sitting or falling.

I manage to say that I have no idea. DI Perivale is asking questions, which I can hardly hear, because, as the dizziness passes, I am left with a roaring confusion in my head.

"Did she come for an interview?" It's the first time PC Morrow has spoken. She's nodding, as if already confident of the answer.

"I wish I could say she had," I say eventually, "but she didn't." I cast my eyes around the tidy kitchen. "If I could lay my hands on last year's diary I could show you who came. Oh I know, I've got a file with their CVs. I could dig it out."

"Just tell us what you remember," PC Morrow says.

"I remember everything from that summer. My mother was ill and our old nanny, Robin, was getting married—which was obviously wonderful, but also meant she was leaving us, so that was sad. For us, I mean."

DI Perivale looks impatient.

"Anyway. I had two days of interviews. I saw about six young women. Actually, that's wrong—five women, one man. Two were English; one was going to university in September, so that was hopeless; the other couldn't drive. There was an older Armenian woman who wanted to come up by train from Croydon every morning. The man was South African: great if we'd had boys. A nice Portuguese lady: she seemed great, but her English was nonexistent . . . I had a few more to see, but my mother's health worsened, and on the third day, we found Marta."

I am talking too much, trying to give them as much information as I can. Then an idea, an obvious thud of explanation. "I mean, maybe this . . . this Ania thought about applying for the job, if that's her profession, and didn't."

"Yeah, that could be it," PC Morrow says. She looks at Perivale. "That makes sense."

"You know," I continue, with relief, "how sometimes you stick things on the fridge and forget about them?"

"Yeah." PC Morrow wrinkles up her nose. "I've got some all-protein diet stuck on ours. Have I looked at it?"

"You don't need to diet," I say, "and that high-protein Dukan thing—terrible for your breath." She gives a squeezed hunch of her shoulders, as if she would laugh if she could. I think again how young she is. "Our fridge" is probably her mum's.

DI Perivale takes the plastic envelope, puts the photograph on top of it, and lines them up in front of him on the table. I can see specs of dandruff in his part. I wonder if he is married, has kids.

"Okay. One more question." He hasn't looked at me, but he does now—his eyes seem to bore into mine. "I have asked you this before, but I am going to ask again. Did you touch the body?"

"The body." I gaze at him. I try and think back. My head is fuzzy. If I can't bear to think about her body now, how could I have touched it then?

"No."

"Are you sure?"

"I know I touched her hair."

"Did you take anything from the body?"

"No." I feel uneasy again. I don't understand the direction these questions are taking. I feel as if I have forgotten something important.

"You didn't take a St. Christopher on a chain from round her neck?"

"No. Why on earth would I do that?"

He rubs his face, his eyes, with his thumb and fingers. "Look—Edmond Locard. The Locard Principle: every contact leaves a trace? Have you heard of that? Well, it's one of the first things you learn at Hendon. Hair, flecks of paint, fibers, makeup—particles travel, move, shift. Every mote of dust has its own identity. Cotton has twisted fibers that resemble ribbon; linen looks like tubes with pointed ends."

"Okay . . ."

"And although the killer seems to have sprayed her neck with bleach—"

"So that was the smell?"

He nods, and continues, "We found certain fibers, certain DNA on her collarbone, which . . . It would just be helpful if you could rack your brains. Now, I know you were traumatized, in need of victim support"—he gives me a gnomic jut of the chin—"but if you could just tell us everything that you remember, it would help us a great deal in our enquiries."

I look up. Nora has tiptoed into the kitchen with a bucket and mop. I didn't hear her coming. She wears slippers when cleaning; her feet whisper as she walks. I get up from the table to rummage around in the hall for my purse and dig out her money. It occurs to me to postpone paying her until next week, but I hate to do that. She has a family back in the Philippines and sends most of her wages home.

When I walk back into the kitchen, DI Perivale asks if Nora is local (maybe he wants to check her papers), and I realize I couldn't tell him, even if I wanted to. She has cleaned for me—emptied my bins, scrubbed my loos—for years and I don't know where she lives. I sit down. Is it my imagination or do PC Morrow and DI Perivale exchange a look?

"So just to be clear," PC Morrow says, "apart from the hair, nothing of you touched anything of Ania Dudek's?"

You know if you forget a word or a name, the worst thing can be to rack your brain; that often it is when you think of something completely different that it comes to you? Maybe it was the reflective diversion about Nora that prompts me. Or maybe I would have got to it anyway, in my own time.

"I did touch her," I say. My head has cleared. "I mended her bra strap. It was one of those bras that attaches at the front and the strap was dangling out; it had come unpinged. So I did touch her. I did it up. I don't know why I didn't mention this earlier. I think it was because you said 'body' and I know I was careful not to touch the actual body." I'm shaking my head. I remember suddenly the stiffness of the hook at the top of her bra, the coldness of the fabric. "I can see myself doing it. I don't know why I did it, but I did, she just looked so . . ."

"Aha." DI Perivale sounds as if he has just solved a clue in the *Times* crossword. He asks if I have suppressed taking the St. Christopher, too. I shake my head fiercely. "Okay." He nods.

I ask if they know *what* killed her, and he says, "Cardiac arrhythmia, caused by pressure on the carotid artery nerve ganglion. The superficially incised curvilinear abrasions: self-inflicted bruises as she struggled to remove the ligature from her neck."

I feel myself blanch. "And what about *who*? Do you have any leads on that?"

Perivale stares at me.

"No boyfriend?" I say. "Aren't they usually the first in the frame?"

"A boyfriend." He nods. "But not in the country at the time."

"And no obvious murder weapon," PC Morrow adds.

I am desperate for them to leave now. I don't want to hear any more, but Perivale starts talking more about fibers—polyester threads, apparently, look like smooth, unwrinkled rods—and then he asks, for the sake of elimination, if he can take away the clothes I was wearing that morning. I fetch the jogging bottoms and the T-shirt and the gray running top as quickly as I can. And then, just when I think we must be done, he asks me where I was the night before the killing, between 4:00 PM and midnight. I don't understand why he is asking this.

"Well, I wasn't on the common," I say, "not then."

"She wasn't killed on the common," PC Morrow says chattily. "She was killed in her flat. We know that from the pooling of the blood in her body."

An exasperated frown knits DI Perivale's brow. "When the heart stops," he continues, in the dum-di-dum tone of someone repeating information for the umpteenth time, "blood settles in the lowest part of the body, causing the skin to become pink and red in that area. The hypostasis on Ania's body suggests she was killed with her legs in a lower position to the rest of her—this is consistent with indentation marks found on the cover on the bed in her flat. There were two cups of tea there, one untouched, and a glass of water that had been knocked over."

"I was here," I say, "at home. I had a nap, a run—just a quickie—then a shower, some supper, read to my daughter, watched a bit of telly . . ."

"What did you watch?"

"I can't remember. *Mad Men*, I think."

"Can anyone corroborate that?"

"Marta. Millie, for the early part of the evening."

"And what about later?"

"I went to bed early, alone. My husband was at work and then out with colleagues." I am being helpful, but I am also wondering why they want to know where I was. I *found* the body. Do they think I *killed* her? I can feel panic and the beginning of fear. Is this what a police investigation is? Pointless queries? Bureaucratic quagmires?

Maybe he just has to ask, though. Maybe it's policy—like having an HIV test when you're pregnant—because then he moves on and asks a couple of questions about my stalker: the file on it "has drifted to the surface." I tell him the stalking, if you can call it that, began at the end of last summer, which DI Perivale at least finds sufficiently interesting to write down.

"It may just be a coincidence," I say, "but I'm sure I saw someone watching the house on Saturday, and when I came in just now, there was a thuggish man, looking a bit suspicious, in a car outside." I try to speak casually; I don't want them to think I'm making a fuss.

They both stand up. PC Morrow makes a circular movement with her shoulders, massaging out the tension.

"That thuggish man outside?" DI Perivale shrugs. "He's one of ours."

After they leave, I take a run. It's like getting back on a horse: I have to do it sooner or later. I don't have my Asics, or my favorite running clothes—I don't know when I'll get them back—but I've got a pair of old Dunlops hanging around and some tracksuit bottoms, which will have to do. I tie Philip's gray hoodie round my waist. I probably won't need it, but it hides my bum.

You can get to Fitzhugh Grove across the common—a path leads from the soccer field into John Archer Way, a new road created out of nothing when they built the modern housing estate, and then along a row of towering chestnut trees. If you take that route, though, you have to broach the police cordon, and even if you work round it, those big chestnuts, with their thick, reaching branches, turn the path into an uninvitingly dark corridor, so instead I pace along Trinity Road beside six lanes of thundering traffic. At the entrance to the grove, rattling in the vibration from passing lorries, is a yellow sign, appealing for witnesses. I jog on the spot for a bit, pretending to read it, and then I walk a little bit farther in—just to where the cars are parked, blocks of flats separated by scraggy patches of grass. I can see the roof light of a police car whirling by the second tower, turning the wall intermittently orange. I feel drawn in, entangled. At the last minute, I turn on my heels and run home instead.

Nearly at my house, just before the gate, a bulk comes out of the shadows, between me and it.

I stifle a scream.

"Oh, don't," the man says, putting out his hand. "Sorry. Gosh. Sorry. Did I scare you? What an idiot. Sorry."

I push quickly past him. He doesn't block me—he moves easily out of my way. I catch a whiff of Polos, and tea, and the artificial bouquet of fabric softener.

"Sorry," I say, when I have put the front gate between us.

"No, I'm sorry. After the shock of what's happened, your nerves must be shot to shit."

I laugh. "Shreds." I can see him properly now. He is not much taller than me, with curly hair and mad, haywire eyebrows. He has big brown eyes, appealing, slightly crinkled at the side, quizzical.

"Shreds. Shit?" He makes a surprised face. "Where did *that* come from? Anyway, sorry to bother you like this." He puts his hand out. "Jack Hayward. We spoke on the phone."

I nod, shake it. "Two worlds collide sort of thing."

"That's the one. I thought it was worth a try to ask you personally. It's such a good story. I've found out a few more things since then. I'm freelance. I need a break. Give me a break." He opens his hands.

"Have you thought of getting a proper job?" I ask, not unkindly.

"I tried a proper job. You know, they make you go every day? And you have to wear a tie and sit at a desk?"

"Unbelievable."

"People go on about the watercooler and how much fun it is around there, but have you been to a watercooler recently? Dead. Nothing. Some guy from accounts, that's all. I'm telling you the party's moved on."

"Maybe you're just going to all the wrong watercoolers."

I'm smiling, but still backing toward the door.

"Please," he says.

"I'm sorry, I've got nothing to say."

"Please?" He pushes.

I've got my key out. "Another time maybe," I say. "When things are quieter."

Philip rings at 8:00 PM He won't be home for supper. He's had a difficult day. He can hardly speak for exhaustion, or stress. His words are stunted and cold.

We haven't spoken much since Sunday lunch. He was so rude to his parents I could hardly look at him. He spent the meal either fiddling with his phone, or leaving the pub to make calls, or staring at the table, as if he couldn't bring himself to engage with any of us. I love Philip's parents, but Margaret, his mother, is no good at confrontation. She just kept smiling as if nothing was wrong and Neil, a retired headmaster from the days when erudition was more important than charm, plowed on with his disquisition on the history of pub names while I desperately tried to compensate for Philip's distraction with an enthusiastic stream of Oh reallys and No, I didn'ts! It was heartbreaking. Margaret and I were the last to leave the table. "Sorry about Philip. Lot on," I said. She looked at me, and for a moment I thought she was going to ask more. The urge to confide, to feel her reassuring arm on my shoulder, was briefly overwhelming. I wanted to tell her what I'm actually scared of: that Philip is drifting away from me. But she smiled again, and gave a cheerfully clipped laugh. "Philip will be Philip."

"The police have been," he tells me now from his desk at work. "I had to come out of a meeting."

"The *police*?" I say.

"It was about the dead woman."

"*Why*?" I ask. "Why did they need to speak to you?"

He doesn't answer immediately. He has put his hand over the

receiver or has put it down on the desk. I want to scream to get his attention, but when he comes back on the line, I force myself to sound calm. "They've been here, too," I say. "They know who she is. A woman called Ania Dudek."

"Yup. They said."

"What did they want with you?"

"Routine. Because you found . . . her."

He goes again. Or I think he does.

"And?" I ask when he comes back.

"Er . . . Just questions, Gaby. Okay? About where I was. Where *you* were."

"Please don't sound so irritated. I'm sorry you've been disturbed at work, but can you just tell me a bit more? Please?"

He lets out a deep sigh. His voice sounds distorted with the effort. "Sorry. Yes. I can't believe this has happened to you . . . Why you?"

"I know," I say.

"You said she was a teenager."

"No, a woman."

Another silence. Is he actually talking to someone in his office at the same time? "The policeman was checking what you told him . . . about finding her and . . ." I can hear a distant clicking, like a ballpoint pen being retracted and extended. "Basically checking details of time and place."

"My alibi, you mean? They're checking on my alibi?"

"Sort of. Not that I'm much good to you." He gives a bitter laugh. "It was back-to-back meetings, followed by work drinks, followed by work dinner. I've got a list of alibis as long as my arm. Pity you can't have one or two of mine."

I long for him so badly to come home, I find myself pretending to be asleep when he finally does. I want him to wake me, to nudge me;

I want him to *want* to. But he doesn't. He slips in almost silently. And later, in the early hours, when I wake of my own accord, he's not there; his side of the bed is still warm, tepid at least. I wait for a while, but when the sheets have gone properly cold, I tiptoe quietly down all four floors of the house. I reach the basement and pause in my bare feet by his bike, which he has had time to hoist carefully onto its special rack.

Philip sometimes works out when he can't sleep, but tonight he is slumped in a chair in front of his screens—Bloomberg, CNN flashing holograms onto his blank face. He's so wrapped in his own thoughts, he doesn't even hear me.

TUESDAY

"Sex. You need a weekend away, and you need sex. All that money people spend on psychotherapy and couples counseling and CBT, I'm telling you there is no marital issue that can't be solved with a good shag."

"You're right," I say

"Honestly. You'll have to sit him down and make him see sense. Do you still have the hotel room?"

I nod pathetically and say, in a squeaky voice, "Freestanding bath. Obstructed view of sea."

"Force him. Use your wiles. And if he won't go with you, I will."

Clara and I are in a café in Exmouth Market—it's so trendy up in this corner of northeast London, the coffee is "artisan-roasted." I have no idea what that means. Perhaps they have an artisan roasting it in the basement. Clara is having a short white, and I have ordered a long black, just to make her laugh. Cake is also being eaten (a yuzu-vanilla ginger loaf: seriously). It's Tuesday afternoon—Clara's half day—and I have taken a cab here from the studio instead of going home. I feel like I'm playing hooky.

Clara is small and slim, her face full of character: deep blue eyes, a pointy nose, the dips and shadows thrown by prominent cheek-bones and a wide, bony forehead. She is the coolest person I know, and the least vain. Next to her, I am just *boring*. Sometimes I gaze longingly at her A-line corduroy skirt, or old lady's tweed jacket, or French fisherman's bag and think, Why doesn't wardrobe put me in something like that? But I know why. It's not the item under scrutiny that's hip; it's her. She has natural hipness.

"You all right?" She's studying, head cocked, searching my face. On the phone to her yesterday, waiting for Philip to come home, our meeting seemed so panicked, so urgent. I cried: nasty, grotty tears. Now I feel bad that I have rallied. The awful truth is extreme emotions can be hard to sustain. I have a memory of Clara turning up on my doorstep after a row with Pete. She sobbed so much in my kitchen, she began to hiccup, like a baby. In the morning, I got her up and gave her coffee, and she toddled off to the Tube, vowing to be back that night, but the next time I saw her, weeks later, Pete was moving in and everything was fine. A friendship can change so gradually sometimes you don't notice, until moments like that come along and define it. Once Pete was on the scene, I realized, Clara and I would be "there" for each other when needed—for "a heavy," as we used to call it in our teens—but not every day, not like it used to be.

"What about Easter?" Clara is asking. "It's so early this year. Are you skiing again, or . . . was it Jamaica last April?"

"No. Philip has dropped his obsession with exotic holidays, thank God. Work." I think about the cottage in Peasenhall, which Philip bought with his first bonus, the snug kitchen, the bedrooms with their wonky floors, a house solid and real enough to have a proper family life lived within its walls, sitting empty, waiting for us like an old dog abandoned on the hard shoulder. "Why don't we all go to the cottage at Easter? Why don't we all go together?"

"Suffolk. Oh, I don't know . . ."

"We could go for walks, trips to the sea. We should fill the house with fun, laughter."

Clara smiles. It's a noncommittal smile.

I try not to feel deflated. I'm a bit too dependent on Clara. I know that. "How's Pete?" I ask lightly.

"He's ow'right." She does a little dingle-dangle with her shoulders. Pete is an artist. He creates installations, but mainly he cooks, and creates washing-up. He and Philip used to be friends. We did lots of things together—we surfed in Cornwall, cycled in Surrey, got pissed in Soho—but things change. Lives go out of sync. And now, well, I feel I have to lie a bit. I skip over the skiing holidays, the trips to Jamaica (actually, it was Nevis), things that cause tight ripples of tension at the top of my rib cage. Recently, over supper at a local Chinese restaurant, Pete ripped into academy schools and how they were "just a means of privatizing state education and handing it to local businesses." Millie's precious prep school, the one Philip insisted upon, with its prissy uniform, its swimming pool, its fleet of bustling blue buses, danced above our heads like a fantasy sequence in a Disney cartoon. I avoided Clara's eyes. I know what they both feel, that Philip and I have lost touch with what really matters. And I know they are right. I'm weak and easily led. I should stand up to Philip more. But I'm scared of annoying him, I suppose.

It's raining outside; a flurry hits the windows with a rattle. The café has floor-to-ceiling doors, which open wide in summer. They are closed now and the lights are on—trendy fittings, which dangle down like naked bulbs, each golden orb throwing a wobbly reflection on to each wooden table. It's stark in here, but cozy. "Real daube weather," I say, a reference to our A-level set book, Virginia Woolf's *To the Lighthouse*.

We cackle with laughter and then, when we stop, Clara asks how I am feeling about my mum.

I look out of the window. Two women are walking by, bent double under umbrellas, as if forgetting they could raise them if they wanted. Clara doesn't often ask. She knows I would rather not talk about it. It's not that I shy away from the subject; I just don't want to be one of those people who is still in a bad mood from their childhood. I take a glug of water. The dry pain rises, despite my efforts, the ugly murkiness. I swallow hard. "Fine," I say, as indifferently as I can. "I'm trying not to feel guilty. I know it wasn't my fault, that I did everything I could to stop her drinking. I'm resigned. Or I think I am. I still feel responsible. I keep thinking, I must go down and check, before realizing that I can't. In some ways it's a relief."

Clara is making a face, pulling her lips in, and it's an expression I've seen somewhere else. It's the expression PC Morrow made the previous day, and I realize, with a shock, that I had taken it to express solidarity in view of something that was *about* to happen—DI Perivale's endless questions—whereas actually, as here, it might well have been a hopeless sympathy for something that had *already* happened, that kept on happening, something I could do nothing about.

"Do you remember the plum chutney the woman next door to you used to make? She used to call us over and give us cheese sandwiches. Double Gloucester and chutney."

It's not the words that matter, but the connections, the threading of time, the fashioning of cheerful childhood memories out of what for me wasn't always very cheerful.

I smile. "She was always trying to feed us up, wasn't she? The plums were from her garden. You had to cook them; they were too bitter to eat raw off the tree. And I should know—I climbed over and tried enough times."

I ask after Clara's parents—still going strong, a reproach to all those parents who aren't. And we talk about Justice and Anna—old friends I haven't seen for ages. "Anna sends her love," Clara says thoughtfully. "She said she left a message . . ."

"I know. I'm terrible," I say. "They just live so far . . ."

"Yeah. I know."

But they don't. Not that far. Not really. It's just Philip didn't really like them and . . . well, it's my fault really. I've let myself become sucked into Philip's world. I've let my own friendships slide.

Changing the subject, I ask after her kids, lightly: it's important not to sound too envious. Her daughter, eleven, has recently discovered boys. Her elder son needs to have a stab at getting enough "points" or they won't let him stay on for A levels. The younger one is driving her mad with his mess. She makes the face of a gormless teenage boy. "'Why's my frickin' Topman top still dirty? I left it on the floor and it hasn't frickin' self-washed!'" Hamming up the awfulness of her children is her way of telling me a big family isn't everything.

We move on to work—some political stuff going on with her head of department; a year-ten group is playing up. She asks if I have heard from Robin—everyone in our life loves Robin—and I say she's doing a brilliant job and that I'm hoping to see her at Easter. "You could, too," I say, "if you come."

Clara wonders if I have got to the bottom of Marta.

I sigh. "I wish I could. I really want to. I want to be her friend. I keep thinking here she is on her own in a foreign country; she must be so lonely . . . But every time I try to talk to her it goes wrong. I get this feeling she doesn't want anything to do with me."

"Maybe your expectations are too high. Robin's a hard act to follow."

"She is unbelievably tidy."

"That should be a good thing, no?"

"I know. It should be. It is. And Millie seems not to mind her. She's obviously different with her. And that's what counts."

"Except you can't live with someone you don't get on with. It's impossible to sustain."

"I should try harder," I say. "Though actually trying seems to make it worse."

A woman near the bar with very long hair and zips at her ankles keeps looking over. She can't quite place me. It's driving her mad. She's wondering if I'm the woman who goes to the gym with her sister. They stare less when they recognize you outright.

Clara hasn't noticed. We've finished our coffee and cake. It is getting darker out there. Clouds are gathering, swirling, lowering, like a call to arms, or home. I pick my bag up from the floor. It's the posh bag Philip gave me for Christmas and I have been slightly hiding it from Clara, in case she knows how much it cost, and put it on my lap under the table, a precursor to departure. Clara has still got a question, though, I can tell.

"What's it like?" she says. "A dead body. What does it *look like*?"

I study her with interest. "No one has asked me that. They've all been more delicate. They've all asked what it *felt* like to find it, not what it actually *looked* like. Maybe that was what they were after and I've just been being dim. It looked like flesh, not like a person, just flesh. In this case, horrible battered, bruised flesh. But nothing else. Everything they say about the spirit leaving the body is true. I think, anyway."

"Was it scary?"

"No. The dying are scary. You know, zombies—arms reaching out of graves—but I don't think the dead are."

"That's something, then," she says.

We say good-bye in the street. She is so much slighter than me; her shoulders feel fragile when I hug her. An old man is pissing against the wall of William Hill, but we are standing by a shop that sells jewelery in the shape of jumping rabbits, and lampshades with birds on. It has stopped raining for a moment—long enough hopefully to grab a black cab—and I feel as if my "nightmare," as Clara called it, is over, that I can sort out my marriage, and put the dead woman behind me.

· · ·

UNDER YOUR SKIN   71

But he's there again. At the back of my mind, I thought he might
be, and it's almost a relief—as things you've been dreading often are.

I should have listened to Clara. She told me to take the Tube.
Once you lose the swing of public transport, it's hard to get back
in. It took forever in a cab. The taxi driver took some mad route,
up to Westway and down through Earls Court. Steve, now safely
home with his wife in Wallington, would have told him what for.
London glittered and blurred through the window. Rain came
in flurries, in waves; wheels hissed and sprayed; the windscreen
wiper scraped. My optimism drained, along with the rain. Fulham
Broadway, where I had my first flat, looked dismal, the worst kind
of urban—veg from the market rotting in seeping gutters, commuters scurrying from the Tube in damp suits. Under Battersea
Bridge, the river churned, beige and pockmarked. Nearing home,
on Trinity Road, the common stretched bleak and gray. As the taxi
ticked, idling in the bottleneck beyond the prison, I could see over
to the tennis courts, where small figures huddled under trees: an
after-school All Stars group lesson halted by rain. The police cordon
must have been lifted, then.

He was sitting in his car and he got out as soon as the taxi drove
off. I was rummaging for my keys—why can I never find them?—
and he came up behind me and said, so politely, "You won't be
needing those, if that's all right." I pretended to be startled, though
I had seen the car the moment the taxi pulled up.

"I've spoken to your help, and she says you're not needed for
an hour or so."

"Marta, you mean."

"If you wouldn't mind, we would like it if you came to the station with us. It's easier down there. Just so we can ask you a few
more questions, properly."

"I've told you everything. I don't know anything else."

"I know it might seem unnecessary to you. I know you're busy, but I'm sure you understand we need to pursue every lead we can. Nobody—you more than anyone—wants to think there is a killer out there for any longer than there need be."

He's right, I can't complain with a killer on the loose, and he has to follow procedure. "I am at your disposal, then," I say, and we climb into the back of his car. It's a beaten-up Volkswagen Golf, not what you imagine for an unmarked police car. It smells of air freshener—there is a cardboard pine tree dangling from the rearview mirror—and of old onions. That'll be all those Big Macs, I think.

Perivale gets in next to me—there's another man behind the wheel, the "thuggish" man from the other day. He has short-cropped hair, the kind that grows in dark whorls at the back of the neck, and broad shoulders.

I talk too much on the way. I always do when I'm nervous.

"Do you like sitting in the back?" I say. "Does he drive you around like a chauffeur?"

"Very funny."

"So you're just keeping me company?"

"Something like that."

"All this rain," I say after a bit. "Must bugger up a crime scene,"

"Can do so indeed," Perivale replies.

At the police station, we hurry straight through past the desk and down a corridor. The room we enter is smaller than the smallest rooms you see on *Vera* or *Scott & Bailey,* and if there is a two-way mirror, it's extremely well concealed. It's not very well insulated either, like one of those 1980s conversions. Sounds of the station drift through the plyboard: laughter, talk, a voice saying, "I'm sorry, but if she thinks she can talk to me like that, she's got the wrong woman."

Perivale steers me to a chair and asks if I want a cup of tea. Then he disappears out through the door, leaving it open, and I stare around me for a few minutes. The walls are off-white, recently painted, though the decorator has missed a bit above the skirting—a calligraphic smear, a missing jigsaw-piece streak of darker paint underneath. My mind has started flickering all over the place, as if trying to find some comforting thought to latch on to. I wonder if they use ordinary decorators from the Yellow Pages to paint police stations, or whether it is in someone's line of duty. "Oi, Robson, you're on paint. Counterterrorism this afternoon. Crown magnolia this morning."

"No offense, but I'm not the one running around like a blue-arsed fly." It's the same voice through the wall.

"I'm sorry, but . . . ," "No offense, but . . ." People only say those things when they mean the opposite. They're not sorry! They do mean offense! The English language is inherently contradictory. How often people begin sentences with "Yes. No . . ." Perhaps equivocation is a British thing. Or maybe not. Trying to buy a train ticket in southern India, just after we married, Philip and I couldn't work out if we could reserve seats. "Yes," the man at the ticket office kept repeating while shaking his head. Perhaps ambiguity is the human condition, a desire to say the opposite of what we really mean.

"Here we go. Can't guarantee its quality, but at least it's hot and wet."

Perivale has come back, with another man in tow. He is as tall, but with less hair, more portly round the waist, as if he spends most of his day at a desk, or in meetings. He has the kind of body type, a python that has swallowed a goat, that Dr. Janey, *Mornin' All*'s resident health expert, says is the most dangerous. He is wearing a gray suit with an electric blue shirt and a thin black tie, an attention to style that suggests he is oblivious to the treacherous fat congealing round his organs. Perivale is wearing a suit, too, an unfashionably baggy black one, unlined: I've only just noticed.

Perivale introduces me to Detective Chief Inspector Paul Fraser.

He has a Scottish accent. I wonder out loud if he is from Aberdeen and he looks surprised and says he is. He opens his mouth to ask how I know, but Perivale, rubbing his hands, says: "Right, let's get going." Neither of them has brought tea for themselves. Perhaps it would be giving the wrong message. This is not a social occasion. I rack my brains to think if Morse ever drinks tea in the interview room.

Perivale switches on a tape recorder. I tell myself it's no different from that "turn over your paper" moment at the beginning of an exam. It'll be finished before I know it. "First of all, you are not under arrest. You are free to leave at any time."

"That's good, then." I make to stand up.

"But if you did, we might have to arrest you."

I suspect he is joking, but I feel a trickle of anxiety. Perivale's manner has changed. It's almost as if he is enjoying knowing something I don't.

He opens a document wallet and lays the photograph of Ania Dudek on the melamine table in front of us. "Just to confirm, you have never seen this woman before?"

A jolt at the sight of her face. My eyes unexpectedly fill with tears. "No. Not before I found her. I've told you that."

"And you've never been in her flat?"

I pretend to rub my eyes, to get the tears away. "No."

I assume he is repeating these questions for the sake of the tape recorder, or the DCI. I look across at Fraser, and he gives me a quick, surprisingly sweet smile. Perivale is just being pompous for the sake of it. I'm only a witness.

Then from his cardboard file Perivale slides out something else. At first, I think it is the advertisement from the *Lady*, but the sheet is broader, the paper thinner, more yellowy, the conflagration of text and photo altogether different. Creases across the cutting suggest it has been folded. Even upside down, I can see the photograph is of me.

"Do you have any idea why Ania Dudek would have had a copy of this—'My Perfect Weekend: TV Presenter Gaby Mortimer Enjoys Her Family Time,' an article that appeared in the *Telegraph* on Saturday the seventeenth of September last year?"

For a moment, I don't understand what he means. Then my heart thumps in the back of my neck. I study it, trying to gather my thoughts. Lines leap out: "Friday night is movie night. As the only child of a single parent, family is vital to my well-being. My husband makes sure he is home early and we order a takeaway; sometimes, we eat it in bed in front of the TV . . ." I think it was June when I spoke to the journalist; they must have kept it on file. It's like a time capsule, a touchstone of a happier time. There's a sidebar Q&A. For "Dream weekend?" I've answered, "Muddy walks with my daughter and husband."

I look up, feeling the color come back. "I can't possibly think why she would have it. It's peculiar. Do you know?"

Fraser and Perivale are both staring at me. I look back down. My brain feels hot. I think it through out loud. "Maybe she *thought* of applying to be a nanny, which is why she had the ad from the *Lady* and then didn't, for whatever reason. Her application was too late perhaps. Then she became, you know, curious. I don't live that far from her. She might have recognized me. Maybe she cut it out to show someone—'This is the woman with the job.' What do you think?"

I look to Perivale hopefully for answers, but he sets off on one of his tangents. I'm trying to concentrate. I am still bothered by the cutting, even if he isn't. He tells me he has searched Ania's flat and that when he searches a scene, "I have a quirk: I tend to follow the left-hand wall round a room. If you go to Hampton Court Maze and follow the left-hand hedge, you get to the middle. You solve the problem. It's a good technique. Blood distribution, saliva, little bits and pieces—I'm not going to miss it."

He has caught my interest, though I am not sure where this is going. Maybe he's just showing off to his DCI.

"Anyway, we didn't find her mobile phone, which makes us think someone decided it was worth disposing of. It's amazing what I *did* find, though. In a pile of magazines, for example, not just that"—he gestures with his chin to "My Perfect Weekend"—"also *this*." From the document wallet he removes a sheath of papers, fans them across the table. Pages from *Easy Living, Metro,* the *Guardian*'s *G2, Vogue*: all interviews I have given in the last year.

For a moment, I can't breathe. A sharp pain in my diaphragm, like acute indigestion, a surge of throat-throttling alarm. I have to force myself to inhale. I try to concentrate on filling my lungs with air, diffusing oxygen into my bloodstream, gaseous-exchange alveoli, intercostal muscles, O-level biology, the life cycle of the frog. Not just one short piece. A file. A whole file of cuttings.

"Why do you think these articles were there?"

I swallow hard. "I've no idea." Why does he think *I* know about all this? He should be telling *me*. Bloody hell, this is weird. "I have no idea at all. I mean–"

"Did you give them to her?"

"No. Why should I? I never met her."

"Please think before answering the next question." Perivale does that slow pulling down of his jowls with his fingers. It means he has something serious on his mind. "Take your time. I want you to think carefully."

From his Pandora's box file he produces two photographs. One of them is of a green cowl-necked top; the other is of a silver cardigan, cropped, with three-quarter-length sleeves. They have been photographed laid flat on what looks like a canteen table. Both items look familiar.

"These clothes were found in the flat of the dead girl. Do you recognize them? Think. Don't feel you have to rush into it."

I don't say anything.

Fraser moves, and the leg of his chair squeaks against the lino floor. It seems to hurry Perivale along because he doesn't wait for me to think any more and the next thing I know he has placed two more items on the table, lining them up next to each other.

"Now do you recognize them?" he says.

The new items are stills from *Mornin' All,* taken from the Web site. In one I'm talking to the singer Tom Jones, gesticulating, laughing, and wearing the cowl-necked green top. In the other I am listening to Stan interrogate the mother of a persistent school-refuser in the silver cardigan.

I can't think clearly. I loosen my sweater at the neck and a gust of my own body scent rises up. It's too much to take in. "I don't know. I'm baffled. This is so disturbing."

"Are you sure you don't know?"

Could it be a coincidence? Or she saw the items and copied me? She had a similar body shape, and they are both tops that suit women with narrow shoulders and big boobs. Or perhaps they were in a bag I took to charity. Or is Marta involved? Could she have been lending some of my things out? And then I think of a solution—it fits both the clothes and the magazine articles—though it's a horrible solution. I don't like it at all. "Do you think she might have been my stalker?" I feel sick.

The two policemen look at each other. Something passes between them.

"Why did you lie about touching the body?" It is the first question DCI Fraser has asked.

"I didn't lie. I forgot. Is she my stalker?" I can't put it all together.

"Why did you say you didn't know the victim when you obviously did?"

"I *didn't* know her!"

"And your alibi." Fraser looks down at some notes. "You say you were with your daughter and her nanny for some of the evening, but for the rest of it you were alone. Is that right?"

"Yes. My husband didn't get back until three a.m."

"That's an incomplete alibi," Perivale confirms.

"What? Does it matter if it's incomplete?"

Perivale emits a sarcastic sort of laugh.

"Why do you care about my alibi?" I get to my feet. Suddenly, I realize where this is going. I feel scared, but more than that, outraged. "You think *I killed* her?"

Perivale says nothing.

"Even if she was my stalker, that's not a motive. I wouldn't have killed her." Are they insane or just really stupid?

"No one, out of television cop dramas, really cares about motive," Fraser says. "In my experience, who, where, and how are more important than why."

Perivale stands up. "We'll see you again. Don't go on any long trips."

The moment I get through the door, I run upstairs to my wardrobe—demolishing neat pile after neat pile, scattering garments in my search. When I have finished, I stand in the middle of my bedroom, clothes tangled at my feet.

Marta and Millie are both in the kitchen. Millie is sprawled on the sofa, apparently doing her homework, though her books are all over the place and she doesn't seem to have a pen. Marta, in latex gloves, is scrubbing the sink. Millie throws herself at me, demanding to know where I've been and what collective nouns I can think of because Marta doesn't know any. I dart a look at Marta, who isn't smiling.

We sort Millie's homework (a quiver of arrows, a squabble of seagulls, a posse of police), and I put her in bed with her pink rabbit and her bear (a congress of stuffed toys). Afterward, I catch Marta on the landing and ask if I can have a word.

"Yes," she says standing on the top stair, one hand on the wall, the other on the bannister, blocking the way, with her pale face tilted, not moving.

It seems bossy to insist she comes downstairs, so in the gloom there, halfway up, halfway down, I ask her whether she has seen the jersey top or the silver cardie, whether she remembers if I took them to Suffolk at Christmas, or gave them away? She shakes her head a few times. "And my bracelet," I say, "the gray thread with the silver balls—have you seen that?" She shakes her head again.

"Did you know Ania Dudek, the woman who was killed? She was Polish. A little older than you, but I thought you might have come across her, moved in the same circles?" Even as I am saying this, I realize it's tactless, possibly even hurtful. Marta hasn't shown signs of moving in any circle at all. I gaze at her, stricken.

"I am here to improve my English," Marta says. "Polish companions do not interest me. Is that all?"

"I . . . yes."

She climbs the last stair and pushes past me, gently, and I catch a faint, but distinctive trace of fig. How odd. She is wearing the same perfume as me. She opens her door, just a sliver, and slips in, closing it behind her, though not before I have a chance to see piles of clothes all over her floor. I stand there for a second, feeling that I have trespassed or crossed a line.

The doorbell goes and I almost fall, face first, down the stairs.

I open the door a crack and there stands a large man with crates full of plastic bags, crinkling as the contents shift. It's the Ocado supermarket delivery. I open the door wide to let him in. He carries the handfuls of groceries into the kitchen. "Where do you want us? Down here, is it?" They are terribly polite now there is a "driver feedback questionnaire." I don't realize the Ocado man hasn't closed the front door until I am back up in the hall. It has been wide open all this time. Gusts of wind, rain, litter, anything, anyone could have come in when I wasn't watching.

In bed, I decide they can't suspect me. It's impossible. They would have arrested me. It's a game. Perivale thinks I need cutting down to size. But I could sense Perivale's arousal. He was like a horse backing up, flaring its nostrils, before a race. What are they waiting for? What aren't they telling me? Something else nags at me. It keeps coming to the surface and flitting off.

In the middle of the night, I sit up in bed. Philip, who has slipped beside me like an invisible man, like a ghost, doesn't stir. All at once, I realize: the rose-pink cap-sleeved T-shirt, with buttons down the front, the casual, summery tank: I can't believe I didn't recognize it the moment I saw it. Ania Dudek died wearing my top.

SATURDAY

Chill winds whip across the Brighton seafront. Seagulls as big as cats perch along the turquoise balustrades with their backs to the sea, as if the drama is taking place in front of them, not behind. It's olive green out there, foaming white, the sky a paler, bluer gray, the swell filling and rising, like the wing of a plane and then rolling in, pulling and sucking on the shingle. A dog noses past, and the stripy gulls flap up, squawking and chaotic, before landing in the same row a few feet farther on. Fresh in the air is ozone and diesel and the smell of hot fried doughnuts.

"I actually think the seaside is nicer in winter," I say. "Don't you? The colors and everything. It's much more romantic."

Philip is trudging with his head down. He has switched his BlackBerry off for the morning. He is almost catatonically silent, but that at least suggests he is making an effort.

"Do you remember when I was on *Newsnight* and had to do all the party-political conferences? Do you remember bunking off work and coming to Blackpool to join me, to that scuzzy hotel on the front? It was all glass except that every window was tinted, and they all had those funny, dusty, vertical blinds, so there were no views anywhere?"

Philip makes a noise that I take to be an acknowledgment that this event did occur, that the hotel with its vertical blinds did in fact exist.

"Where shall we have lunch?"

"I don't mind." He clears his throat. "You choose." I try not to think there is anything wrong with this. I try to believe his indifference is about the venue and not me.

I grab hold of the small portion of my soul that's trying to slip away. We have the Pavilion to look round, the dinky-do shops in the Lanes to browse for secondhand books and vintage frocks and designer kitchenware.

"I'm not very hungry yet," I manage to say cheerfully. "Let's decide later."

My life has returned to normal. If it is possible to believe that the horror of Ania Dudek can ever go away, it appears to have gone away. Philip has been an absence, or an absent presence (he has hardly slept), but I have had three days of routine—work, home, Millie, supper, the occasional run—to distract me. Much of the time, a man has been stationed in a car outside our house, or as close as he can get (parking being a competitive sport in the Toast Rack). From his number-one cut, I think it is the policeman who drove me to the police station on Tuesday, but I'm not sure. I also don't know, and I am not going to ask, if I'm being guarded or watched.

It is at the back of my mind much of the time—this feeling that the police want or need me for something—but there have been moments when I have forgotten. Whenever I catch myself thinking about the case, I block it out.

My "terrifying ordeal" has also been off the agenda at *Mornin' All,* largely, I'm afraid, thanks to a tragedy in the American Midwest, combined with double-dip recession here and economic chaos in Europe. On Wednesday, Terri said, "Okay. Directive from on high. We are to be the light at the end of the tunnel. Dancing bears, cotton candy, cupcakes—you know the score." What with all the scurrying to secure that *Hollyoaks* actress who is storming *Dancing on Ice,* my discovery of a dead body went out of everyone's mind. Thank God.

On the personal front, there have been no more enquiries from journalists, no more photographers. Philip's parents left on Wednesday for their cruise, and when I spoke to Margaret in the middle of her packing, I told her there was nothing to worry about, that it was just a typical media circus. By the time they come back, I said, it would have all blown over.

"Do tell us if there is anything we can do."

"Of course. Now you have a fabulous trip."

On Thursday, Jude Morris rang. Ostensibly, she was phoning to talk about the fund-raising evening at the school. She had forgotten to ask if I wanted to "join a table" for the quiz before the auction or whether I wanted to perch in the wings, before my slot, with her and some of the other PTA squaddies. I told her that, no one having actually invited me to "join a table," the squaddies' perch sounded perfect. Particularly if she was on it.

Then she said, "Everything all right?"

"Yup. Fine. Calmer, thanks."

"It's just Rachel Curtis, who was walking her dog, saw you going off in a police car on Tuesday." She made a police car sound as extraordinary a proposition as a pimped-up double-stretch candy-pink limo.

"Oh," I said. "Blimey. Yeah. That was a thing."

"So what's going on?"

I should have told her. I'd promised not to lie. And if I wanted her to be my new friend, this was an opportunity. Yet the thought of any more information slipping out, of the production company hearing, of it being blown up into more than it was . . . "It's all so horribly stressful," I said vaguely.

"I'm sure . . . if there is anything I can do."

"I'll spill the beans over a bottle of wine, when things are a bit calmer." Could I get away with that for now?

"Of course. Poor you. I'll speak to you soon." Apparently I could.

Lunch is butternut squash and ginger soup with homemade rye sourdough in a homey health food shop at the top of North Laine. Our table, honey-colored varnished pine, is sticky to the touch. The saltshaker and pepper shaker, one black, one white, are halves of a naked body that slot together to make a whole.

"Is that erotic?" I ask Philip.

He screws up his nose. His eyes are red-rimmed. Hay fever season is beginning. "Bit hermaphrodite-y."

Despite everything, I still love him. I think this in a detached way, as if from a great height. There's a clenching deep in my stomach as my muscles contract. It was the wrinkling of the nose and the "y" at the end of *hermaphrodite,* a verbal tick, that did it. They say, don't they, that in a good relationship the partners meld, become one? What was it Plato said? "Love is the pursuit of the whole." There have been times, years, when I stopped noticing that I loved him. If only reciprocated love could feel as intense as love that isn't, how blissful I would have known myself to be. Now that he has pulled away, I can see him more clearly, am reminded, with a sweet pain, of everything—his face, his skin, his mind—that I fell for in the first place. What is agony is that it should be mine and it's not.

Last night, I wore the Myla underwear, the "boudoir lingerie" he bought for my birthday last June. I would say it hasn't seen much daylight since, but it hasn't seen much darkness either. I wish I hadn't put it on. A Marlene half-padded demi-bra and matching thong in "LA Rose" only adds to the humiliation when things go wrong. We were both exhausted, or that's what I told him. He turned away. For a moment, I thought he was crying. He was soon asleep, or pretending.

I lay there yearning. I felt quite tragic in my longing, like Sylvia Plath. One touch and I'd have died. His naked body—I hadn't packed his pajamas—thrilled me. Revellers caroused drunkenly below our window. Silently, unmoving, he slept on. The room was hot.

"So, the Easter hols," I say chirpily, putting the salt and pepper cadavers back together. "I vaguely invited Clara and Pete to come to Suffolk with us."

He raises an enquiring eyebrow. "Sorry?"

He's not even listening to me. "Clara and her family—invited them to Suffolk for Easter?"

"Oh, did you." His tone is not encouraging.

I can see thoughts flickering in his eyes, like figures on the NASDAQ. He could be remembering what a stressful week I have had, or how bad he feels for me. He could be feeling guilty, or sheepish, about last night.

"Philip—"

"No. Yes. No. I can see that that might be a good idea." He has lost interest. I remember a fight we had with a packet of Maltesers the first time we came to Brighton, trying to throw them into each other's mouths, Philip howling with laughter. It's unnerving how the warmth of that memory makes him seem colder now.

"Great. I'll see if Robin and Ian and baby Charlie can join us for Easter lunch, though Ian might be busy with lambing. Perhaps an Easter egg hunt in the garden, if Clara's lot aren't too old for it."

Philip keeps adding salt to his soup, leaving the white hermaphrodite alone on the table after he's done. I keep slipping it back. The bottom of the pepper is chipped, so they won't fit together properly, and they never will. The café owners—the woman behind the counter with the blond dreadlocks—should throw them away and buy a new set.

With sudden certainty, I think he is about to leave me. It is over. It's too late. There is nothing I can do.

He sighs; his whole body shakes. "Hon," he says, "I've got to go away again this week, to Singapore. Only a few days with any luck. Less than a week, or maybe . . . a week. Back-to-back meetings, important ones. Will you be all right in the house on your own?"

My body feels as if it belongs to somebody else. "I won't be on my own. I'll have Millie. And Marta."

"You will make sure you lock the doors properly at night—put the chain on, won't you?" He knows I always forget.

I'm biting the inside of my cheek. "We'll be fine. Safe as houses." He hates complainers, "whiners." He fired his last PA, a fearsomely efficient Harvard grad, because she was always moaning about the office air-con.

He pushes his soup bowl away. "Don't make light of it. There's some maniac out there."

"I know. God, Philip, you don't have to tell me."

Something passes between us. In his face is a desperate vulnerability. With a stab at spirit he says, "Shame you have to work or you could come with me, like in the old days."

The old days. The woman with the blond dreadlocks clears our bowls. She asks if we enjoyed our soup, and Philip, who has hidden most of it under (or in) his bread, says it was delicious. You can get by on pretending.

My stomach settles. He's not leaving me, not quite yet. I have a sense of possibilities, of things cranking up, starting again. For the first time in ages, sitting with Philip in a café in Brighton, I try to imagine an ordinary life.

WEDNESDAY

They come for me soon after dawn. It is as if they were waiting for Philip's taxi to tick, tick, tick up the road and stutter off round the corner before they knocked.

I'm half dressed. I have come to the door holding my tights. The light out here is pinky, as if the sun had risen early for once and was thinking of poking through. "I thought you were my husband," I say. "I thought he'd forgotten his passport."

"Gaby Mortimer?"

"Y-es," I say, confused. Perivale knows full well I am Gaby Mortimer. He isn't looking at me. He is gazing at the wisteria, at the twisted wooded stems, the hopeful lime green new fronds, as if inspecting them for buds.

"I'm arresting you," he says, "on suspicion of murdering Ania Dudek on the night of the fifteenth of March. You do not have to say anything, but I should warn you that it may harm your defense if you do not mention when questioned anything which you may later rely upon as evidence in court."

Is that the right sentence? It sounds wrong, mangled into a hideous pattern. Random, ugly words. Or is it the roaring of neurons, synapses, electricity fizzing through my nervous system. I try to speak but my mouth is full of teeth and tongue. My knees buckle. My limbs turn acid and dissolve. My body, thick, flesh, bones, seems to belong to somebody else. I can still see Perivale in the center of my vision, but the rest of the world has gone black.

PC Morrow comes out from behind him and takes my arm and steers me into the house. She is talking to me quietly, as if I am a confused old lady who thinks her care home's a hotel. Am I a confused old lady who thinks my care home's a hotel? She is guiding me up the stairs, still propping me up. "Here. We go. Up the stairs," she says. "We'll get you properly dressed and then we'll pop down the station and we'll have a nice cup of tea there." Or did she say hospital? Or day center? I don't know what she said. It's like a migraine without the headache, when you can't trust yourself to know what's real and what isn't.

I sit on the edge of the bed, aged 110, and she tries to put my tights on me, struggling to get a purchase. Suddenly, the black clears. "I can do it," I say, almost kicking her. "I'm sorry. Oh God, I'm so sorry. Did I hurt you? I'm sorry. I mean, why on earth? What is happening? Why? This is just absurd, it's completely *mad*."

Now I've got over the shock, I am outraged. Out the window, I can see Perivale and the knuckleheaded man from the Golf through the open slats. The police car is parked in the middle of the road, with its lights flashing, its engine running, its Day-Glo stripes throbbing. It will wake the entire street. If Rachel Curtis is walking her dog, she'll have a field day.

"I know," PC Morrow says, wrinkling her friendly, freckled nose. "I'm sure it'll all be cleared up and you'll be home for lunch."

"I've got *work*," I almost shout. "I don't have *lunch*."

"God, I do. I'm a real stickler for meals, starting with a good breakfast. Today, I had porridge with milk and golden syrup, which has less calories than you think. It's only one point on Weight Watchers. I try not to snack in between." She gives the concave swell of her stomach, encased in its unfashionably high-waisted policeman's trousers, a little rub. "That's the problem—the machine in the canteen. A Kit Kat here, a Bounty there . . . maybe a two-finger pack of McVities All Butter Shortbread . . ."

I stare at her, lost for words.

After a few seconds, in which I am not sure I might not scream, I say, "I think you've got a lovely figure."

Perivale has left the front door wide open. Why? So I don't make a run for it? Or maybe he just doesn't care, concern for normal door-closing etiquette not being part of his remit. A change in acoustic—the vibrating hum of the police car, the rising snarl of the first planes out of Heathrow—has woken Millie. She is sitting on the stairs, clutching her pink rabbit when I come out of my room. "What's happening?" she says.

I take my daughter's sleepy face in my hands and kiss it carefully all over. PC Morrow steps past us. "Nothing, Mills. Nothing to worry about," I say. "I'll knock on Marta's room and ask her to get up. I've got to go out for work. Just work."

"Really? Has Daddy gone?"

"Yes. Marta will give you breakfast."

"Time to go," PC Morrow says.

"I love you, Millie," I call, trying not to sound desperate.

"You have got to be kidding," I say to the man from the Golf when he puts his hand on my head. I twist away from him and he clamps it back down and steers me into the back of the car. I am shaking, but I'm aware of it being funny, the sort of thing I could tell Philip. "I can't believe you did that! Put your hand on my head! Do they teach that at Hendon? I thought they only did it on *The Bill*." Apparently not. Apparently they do it in real life, too.

PC Morrow and Perivale are both in the front, Perivale this time in the driver's seat. "I've got to be on air in four hours," I say. "I'm coming willingly because I didn't want to upset my daughter any more than she already was. I am a good, helpful citizen. You have everything wrong; you must have. I haven't done anything. It's madness. And, come on, guys, you woke up my daughter, and she's got school. Oh God, what would have happened if I had had no one to look after her?"

"Arrangements would have been made," says Knucklehead, who is sitting next to me, slightly too close.

"Another thing, my driver will be here in less than an hour." I rummage for my phone. "I'll just ring him and tell him to pick me up from the station. We'll clear this up quickly, won't we? It must be a misunderstanding. You won't need me for long, will you? Actually, can I ring my husband? He's about to get on a plane."

Knucklehead takes the phone out of my hand and puts it in his pocket.

Morrow twists round in her seat. "We'll sort it all out for you. Don't worry. You won't have to do a thing. We'll take care of everything."

I've heard those words before. It's the mantra of the travel agent Philip is so keen on, the one specializing in "handpicked, tailor-made luxury."

Funny how the same combination of syllables, in a different context, can sound so chilling.

Who ever thinks they're going to see the inside of a cell? I've got a bench to sit on. A tiny square window up high. That little tent of blue. Except it's white. The sky is white. Distant drilling. No bucket. Apparently, I can knock on the door if I need to go. I'm so tense I don't think I'll ever go again. I've got nothing with me. No phone. No pen. No book. You'd think there would be graffiti: "Dan woz here"; "Fuck off." Not even that to read. Nothing to do, except look at the four blank walls and worry about what is happening to me.

I ask myself out loud if the police have gone mad. I'm Alice down the rabbit hole. I try and think of more cheering precedents, but I can't. In the last hour, I have been cautioned, informed of my rights, had my photograph taken—click: full frontal; click: turn to the side. I tried, as it was happening, not to think of the reprints. This picture will be shown, like Hugh Grant's after his dalliance with the LA prozzy, in every piece about me ad infinitum. I tried to come up with something funny to tell Philip. I'll tell him, I decided, that I kept turning my head, flashing that over-the-shoulder smile that any pro knows is the most flattering of profiles. I didn't, of course. I looked as glumly petrified as I felt. I couldn't have raised a smile if you'd paid me. Not a mug shot, a snapshot into my soul.

I have given my fingerprints—and made a thumb of ink on the hem of my skirt by mistake. One of us is never coming out, I thought to myself. There you go: a joke! I could tell Philip that. PC Morrow asked if I wanted to see a copy of *The Codes of Practice and Procedures*.

"Nobody ever does," she said. "Or I did have one bloke, pissed to the tits, mouthing off all over the place, thick as shit, mind my French. I said, 'Certainly, sir. Do you want help with the big words?'" She giggled. I told her I was all right, thanks.

I've turned down legal representation, too. Philip has his own firm of solicitors, posh ones like his travel agent: a sparky solicitor on the third floor for wills, another on the sixth for conveyancing, and presumably another equally sparky on the eighth in the event of murder charges. Only the best for the golden couple. But I don't want a sparky solicitor. It would be a statement of guilt. I don't even want to see the duty lawyer. I don't need to.

"But the duty lawyer's free!" PC Morrow said, as if they were a sample of a new type of yogurt being handed out in a shopping centre.

I close my eyes. The cell is too small, so I pace in my head. Up and down. Up and down. It doesn't soothe. I am back in the exam room; the paper's turned over, but I haven't revised. When Millie was first born, I kept having this nightmare that I was in the middle of Bombay, thronging with people, traffic, noise, and Philip was trying to make me jump on to one of those teeming top-heavy buses they go in for in there, but I couldn't because I was holding a cat, a stray I used to feed in our shed when I was a child, and it was struggling to get free, and I knew if I dropped it, I would lose it. It would be sucked up by the heaving city. I would never find it again.

It was a stupid dream because of the cat—Philip accused me of "moggish sentimentality"—and yet that giddy feeling of standing on the edge of something terrible and inevitable, of a loss waiting to happen, is what I have now. I'm out of control. All that I have— money, house, job, connections—none of it means anything.

Calming thoughts, calming thoughts.

I was allowed one phone call. I tried Philip first, but it went to voicemail. There was a time he would have rung me from the station and the train and the airport, when going away would have made him homesick. That doesn't happen anymore. He doesn't have room for that sort of emotion. He didn't even say good-bye this morning. When he went downstairs, I was expecting him to come back up. I prepared a loving speech about how space would do us good. I was going to hug him hard, just in case it was the last time I saw him. He knows I'm pathetic like that. But this morning he didn't come back into the bedroom. I heard the taxi outside the window and the front door close.

So I didn't leave a message. And anyway, what good would it have done? If he had gone through security, they probably wouldn't have let him back out, and that would have been unbelieveably stressful. And even if they had, perhaps it would end up being for nothing. He would have given up his trip, gone through all the inconvenience and annoyance of that, and I might be home before he got here. I might be having *lunch*.

I hung up.

"Not leaving a message?" PC Morrow asked.

"Didn't want to use up my go," I said. I smiled at her.

"You kill me," she said. "Go on, then. Try someone else."

Marta answered the home phone on the first ring. Millie was dressed and eating Cheerios. Yes, she had calmed down. "I said to her, 'Silly girl! Your mother back later. She out all the time anyway.'"

I didn't have the energy to take umbrage, so I laughed and told her I didn't know how long the police would need me—they had a few questions, that was all—but could she "hold the fort" until I got back? This delayed things a little while, idioms, along with collective nouns, not having yet been covered at the Tooting School of English.

PC Morrow took the phone out of my hand, quite abruptly then, as if I had taken advantage of her benevolence. She said if I wanted she would inform my work that . . .

"Will I be late in today?"

". . . you won't be coming in at all."

We were on the station side of the front desk at this point. She was sitting on a high stool, raised up higher than me, even though I was standing. "Thank you," I said. I thought about Terri's panic and Stan's glee, and Alison Brett, that efficient woman in publicity, and what she would say about all this. Leaning my elbow on the counter, I thumped the palm of my hand on my forehead and rested it there for a moment.

"Oh Lord. Will they be really cross?" she said. "I have no idea what happens in these circumstances. Will Stan the Man be all on his own on the sofa? Poor Stan . . . Oh!" She moved her chin to one shoulder suggestively. "Maybe if I ask nicely, they'll let me cuddle up next to him instead."

"Not you, too," I said.

"Now, what about hubby? Do you want me to keep trying his number and give him a message?"

I went quite still. I thought about Philip being late for my mother's funeral, how he promised to come home for Millie's birthday and forgot. His distance, the feeling I have that he is on the verge of a decision. I thought about how important he'd said these meetings were, how tense he has been, how, possibly, if our marriage has any chance at all, he needs time away. I thought about him leaving today without saying good-bye.

"Don't worry," I said. "I'll ring him later when I'm home."

An hour in a cell is a million years outside. I don't know what I am being kept waiting for. My mind wanders wildly. What would a TV detective say? "Let's leave her to kick her heels for a bit." But then what does "kick your heels" mean? Or is it "cool your heels?" Do they want me to be bored? Or calm down? Or do they want me to express exuberance, like a horse?

What do they want with me? Time expands. I can feel every atom moving. Particles shifting.

I don't eat, even when Knucklehead brings me a completely circular slice of boiled gammon under a completely circular ice-cream scoop of mashed potato.

A young, anxious policeman, still wet behind the ears, calls for me when it is time. He blushes almost girlishly—two pink spots high in his cheeks—when I smile and ask his name. I'm not wearing makeup. My hair is in tatters. He probably doesn't even recognize me. Who cares what he says about me to his girlfriend, or his mum and dad, when he gets home? I don't need to play a part. But I have to smile. I don't know what else to do. Partly, it's to stop myself from crying.

Perivale gets to his feet when I come into the room—the same, bland interview room as before—dwarfing the space. I pretend to look around. "I like what you've done," I say. "Have you thought of knocking through?"

It's a terrible joke. What's wrong with me?

"Take a seat."

Knucklehead enters. It is 1347 hours. I know that because Perivale leans forward, hair flopping, and says it into the tape. I also learn that Knucklehead's real name is Detective Constable de Felice. His parents might be Italian, but he must have grown up here because he speaks with a South London accent. He has hooded green eyes and one of those triangular-shaped faces that Pixar uses for its superheroes—a ridiculously broad forehead tapering to a squarely pointed jaw. I bet his mother hates his hair.

Perivale has been running through the preparatory guff I've heard before, plus all the instructions about remaining silent if I want to. I recite my name and my address, and I say no, I definitely have never been to Ania Dudek's flat before; no, I have never crossed the threshold; no, I had never met her before; and no, I didn't know her from Adam.

I'm beginning to relax a little. I'm even thinking, Been there, done that, when, with an alacrity that nearly sends the tape recorder flying, Perivale pushes forward across the table and says, "She was pregnant when she was strangled. Do you know that? Eleven weeks pregnant."

The world stops turning. The edges of the room blur. I hold tight to the edge of the table to stop myself from tipping forward.

"I'm sorry," I say. "I'm so sorry." It is so much worse than one could possibly imagine. Two bodies. Innocence. Life. Death. A double murder? I don't know. A dreadful poignancy, a waste.

Perivale's face comes back into focus. His nose has a bump halfway along it. His skin is blotchy. His hands are shaking slightly. He is as agitated as I am.

"So if you could be a bit less flippant, it would be appreciated."

"I'm so sorry," I say again. It is all I can think to say. All the worry about *me,* and what is happening here, and now her again. I don't want to have to feel any attachment, any pain for her. All along, I realize, it has been easier to block her out.

"Did you know she was pregnant?"

"No. No one has mentioned this before."

I gaze at Perivale. I wish I could read him. I can't get a purchase. The boyfriend, the one who wasn't in the country when she died. Is he back? Is he somewhere grieving? Or could he be involved? I wish I didn't have to think about these things. I wish I'd never heard of Ania Dudek.

"And you have never set foot in her flat?"

I resist the temptation to scream. "No."

Perivale and de Felice have exchanged a glance. I wonder if Perivale realizes he is repeating himself. Shouldn't he be letting de Felice talk? Good cop, bad cop? Forget that. He shifts the papers in front of him.

"So, I'm just interested. You have recently had your garden re-planted?"

"Yes." I have no idea where this is going, but at least we have left her fucking flat.

"Could you tell us a little more about that?"

"Okay." I will humor him. Perhaps it will help us both. "Front or back?"

"Front, please."

"Um, yes. Well, we've had our basement dug out—took ages, and the builders made a mess of the garden, so we got a special company in called Muddy Wellies—Roger Peedles, the gardening expert at work, recommended them—and they took care of the lot. I told them what sort of thing I wanted—"

"Olive trees?"

"Yes, and a wisteria, which we are hoping"—I cross my fingers in the air, the kind of cozy gesture I use all the time on *Mornin' All*—"will flower. They can be stubborn when transported." I feel on safe ground now. I have my TV face on. I am far away from pregnant murdered women. I am in control. I direct my explanation to de Felice, trying to pretend he's actually interested. "And a line of lovely green *Alchemilla mollis* interwoven with heuchera 'Purple Palace,' and two large pots on either side of the door with French lavender in."

"Okay. Yes." Perivale has found the right notes. He looks up. "Are you aware of where Muddy Wellies sourced those plants?"

"No, not really."

"Well, let me tell you. The olive trees and the wisteria were both purchased at Evergreen, a wholesale nursery in Banstead. They don't grow their plants on-site, but procure them from specialist growers. Quite often from . . . Italy. The olive trees are propagated in gravelly shale—sandy orange in color. Quite rare, that soil. And the wisteria: now here's a thing. It comes from one spot in Tuscany, the Pistoia Valley, where the soil is different. It's heavy, silty, beige in color."

I don't like not knowing where this is going.

"And on the floor in Ania Dudek's flat," he continues, a light in his eyes that is almost like excitement, "just inside the front door, we found mud shavings—minuscule, curved in shape. And here is an interesting fact, our laboratories, ooh, they are clever, they've looked at that mud under the microscope and it's almost striped—sandy orange mixed with beige. And when I visited you the other day, blow me down if I didn't pick up some dirt on the bottom of my shoes. And guess what?"

"What?" I can't tell, unless I look under the table whether he is wearing those brogues now.

"It's a match."

"Really?"

"Yes. Not to mention tiny fragments of volcanic pumice stone that they add to pot plants."

"Like my lavender."

"Like your lavender. So, we now know, thanks to the miracle of science, that those grooves of mud we found in Ania Dudek's flat came from your front garden. And one more thing." He slightly lifts his shoulders, like a parent telling a child they can have ice cream. "How do you think those grooves of mud got into the flat?"

"On the bottom of someone's brogues?"

"Almost but no. Asics, Gaby Mortimer. Those clods of earth, they slot exactly into the ridging on the bottom of trainers like the ones you gave us. Asics."

"But everybody has Asics," I cry.

"So I ask you again—this is your last chance—have you ever been inside Ania Dudek's flat in Fitzhugh Grove, London SW18?"

It would be easy to say yes. He so wants me to. He's longing for it. He's desperate for it. All that work on the soil. Perhaps they would let me home if I said yes. Is this what torture is? I haven't even been water-boarded and I am almost willing to say whatever they want. Who knows how that sodding sod got there?

"No," I say wearily, apologetically even.

But I'm wrong. Perivale doesn't look disappointed. He wasn't longing for me to say yes. He looks triumphant. "How, then," he says, producing a sliver of paper from his file and thumping it on the table, "do you explain *that*?"

The sliver of paper has curled up like one of those dark red mood-reading fishes you find in crackers. I try to remember what curling-up means. Millie would know. Shy? Passionate? Or maybe just Utterly Bewildered.

"Am I allowed to touch it?" I say.

He tuts, smoothes it out with his hand, holds the errant corner down so I can read it. A Tesco receipt:

MARGHERITA PZA: £4.50
ISLA NEGRA: £9.49
Total: £13.99
Every Little Helps

"Can you see what it is?"

"Yes. It's a receipt for a pizza and . . . er, a bottle of wine."

He is just smiling at me, that almost-foppish face contorting into a grin. He hates me, it occurs suddenly; that's what this is about. He actually hates me.

"Yes. Correct. Found on the bedside table of Ania Dudek, along with a few coins. And what paid for that pizza and that bottle of wine?"

I scrutinize the second half of the receipt. "MasterCard Sale." The last few numbers. I stare at them, trying to make sense of what I can see.

"Do you remember what you were doing on Wednesday the eighth of February this year?"

"I'm sorry . . . I don't. Not without . . . No."

"Perhaps you could check. Have you worked it out? The credit card that paid for the pizza and the wine is registered to your name. Isn't that a strange and peculiar coincidence, seeing as you have *never been inside Ania Dudek's flat*? They were paid for with your credit card. So, you can understand, can't you, why things are beginning to stack up? We've got the advert from the *Lady,* the newspaper interviews with you, the clothes, the mud from your shoes, and now a receipt for items purchased with a credit card in your name." He rocks back, studies me as if from a great height. "What do you have to say about that?"

I know I am still sitting on a chair because my fingers are gripping its sides, but I could be floating: the rest of my body flickers and melts, as if I am looking down at it through water.

"Do you have anything to say?" Perivale repeats.

"I'd like to see a lawyer."

THURSDAY

Oblongs of light. The panes are bottle-bottom thick, hardly glass at all. Only whiteness penetrates.

Grit in my eyes, or so it feels. Ash, sulphur, at the back of my throat. Neck so stiff I can hear it crackle as I move.

I peel myself off the mattress—my skin has stuck to the plastic; it's like pulling off Scotch tape. A stench of sweat rises from the blanket. It is twisted under my armpits. It's me who smells.

It has quieted out there, just the sound of muttering. Praying? All night, it was shouting and hollering. A gravelly voice down the corridor singing off key, "Roxanne." Another, a higher scream: "Shoot me. You hate me, don't you? Come on, fucking shoot me between the eyes."

It's peaceful now. They're asleep. Or someone shot them between the eyes.

I have to pee. Cold, shiny aluminium. No paper to wipe the seat with. It's a different cell from yesterday. I've been upgraded.

Last night's plate of lasagne congeals a foot away by the door.

I perch on the edge of the bench. I am in yesterday's clothes. You don't get pajamas in a police cell. Who knew? My teeth are furred. I asked the custody sergeant if I could have a toothbrush and he said if I were desperate, I could see a doctor; I was entitled to a medical examination. But not a toothbrush. You'd think it would be a contravention of European law. Isn't dental hygiene a human right? It doesn't have to be fancy. Just the sort of compact fold-up they give you on airplanes would do. Or even that chewing gum you get next to the Durex machines at motorway service stations.

I miss my daughter.

I wish I had got through to Philip. I wish I had told him and he was on his way home.

Fear and panic begin to well again, pooling, spilling. I can't comprehend it. The series of events that set this in motion was a drip, drip of oddities, I can see that. But they were explainable, an interlacing of coincidence. We looked alike, Ania and me. What did that add up to? Nothing. The ad, the cuttings, the clothes . . . Maybe she stalked me. Maybe she didn't. The world is full of peculiar things. We had a cat on the show once—Mr. Paws—who got lost after his owners moved and managed to find the way back to his old home, a hundred miles from Norwich to Luton: a real-life incredible journey. Or those twins, separated at birth, both married to women called Linda, both with sons called Guy and dogs called Badger. I mean, just extraordinary.

But the soil . . . the receipt? How did they get into her flat? How do they link to me? This is the worst kind of nightmare, this piling of seemingly impossible evidence.

Last night, when she arrived, Caroline Fletcher, the duty solicitor, wrote it all down, listed it, then looked up at me with an expression that seemed to say, "Well?"

I made a gesture with the cuffs of my blouse as if to say, "No, nothing up there."

I had—have—no explanation to give. Why should a receipt from my credit card be found in the dead woman's flat, unless someone else used it? It lives in my wallet, though I have been known to leave it by the front door, when I've paid for a takeaway. Someone else must have used it.

Caroline Fletcher, with her choppy salt-and-pepper bob, her black trouser suit, is a decent person. She has a good heart, I am sure. She has never watched an episode of *Mornin' All,* she confessed. "Too busy. Family, though the last is about to leave for uni, thank God. Work. The eternal juggle." Sharp, too, I suspect. Mistakes have already been made, she told me: "We'll have you out of here, don't you worry." Then, returning into the room after her discussion with Perivale, after "full disclosure," with slightly less confidence: "Quite ridiculous. Perivale says you are a flight risk, that you are a wealthy person with the means and the wherewithal to escape if you were so inclined."

"What does that mean?"

Her mouth set in a grim line. "That he will fight bail."

"But . . ." I couldn't speak. "They can't keep me here."

"They can."

"But my little girl." It came out like a wail.

"It's quite absurd."

Some of the mistakes, she went on, watching to check I was pulling myself together, were mine. I should never have agreed to be interviewed without a lawyer present. All those casual little chats I got sucked into: they all counted. I wouldn't have been "emotionally fit." In her opinion, he was determined to catch me out. "He's obsessed with this 'lie' about not touching the body. It happens all the time."

"What, people lie about touching bodies?"

"No. People miss things out, or they exaggerate—an overdramatization here, a little fib, an egging of the pudding there. It's human nature. Confusion, self-consciousness, a desire to talk. Not enough people deploy their right to silence. More cases are won or lost in the interview room than in the courtroom. And you had suffered a shock. You should have called . . . Who did you say your lawyers were?"

"Withergreen and Spooner."

"You should have called Withergreen and got them down here."
With her "Withergreen" she was letting me know she'd been round
the block a few times. I wasn't just slumming it if I stuck with her.
She could Withergreen with the best of them.

"I've got nothing to hide."

"Irrelevant," she said.

It was the most chilling thing she said. *Irrelevant*. It hardly mattered if I had done it or not. I was embroiled. I had entered a
process, parallel to the normal enterprise of my existence, with its
own directives. You muddle along; you think your life is your own
possession, that it has its own discrete identity, that the police, the
law, are part of the community, an embellishment, there for when
you need them, like hospitals and crosswalks and shops selling
ready-made frozen meals. But they are not. They are waiting, all
the time they are waiting, for something like this to happen, to
trip you up and snatch you and show you that it was the life you
thought you were in control of that was the embellishment. Your
life was just *nothing*.

One discovery has set in motion all this. If I hadn't gone out for
a run, if I hadn't found the body, would I even be here? I let out a
deep groan.

Breakfast is a bacon and egg sandwich—in one of those sealed triangular boxes—and a packet of prawn cocktail crisps. I eat both, actually. On the tray is tea in a paper cup, the circular tea bag attached
to the side with a dangling piece of metal—the sort of tea bag you
get from the hot-drinks trolley on a train. It tastes harsh, but then
so does my mouth.

The policeman who brings it in backward, pushing the door to
my cell open with his elbows, is the same young chap as yesterday.

He has a pale, peaches-and cream complexion; you can't imagine him shaving.

"Oh lovely! Breakfast in bed," I say. "You spoil me."

He blushes. "Sorry. It's not much."

The effort I am putting in to keeping my face up, when I would rather curl into the fetal position, reminds me of being in hospital the morning after I gave birth to Millie, smiling at well-wishers, thanking them for their muffins and teddies and flowers, and all the time in pain from the stitches and worrying if I'll ever pee again.

I say something about this to the sweet constable.

He looks flustered: too much gynecological detail. I'm not convinced he even locks the door. I could probably make a run for it if I were *so inclined*.

Caroline Fletcher is later than she said she would be. When she finally comes, I am brought to her in another interview room—a different one from yesterday, less freshly painted.

She is wearing the same black suit with a different shirt. Yesterday's was rich dusty pink—silk or polyester; this one is cotton with a fine blue-and-white stripe. Same shoes—black loafers, but no tights or pop socks. Her hair is a little less ordered, slightly oily, her parting askew. When you've spent the night in prison, when you don't know if you are ever going to come out, these tiny details tell you everything. The cotton shirt, the bare feet, they talk about a shift in the barometer, a rise in pressure—it's warmer out there today, sunny even. Spring may be pushing through. Fletcher's messy hair, her lack of punctuality—she's been busy this morning. The world turns without you. It doesn't even notice there's one person not there.

It's day two. Two days not at work. Yesterday, I could hardly believe it. I watched the minutes tick by. I kept thinking, Stan will be flirting with the entire Flash Mob, which was my idea anyway. Now it's time for India's 'Appening Apps . . . Thursday, so it'll be "Up the Garden Path" with Roger Peedles . . . Who is in the kitchen today? . . . I *can't remember*. When 12:30 p.m came and went, I almost wept with relief.

Today, 10:50 a.m already, well into Gok Wan's Spring Trends and I've hardly thought about it once.

She is wearing glasses, too. I don't think she was yesterday. Blimey, did she not even have time to put in her contacts?

"So, we have no witnesses. I've got that absolutely on Perivale's authority. He's not pissing about anymore. I can't bear it when police start mucking about with limited disclosure. It's so sodding tactical. Just being silly buggers for the sake of it."

I like her, I realize. It's the swearing that swings it.

"And CCTV: they've got none. Nada. Zilch. There aren't any at Fitzhugh Grove, and the ones at Tesco Express on Balham High Road are on a twenty-four-hour loop, so have already been wiped. I expect he's narked off about that."

"So much for all that following the left wall, pretending he was at Hampton Court."

"Did he tell you that?"

I nod.

"Silly sod. Yeah. No. But you need to get back to him with an alibi for the eighth of Feb.—if it turns out you were in Honolulu for the entire day, all well and good."

"I'm not sure that I *was* in Honolulu."

"Also, he has no murder weapon. They've turned Ania Dudek's flat inside out. They've searched the common. Yesterday, they went through your house with a fine-tooth comb. Guess what? No murder weapon there either."

"You're joking."

"Nope. Wouldn't joke about a thing like that. He had a warrant.

Your cleaner was there incidentally. She wasn't happy about them keeping their shoes on. They're looking for a bit of a string basically. Anyway, he found not a thing. No murder weapon. And not this St. Christopher he's obsessed with. Also"—she turns her steady gaze on me—"they have no confession. It's what he wants: a confession. It's what he's depending on."

"Well, he's not going to get one."

She is still looking closely at me. "Excellent. So, Gaby—if I may call you Gaby?—all his evidence is circumstantial. Plus the fact that you have an incomplete alibi for the murder. That is right, isn't it? I know it's hard because of the time frame. They're not quite sure what time she was killed. The heating was on high in the flat, which muddies the issue. But no one was with you the entire time?"

"My daughter and the nanny were in bed. I went for a run at some point. And my husband didn't come home until the early hours."

"Yeah." She consults her notes. "Perivale has spoken to your nanny, who thinks you were in all evening, though she is not sure. Your husband has corroborated that he was also out. He was at work and at a dinner. His alibi, were one to need it, is pretty solid, a list of colleagues and clients and waiters. He says you were asleep when he came in. Is there anything you can think of that might go some way to explaining . . . ? To be honest, it's the receipt. Everything else—well, it would take a barrister two seconds to dismantle the Italian-soil malarkey. Sounds fancy, but there's a garden center just across the way. Bet it's awash with Tuscan loam. Your theory that she was your stalker is also interesting. But the receipt? I won't lie to you—it bothers me."

I tell her that I have thought about it a lot, that I have spent most of the night thinking about it. "Two people could have had access to my card. My husband—but he is never back that early. It is just an absurd thought that he might have been at Tesco Metro in the late afternoon." I give a hollow laugh. "And the other person is our nanny. It would be such a simple explanation. I'm not saying she killed her, just that she might have known her. It would tie into everything. She says she doesn't, didn't, but if she is lying, everything could be explained. The clothes: Marta could have given them to her. The newspaper articles: well, I don't like thinking it, but maybe, if Ania was her friend, they were both intrigued by my job . . . whatever. Or they were collecting them to show someone else."

Caroline Fletcher nods. "Go on."

"As for the receipt, she could have taken my credit card. I, you know, sometimes leave it out. If I've been on the phone and needed it . . ."

"What about the PIN?"

"It's two-five-oh-three, my wedding anniversary."

"I'm not asking for the number." Rather comically, she puts her hands over her ears. "Could she have known it?"

"She could have seen me key it in—at Pizza Express or somewhere. She's been with me a few times when I've used it. If she is lying about all this, maybe she has something to hide."

Caroline Fletcher has been watching me carefully. She is holding her glasses on the tip of her nose and has been looking over them. Reading glasses, then, not contacts. She closes her notebook now and nods. She says I am to leave it with her and not to worry. "The most important thing is to get you out of here. They can't keep you for longer than thirty-six hours without charging you. They've only got until one o'clock to make this stick." She looks at her watch. "Less than an hour."

I'm back to pacing, only this time not in my head. Up and down the pathetic little cell—a new one. Up and down. I pretend I am at a step class. I am using the bench. I've got a stupid song spooling in my head: "Build me up, Buttercup . . ." It's one of the numbers they used to play during weekend aerobics sessions at the Harbor Club. Why on earth am I a member of the Harbor Club? The prissy women on reception and the mothers in their skintight Lycra and the screamingly spoiled alpha brats in the pool, and the Nikkei-indexed fathers *thrashing* the living daylights out of each other on the indoor all-weather tennis courts . . . Philip was so keen, but why did I go along with it? I've let myself be sucked into his world.

PC Morrow lets herself in, poking her head round the heavy door, like someone checking to see if their baby is awake. "Let's be having you, then," she says.

I don't want to know what is happening. I don't want to ask. For the few minutes that it takes to walk along the corridor, and up some steps and into the room where Caroline Fletcher and Perivale are waiting, I can pretend that it is all going to be fine, that Steve will be idling out there in the street, and in a minute I will be gone, leaving this horror, this nightmare behind, speeding away like Jackie Kennedy whisked off in her motorcade in Dallas. The alternative is too dark to contemplate.

"Your bag—check it. I wouldn't trust any of them in here as far as I could throw them."

The bag Philip gave me is sitting on the table. It takes a few seconds for her words to sink in. My hands are shaking so much I can hardly unzip it. I've no idea what it contains. My nervous system is in pieces. I rummage, but no electrical impulses connect. I push my sleeves up my arms to try and get sensation back, but my brain isn't charging. I could be fondling my phone, my purse, my Dodo Universal Organizer, a gaggle of Tampax, or I could be massaging the sort of wadding they use in medical dressings.

"All there," I say, because it is easier than saying anything else.

"Right." Caroline Fletcher stands. "Perivale?"

He looks glum. He intones, almost mechanically, "You are

bailed pending further enquiries. Don't go on any long journeys. You are free to leave."

The relief is, for a moment, almost as unbearable as the dread. I make a noise that is a bit like a gasp and a bit like a sob.

He can't drop it, though, Perivale. He can't let it go. He has to have the last word.

"Scratches have healed, I see."

Oh, it is a learning curve. The 219 is what I need. PC Morrow is a walking encyclopedia on bus routes. I could get the 319 and change, or the 432b or something, but that goes "round the houses." I always thought that was the point of a bus, but there you go. The 219 is a bit of a walk, but, "It's a nice sunny day. It'll clear your head." Caroline Fletcher would have driven me, only her car was in the garage, having its suspension sorted. (That's why she was discombobulated. There's an explanation for everything if you wait long enough.) And then on the bus, it's a flat fee these days. Who knew? And they don't like giving change. I had to rummage around in my bag as the bus lurched off to dig out the right coins. Everybody else seemed to have an Oyster card. In my new life, I am going to get an Oyster.

When you walk out of the cinema and you aren't expecting it still to be light, it's as if the world has spun a whole cycle without you knowing. For those first few moments, as you go down the steps or the escalator, the day itself is a surprise—even if you are only looking at it through the windows of the Southside Shopping Center. Well, that feeling of wondrous incredulity is what my liberty feels like. Clapham Junction is a great bright, brilliant ball of activity. The low sun catches the shop windows. A row of awnings is as jaunty as bunting. Wads of pink cherry blossom bunch over the walls of back gardens. Across the common, where the light turns hazier, trees show tips of acid green against the Chelsea-blue sky.

In the bottom of my bag, I have found one of Millie's school hair ties and I've pulled my hair back into a ponytail. My lips are dry and cracked; I keep licking them, which makes it worse. My eyes, shrunken and puffy, hurt when I move them. It's busy—all these people with their bags of shopping, a lad in a school uniform next to me eating fried chicken from a box, but no one spares me a peep. No nudging or sideways glancing.

I'm desperate to see Millie and speak to Philip. I should wait until I'm home, but I can't. My worries about our marriage seem to have been swept away by the enormity of what has just happened. I need to hear his voice, even if I can't speak openly yet. And then, as soon as I know she is out of lessons, I'll ring Clara. I rummage around in my bag. No answering light flickers; perhaps the battery is dead. I search the pockets, feel my way along the lining. I take out the heavier items one by one and then I know for sure: it's not there.

My first thought is that I need to go back to the police station—I half stand to get off the bus—but my second thought is that I can't possibly do that. It's the opposite of what I want to do. I want to get as far away from Perivale as possible. I will have to phone from the landline when I get home. Perhaps they can pop it in the post.

It has knocked a little dent in my relief, but only a little. There's a stop just past the end of my road and I get off. The magnolia in the garden on the corner seems to have blossomed overnight, unless I just haven't noticed it before: a spectacle of blowsy magenta cups, the sort of show-off flowers you should have in midsummer, almost indecently magnificent. I pause to bury my nose in a bloom. Honey and lemon with a medicinal note! All the years I have lived in our house and I've never smelled it. I don't normally even walk up this way.

Then I turn the corner. For a fraction of a second, I have time to turn and run, but the fraction multiplies, splits into a million numerators, a trillion denominators, and then it is too late.

The woman in a beige trench coat spots me first. I think she must have moved up the road a bit to have a cigarette. As she sprints toward me, I see her chuck it, still lit, in an arc over her head into the middle of the tarmac. "Gaby! Gaby! What was jail like, Gaby? Gaby!"

She is in my face in seconds. Her skin is yellowy-gray, all perpendicular lines—from her nose to the outside of her mouth, from her mouth to her chin: ventriloquist marks. The rest of the pack is behind her now. Cameras are whirring. Someone is trying to thrust a Windjammer microphone over the lot of them. It's too late to smile, to turn and glance over my shoulder. It's full frontal, not slept, bad-hair-day horror.

More shouting. Male voices, pretending they know me. "Gaby. Gaby. This way, Gabs. Any comment, Gabs?" I close my eyes. "The Running of the Bulls" in Spain, filming it for *Panorama* years ago. The noise of the hooves—like standing under a bridge when a train is going over—the muscles straining in the beasts' necks, the sweat flying off them. People jostling, pulling. Crowd control.

If I push forward, I might get through to the empty pavement beyond, but the throng moves with me, ants transporting a crumb. Aside from the woman in the trench coat, it's all men in black—black jackets, black Puffas, a sprinkling of fur-trim hood. A king rat. Tails twisted. Some of them are trying to reach me from the other side of the parked cars, round the side, over the top. The scratch of microphone on metal. Thumping of bag on boot.

I should be smiling, half smiling but still sad—humbled by my ordeal, relieved to be out of it—but my muscles have seized. I'm just trying to get through, to get into the safety of the house. It's how far? Fifty yards. If I can just do that without breaking . . . I mustn't crumble or cry. What do I need? Dignity, grace. Mournful but plucky. Come on. Order. Control. The life cycle of the frog. The origins of the Second World War. I've managed so far. Where is my dignity? Where is my grace?

At the back of my throat a lump is growing, making it hard to swallow. I am losing control of my mouth. It's trembling and contorting. I want to shout at them to let me pass, but I must keep quiet. I must remain silent.

It's like a wall. I can't get through it. All those faces in my face. No one is on my side. The panic rises. I'm back in that cell. Nuclei. Cytoplasm. External gills. Lungs. Images flash through my head: Millie, Philip, Clara, Robin, the people I love. My house—the gate, the front door—is only a few yards now. Stan, smirking, Perivale. I can't get there. I can't move at all. I'm twisting and turning.

"Gaby, Gaby, are you free? Gaby?"

It rises, the strength, from deep inside me. It rises and changes color, turns red, and, flickering, enters my blood. "Go away!" I hear myself shout, in an ugly voice that isn't mine. I am pushing through them. My foot impacts with shin. "Leave me alone, all of you. Just go away."

Inside, I lean against the door, shut my eyes, and wait. It's so cold it's like a smell, the sort of cold that stops you in your tracks. An abandoned house, unlived in. How long have I been gone? A year? A month? No, thirty-six hours exactly. My eyes open; I can't keep them closed any longer. The noise has abated. A picture of Millie is at an angle on the wall. A faint footprint on the bottom stair.

I find myself in the kitchen—an instinct, I suppose, the heart of the house. The floor is grubby in here; not filthy, but slightly scuffed, as if Robin has been to visit with her dog. Perhaps the police brought a dog. Oddly, on the counter, the top of the Frosties box is open. Did they search the cereal? Hoping to find the murder weapon lurking in a plastic wrapper like a free toy? Or maybe someone was peckish. I imagine Perivale nipping into the kitchen and grabbing a quick handful.

I look for his markings but there are no dirty fingerprints. He will have washed his hands, or worn gloves. In the sitting room, the sofa cushions are lopsided—pointy-up triangles, not face-on squares. One of the silver-framed photographs on the piano, a picture of the three of us, is missing. The keyboard cover is down.

Near the window, I hear shouts. Whirring. They're still out there. I close the shutters with Philip's remote. My hands are still shaking, blue veins snaking down my arms. I catch movement in the mirror above the fireplace. My own white face. I am clenching and unclenching my teeth. The muscles in my neck flex like rope.

Upstairs, in Marta's room, her TV is on the floor, and the shutters are opened out—her naked window stares back at me. The mysterious piles have gone, though I doubt it was the police who tidied them away. A floor away, Beechwood Hall, home of Millie's Sylvanian creatures, has been shunted sideways, like one of those whole-house moves they go in for in America, all the furniture tipped forward. Her bookcase has been rearranged; one book by her bed has been shaken with sufficient force to rend the binding, for the original hieroglyphic cover to be ripped.

Initially, my bedroom, *our* bedroom, looks untouched, but there's a cigarette butt floating in the loo in the bathroom, and for some reason Marta's toothbrush has made its way here. The glass of water on my side of the bed has a mottled surface, like a piece of old Scotch tape, a skin of fiber and dust. There is a faint herringbone stripe in the weave of the duvet cover. I always lay it so the stripe lies vertically, but it has been put back on the horizontal, and when I move the top pillow, the lower one is dented, as if someone has slept on it.

I open the wardrobe. Philip's side is untouched, his piles still neat. But someone has gone through mine. Blouses are scrunched with trousers, skirts in between jeans. A dress: crumpled on the floor, wrinkled up like a sock. Silk and satin, wool, twill and cotton, they've fingered it all. Even my undergarments. The shelf where

M&S pants and Myla Marlenes should be neatly piled (a pile for every day and a pile for . . . well, *never*) is a jumble. My knickers are literally in a twist.

Embarrassment, pity for whoever had to look through all this, irritation. I work on this as I tread back down the stairs, in the way of Philip when he's kept awake by a neighbor's music, and after a while, it's not the noise that becomes the problem, but his own forensic scrutiny of their inconsideration. What right do they have? Millie's toys, her *books*. In the garden, they've tramped the hellebores, and two of the new tulips lie on the grass, snapped. How dare they? How *very* dare they?

I sit at the kitchen table. I want to see Millie. It is all that matters. I think hard. It's Thursday. She has hockey after school, but I want her pressed in my arms. I feel in my pocket for my phone, but of course I haven't got it and thus, not Marta's number either. Panic starts again at the tips of my toes and works up. Where *is* Marta?

I put my head down, feel the wooden surface cool against my chin. I'm so tired I can't think straight. Is this shock? Exhaustion? The horror of my own behavior out there? The tulips. The Frosties. The rummaging of my smalls. I wasn't expecting this. I had thought myself in control, but things keep happening. The strings of my life are being pulled. The connections, the oddities—they may be circumstantial, but they are still weird. I need answers, but I don't know where to find them. I can't see my way through. I am powerless, trapped inside my house, and I don't know what to do.

Philip. In the police station, all I could think about was the bad things, but now other memories fill my head: a long wait in casualty once when I chopped off the top of my finger, the one-word impressions Philip did of his colleagues to take my mind off the pain. The time my train broke down in Leeds and he drove up to collect me. Persuading me to dance at that wedding, pulling me up some hill in Wales. People talk about "alpha males" all the time

these days, and that's what Philip is. That's what I fell for. Philip's
strength, his capability. He's a man who takes control.

His mobile number is the only one I know by heart. It takes
a while for lines to connect, satellites to align, and when I finally
hear the long, low dialing tone of abroad, I'm already crying with
preemptive relief.

No answer.

The time difference. It's eight hours ahead in Sinapore, past
midnight. He traveled all day yesterday, arrived late last night,
morning there, hurtled into meetings. He will have gone to bed,
exhausted, two hours ago at least. I leave a brief message on his
voicemail, asking him to call: it's enough. It would be selfish to keep
trying, to ring the hotel switchboard . . . If I had my mobile I could
text him, but I don't. I'll speak to him tomorrow. He should sleep.

The act of deciding this, the shape of kindness, makes me feel
a little better. I'm home now at least. I sit up. I think of the things
I've dealt with in the past. I might not get through this entirely on
my own, but I can make a start. I will be organized. One step in
front of the other.

Philip will say I've been brave. And even in my imagination,
that feels like love.

I start with practicalities. I know when I handed over my phone—it
was in the car on the way to the police station. I gave it to de Felice.
It's probably still in his pocket. All I need is a number for the phone
at the front desk where PC Morrow perched—I rang Philip and
Marta from it—but it turns out this number is unavailable. I ring
a three-digit code, which puts me through to a central hub where
my call is recorded, and a helpful person says they will patch me
through. Except they patch me through to a recorded message and,
before I go mad, I hang up.

Caroline Fletcher has gone home.

To get hold of Terri, I ring the main number for the studio, which involves more choices than I thought possible and the pressing of more buttons. Then I speak to the downstairs reception—spelling out my name (she must be new)—and then a brief exchange with Hal, the floor manager, and then an agonizing wait.

"Thank God," I say, when I hear Terri's voice. "It's me."

"Gaby!"

I sit up straight. I can see my reflection in the window, the shape of my face, though not my features. My heart pounds in my ears. "I'm so sorry, Terri. I would never have let you down for the last two days if I had had any control over this at all."

"You're all over the Internet!"

"They did ring to warn you, didn't they? PC Morrow promised she would. Has it been okay? I'm so sorry for landing you in it. The weirdest things have been happening, but this end is almost sorted out now. I suppose I should speak to Alison in publicity. She must be going mad."

"I know she has had a lot of enquiries. The police rang to inform us yesterday . . . But yes. No. We're fine."

"Good. I'm so glad. Did Stan have to go it alone?" (*Please* let him have gone alone.)

"Well. Actually . . ."

"Did India have a tryout?" It's easier if I say it myself.

"She needed some persuading, but we got her on the sofa in the end."

"That's good," I say, thinking, shit. "Was she any good?"

"She did well . . . But how are *you*? What's going on?"

She did well . . . what does that mean? I'll have to dissect that later. "It's been horrid," I say, "but you have to do what you have to do. If it's all over the Internet . . . that explains the welcoming committee of reporters outside my house."

"So you're at home at least. That's good."

I'm still smiling; my facial muscles ache with the effort, but the conversation seems strained. She makes it sound like I've been in hospital or the Priory.

"I'm bemused by the whole thing, I must say. Such a storm in a teacup. I don't know what the police thought they were doing arresting me, but I've tried to help as much as I can, and it's just awful what happened to that poor woman, though there is a limit to how involved they can expect me to be. I have a life, a job. Other people—you!—are depending on me, so—"

"Gaby—"

"Anyway, I can come back to work now. If that's okay. So, you know, let India down gently . . . tell Steve to be here tomorrow normal time."

"Gaby . . ." She pauses. "Are you sure it's not too soon?"

"Work is what I need! I know I've been a bit distracted recently." My voice is cracking and I clear my throat, try again. "Have we got anything good lined up for tomorrow's show?"

"Have a day or two off. No one is going to blame you."

"I'm up and at 'em. You know me, Terri, old pro." I close my eyes. "Please."

"Let's see how things look in the morning. Ring me first thing."

"Okay." I'm pressing the ball of my hand into my forehead. "No biggie!"

She hangs up before I can ask her to patch me through to publicity. It was an awkward conversation, but perhaps that was only to be expected. I will worry about it tomorrow, deal with Terri and Alison when I'm there.

I have an overwhelming desire to hear a friendly voice after this. I wish I knew Clara's mobile number off by heart, or had it written down. How idiotic to be so dependent on technology. Philip is always talking about "backup." He's right. I try her at home, but there is no answer. She could be watching one of the boys play football, or she could have a meeting after school, or . . . she could be *anywhere*. There are other friends I could have rung—Justice and Anna, but it has been so long since I've seen them I can't just ring them out of the blue with this. At moments like this, I am painfully aware of my lack of family—if only I had a sister, or a brother. Philip's parents would help, they would drive straight up—but they are unreachable, floating on their cruise, somewhere in the Ancient World. I can't ring Robin. She has a new baby. She has enough on her plate. And Jude? Well, I just don't know her well enough.

I look at my watch. It is 5:30 PM and Marta isn't here, nor is Millie, and I have no idea where they are. I'm alone. I can't leave the house. I haven't eaten all day, and I have no phone. I let my misery zero down on to that. "I've got no phone," I wail like Andromache in that production of *Women of Troy* we saw at the National Theatre, howling in anguish as her infant son is wrenched from her arms to be butchered by the murdering Athenian forces. "No phone," I cry again. I know I am being ridiculous, but at least I'm alone. I put my face in my hands and feel the wetness seep through my fingers. For the first time since it started, I bawl.

It's a flicker I notice, more than a creak. I look up. Marta is standing in the doorway to the kitchen.

"I've lost my phone," I say pathetically.

"Yes," she says. "I heard you."

"Philip's not here." I'm still weeping, can't quite stop. "And I didn't know where Millie was." The sobs are coming out like hiccups. "Or you."

She looks at me with interest. "Millie is with her friend from hockey. Izzie Mathews."

I haven't got a tissue, but I squeeze my nose between my thumb and finger. "Isn't she the one she hates?"

"Not today," Marta says flatly. I'm not sure she means to make a joke, but I laugh through my tears anyway.

I grab some kitchen roll to wipe my nose, try and control myself. "Do we need to pick her up?"

The "we" is rhetorical. I couldn't leave the house, thrash a path through those men, if there were a Royal Television Society Interview of the Year Award at the other end of it.

"Her mother, Mrs. Matthews, says a sleepover is okay. Izzie is not normally allowed sleepovers in the week, but she understood the circumstances are difficult. Also, tomorrow they have the Easter holiday."

"Easter!" I had forgotten that. It had flown out of my mind, flapped up into the ether like a skylark disturbed by a dog.

"So . . ." Marta says. She looks over her shoulder.

Is she planning to escape before I veer into a colloquy on the local bars? No. She walks across the kitchen floor, gingerly, as if the smears on the tiles might contain germs. She is in a blue shirt with a paisley pattern, quite diaphanous, and a pair of jeans that remind me of mine. When she gets close, I smell fig again. I wonder if it *is* my perfume, or just one that's similar. She sits down and explains, in her broken English, everything that happened while I was in custody. I once told her I liked to be kept informed of Millie's "daily doings" and there is a dutiful precision to her narration. The police searched the house, but Millie was still at school, so she was not affected, but this morning, people started knocking on the door and once she had dropped Millie off—early because she had running club—Marta found the class phone list and rang Mrs. Matthews, who had been happy to look after her. "I have taken her toothbrush to hockey and handed over her bag. It seemed best as I was"—it's almost a smile; I should catch it and cage it—"holding the fort."

I don't say anything for a moment. I miss Millie. I long for her. I want her here. But maybe this sleepover is a good idea. It gives me time to pull myself together. I can ring Mrs. Matthews, using the invaluable tool of "the class list," to thank her, and speak to Millie, say good night to her. In the meantime, I could make the most of this: a moment on my own with Marta.

"Thank you," I say, and then, "and are you okay?"

"Yes," she says.

"It must have felt horrible in the house after everything, and I don't mind at all, but did you sleep in my bed?"

"No."

"Oh. It's only . . . never mind."

"I have seen the police," she says. "They came here and asked me questions."

"What did they want?" I ask.

"They had many questions. They want to know about you—"

"About me?"

"The night the woman was murdered. They want to know if you left the house."

"What did you say? Did you say I was here?"

"I don't know. I say I think you were here."

"Okay. And did they ask you about Ania Dudek?"

"Yes." She gives an annoyed tug to her collar, as if it has caught at the back of her neck. "Like you ask me before. They go on and on and on." She is frowning. "Do you know why?"

"I think they think that maybe you did know her because of some oddities that have arisen in this murder case . . . It's why they wanted to see me. It would all be cleared up if one of us had ever been to her flat, or given her clothes, or had a meal with her."

Marta's eyes flicker away.

"So she wasn't your friend?"

She shakes her head, chewing on the skin to the side of one finger.

"Are you sure? You never had any contact with her? I thought perhaps you might have been friends and fallen out."

"She may have attended my church . . . I don't know."

"The one on Balham High Road. Near Tesco Express?"

She shrugs. "Many, many Polish people go to my church." She says it with some disdain, as if she isn't Polish herself. "Maybe I met her once or twice. I don't know."

"Did you tell the police that?"

She nods again. For a moment, I think she is going to add something, but she seems to change her mind. She looks at me, almost as if she is waiting.

I decide to risk it. "Did you ever borrow my credit card, Marta? I don't mind. I would much rather know, and it would explain so many things."

"I don't use a credit card. I don't own a credit card."

"So not the one in my wallet? Or perhaps I left it on the shelf by the front door? I know I sometimes forget to put it away."

"No." She is looking down, concentrating on a tiny scattering of crumbs on the table, corralling them into a corner and scooping them into her hand.

I let out a heavy sigh, release it through pursed lips, feel the breeze of it on my hands. "I'm sorry. I'm just trying to get to the bottom of it all, trying to find answers. Someone has used my card, you see, and if it was you . . . well, that would be fine. I'd be relieved."

Suddenly, startlingly, she's off. She stops combing the crumbs and starts talking very quickly about identity fraud and about a friend from her language course who lives in Colliers Wood and how a person in a shop had taken an imprint of this Colliers Wood person's credit card and used it to run up bills, buying flights to Lagos and—she says this with increased shock and indignation—a Kärcher high-pressure water cleaner, "very, very expensive" in B&Q.

"Golly," I say. "I suppose it's a possibility." And it's true. It *is* a possibility. Only I am distracted by her delivery. Her English is better than I thought. It's not broken at all. It's glued together, like a badly mended vase; you can see the globs of adhesive along the cracks.

"Yes." She stands and sweeps the crumbs off her hand into the bin. Then she opens the tall cupboard for the mop and fills a bucket and starts swiping it in large regular swoops over the floor. "So be careful," she says.

I lift up my feet when she reaches me. "Oops," I say as streaks of shiny wetness engulf my chair. "Now you've got me trapped."

She doesn't smile. I watch her, still turning up the corners of my mouth, aching with the effort to prove I'm joking, but her face doesn't crack. It has the faint flush of someone who knows she is being studied. I wonder again if she's lying, if she has something to hide, or whether it is just the cultural difference between us that makes it seem that way. Not everyone conducts their social life with smiles; not everyone makes their face do half the work. I feel a twinge of guilt, and doubt. Is Martha a liar? A thief? A plausible suspect? *Really?*

Before we go to bed, we clean the house. We are uncomfortable allies. Marta vacuums the stairs, and I go through every room, re-arranging and adjusting. We don't talk much—the odd word here and there: "Can you pass the Pledge?" Marta closes all the shutters, blocking out the eyes and lenses. She checks the basement, too, which I haven't done, not with the lights on the blink. All those Saturday night TV thrillers of the 1970s—*don't go into the cellar*—have a lot to answer for. A basement remains a basement, even when it has been dug out and fitted with a high-tech gym.

Marta doesn't flinch. I hear her moving around in Philip's of-fice—small sounds, the puff of the spray, the squelch of a mop.

While she is down there, I phone Mrs. Matthews, Izzie's mother, who manages to express concern about my situation without completely concealing her consternation at being caught up in it herself. I'm too grateful to mind. She calls Millie to the phone and just the sound of my daughter's breath before she speaks makes my heart sing. She is completely herself, as if yesterday morning never happened, chatty, cheerful, upbeat. She got twenty-one out of fifty in her spelling test, but "that's good, Mum, Sophia got fifteen!" Izzie has a bed on stilts. "But not with another bed underneath. A *desk*!"

She asks if Dad is back yet and when I say, "no, Mills darling, not yet," she replies, with sweet indulgence, "Busy old Dad."

I tell her I love her, and she makes a noise that is half tut, half groan. Even her contempt is soothing to my soul.

I change my sheets. They are cool and smooth and smell of laundry, but I miss the old ones. I find one of Philip's shirts in the closet and wrap it round my pillow. I breathe in the scent of him. I know I shouldn't.

He'll be awake soon—11:00 PM our time will be early morning there—and he'll ring as soon as he is.

FRIDAY

It rains in the night. I'm aware of the drops pattering against the window, gusts going down the chimney. The window is open a crack and the wind creeps in, touches the duvet cover, crawls across my skin. When I close my eyes, all I can see is Ania Dudek's face—the milky membrane that covered her pupils, her protuberant tongue, the gouges and livid cuts across her neck. In my half sleep, her hands claw at me.

I keep the shutters closed and dress in the light that slips in around them, a set square of luster. In the kitchen, I eat breakfast—a bowl of muesli—standing up, looking out. Philip didn't ring. Perhaps, if he didn't get my message until after breakfast, he didn't want to wake *me*. He'll ring in a bit. I know he will.

The hornbeams and the taller trees in the gardens that back onto us block the lower windows of the houses behind, but if you were standing on the upper floor, you could see into my kitchen. Once, I saw a man at that top window, half naked, no details, a blur of flesh, monochrome, pale against dark. Our kitchen wall is all glass. What was it the architect said? "Inviting the garden into the kitchen." Well, the garden can bugger off. I'm getting blinds.

I'm early for Steve, and so I sit on the bottom of the stairs, looking at the front door, tensing for the tinkle of the gate, the sound of his footsteps. The newspapers stare reproachfully up at me from where they have fallen on the doormat, half curled, half splayed, like rolls of defrosting pastry. I wish I could thrust them deep into the bin, or hide them, as Millie did with *Struwwelpeter,* that gruesome collection of cautionary tales, which I once found tucked behind the bath. I have to read them, though. It's my job. Current affairs, or the flotsam and jetsam that follow in their stream, are my life. I'll go through them in the car, Steve as moral support. I shall incorporate them, and whatever cautionary tales they contain—"The Dreadful Woman Who Found a Body"—into the bustle of the day.

Work. Work will help. I'll feel better at work. But Steve is running late, each extra minute agony. Five minutes . . . ten . . . fifteen . . . Where is he? Then a niggle, a thought blooming like a bruise. Terri had given me her number and said to call.

She answers on the first ring. "Terri," I say quickly, "only to say I'm fine. I'll be with you shortly. Just waiting for Steve to roll up."

"Gaby," she says, in a tone I don't like: too friendly, too surprised, "Gaby, honestly, as I said in my text, take the day off. Take a few days."

"Not necessary. Tell you the truth, I need to come back. I'm ready. Oh, and don't text, I've lost my mobile, remember?"

Her voice fades slightly as if the phone has slipped, or her mouth has turned. "I think you should have a few days at home."

"Honestly, I'm totally fine. I haven't read the papers yet, but I'm going to get on to them in the car. I am going to be hot with ideas, I promise."

"What about the police?"

"I'm on bail!"

She doesn't answer. I hear clattering in the background, cameras moving, doors shutting. A long, uncomfortable silence in which my hand clutches the banister so tightly I hear it creak, feel the post beneath it shift. I think of India, with her bright, white smile. Something inside me cracks open. Finally, Terri says, "I'm sorry,

Gaby. The big cheeses don't think it's right for you to come in, not just at the moment, not while the enquiry into this murder is still ongoing."

My mouth is dry. "If you want me to be the story," I manage to say—"'The Foolish Woman Who Thought She Was Safe'—then I'll be the story."

"Gaby, I really . . ." She can't say it. She's too embarrassed. The silence gapes between us. I imagine her perched on a desk, staring out the window, staring at the wrinkled surface of the Thames.

I think back to before this phone call. How did I imagine I could go to work, carry on as if everything was normal? "You're right. It doesn't matter that I'm innocent. It's the wrong type of publicity. The show must come first," I say. A list of statements, not questions.

I can hear her relief. "Have a few days' rest, clear things up with the police, speak to Alison Brett, do some damage control. I'll keep you in the loop."

"TV Gab Loses Cool," "Gaby Mortimer in Police Investigation," "*Mornin' All* Presenter in Dawn Arrest." Worst of all: "Gaby Lashes Out." My teeth are bared in that photo, like one of those Rottweilers that mauls kids. An insert pic provides a close-up of the shin with which my "vicious foot" made contact: a plum of a bruise, plus a nasty nick. The reporter in question "sought medical treatment." Bless.

I go back to bed. I don't know what else to do. My life, so solid, so impermeable, is dissolving, slipping between my fingers. Was it ever solid? Was it ever impermeable? I feel like I am falling, with nothing to cling on to. This murder enquiry has affected everything. It has stripped me down to nothing. Who am I? Who are my friends? I thought I was a nice person, kind, the sort of woman people liked. I thought I was safe in that. And it matters to me. I realize that now. I care what people think. I really do. I'm generous to the people I work with, the receptionists and the ADs and the stylists. I bite my lip with Stan. He has nothing on me. Nothing. I'm *fucking* charming. The effort I have gone to maintaining my poise, my cheerful, unruffled stance, smiling for the photographs, p's and q's, and all it took was those few blinding seconds outside the house. A personality, a persona unraveled. I'll never be "that nice Gaby Mortimer" again. Even when they have all forgotten poor Ania Dudek, when she has slipped from the public memory, I'll be the TV presenter who may or may not have killed someone, and attacked a photographer.

I try and sleep, but I fail. I cry a bit.

At 10:00 AM, I ring Alison Brett in publicity. Her assistant answers and says she is in a meeting. I turn over in bed, lie on top of my hands, bury my face in Philip's shirt. It's 6:00 p.m., the end of the working day, in Singapore. Philip will have got my message eight hours ago at least. Why hasn't he rung? I know I didn't say what had happened, but he must have heard from someone else—a text from a friend, a snippet on Sky News? *Surely*. And then, *not to ring*? He could have been in meetings, I suppose, in a world of numbers, cut off from *Daily Mail* gossip, and he thought he'd ring me later. I should have been less cool in my message, but then that's how he likes me: cool, poised, successful. His celebrity wife. Would it be so wrong to break that?

I think about how things are between us—the distance, the lack of connection, the dark ravines and jagged edges. I search my brain—the day he came to surprise me after work. I saw him in reception before he saw me, leaning forward in his city suit, a fish out of water, a look of slight confusion on his face. Or the time another cyclist knocked him off his bike at Waterloo. He limped home, stood in the doorway calling for me, his elbow at a funny angle, blood pouring from his knee. My heart turns. The distance between us doesn't seem so gaping.

I pick up the phone before I can stop myself. He doesn't answer. I should hang up, but I don't and I do everything I have told myself not to. I leave a garbled message, begging him to ring, my voice choked with tears, thick with need and panic and self-pity: all the things he hates.

After I hang up, I realize too late that the intimate memories that gave me courage were about *his* vulnerability, not mine.

And then Clara calls.

I will be bobbing on a raft in an ocean, shipwrecked, my skin blistered, a seagull for lunch, and Clara will eventually find me.

"Gaby!" It's all she has to say. Her tone tells me she has seen the papers, that she knows I'm in a state, that here she is, my friend, ready to give me what I need.

"I texted you yesterday. Ken, head of physics, told me you hadn't been on *Mornin' All* and I thought you were ill, but then when you didn't reply, I thought maybe you and Philip had gone away or . . . I've been in lessons. I had no idea, Gaby, until I saw the papers in the staff room just now."

"I've lost my mobile . . ." I wail. "I rang you at home . . ."

"I'm so sorry, Gaby. We took the kids to the theater. If I'd known I—"

"It doesn't matter."

"It does, though. I can't imagine what you've been going through. Are you okay?"

"I'm fine." It comes out high and artificial.

"What are you doing?"

"I'm tidying."

"Are you? Are you really?"

I swallow hard. "Just emptying the dishwasher."

"Okay, good. Domestic tasks, always more absorbing than you

think. The other day, the cat tangled a ball of wool round a chair leg . . ." She gabbles for a while about the pleasures involved in untangling wool, how it took two hours and they were the "happiest two hours" of her professional life. She is giving me time. When we were growing up, I would just turn up at her house sometimes, and she would always know, by instinct, when I needed to talk and when the best thing was distraction.

I hold my hand over the receiver and blow my nose on a piece of tissue I find snailed under my pillow.

"Ken says your replacement, the girl who does the tweets, isn't half as good."

I clear my throat. "Really?" I say.

"Not a patch."

"Is he a fan?" I ask, a little squeeze of vanity to show her I'm all right.

"Everyone's a fan," she says softly. "You know that. So, Gabs, what's been happening? What's going on?"

"How long have you got?"

She answers literally. "Fifteen minutes."

I tell her everything—almost. I explain about the arrest and the interview and the smallness of the cell. I don't mention the credit card or the Italian mud. I don't give many details about Perivale's questioning. When I get near that point, everything inside me tightens. I realize he makes me feel as if nothing about me as a person matters, that he can mold me into anything he wants, and that that is his aim.

"Did the cell have a loo?" Clara asks gently after I have fallen silent.

"One of the cells did."

"Did you go?"

"I had a wee. Couldn't keep it in. I didn't have anything else."

"Loo roll?"

"No." I laugh. "I had to give a little shake."

"It's inhumane! No loo roll in Battersea police-cell shock! You should write an exposé."

"I think a different exposé might be in the pipeline."

"The tabloids still outside your house? I can see the olive trees in the corner of the pictures—they're looking good."

"Yes."

She says, now the police have "seen the error of their ways," I should talk to one of the hacks, do an exclusive, so the others go away, like they do when they come out of the Big Brother house. "Mystorymyagony," she says, turning it into a single word. "Go on, do it. Get it done. Mention the lack of loo roll while you're there. Lobby. Get questions asked in Parliament."

"I could become known as the woman who reintroduced Andrex to the arrested masses."

"Or Cushelle," she says, enjoying the name. "Or those tissues with aloe vera built in. Or quilted. Or bloody hell, why shouldn't felons be allowed Wet Ones?"

We both laugh. My eyes feel tight and small. When my chest contracts, I feel an ache like a stitch.

"When are you going back to work?" she asks finally.

"Terri has given me a few days off. India, the tweeter, has been longing for the opportunity to take my place. Did Ken in physics really say she wasn't any good?"

"Yes."

"I feel so pathetic." My voice catches. "What am I going to do, Clara?"

"Don't do anything. You've had a traumatic experience. You'll be back at work before you know it. You need to rest. Spend some time with Philip."

The bell goes. She's got Resistant Materials with her year nines. She'll ring me later to see how I'm "faring." It is a good choice of word, "faring." It calls to mind sea voyages and fair, clement weather. It has optimism built in. She doesn't know Philip is away.

"You're a survivor, Gabs," she adds, with a concern that has been there all along, underneath the joking. "All that stuff you did on your own when we were growing up. You'll get through it. You've got through worse."

After I hang up, I get out of bed and wash my face. It stares back at me, hollow cheeked and red eyed. I get dressed. I can't find my favorite jeans, so I put on tracksuit bottoms and a sweater. I peer out of the bedroom window, through the slats in the blinds. The clouds have shifted and it looks like a sunny day—sky the color of Aertex shirts. How many are still down there? I look down at the tops of heads. Bodies leaning against cars. Camera equipment splayed on warm slabs. Puddles in the gutter. Boredom. Cold hands. Pop music from someone's iPod. Idle chatter reaches up, the possible convolutions of tomorrow's game: "Yeah, they should put McEachran in midfield, give the kid a chance."

Should I choose one to talk to, I wonder, as Clara suggests? I'll ask Alison Brett when she calls back.

And then I see him.

Perivale. And I realize I have been so acutely dreading this moment that I feel no real surprise at it actually taking place.

He is standing across the road, by the alley to the common, leaning against an ivy-clad wall. His hands are dangling by his side, the low crotch of his jeans foreshortening his legs, head tipped back. He looks, with his hangdog demeanor, his hanks of thick hair, like a character from a Dickens novel. He is scuffing the ground, turning something over with the toe of his shoe. And then he looks up and stares straight at me.

I dart back into the room. The mattress sighs. I lie flat, stare at the ceiling without moving. It's not over. The police haven't seen the error of their ways. It's still going on. My stomach muscles contract, wither in on themselves, shrink into my pelvic floor.

I wait for the air around me to still. It is ridiculous. The slats are closed. He can't see me. I am clenching and unclenching my teeth again. As soon as my legs can take my weight, I creep out of the room and go downstairs. I pause in the kitchen and then I let myself out into the garden—a whole house stands between us now, but it doesn't seem enough. I can still feel his eyes, but he can't be there, out the front, and simultaneously up there, in that top window in the street behind us. It's impossible. He has just spooked me. I move under the cover of the apple tree, where I can't see any windows at all. New growth is fizzling, the cherry knotted with buds, the ivy unfurling against the wall, each leaf a little clawlike hand. A robin perches on a lower frond, head hopeful.

It's cold. From inside, it looks like summer, but out here, it's as bitter as midwinter. In the shadow of the house, the grass is sodden.

There is a door in the back wall behind the hornbeams and the tree house. It leads on to a passage, where the street used to keep the bins. A few years ago the council—or rather the company contracted by the council—declared the passage too dangerous (too much bending, or ivy negotiation), and many of our neighbors, concerned for "security," have bricked their back doors in.

I fought for ours. I imagined Millie as a teenager, nipping out there for an assignation or a secret cigarette. I felt in touch with the history of the house, in tune with coal deliveries and milk in metal urns, for a time when Serco was just a twinkle in the public service market's eye. Philip agreed back then, but last year, when we redesigned the garden, he fell in line with the neighbors, and I was too preoccupied with my mother to fight. The door is still there, but buried behind the tree house; you have to arch to reach it, contort round a wooden corner, bend your neck, bash your elbows. To bother, you'd really have to want a cigarette.

The damp seeps through my sneakers. I wriggle through the undergrowth, raindrops scattering, and stretch my arm far enough to draw back the bolt. I bash the door about a bit, tearing beards of ivy from its joints, until it opens.

Millie is home. I rang Marta and she brought her back along the alley, through the secret door. Neither Perivale nor the tabloid journalists will have seen her come in—a pathetic little triumph, a wresting of control, a spark. I hug her and hug her, breathe in the smell of pencil sharpenings and floor wax and that particular form of processed garlic they use in school dinners. She is all that matters. I tell myself that over and over. She pulls away. "Too tight," she says, "and you're dribbling on my neck."

Marta is watching from the door to the kitchen. She has an expression that is almost distaste, but not quite. Perhaps she is feeling homesick. "Listen," I say, turning to her. "As I'm here, have the rest of the day off. You probably have lots of things you'd like to do."

She is standing very rigid. She pushes her shoulder back. "But Millie and I, we had a plan to go swimming,"

"Do that another time," I say kindly.

She still doesn't move. "But I told her we would go."

"I'm sure she won't mind. Mills? Do you?"

But Millie, searching the cupboard for biscuits, isn't listening.

I turn back to Marta and smile. I'm expecting her to smile, too, but she doesn't. "It is the pool with the wave machine," she says. "You want to come, don't you, Millie."

I feel a little bit lost for a moment. I look back at Millie. "Sweetie, Marta's talking to you. She's offering to take you swimming, or you could stay here with me."

Millie has a mouth full of Jammie Dodger. "Are you working?"

"Nope."

"I'll stay," she says.

The wind must catch the door because as Marta leaves, it closes behind her with a slam.

Millie and I sort through her end-of-term schoolbag. We marvel at paintings of trees on brown crumpled paper, chocolate eggs from her teacher, a bit bashed from the journey home, a project book, containing stuck-in pictures of bread and vegetables, "A Food Web," a letter to Santa left over from Christmas, a wonky elephant made of clay that has lost an ear. We lie these treasures out on the floor and sift through them like Howard Carter and his young assistant in the Valley of the Kings.

She plays in the garden, swings a bit from the struts of the tree house and watches some TV. She reads to me and I read to her. We make complicated creatures involving plastic laces and metallic beads. We talk about Izzie Matthews and whether her hair is longer than Millie's or not. Even as I am engaging with the issue—perhaps Izzie's hair is very slightly longer, but I'm sure Millie's is thicker—I am worrying about why Philip has not rung back. Or, a different sort of anxiety, Alison Brett.

Twice, in the course of the afternoon, the letter box rattles and a voice sinews into the house. "Gaby! Any comment, Gaby?" Both times Millie is concentrating—once on threading a bead, once on Miley Cyrus. I don't know if she hears. She doesn't say anything if she does.

She asks if we can go swimming and I say no. "What about the playground?" I shake my head. Millie, picking up the early traces of her own boredom, slips into petulance. I am aware of feeling panic, and an edging despair, the inner sapping of my own resources. I should be returning to the house about now, sweeping in on a breeze from the world outside. If I had had a proper day at work, these hours before bed would have a different flavor; an intensity and speed, not this languor. Time has varying tastes. I wonder whether India really wasn't any good. I wonder if she missed a cue. Or giggled uncontrollably. I hope she did. How horrible I am. How can I be a parent when I can't even operate as a person?

A neighbor rings to complain about the reporters, "this unsavoury mob." She asks what I am going to do about it. They are smoking outside her house. It's an invasion of her privacy. I don't know her. She'll have got my number from the school list, or from Philip's squash ladder at the Harbour Club. An invasion of *my* privacy. She says, with the whine of someone used to getting her own way, "It's not fair on the rest of us, and I've got people coming. It's my book club tonight."

"I'm sorry about your book club," I say, "but I don't really know what I can do."

"What about the police?"

I smile wanly. "They're already here."

I try publicity once more, and this time—at last—I manage to speak to Alison Brett. But she took a long time coming to the phone and she sounds less efficient than usual, more distracted. "Alison Brett speaking," she says, though I've told her assistant who I am; she knows it's me.

"Presumably we need a plan," I say. "Damage limitation. Should I be talking to anyone in particular?"

"Yes," she says. "That's a good idea. Probably best if you do it direct."

"So there isn't a journalist you would recommend? No particular newspaper or magazine?"

"God," she says. "Tricky one. Listen, leave me your number and I'll get back to you."

I have a horrible feeling I am being fobbed off.

Just after 5:00 PM (1:00 AM in Singapore), when the sun is flashing low through the branches of a distant sycamore, catching the catkins on next door's silver birch, and Millie and I have worked our way through a packet of chocolate digestives, Caroline Fletcher comes to the door. I let her in, pressing myself against the wall so as not to be seen. "Animals!" she says, then turns and over her shoulder spits, "Go away." The gate clatters. "Fuck me!" She is wearing heels, with thick black tights and a frilly sailor-suit-style dress—a stranger, if ever I saw one, to Gok Wan's Spring Trends.

She rejects tea, or coffee, or something stronger—she won't stay long. She has brought my phone. It is wrapped and bound in plastic cellophane, like a miniature version of that luggage you see on long-haul flights. She hands it to me with a roll of her eyes. "Evidence," she says. "He wishes. Anyway, we've got it back. Any news on your alibi?"

"My alibi?" I am holding my phone against my heart as if it were a fragment of the True Cross.

"For the pizza and wine receipt? The eighth of February? Early evening, I think, seven PM?"

"Right."

She stands in the kitchen while I rummage around for my diary. I find the date. It would have been amazing to find proof that I had actually been in Honolulu. A late production meeting, drinks with friends, *anything*. The day before, Tuesday, I had had a parent/teachers meeting at Millie's school. But there are no appointments, nothing to jog my memory, on Wednesday at all. I rack my brain. Millie had extra gym, so she and Marta would still have been out. Philip is never home before 8:00 PM. But nothing else. Just a blank.

"I haven't written anything down," I say.

"Can you remember doing anything you *didn't* write down?"

"I probably went for a run, or had a bath, made supper. It seems terribly unfair." I hold up my arms. "It was ages ago. Do I get penalized now for having a bad memory? Is this what happens to people?"

"Perivale says he wants to see you. He'll be in touch over the next couple of days."

"Is he still in the street?"

"No," she says slowly. "When I spoke to him just now, down at the station, he said to tell you not to go anywhere."

"Is he down at the station, then?"

Did I *imagine* him outside?

"Yup. I got the impression he's running out of ideas, but he's persistent, I'll give him that. He seems to have no interest in looking for a motive, or in pursuing any other suspects. I don't know what you've done to piss him off, but he's obsessed with you. He won't let it go. He's like a dog with a bone."

"*Someone* killed that poor woman," I say.

"Anyway. I'm here if you need me." She is standing, checking her watch and, with a haste that could almost be said to contradict her words, heads back toward the front door. "Don't, whatever you do, talk to him on your own."

After Caroline has gone, I switch on my phone. Several texts, a couple from Clara ("Not on the sofa then, you cheeky minx?," another, a little later, "You alive?") and one from Terri, left last night, telling me not to come to work. Two missed calls—both from Clara. None from Philip—just a single text, sent late on Wednesday: "Arrived safely. Will ring you later." Nothing else. *No voice*mail, no sign that he was thinking about me at all. I can only think perhaps he's lost *his* phone. Or fallen off the edge of the world. But of course he hasn't. I stare at the screen. I grit my teeth. I'm sick of making excuses for him. Millie is dancing around the kitchen, and I think, to hell with him. I'm better than this. I can manage on my own.

I cook supper—an unadventurous pasta with tomato sauce. Banned from watching more TV, Millie finds her own entertainment, skipping to the front blinds, peering through and springing away again, squawking if she's spotted. It's like that car game she plays, Sweet 'n' Sour, when she makes faces at pedestrians and scores their response. In the end, I join in, stand and squint out, too. There are two reporters at the front gate, leaning against it, chatting. Another's legs are poking from a car. He's listening to the radio. I can hear the burbling voice of Radio 5. A can of Pepsi Max is spiked on one of the wrought-iron railings, like Oliver Cromwell's head.

Then a shape goes by, clashing colors, a familiar gait. I hear a jaunty voice—"Excuse me! Thank you!" It's an impression of Miss Hyatt, my primary-school headmistress, the way she used to jolly up her imperatives, corralling her charges with a sort of bossy exuberance that brooked no complaint. There is only one person on this planet who still quotes Miss Hyatt, who could part a gaggle of tabloid reporters with that intonation, purely for her own amusement.

"I got the Tube from work," Clara cries, after I have let her in, "and then the train and then I walked. Sauv blanc." She thrusts out two bottles of Blossom Hill and, from her Daunt Books bag, wrestles several enormous packets of Kettle Chips. "And salty snacks."

"I can't believe you've come." She's wearing a duffel coat and a bobble hat, a woman who knows a deceptive sun when she wakes up to it. North to South. London is a forest, a desert, a blasted heath. She's crossed the Sahara, the frozen wastes of Antarctica. "I can't believe you've come all this way."

"Do you like my disguise?" She pulls her hat down over her face. "They let me walk straight past. They didn't realize I was *the* Clara Macdonald, DT supremo of Highbury Tech."

I hug her, my nose prickling with unexpected tears, and she emits a self-conscious "Aw," still stirred with the adrenaline of her own surprise, still carrying the imperious breeze of Miss Hyatt.

We go into the kitchen, and with my back to her, wiping my

eyes on a tea towel, I open the Blossom Hill, "Nisa Local's finest."
Millie sits on Clara's knee—"Auntie Clara" she calls her, which has
always irritated Philip: no "aunties" allowed in his family, related
or otherwise, far too common. Millie eats the crisps, to make up
for the appalling pasta, and Clara tells stories from our childhood,
about the summer my mother was sick and had to go to a special
place to get better and I stayed with her family for *a whole month,* "a
month of sleepovers, though we called it 'staying the night' then,"
until, finally, we coax her off to bed.

I tuck Millie in and kiss her carefully. She puts her arms round
my neck. The talcy smell of her pajamas fills my nostrils. I breathe
it in deeply until it seems to knot around my heart. Nothing will
ever come between me and my child, I think. For a moment, I wish
Clara hadn't turned up, that I could snuggle down with Millie and
close my eyes. All my worries, all the trauma, if it could just boil
down to this.

"I love you," I say.

"I love you more."

"I love you more than that."

I stay there for a bit longer than I should. When Millie was very
little, Philip and I used to lie on either side of her until she slept.
Sometimes he fell asleep, too, and I would watch them both, the
movement of their chests, the flutter of their eyelids. I have to stop
remembering things like this. I rub my eyes. I must go downstairs.
I will tell Clara everything that has happened since Thursday, but
I want to order it in my mind first. As long as I can keep it clear in
my head I'll be all right. If I start splurging everything out to my
oldest and dearest friend I might not stop. All these fears about
my marriage, my job. This murder has set it all in motion. Being
selective might be a lapse of faith in our friendship, but that trendy
media scientist we had on the show recently said something about
atoms and electrons and nuclei and how an atom will react to fill

its electron shell. Well, that's what I'm doing. I'm just trying to shift the energy level, trying to keep my nucleus happy with a full electron shell.

Clara has moved places when I get down and is sitting with her back to me, looking out at the garden. The light is on in that upstairs window across the two gardens. It's a bathroom, I think. It must be, with that flat, white light. Or an office. I look for shapes moving, but the rectangle is blank.

Without turning round, she says, "Where's Philip? Is he not here?"

"He's away."

Something flashes in her eyes as she turns, or maybe I imagine it. "And he didn't come back when he knew you'd been arrested?"

"Not so far." My tone is so light you couldn't catch it if you tried. "To be honest, he hasn't even rung."

"That's just *ridiculous*."

"It's just possible he doesn't yet know. I haven't been able to get through . . ."

I have this feeling again. It comes from nowhere. It's as if I am standing on the top of a precipice. I could tell her anything and she would be on my side.

I sit down and refill our drinks. Condensation pearls on the outside of my glass, and I run my finger across and down it in patterns while I talk. I explain that I missed out a lot earlier. I tell her that I think Perivale hates me, and I run through his coincidences: the physical similarities, the clothes, the cuttings, the Italian soil, the credit card receipt.

Clara puts her glass down while I am talking, and when I have finished, she looks at me intently. "Why do the police think you did it?"

"They don't seem to be interested in motive at all. They have some vague thought, I think, that . . ." What shall I say? "That she was my stalker and I killed her to . . . stop her stalking?"

"It's a bit far-fetched."

"I know." I haven't talked much to Clara about my stalker. It makes me feel uncomfortable, as if I am drawing attention to my semicelebrity status. When Philip mentioned it at that Chinese meal the other week, I saw the same look cross her eyes that she gets during discussions of a particular form of learning difficulty she refers to as "middle-class dyslexia."

"Was she 'stalking' you?"

Inverted commas.

"I don't know. One always assumes a man . . . A report in the US a couple of years ago said sixty-seven percent of stalked females were stalked by males. But—" I break off, frown.

"So what's your explanation?"

"The coincidences tie Ania Dudek not to me so much as to the *house*. I don't live here on my own. Marta is a possibility—for some of it anyway."

"And what does she say?"

"She denies everything. She denies knowing her, giving her clothes, nicking my card to buy pizza . . ."

"And do you think she's telling the truth?"

"I don't see why she'd lie. I don't really like her. I do have this feeling that she's hiding something, but I haven't got any proof. And . . . I don't know, perhaps it's all my fault."

Clara is looking at me.

"Not liking her, I mean."

But she is still looking at me, waiting.

"Philip," I say, after a moment. "You're thinking about Philip."

"He does live in this house, too. All the evidence could link equally to him as you."

I take a big swig of wine. I know Clara dislikes Philip, but I can't quite believe she would suspect him of murder. "True," I say.

"Gaby."

"Philip's not a murderer," I say. "He's a wanker and he's ob-sessed with money and status and he's probably fallen out of love with me, but he's not a murderer."

She laughs and I do, too, though I didn't mean to be funny.

"Also, he's so organized and cool and considered. If he wanted to kill someone he'd do it cleverly. It wouldn't even look like a murder. Not messy and raw, like this one. He wouldn't make any mistakes. It's just not Philip."

"Fair enough," she says.

"Plus he's always at work and he has an alibi."

Clara puts her hands in the air in surrender. "Okay! I think we've established you're not married to a mad ax murderer!"

"That's a relief. More wine?"

I refill her glass, and she smiles at me above it. But when she puts it down, she says, "He has to come back, though. He needs to be here. He is your husband. I don't understand why you haven't rung the hotel, his office, his colleagues. Wouldn't he be useful, with the legal situation, not to mention moral support? For Christ's sake, Gaby, it is okay to ask for help. Occasionally, for once, it would be nice if you let someone else look after you."

I lick my finger and use it to pick up a shard of crisp from the table. I put it on my tongue, where it rests like a fragment of card. "I've forgotten how to behave normally. I can't be myself. Every action when I'm around him is self-conscious."

"Why, Gaby?"

I brush the tips of my fingers together, gritty with salt, try again to swallow the crisp. "I don't think he likes me anymore—that simple. He's going to leave me, I think. He's building up to it. Not sure, but probably."

"Gabs."

"It's fine." The crisp sticks at the back of my throat. I look at her again and smile. "Possibly there's someone else, I don't know."

Color rushes to her cheeks. She's been thinking this for months. "Probably at work," I add. "He definitely seems to live there."

Possibly. Probably. *Definitely*.

"Oh, Gaby."

"Honestly, Clara, I'm okay. I've got Millie."

Something ripples beneath her features, a spasm. "And me."

"And you." I put on a crinkly old-lady voice, wrinkle my shoulders. "I've still got my eyesight, my *health*."

"We need to get you through the next few days," Clara says. "Don't think about Philip—he really *is* a wanker. We'll worry about that later."

"I can move to Suffolk with Millie, start again."

"Exactly. But in the meantime, you need a plan. Two plans. Several plans." Clara plunders her bag for a pad and pen. The pen is sparkly with a feather on the top. "Nicked from one of my year sevens. Right. Churchill's War Rooms." The sentiment that floats between us is swept away by activity. This is how Clara copes, how she always has. I think about her lists and her mind maps, her index cards and revision cards. She was the first person I knew to buy a Filofax.

We agree that, for the immediate future, I am stuck at home. Perivale has said I am not to stray too far, and I don't want to annoy him any more than I already have. I should win him over, prove reliability, shake off this image he has of me. We can't accuse Marta of anything. We have no proof. For the next few days, though, until it is all sorted, it would be good if Millie were somewhere else, somewhere safe—a place where there weren't predatory journalists or police officers on every street corner. My heart aches.

Clara suggests Philip's parents—until I tell her they're away—and says her parents would help (they were lovely to me when I was growing up), but that her dad is in hospital for his dodgy knee. She asks then if any of my local friends might leap into the breach.

A small chasm opens up. I think about Jude, whom I never got to know, and say, "Local friends? What local friends?" and she stares at me.

"Do you have local friends?" I say.

"*Yes*. Everybody has local friends. Local friends, Gabs, are the secret to happiness."

"I've been busy. And it's awkward, being on the telly. And Philip—"

She raises her finger. "No excuses. When this is over, you're going to sort yourself out."

For now, she says, she could take Millie home to Islington, tonight, this minute. Pete could look after her while Clara's at school (she doesn't break up until Wednesday). Something delicate crumples in my chest at the immediacy of that. The dream I had when I was pregnant, the cat struggling out of my arms in downtown Bombay . . . waking her and kissing her good-bye, the confusion on her sleep-pouched face.

Clara's still working it through. She has another thought: Suffolk. Robin. I could ask Robin anything when she lived with us—to work the weekend, to move her holiday and she would be saying, "Sure," even as the words left my mouth. It was up to me to decide whether she minded, to calibrate the disappointment behind her eyes, the shifting of plans. So now. Is the baby too young? Is it too much of an imposition?

Clara rides across my hesitations. We ring her.

"Sure," Robin says. "Of course. What's one more? What better helper with Charlie could I have than Millie? I'd love to have my girl."

As for getting her there, Clara will take her up on the train tomorrow.

A lifting sensation in my shoulders. "Above and beyond," I say. "Definitely."

"Don't be silly." Clara reaches to tap my knuckles with the feathered pen. She misses, knocks the crisps over instead. We're both a little drunk.

And Marta? I should give her a few days' holiday, suggest she go—where? Colliers Wood to stay with her identity-thefted friend.

Clara has to set off. Pete has been cooking chicken jalfrezi for the kids. He went to Southall especially for the spices. There'll be washing up. "Fuck me, there'll be washing up." She decides to leave out the back, just for the fun of it. "All these people going in and no one coming out. It's like that Beatles movie."

We stand in the garden, in the middle of the lawn. Wispy clouds scuttle across the sky like smoke. We giggle. I'm thirteen again. Knock Down Ginger. Kissing Johnny Riggins. Fake ciggies from the health shop. Nicking my mum's booze. We used to wander Yeovil pretending we were French.

Clara hovers in the alley. "Spiders!" she yelps, and then she is off, dancing to the end of it. She waves, turns the corner, and disappears.

When I was little, when the mood took her, my mother used to take me to the seaside. It didn't matter if it was a school day, not to my mum. She would put the radio up high and sing at the top of her voice and stop for chips and Tizer. I would sit on the edge of the backseat, searching the skyline for the first hazy line of blue. But quite often it would all go wrong. I might have dropped tomato sauce on my top, or it might not be the right song, or she would see someone out the window she didn't like. She would change her mind, turn back. The ozone would be blasting at the window, but in the car, the air would turn black and sour.

I think about that when Philip calls that night, how things that one longs for can sometimes tip, the moment you reach them, into disappointment.

He says everything I have waited to hear. He just got a text from Rog. He has heard what happened. He's sorry I've been through such hell. Thank *fuck,* it's over. What did the police *think* they were doing arresting me? Why did they think for a minute . . . ? He's *so* sorry he didn't ring earlier. His phone was charging. Back-to-back meetings, then forced to a karaoke club—this *endless* corporate entertainment. He hasn't even showered. He saw that I'd rung, but he's only just listened to my message. Of course, he'd have phoned back if he'd known. Am I all right? I sounded so *distraught.* Did the police take me in because I found the body? Is that what it was?

I don't know. It doesn't matter. Yes. I'm sorry. Yes.

He's coming straight back, he says. He'll be on the next flight.

I'm so calm. It's as if I am looking down on myself, from the cockpit of the Boeing 747, or whatever it is he would fly home on. He doesn't sound like Philip. He sounds like a representation of Philip, the real Philip buried in there, beneath the mannerisms, the pat phrases, the real Philip thinking and feeling something completely different. I think back to a difficult conversation we had in Brighton. I said, "You're being odd." And he said, "No I'm not being odd. But by saying that you're *making* me odd." Everything seems artificial. Images of us before. All these memories I keep dredging up. They are all filtered. It's all words and posture.

"Stay in Singapore," I say. "It was a storm in a teacup. I'm sorry I cried in my message. I was overemotional, tired. But it's over now. I don't even need a lawyer. It was a misunderstanding. It's enough that you've offered. Millie has gone to stay with Robin and . . . Don't come home unless . . ." I want him to fill in the gaps, to sense there's something I'm not saying, to care enough.

When it is silent on his end, I add: "Stay."

"Well, if you're sure. I suppose, having come all this way . . ." He yawns, an ache of silence, a sob. "And if you promise the police have let you go . . ."

"Stay," I say again.

"Okay, old girl."

Old girl.

I'm in the kitchen and I look out into the black garden, at that square of banded light above the apple tree. I'm digging my finger-nails into the palm of my hand and the pain is so ordinary, so easy to bear, I almost laugh.

SATURDAY

I don't sleep well. It's racking up, the lack of sleep. Phrases from my phone call with Philip keep coming back to me: his reference to a missed shower, the indulgent self-importance of this "endless corporate entertainment," his yawn. Somewhere Ania Dudek's parents are suffering, and Philip is "forced" into karaoke. I told him to stay away, and I meant it, but he should have insisted on coming home. He should have realized I was in trouble. Or even if he didn't, he should have wanted to be by my side. Nothing should have kept him away. My longing transmutes to hate. They were never that far apart, it turns out. You think it's a continuum, a long arc, a process, but it's just the flip of a switch. I ball up his shirt, the one I slept with last night, and hurl it across the room.

All this anger is oddly soothing, and in the morning, I am up early. Marta's door is closed. I pack for Millie and we watch television quietly—I don't want Marta coming down before Millie has left. Clara rings to let me know she's at the garden door. Millie skips across the grass. I carry her bag. I'm in my dressing gown, and I have to hold it closed because I couldn't find the belt! My daughter's bag bumps with each step against my bare leg. I don't want her to go, but she's excited. Clara has come all this way—again. She has the train tickets, flapping them in the air as if she has won the lottery. I'm in too deep.

Millie won't wear her coat; she shrugs it off. I get cross. I pick it up, tell her it's cold, she'll need it. Clara says, "We'll have to run if we're going to catch that train. We'll soon warm up."

When I walk back across the lawn, I catch sight of Marta at the kitchen window, watching.

"What is happening?" she says. "Where is Millie going?"

She is fully dressed, even down to the latex gloves. I feel at a disadvantage in my dressing gown, as if I have been caught out. I close the door and lean against it. "She's gone to stay with . . ." I pause. I'm worried about hurting her feelings. "With our old nanny, Robin."

"Why?"

"Just for a couple of days, while the police are getting to the bottom of . . . things."

I gesture to the coat, thrown over my shoulder like a body. "She wouldn't wear her coat."

"It's cold."

"I got cross. I wish I hadn't."

"Sometimes she is spoiled girl."

I sit down at the table. Do I mind Marta criticizing my daughter? "She is only eight," I say.

Marta makes a dismissive noise, a hrumph at the back of her throat.

"So I won't really be needing you for a little while. You should take a holiday if you like. Go away somewhere."

She is still standing by the window. "Where? Where do I go?"

"Your friend?" I suggest brightly, "the one in Colliers Wood?"

"No. I think I stay here."

Panic rises inside me. I don't want her in the house. It's awful I know. This is her home, but I would like a day or two without her. The table is tacky from last night's wine. I shift my elbows. "Might be good not to be here for a while," I say more firmly. She blinks slowly, moving her head slightly at the same time. It's hardly a gesture at all, but it conveys contempt.

I clear my throat, look down. "If it is possible for you. It would be better."

I hear her cross the room. The dishwasher shuts with a loud clack. When I look up, she has peeled off her latex gloves, thrown them on the counter, and left the room.

I lie on my bed, tensely reading a book—I hid the newspapers under the sofa without looking at them, a possible sign of madness. I am alone in the house. I heard the front door slam. I miss Millie, but she will be happier where she is. I tell myself that like a mantra. My senses have become alert to the smallest of details—a tap dripping in an upstairs bathroom, the lonely corkscrew gurgle of my own stomach. A slight shift in temperature has brought goose pimples to my arm. Noises. Shouts in the street. A scrape of the letter box—a note poked through, which I threw away without reading. The motorbike buzz of a neighbor's leaf blower.

Despair slips in and sinks like a stone. What if I don't escape all this? What if Perivale never lets this go? What would happen to me then? *Prison?* I get up quickly, cast off my dressing gown like a snake's skin, like a bad thought, and snap on my running gear. No Asics still. I wear the green-flash Dunlops. I look out of the window. A few journalists are still there; one of them wrote that note. I can't see Perivale. I charge down the stairs, grab a woollen hat from the cupboard, clatter out the back, streak across the garden, and wriggle behind the tree house. I bash my shoulder on a wooden post. I know I've grazed it, possibly drawn blood, but I don't care. I pause in the passageway. No pockets, so I leave the key on the garden side and pull the door shut. It will look as if it's locked; no one will know it isn't. The house doesn't need to be fortressed now I'm out of it.

The pounding of the pavement, the vibrating jolt of my own breath. I'm not that comfortable—I'm wearing the wrong bra, the underwire is digging into my armpit, and I've got that peculiar teeth-joggling thing I sometimes get while running. The beanie keeps slipping down my forehead. I leave it until I can see only a slit of feet and gravelly earth and then push it back up; it waits, a haze of itchy fabric, before sliding down again. As soon as I am on the common, I feel my mood shift. The minutes, which stagnated in the house, speed up. For the first time in ages, I am out running and I am not worrying about what Philip is thinking or feeling. Today I just don't care, and it's liberating. There is fresh air in my lungs—or as fresh as Wandsworth Common gets. The diesel from trains and traffic mingles with the birthing of leaves, the pinking of blossom. Above me, wood pigeons coo, and in the bushes, blue tits dart and squeak.

It's not too busy out here. I've timed it well—post-football club, pre-afternoon stroll. A dull day, too, a day for jigsaw puzzles and shopping centers. Layers and layers of fleeting gray cloud, a leaden gloom. I think about arriving back at Heathrow from Nevis last Easter, plunging from all that light and horizon-dazzling blue, down through the dirty milk shake of cloud, into the flat black-and-white world of Hounslow and Slough. The woman, an American, next to me said, "Can people really survive in such darkness?" Yes, they do. *We* do.

It's a relief to clear my mind. Keep it clear. Exercise your limbs; don't think. Over the bridge and down the path along the railway. They have resurfaced since I was last here—since that morning two weeks ago. Smooth tarmac, easy under foot, liquorice bubbles of tar by the weeds. End of the tax year—council's using up its quota before the government grabs it back. Shouts reach me through the trees from the soccer field to my right—hairy men in small shorts hollering, "In. Slide him. Russell, he-re." Two syllables for "here."

I manage my usual circuit. I've crossed the common from road to road—2.5 kilometers, once round—and I'm pacing along the railway, approaching the bridge again, the beanie back across my eyes, when footsteps rasp behind, a jangle of coins. I quicken, assuming I'll outpace them, but the footsteps quicken, too. I slow right down. Some runners don't like other people's slipstream—the boy racers of the running world. There is no satisfied intake of breath, though, no jostle of air. It's a man. I can hear him breathing. There's a pitch to a person's breath; I have time to reflect on that. I'm still a hundred yards from the bridge. Flight or fight? Is this nothing? Or everything? Is this the moment I've been dreading? I could run. I push the beanie out of my eyes. Or . . .

I stop and turn. One of my feet is still facing forward; it's a comedy reversal of a racing start.

"Sorry." He's almost on top of me. His arms brake with a Woody Woodpecker windmill. "Sorry."

"You," I say. "Again."

"God. Bloody idiot. Sorry." He clutches both hands to his head in mortification. Or—the gesture turns into less of a smack and more of a smooth—to dampen the exuberance of his curly hair.

"What are you trying to do? Kill me?"

"No, of course not. No. Did I . . . ? I'm not wearing the right shoes."

"For killing me?"

"No, for running. And you're bloody fast. In training or something? And then I thought I'd wait until you reached the bridge, that you might walk over it because of the railing things and that that might be a good time to catch you."

I study him. Jack Hayward—I remember his name. A nice voice, a bit of Yorkshire in there. A short *a* in *fast*.

"Why do you want to catch me? Have you been following me?"

"No. No, of course not. Sorry. No. I wasn't. I mean, I have been outside your house, but I came over the common for a cup of tea and a flapjack, saw you running, waited on that bench. I didn't want to ruin your . . . keep fit."

I have started walking on now, at quite a clip. "'Keep fit!'" I say, over my shoulder. "How old are you—sixty?"

"Don't we call it 'keep fit' anymore? Okay, so what is it? I didn't want to ruin your jog."

"Nope."

"What, we don't jog anymore?"

"*Jogging*'s dated too. It's a run, even if you're jogging it."

"Okay, I didn't want to ruin your run."

We've reached the bridge and I turn. "Well. It's a bit late now." Good God, I'm flirting.

He puts his hands out in surrender. "Five minutes," he says. "Just give me five minutes."

"No. Sorry."

I keep walking. Not running, though. That's interesting.

He keeps pace. "I know you think journalists are scum."

"I don't think anyone's scum." Animals, Caroline Fletcher called them. "Anyway, I'm a journalist myself. I'd never use that term."

"But we're not all bad," he continues. "I mean, some of us are. Probably me." He has prepared what to say, self-deprecation at the ready. "And post-Leveson, we're all better behaved. We're not hacking your phone. We're not even knocking on the door. We're just hanging around, waiting, living in hope." He sighs, less like hope, more like disappointment. Maybe the speech sounded better in his head. "I know you're using the back," he adds. "I was parking when I saw your daughter and that woman leave this morning."

My head turns sharply. "You saw them?"

"Don't worry. I haven't told the others."

"Consideration, or self-interest?"

He laughs. "Bit of both."

The admission of ambiguity, the humor or self-knowledge: it's like a salve. I mean, none of our motives is ever straightforward. I think about Clara's suggestion to sell my story to one hack to be free of the rest. Does that tactic work? I don't know. I would ask Alison Brett, if she showed any interest, which it doesn't look as if she's going to. It's not my reputation she cares about anyway; it's the show's. She doesn't care who killed Ania Dudek. I'm on my own in that, but I also need to do something if I am to be rehabilitated, if I am ever to be that nice Gaby Mortimer again.

We pass a piece of apparatus for Wandsworth Common's "Trim Trail": a horizontal plank of wood on two struts, just off the path near the pond, meant for sit-ups. I walk across, balance my bum on it, and say, "Five minutes. Not to talk. This is off the record. You have five minutes to persuade me."

He sits down next to me with a sigh of what I can only imagine is heightened hope. He is wearing a suit with a thin waterproof jacket over the top—the jacket puffs up like a buoyancy aid. He'll be getting mossy stains on the seat of his trousers. I'm oddly touched by the fact he doesn't seem to notice.

"Listen, then," he says. "I believe you are innocent." His expression is so earnest and heartfelt, I laugh. He grins, his eyes disappearing, brackets around his mouth. "Give me an interview and other people will see that, too. I can help you prove it."

"I've got a lawyer for that."

"Yeah, well"—he winces—"you haven't really. Caroline Fletcher is only the duty solicitor."

"Caroline Fletcher?" I'm startled, rattled he knows her name.

"What do you think we all talk about, hanging around for hours outside your door?"

"The football?"

"Mainly that, but the odd other thing slips in. A duty solicitor is always on to the next job. They only care about getting a suspect off the charges. In your case, Caroline Fletcher won't give two hoots about your public profile."

"I suppose you're right. Even an innocent person needs the best legal representation . . ."

"I could give you a list of celebrities whose careers have been ruined, regardless of whether they did what they were accused of or not." He looks quite grim for a moment, a dark set to his mouth. Not all cheerfulness, then. "I could write a sidebar on it."

"Well, thanks for the advice. I'll get a better lawyer." And agent, I think to myself: I won't make that mistake again.

"No! You don't need that. You just need me. Give me an exclusive, a nice in-depth profile, and I'll turn this thing around."

I look at his face, trying to read it. A handsome face, but one Philip's mother would call "lived in"—a large nose, smile creases on the cheeks, wild eyebrows, brown irises with strikingly dark rims. "How do I know you won't do the dirty? You might be stitching me up."

He shrugs. "You just have to trust me."

He holds my gaze for a moment and then looks away. A firm chin, broad shoulders, a determined mouth: the sort of man who in a previous generation would have run a battalion, earned the respect of his troops. Journalism: the new armed forces. Is he to be trusted? Who knows? How old is he? The pent-up energy, the enthusiasm of a young man, but a fan of weariness around the eyes. That bitter flash earlier. About my age? But then I've started thinking everyone is "about my age," until I find out they're actually twenty-eight.

"How old are you?"

He shrugs. "Forty. Old enough to know better."

About my age. Well, *almost*.

On the path, two young women with frog-shaped buggies have stopped, their heads turned toward us. There is a second when my face falls into its muscle-memory minor-celeb smile, but there is no smile back, no bashful dawning of why they recognize me. Their eyes narrow. I can hear whispers. They think I can't see their lips move, or they don't care. What do you think she was doing, getting mixed up with that dead woman? Obviously unhinged. Kicking a reporter like that. Did you *see* the bruise?

I do need somebody, even Alison Brett agreed with that before she hung up. Perhaps Hayward knows how to tinker with search engines—bury my bruise way down on page twenty-three, where no one ever looks. Google-washing, Google-bombing, Google-bowling. We had a media manipulator on *Mornin' All* a while back—some story to do with George W. Bush. I know it can be done. We can use each other. A symbiotic relationship. Goby fish and snapping shrimp. Or those birds that sit on the heads of African wildebeest.

A large brown dog barrels over and starts digging the bark with its two front paws, pausing to sniff the newly formed hole and then frantically redigging. Earth is spraying onto Jack Hayward's suit trousers; he's collecting mulch in his cuffs.

He laughs and calls the dog to him. "Come, boy." The dog, tail wagging insanely, noses about a bit in his crotch, licks his hand, and gambols off. Hayward watches him disappear. Somewhere in the distance, a voice shouts, "ROGER!"

"Okay," I say. "I'm probably mad, but okay."

"What, you'll do it?"

I nod. I shall have to be alert. That's all.

He makes a gesture with his elbow, and his fist and says, "Kerching!"

"If you do that again, I'll change my mind."

"Sorry," he says, and then does it again, more mutedly, as if behind my back.

He is pretending to be more carefree than he is. I'm intrigued. Perhaps he is playing a part, but he's hardly alone in that. I will have to keep my eye on him. We will just have to see.

I get to my feet and sweep a few globules of dog-displaced grassy mud from my lap, and we start walking back in the direction of the house. It has begun to rain. He is talking, with the attention to detail of someone for whom food is important, about the various goodies he has in his car—Italian sourdough from the bread stall on North-cote Road, some Somerset brie from the cheese shop—"thought it was worth trying"—and a couple of bottles of Belgian beer—"not very cold, but beggars et cetera."

"Are you thinking of coming back now?" I say. "This minute?"

"If that's all right?"

Dark spots of rain on the path ahead, a rushing in the top of the trees. I frown, trying to look as if I am considering the matter, weighing the pros and the cons, still in control of the situation, while inside a tightness I hadn't realized was there eases a little. Maybe it is loneliness, or despair, or the dread of an empty house, but I have that feeling—one I haven't had in a long time—when you don't want to let a person's company go.

Jack goes to the car to collect his gubbins—as he calls them—so I am alone for a few minutes. I try Alison Brett again, but she doesn't answer. I didn't think she would. I pull a comb through my hair and make a stab at lunch. I chop tomatoes and slice mozzarella, chuck on salt and olive oil. I grate a couple of the zucchini-substitution carrots from the supermarket delivery, grating my finger along the way. Now they're grated zucchini-substitution carrots with extra finger. I rack my brain. Didn't Carol Vorderman do something clever with carrots in the *Mornin' All* kitchen? I throw in some dried tarragon and a slop of orange juice from the fridge. I'm hurrying, which is ridiculous, because there is no hurry—no one, it seems, is going anywhere.

I look up and see Jack crossing the lawn. I must have left the back door open. I'm disconcerted—it seems a bit *forward,* if nothing else—but I don't have time to think because in seconds he is in the kitchen. His hair and clothes glisten. He makes one of those horsey *brr* noises that people make to express any sort of cold or discomfort, and unzips his mac. I ask if he needs a towel, but he says, "I'll survive." Unlacing his shoes, he bends over the edge of the bench. Rain scatters against the window, blurring the garden into green clumps. I chuck him a clean tea towel, whether he wants one or not. Overarm. See how casual I can be? It floats to the floor a few feet from him. He stoops to pick it up and gives his face a quick rub before handing it back.

"Thanks," he says.

I'm rootling around in the fridge for a bottle of wine when he says, "Top salads. Where did they come from? It's not bread and cheese. It's a feast."

That's why I was hurrying. I wanted him to see the salads spirited onto the table and be impressed. I was showing off. And now he *is* impressed—"a feast," he said—and I feel foolish. It's just carrots and orange juice and he's just a hack. I am not the sort of woman to need male approval. If Jack Hayward thinks I'm nice, that's enough. I don't need him *to move in*. What is the matter with me? Why am I flustered?

I'm holding a bottle of rosé, but I slide it back in next to the milk and take out the carton of juice instead. "Orange juice okay?" I say. "Though you've already got some of that in the carrots. Or would you prefer tea or coffee?"

"A hot beverage," he says in a funny voice, which makes me think he's feeling awkward, too. He has laid the bread and the cheese on the table, spreading out the wrappers as if they were bone china platters. He is browsing the recipe books on the island shelf. He isn't a big man—a little less than six foot—but he's stocky, broad in the shoulder. He seems to take up more room than I'd bargained for.

"I've got a Nespresso machine," I say pointlessly. "Krups."

"Or I've got these Belgian Trappist ales, but they could do with chilling."

He crosses to the fridge and, clinking them out of a carrier bag, finds space for them inside. If he sees the bottle of rosé, he doesn't say anything.

I click on the kettle, just for something to do, and find plates—wincing with the clatter—and the two of us sit at the kitchen table. He has hung his waterproof politely over the back of a chair.

Serving, I hold the spoons at a self-consciously high angle. I'm beginning to wish I hadn't said yes. There are stages I have missed. I should have checked his credentials, confirmed Jack Hayward exists, that he hasn't made up the name, or co-opted someone else's, that he is who he says he is. I remember Alison Brett saying never to let a journalist in the house. Even writers on the high-class Sundays want to make jokes about your bathroom fittings. Too late now. We eat. It's an odd feeling—the rest of the house is so shuttered and dark—peculiarly domestic. "Pass the salt," he says. "A pinch of salt is bloody good with these toms."

Philip and I haven't sat at the kitchen table in months. If we've eaten together, we've eaten out.

"They're Riverford," I say.

"River what?"

"You've heard of Riverford—organic veg boxes up from Devon, left on the doorstep every Tuesday. Our old nanny, Robin, introduced us to them."

"Very posh. Muddy veg for the middle classes."

"Don't give me that—you and your Somerset brie that you 'thought was worth trying.'"

"All right, you've got me there. And yeah, I've seen their vans."

This exchange makes me feel better, less twitchy. This man isn't looking around—sizing up the house, valuing the Craigie Aitchison. I'm the one studying every gesture, dissecting every word.

"What do you think of the brie?" he asks, stabbing a chunk of it on the end of his fork, studying it like a botanical specimen. "Pleasant but not quite brie-y enough, is it?"

"Oh, I think it's quite brie-y," I say.

"I know what it needs." He jumps to his feet and collects the beer, which can't have had time to get much colder, and unscrews the tops.

"Can you cook?" I ask, taking one from him.

"Not bad," he says. "I'm an everyday cook. I like simple ingredients, seasonal."

"Saying that these days has become tantamount to a moral code."

He laughs. "True. My mum was good. Four kids. I'm the only boy. She taught us all to cook. You?"

"My mother wasn't really the teaching-to-cook kind. More of a baked-beans-out-of-the-can sort of person."

"I'd say you have natural talent. The . . . er . . . carrot salad has an interesting flavor."

I sip the beer straight from the bottle. It tastes like caramel. I can feel it slipping down my throat, like that ad they used to show for Castrol oil. "Do you live locally?"

"Brixton. For now. I've got a flat above a launderette, which is handy."

Intriguing: a man of his age in a flat above a "handy" launderette. "No Mrs. Hayward?"

He prongs another corner of brie onto a torn piece of bread. "No current Mrs. Hayward."

Divorced, then, getting back on his feet. "Kids?"

"Ah." He wipes the olive oil juices on his plate with a piece of bread. He has barricaded the carrot in one corner. He's working hard to avoid it. It wasn't tarragon Vorderman used, now I think of it, but coriander. "Really good those toms. No. No kids."

I ask him how he ended up as a reporter and he launches into his life story—South Yorkshire, youngest child, mother dead, dad still alive, did a journalism course somewhere, a London evening paper, followed by the *Express*—or does he say the *Mirror*?—freelance these days. I don't take much in. I'm after different sorts of information—how clever he is, how kind. Can he really disentangle me from this mess? Will he write a good piece? Is he to be trusted? That slight Yorkshire accent, associated with honesty, sharpens when he talks about his family—the short vowels, the *g* in *youngest* clung to like a security blanket.

"Anyway," he says after a while, "enough about me." He gives a quick shake of his head, as if to say "I'm being boring," though I am not finding him boring.

"Ania Dudek," he says abruptly.

A ringing starts up in my ears, a surge of panic. I feel guilty. I had forgotten this was about her, as well as me. I have managed to put her out of my mind for a bit. "Ania Dudek," I repeat, waiting for something inside me to still.

He pushes his plate to one side, reaches into his pocket, and stops, brings his hands out again. Cigarette-less. "Now there's a conundrum. From what I've picked up, hanging around out there, she was a hardworking Polish woman, training to be a teacher at Froebel College in Roehampton, doing jobs all hours of the day to make ends meet: nannying, dog walking, babysitting. She was learning ballet and had applied for British citizenship: get that. She was intelligent, making something of herself, putting down roots, and she ends up dead, strangled with a narrow ligature in her own flat and dumped a few feet away in the middle of Wandsworth Common. Pregnant," he adds, as if the fact needs its own pause around it.

I just wait. Sometimes I close my eyes when I think about her being pregnant.

"And the police think you did it."

I let out a small involuntary noise because the juxtaposition of that is hard to hear.

Hayward has moved the cheese wrappers and the bowls of salad farther down the table, as if clearing the decks. "Word is it's an *idée fixe* with Perivale."

"An *idée fixe*?" I say, raising an eyebrow.

He gives me an old-fashioned look. "An *idée fixe*. Mickey Smith of the *Mirror*—he's a proper crime reporter, been around the block a few times—says DI Perivale has got a handful of facts and is determined to slot them into place. The policewoman—what's her name?"

"Morrow. PC Morrow."

"PC Morrow is not happy with the way the investigation is going. Mickey overheard her in the pub talking to one of the other coppers about how 'blinkered' Perivale is. Most people are killed by someone close to them—husband, wife . . . The big question is Ania's boyfriend. I don't know why they're not looking at him. Ninety-nine times out of a hundred it's the boyfriend."

"He wasn't in the country when she was killed," I say. "Perivale told me that."

"Ah."

I laugh. "So there goes your theory."

He looks thoughtful. "Odd, though, his obsession with you. Mickey thinks it goes back to the morning you found the body."

"That was my big mistake," I say, "finding the body."

"Your DNA all over the place . . . didn't look good."

"I fixed her bra and I forgot to tell him. I touched her hair . . ."

"A simple explanation. Then there are these other clues. The soil—I'm sure if we did a survey along every street round here we'd find traces of Italian mud on the front path of every other house. Anyone could have trodden it in: the milkman, the postman, someone delivering pizza flyers."

He has been busy. He seems to know *everything*. "What about the other connections?" I ask, intrigued. "The cuttings . . . the physical resemblance between us . . . The police think maybe she was stalking me."

"Here is what I think. She told her neighbor that she was going to apply for a job as your nanny. She was excited, nervous. She'd seen you on the television." He catches my expression. "You have no memory of this?"

"None. I promise you. She didn't come for an interview. I would remember, even though it was a bit of a hard time for me. I can remember everyone I saw and I didn't see her."

He is looking at me expectantly. "Hard time?"

I've slipped up. "My mother had been taken ill. She died that week." I say it as flatly as I can, but of course anything with death in it is loaded.

"I'm so sorry," he says. "Cancer?"

"Something like that."

"Nothing prepares you, does it?"

"You're right." I smile, a woman coming to terms with the loss of her mother, but he is wrong. I could tell him how prepared I had been, how for years I had known it was coming, but I won't.

He leans back in his chair, the pose of someone at ease with his own body, who has had enough to eat and is quite enjoying stretching his muscles. Where his shirt parts from his trousers, between two buttons, is an arrow of bare flesh.

He sits forward again. "So you were distracted. Maybe you did interview her, or she turned up and there was no one here? Either way, I can understand why she might have become intrigued by you, cut out the occasional article to send home to her mother." He shakes his head. "The clothes, the pizza receipt, on the other hand: baffling."

I don't know if it's the beer, but the way he shakes his head sends a shiver of relief through me so intense it's almost delight. To be in the company of somebody who knows so many facts, in such forensic detail, and still believes in my innocence: I could sing. My friends might believe me, but it's my version they have heard, whereas Jack Hayward's information is unfiltered. An idea begins to grow.

"Listen," I say. "How about this. I give you your interview; we agree you can ask me anything you like. But before that, you help me dig about for a few days. You seem to have the contacts. I wouldn't know where to start. And I'm not saying *investigate*, just do a bit of poking, ask a few questions, look where the police aren't. Maybe we'll find something that clears my name, maybe we won't. Maybe we'll just kick-start Perivale. But at least we will be doing the right thing by Ania. I . . . I owe her that."

Jack doesn't answer at first. He looks troubled, possibly a little panicked. I wonder if I have made a mistake. All this chat, all these opinions about the case, were they just to win me over?

"But you'll be back at work on Monday," he says. "How much time can you really spend on this?"

"I won't be at work, sadly."

He makes an enquiring gesture with his head.

"I've been . . . suspended."

A long pause. He seems to scrutinize my face. I've almost given up hope, when he says, "All right."

I breathe out. "Really?"

"Yeah. It's not like I've got anything else on. And I can see how it might work. Two worlds collide, but in more detail, with a bit of investigative journalism thrown in. Might even flog it to the Sunday *Times* News Review." He reaches into the inside pocket of his jacket and brings out a small dictaphone. "Where shall we start?"

The dictaphone makes me feel uncomfortable and I am about to ask him to put it away, when my mobile rings. The phone is on the table and Jack looks at the screen before I do. It's Philip. "Oh," I say, "that can wait," and I put the phone in my pocket.

"Yes, where shall we start?" I echo. "Well, I have one possible explanation for the clothes and the pizza receipt, which is Marta, my nanny. But don't tape any of this. It might not be for the article. It's not that I think she killed Ania, just that maybe she knew her and has some reason for keeping quiet about it. She told the police she had never met her, but she told me she might have seen her a couple of times at church."

"Where's Marta now?"

"She's gone to stay with a friend in Colliers Wood."

"Colliers Wood." He deepens his voice, as if I have said Voldemort's lair. I can feel the whole thing edging from the Gothic to the comic, tensions loosening. "Show me where she sleeps."

"The police have already been in there. What are we going to find that they didn't?"

"Fresh eyes, new perspectives. The smallest thing can mean nothing to one person and everything to another. And inconsistent evidence is always suspicious. Come on!" He scrapes back his chair. "Are we going to investigate, or are we going to investigate?"

I make a gesture with my hands to say "I surrender," and lead the way upstairs. He follows behind. I'm aware of the weight of his steps. I climb the stairs with a sort of self-conscious agility. When I push open the door to Marta's room, I start. For a moment, I think she is lying on the bed, but it is just the duvet—she has folded it in a strange way, with the pillows on top.

Jack crosses to the window and opens the slats in the blinds. Rain dribbles down the glass. "You can see the common from here," he says, "over the roofs of the houses."

I'm still standing by the door. There seems to be a line one shouldn't cross. But Jack apparently has no qualms. Maybe that's because he has never met her—does that make a difference to the ethics of the situation? He is at the wardrobe, flinging open the door, ravishing the room. A roll of brown paper tumbles out.

He looks up. "What are you waiting for?"

"I suppose it's okay." I cross the threshold and join him at her closet. Still feeling ill at ease, I go through the shelves at one side, starting at the bottom: various textbooks called things like *English Without Pain,* an *A-Z,* a pile of leaflets—Madame Tussauds and the London Dungeon, a card for a cab company. At the back is a pile of padded brown envelopes, a thick roll of white stickers, and several Scotch tape dispensers.

"Why would she need so much stationery?" I say.

"Hm. Don't know."

Jack is flipping idly through clothes on hangers. "How many pairs of leggings does a girl need?"

"That," I say, "is a matter of opinion." I have searched a pile of towels and bed linen and a collection of toiletries and have got to the top shelf. I have to stretch up and feel to reach the back of this one. There is a garment bundled up there and when I pull it out I see it's the pair of jeans I've been missing. I stare at them. "I wondered where these had got to," I say, after a bit. "She must have put them away here by mistake."

Jack closes the cupboard door. "What were we looking for anyway?"

"I don't know. It was your idea."

"What's this?" He points to a shoe box under the bed.

"Should we really poke about?"

"You're right," he says. "We shouldn't, but I'm going to open this anyway. Don't look at me like that. For Christ's sake, Gaby."

It's the first time he's used my name.

I stand by the door, already leaving in my head, already downstairs with the kettle on, as he bends and slides the box across the carpet. I suspect Marta is lying to me, but even still, I don't like the fact that he is doing this. It reminds me that I don't know him. He probably shouldn't be in the house, let alone in Marta's room. But I'm paralyzed. I don't do anything. I just watch. He pushes the duvet to one side and sits on the bed to open it. When he removes the lid, a couple of thin slips of paper float out.

"Post office receipts," he says, flicking through. "Tons of them. Twenty, thirty, all for items posted in the last couple of months. And a stash of money, too. There must be five hundred pounds in notes."

"Who would need to go to the post office with so many packages?"

"A mail-order company. Or"—he makes a face—"someone sending an awful lot of presents home."

"Bloody hell."

I cross the room and sit next to him. I'm intrigued now. A spring deep in the mattress upholstery twangs. I lose my balance, fall into the side of him. "Oh dear, too much lunch," I say, without thinking.

He looks up. Our faces are close, his arm grazes mine. And then a noise. The rattle of a key, and the creak of the front door, a small vibrating bang as it hits the far wall, the reverberating crunch as it closes. A familiar sequence of sounds. Jack and I stay very still. I feel the pressure of his arm. There are footsteps in the hall. A clatter. A wait and then, coming up the stairs, a slow, heavy tread.

At my feet is a stain on the carpet that Marta has clearly tried to get out. The smooth nap of the carpet has been twisted into drawn fibers like a towel.

I stand up. The floor creaks.

Nora, on the other side of the door, gives a small yelp.

"Sorry, Nora," I say. "God, I didn't know you were coming. Did I scare you?"

"No," she says, shaking her head, though one hand is clasped to her chest. She is wearing her gold lamé slippers and holding a cloth. "I've come back because on Thursday it was too difficult to clean."

"That's incredibly kind of you."

"Sorry," she says.

"No. No, I'm sorry."

She is holding the cloth out—only it is unraveling. It isn't a cloth. It's the missing belt to my dressing gown. "I found this," she said. "On the coat rack. I take it upstairs. Okay."

"I wonder how it got there." All these possessions that keep turning up in odd places. I'm losing control of my own life. "But that's brilliant. You're brilliant. Thank you." It wouldn't occur to me to be anything but grateful to Nora, but even as the words leave my mouth, I wonder if they are being registered, documented. Behind that door, Jack Hayward is listening.

That evening, when the house is full of creaks, I run myself a bath. Deep Relax. It doesn't always work. I lie for a long time, looking down at my limbs, flickering under the water. I raise my hand, trying to be as quiet as possible, listening to the droplets fall. The freckles on my arm look dark against the pallor of my stomach. I think about Ania Dudek. Did she have my coloring? Was her body as white as mine?

Philip left a message—"what news, my darling?"—but I haven't rung back. I put my head under the water, blocking out everything but the gurgle of the pipes. Out of the window, I can see violet clouds rushing across the street-lit sky. Blue, or gray, or orange: a night sky is never black in London. A splattering of rain. A helicopter whirrs, circling, the scissor-drone louder and softer in sequence. A prisoner escaped from Wandsworth. A drug bust in Brixton. An Al Qaeda cell in Tooting. Nowhere is safe.

After my bath it's raining properly, and I walk through each

room of the house opening shutters. The journalists seem to have
scattered. Rain sees off hacks like it sees off rioters. Jack left by
the front door and had a hurried conversation with the man at the
gate—Mickey from the *Mirror,* I suppose. Afterward, one by one,
they got into their cars, doors slamming, engines starting, and drove
off. I should feel relief, but I don't. They were a buffer, those bodies;
they kept something, or someone, that I was fearing at bay.

Passing the front door on my way up to bed, I think I see a shape
against the etched glass, the contour of a hand stretching out to press
the bell, but it's only the rippling shadow of an olive tree, thrown
by the streetlamp.

SUNDAY

Philip rings again in the morning, and this time I answer. I tell him things have quieted down. "Oh good," he says. "It's awful, worrying so much about you and being so far." Fake concern. *If it is so awful, why don't you come back?*

"Is everyone at work being supportive?" he asks and in my head I reply, "*Supportive*? Are they being *supportive*? Is telling me they don't want me anywhere near them *supportive*?" But I don't say any of that. I say, "They've given me a couple of days off." I sound like a petulant child.

"Oh, good of them."

I rest my forehead on my palm. I feel irritated and drained at the same time. He is so far from understanding what I am going through. "I suppose so," I answer in the end.

How different I am on the phone to my daughter. Millie is bursting with it: baby lambs and Easter bonnets and bike rides with Ian's niece, Roxanne, who's only nine and *she* has pierced ears. I delight in every joyous word. In the background is the clatter of Robin's kitchen—the scrabbling of the dog and the snuffling of the baby, plates clattering: the rattle and hum of family life.

"That's because she's half Spanish," I hear Robin shout. "They get their ears pierced at birth."

"Like circumcision?" I say when she comes on the line.

"Oh, don't," she says. "Are you all right, Gaby?" Her tone is serious.

"I'm fine," I say cheerfully.

"Are you sure? You're having a nice break from work?"

"Yes! What's happening up there?"

She tells me Millie is being awesome, brilliant with the baby and scarfing all her veggies. I ask if she is cleaning her teeth properly. They are at such funny angles; now that the big ones are coming through, she tends to miss some. And Robin, who knows me well enough not to mind me fussing, says Millie has been giving it her best shot. She calls out to Millie, to include her in the conversation: "I had to send you back, didn't I, yesterday, to have another go at that one that's growing behind the little tooth?" I can hear Millie's distracted agreement. "She's feeding Charlie," Robin says by way of apology. "We've started solids."

"What's he eating?"

"Carrots."

"I've got loads of those."

"Bring them! We don't have many carrots up here in the boon-docks. When do you think you might come?"

I let out a small groan.

"Come now," she says softly. "Get in the car and drive. If you bust a gut, you'll be here in time for midmorning coffee. I've got those yum-yums I know you're partial to."

"M&S?"

"Sainsbury's. Not quite as delish, but almost."

"So more of a yum?"

"Hop in your car and get here for midmorning coffee and a yum."

I groan again. "I can't. I'm stuck. I have to wait . . . Next week-end—I should be able to come up then. I miss my little girl."

"On Wednesday, I've got to come to London to see my ob-gyn

guy. I could pop in and see you. I can't let you have Millie back because it's Roxanne's birthday on Friday and I've promised Millie she can come to the party, but I could bring her up for the day. If you're missing her enough by then."

"Oh, yes, do that. Do that."

"If I can coax her away from Roxanne and the baby . . ." Her voice fades. "Do you want to say good-bye to Mum?" Then, gently breaking the callousness of my little angel, "She'll ring again later."

I put my hand to my heart. A tiny dagger of disappointment.

"Okay," I say cheerfully. I forgive my daughter everything. "I love you both."

I forgot. I thought, now the hacks had gone, I was safe. I leave the house, my head still in Robin's kitchen, through the front door as if life were normal. When the door closes. it's already too late. A silver Mondeo is parked outside the gate, and Perivale is inside. A prickle of fear slowly climbs my spine, pelvis to skull, vertebrae by vertebrae. My neighbor was parked in that space last night. Perivale must have waited for them to leave, or *circled*.

He's wearing his dirty green waxed jacket, and his face, in seated repose, looks more jowly than I remember. On the passenger seat is a heap of newspapers, and in his hand a takeaway polystyrene cup. I smile, my heart hammering. He nods tersely and looks hurriedly across at the newspapers, splashing a tiny bit of coffee with the movement, as if embarrassed at being seen.

I run to my own car, which is parked round the corner. I sit for a moment until my pulse settles. I think he might tap on the window, but he doesn't. Why hasn't he approached me? What is he waiting for? I contemplate going back and tapping on *his* window. I'd rather know what he wants, get it over with. I imagine myself screaming, "There's a murderer out there. Don't waste time watching me, or *circling!*" And then I think, Why, as an innocent person, should I care? Just the thought exorcises something inside, makes me feel better.

The sky has cleared and it's a bright blue day. Sun, but air as cold as the sea after a downpour. Children on miniature scooters trickle past, expensively shaggy small dogs taut on leads, ambling parents shouting, "Stop!" Any minute one of them is going to see me, sitting here like a dressmaker's dummy, so I put the key in the ignition and pull out.

I don't notice at first. I am driving down Trinity Road, hugging the central reservation, when the filter light looms. I will be forced to turn right if I stay where I am. I put on my turn signal. The car behind, a small red Renault driven by a short-haired man, puts on his turn signal, too. A horn blares. We both swerve. The Renault pulls back a bit and puts some distance between us.

It is still there, two cars away, when I swing left onto East Hill, and still there, hugging my tail, after an erratic speed-weave into the bus lane. My hands grip the steering wheel; I change gears with coiled fury and fear. I pull back into the main stream of traffic and immediately right into the Tonsleys, a grid of residential streets choked with one-ways and no entries and commuter-blocking barriers. I turn this way and that, nip and tuck, and scissor back. I can feel a wildness in me, a sort of rage. The gears growl. The steering wheel jerks beneath my hands with a life of its own. Who is it? Perivale? Could he have changed cars? A tabloid reporter, hulking out there, out of sight?

I wrench into a parking space and wait, engine throbbing. Around me, the street is still. An airplane spirals. The squeal of a distant bus braking. I scan the street once more, pull back out, manage a wobbly three-point turn, and drive slowly back through the Tonsleys the way I came, eyes scouring. Nothing. I turn right onto East Hill and continue on my way. I begin to feel oddly bullish. Action is good. I can beat my opponents. If I can throw off a tail, surely I can withstand Perivale, fight for my reputation, wrest back my life.

At East Putney Tube Station, I pull in on a double-red line. No sign of Jack. I'm late, but then so is he. It hasn't rained all morning, but the gutters are still flowing and the striped awning above the flower stall sags. Gloves warm the hands of the young florist; she is bashing them together in a sort of clumphing clap.

Behind her is a newsagent, and I leave the car quickly and run in to get a bottle of water. I grab a few random things at the till, including a packet of Polos. My throat is dry with thirst: must be nerves.

I'm back in the car, purchases stowed, before Jack arrives. I see him before he sees me. His head's down, and he is walking with a lopsided gait, an Adidas messenger bag hanging over one shoulder. He scrunches up some sort of wrapper—a sausage roll?—and throws it into the closest bin. Then he looks up, clocks me, and heads over, almost at a run. He leaps a puddle, rather unsuccessfully; mud splatters up the back of his jeans. He's wearing a warmer jacket today, which he brushes for crumbs, and a trendy reworking of a deerstalker hat. In the car, he yanks it off, and his hair bounces out as if it's been restrained.

He rearranges his feet to avoid the empty cans and sweet wrappers, the pay-and-display tickets stuck to chewing gum. It's a cleaner-free zone, my car, a glimpse into my grubby little soul—the bit Philip could never begin to understand. Jack doesn't say anything. Maybe he's at home in such a mess. Instead, he apologizes for being late. It was more of a journey than he'd anticipated: long wait for a Wimbledon-bound tube at Victoria, and the District line, so slow, chugging along like a rural train.

If he had been standing there waiting for me as I drove up, I would have told him about the red Renault, shrieked a little, but now I feel the tension of it slipping out of reach. Am I being paranoid? Have I made the whole thing up? The sense I have of being followed, watched, may be getting worse . . . am *I* the problem? Is it in my mind? The bullishness I felt earlier has gone. If I don't know what's real and what isn't, how can I be sure, *make* sure, of anything?

I've reached the lights. "Where to?" I say. I look straight ahead. I feel jaw-achingly self-conscious. I realize that I am without parameters. I have no idea what he thinks of me at all. I have lost my bearings. I don't know what to do with my face.

"Ah, yes." He pulls out his phone and fiddles until he finds what he needs.

The Baxters live in a pretty tree-lined street of semidetached Victorian villas in West Putney. We are not followed. I keep checking. Their house, painted one of those tasteful National Trust colors—Clutch, or Bone, or Dead Skin—is set back from the road behind a gate and a small drive. An ornamental cherry, its boughs laden with clusters of candy pink blossom, squats in a raised flower bed by the front door.

"People's taste in plants is often so much more vulgar than their taste in anything else," I say. My voice sounds strange. I'm quoting Roger Peedles: off camera, he's a big one for the arch, withering generalization.

Jack looks at me and shakes his head. "I can't believe you said that. I'm sitting in a beaten-up Nissan with a plant snob."

"'Beaten-up Nissan?'" I say, raising an eyebrow. "Could I possibly be sitting in a 'beaten-up Nissan' with a car snob?"

He grins and I realize we're both more comfortable when we've had a go.

We've agreed I should wait in the car. Jack leaps out and negotiates the gate. Children's shouts reach me through the open window. The back garden: that climbing frame from the photograph at the police station. A toddler's red plastic car. Millie was desperate to have one of those. Why didn't we let her? Philip probably thought they were ugly. The front door opens. A slim woman greets him. They're expecting him: he rang ahead. He's writing an in-depth profile of Ania Dudek, cutting through the tabloid mulch, getting to the real woman. Mrs. Baxter was open to persuasion. She loved Ania. They all did. The children miss her madly.

I close the window and lean back in the seat. I am in a backwater. No one followed me; I tell myself that again. I should have told Jack. Now it's too late. *No one followed me.* The pavements are deserted. The residents of West Putney are in their houses, cooking lunch, doing homework, gardening in the new spring air. I am safe for a moment. The car warms. I yawn.

When Jack gets back in, his breath smells of coffee. Wet cherry blossom adheres to the soles of his shoes.

"Did you learn anything interesting?"

"Let's get out of here."

"Okay." I put my foot on the accelerator and screech off. I'm pretending to be the getaway vehicle, but I'm not brave enough. The spirit that moved my limbs earlier has drifted, dissolved. The speedometer says fifteen miles per hour.

He gets it, though, or at least offers this tame reprise. "Quick. They're after us," he says, teeth gritted.

"Where am I going?"

"The pub. Don't you think?" He is holding a spiral-bound notebook. He flicks it like a Spanish fan. "I can debrief."

I turn left and right and wiggle through the backstreets of Putney until we reach the river. "The pub": it's funny how people use the definite article, as if carrying a Platonic ideal in their imagination that any old establishment can slot into. The Duke's Head, large and airy, nice enough. Philip and I came here once, years ago, to watch the boat race. I park on the slope of the embankment closest to the bridge. A red bus crosses. Its reflection ripples in the water below, clouds scudding, like an advert for London.

The tide is in, lapping the balustrade, and there's an amount of frenetic activity by the boathouses—hulls being hoisted, legs getting wet, muscles flexing, ducks waddling. The pub is still quiet—not yet noon—though a group of broad-shouldered rowers guffaws at the bar, pints of beer held in that way some men have, all gripped fists and elbows at right angles. They recognize me as we enter. Pulled-back hair, no makeup—as a disguise, it used to work. Not now. Not now I've been photographed teeth bared. I smile into their stares. Nothing back. One of them, in shorts and a T-shirt that reads FIT, nudges his companion.

"What you having?" Jack asks. I want a Diet Coke, but it seems so small and mealymouthed, everything this man seems not to be, so I turn my back on the rowers, in all their poker-faced meanness, say, "Oh, go on, half a lager shandy," and find a seat in the window.

He crosses the room with a sort of lopsided skip, and then shouts over his shoulder: "What kind?"

There's a moment of panic when I can't remember what shandy *is*. "Lager," I call pathetically.

"Lemonade or lime?"

"Oh, yes. Lemonade, please."

Jack keeps looking over at me, rolling his eyes impatiently at the slowness of the barmaid. He spills a drop of my drink, smashing it down too fast on the table, and mops at it with the sleeve of his jacket. The rowers have lost interest now, resumed their banter.

"Right." Jack, oblivious, takes a swig from his pint of Guinness. Froth arches on his upper lip. He takes his notebook out of his pocket. Are there clues in there, or is it all just words and make-believe? He launches straight in. "So, Ania had worked for them for seven months. She had answered an ad they placed on Gumtree for a weekend nanny. Mr. Baxter, who is in advertising, has been spending a lot of time in Düsseldorf, working on the BMW account."

I raise an eyebrow to acknowledge what that account might mean to a car snob. "Yeah, yeah. And Mrs. Baxter had had ill health, bit of postnatal depression, and been told by the doctor to take it easy. At first, Ania just worked daytime, but she was so brilliant with the kids—the boy, Alfie, is a bit of a biter apparently—she became their main babysitter, too."

"A bit of a biter?" I say.

"Yes. Issues with discipline. Anger management. Ania had a way about her, they said. She coaxed Alfie to do things that other people couldn't, like eat his dinner. She was selfless and warm, the sort of person who really engages with the world. She bought the kids presents at Christmas, made biscuits with them. She took them to Chessington on the train a few weeks ago. On another occasion"— he checks his notes—"they collected frogs' eggs in Richmond Park."

"Issues with discipline?" I can't help laughing. The man who thinks he's FIT looks across at the sound. "Anger management? He only looks about five."

"Enough about Alfie!" He eyes me over his Guinness. "Alfie is not the focus of our enquiries. They had no idea of anyone who would do her harm. To know her was to love her."

A sharp twist inside. I think about the photograph Perivale showed me, the children on the climbing frame, Ania smiling. Her whole life was ahead of her. What kind of a mother would she have been? A wonderful one: young, full of energy and enthusiasm. *To know her was to love her.* I start thinking about Millie. I force myself to focus. "Did they know anything about the boyfriend?"

"I was getting to that." He taps the table a couple of times, with both index fingers, drumming in miniature. "Yes. Tolek, a man from home, her childhood sweetheart. I think he followed her to the UK. A builder. They were engaged, though she didn't yet have a ring, and it seemed to be one of those engagements that drags on and on, without any sense of it going anywhere in particular. One of those Catholic engagements, perhaps, that's just an excuse to have sex."

"Had they met him?"

"He picked Ania up from work a few times in his van, though Mrs. Baxter said she hadn't seen him recently. He was on a big job, working funny hours. Nice enough."

"'Nice enough.' Is that all? Poor Ania. It's not much, is it?"

"We should talk to him. Even if he didn't do it, he might know something."

One of the men at the bar emits a gutturally pitched bellow. Another doubles up. The FIT rower bangs the bar with the palm of his hand.

Jack raises his eyebrows. I try to look just at him, to imagine we're alone. "What else?" I say.

"She hadn't told them she was pregnant. The police were the bearers of those glad tidings. She had started behaving differently, though. When she first came to them, she seemed short of cash. She bought her clothes at charity shops. Mrs. Baxter complimented her on a coat she was wearing, and Ania told her she got it in Fara, that charity shop on the Northcote Road: 'Rich pickings, apparently,' Mrs. Baxter reported. 'Kept thinking I should pop over there myself.'"

"Even without meeting Mrs. Baxter, I can imagine her saying that. But *my* clothes, do you think? Do you think my clothes found their way to Fara and Ania bought them?"

He shrugs. "It's a possibility, isn't it? Just an extraordinary coincidence. But either Ania or her boyfriend seemed to have come into a chunk of money. An enormous bunch of flowers arrived for her at the house a month before she died."

"I suppose if he had been working on a big job . . ."

More rowers have joined at the bar. Whispering takes place. The newcomers turn to me and stare.

"True," Jack says, oblivious. "It would explain why Ania was more flush." He checks his notes. "She started taking taxis home, and she was dressing in a more stylish, upmarket manner—designer, Mrs. Baxter decided, and definitely not secondhand. And once—she was a bit sheepish about noticing this—when Ania came to stay the night, she brought her sleeping things in an Agent Provocateur carrier bag. Mrs. Baxter was impressed. Agent Provocateur—posh undies, aren't they?"

"Very posh undies. Expensive. Sexy." There is something about the way I say *sexy* that makes me want to hide under the table.

"They didn't have a number for the boyfriend, but they did tell me Ania had a friend, a woman called Christa. She babysat for them once when Ania was busy. And"—he stabs a page of his notebook with his finger—"here is her number!"

He looks at me expectantly.

"Good work," I say. And I mean it. He has surprised me. He is taking this more seriously than I expected. I'm grateful. I wouldn't have known where to start with the Baxters. And this is something, this is a beginning. If the few facts he has collected make us both feel closer to Ania then, surely, that must be good.

"Are the Baxters kind?" I say. "I know it's not strictly relevant, but I would like to think that they were kind to her."

"Yes. Do you know, I think they were."

"Are you sure you're not just one of those people who sees the best in others?"

He looks thrown, opens his mouth and closes it. "I think they cared about her. I would say they were good employers, yes."

"Had they been to her flat?"

"No. Never."

"It's weird how lopsided this sort of relationship is, isn't it? I mean, she will have known so much about them, been part of their lives, been bitten by little Alfie, for God's sake, and yet they will have stopped thinking about her the moment she walked out of the door. The Baxters thought they knew Ania, and yet did they have a clue about what she was really like, or what was really going on in her life? And were they natural with her, or did they put on the act of employer? We all present such different faces to each other. Marta, for example—maybe she finds me as evasive and weird as I find her. We are all lots of different people, and sometimes we pretend to be something we're not."

Jack looks alarmed.

"Sorry. Bit heavy. I keep thinking, you know, she's dead, that's all. She was murdered."

He stares at the phone number scrawled across the page of his notepad, under- and over-scored with double lines.

"Let's ring Christa," I say. "She might know something. At the very least, she might have a contact for Tolek."

He nods. The pub is filling, the noise level rising. The Lombard reflex: an instinct people have to talk louder and louder over themselves to be heard. (We had a sociologist on the show the other day to talk about a southeast England survey on noise pollution.) Jack has gulped down his Guinness and I can't pretend to sip my shandy any longer. A bare-legged couple, fresh from the river, have been eyeing our table. I give them a signal and wait for them to barrel over. They look away when they reach me, don't even say thanks.

It's not as cold, or as blue, outside as it was. The wind has dropped. A haze of disconsolate cloud covers the sky. There is a bench, and we walk over to it and sit down at opposite ends from each other. Why did I have that outburst? It has left an awkwardness. While Jack punches in the number on his phone, I stare at the roiling expanse of brown river. The people in the pub, they have got to me. After a few moments, Jack says, "Shall I leave a message?"

I shake my head. I feel a wave of despair.

He puts the phone in his back pocket. "You all right?" he says. "Those men in there—no style."

So he *had* noticed. Perhaps he picks up on more than he pretends to.

"I'm fine," I say. "You know—if you put yourself out there . . ."

"Sundays are always the worst," he says. "Full of lies."

More pictures of bruised shins today, then. "I haven't looked at them," I say. "I've been stuffing the papers under the sofa."

He grins. "Good ploy."

We sit for a bit longer. Jack says something about lunch.

"Didn't you have a sausage roll only a couple of hours ago?"

"No . . . How . . . ? It wasn't a sausage roll. It was a homity pie."

"A homity pie! What's that when it's at home?"

"I was hungry," he says, aggrieved. "It's giving up the cigarettes. Plus I didn't have time for breakfast, and there's this great organic bakery near Brixton tube."

"I'm amazed you're not fat."

"I work out most mornings. Feel."

He thrusts a bicep toward me. I squeeze it, a clutch of muscle, and then immediately look away, flustered.

"Quick stroll?" he asks.

"A stroll rather than a walk?"

"Let's start with a stroll and see how we get on."

The tide has gone down since we arrived—an arc of beach at the bottom of the slipway. Debris—tires, splintered wood, old plastic bags, the occasional dead rat—dots the water's edge. A woman with bare tanned arms sculls past.

"Tolek," Jack says. "We need to find Tolek."

"If only Tolek hadn't been in Poland. If he had been in the

country maybe Perivale would never have fixated on me. He could have fixated on *him*."

"Can't really beat Poland as an alibi, pretty cast-iron."

"What is a 'cast-iron' alibi? It's such a cliché, stops people from looking any further. I mean, he could have slipped back into the UK in the trunk of someone's car, and then been smuggled out again. Couldn't he? And *not* having an alibi—like me, both for the night Ania was killed, and for the credit card receipt: it doesn't mean I'm guilty. It just means I don't have enough friends." I laugh to show I'm not being completely serious.

"Any sign of Perivale recently?" Jack asks.

"He was outside the house again today. I wish he would be more obvious, get it over with. It's like waiting to be called into the headmaster's study." I turn to face him. "Am I being paranoid to think he's out to get me?"

"No." He stuffs his hands in the pockets of his jeans with a sort of confirmatory vigor. "I don't think you are. He's got some weird twisted agenda."

"I feel so jumpy all the time. I felt like I was being followed this morning."

"I'm sure it's just your imagination. You're bound to feel twitchy."

"Like an itch in a missing limb. Or that kids' book *The Hairy Toe*? You know the one," I say, putting on a scary voice: "'Who's got my hairy toe?'"

"No, don't know it."

You can't talk about kids' books to a man who doesn't have kids. "Not a very good book," I say.

We pause to wait for a rowing crew to pass in front of us. We watch them shoulder their boat, like a trophy, a ceremonial dead shark, into the bowels of the boathouse, and then we walk for a few minutes in silence. We pass a playground: the cries and shouts of children, the distant whack of balls.

I wonder what Millie is doing. I hope she isn't homesick. I feel a sharp pang of longing.

"What about Marta," Jack says. "Does she have an alibi for the time of the credit card receipt?"

"I don't know. I can't remember."

"And Ania's increased wealth. I'd like to know more about that."

When we have reached the place where the road ends and the towpath begins, I lean on the balustrade, rest my chin on it, look down into the eddying waters of the Thames. I'm wondering if this is all a bit pointless. Can Christa really tell us anything useful, even if we do get through to her? It smells here of deep, dark mud. I imagine we will stay here for a moment or two, reflect on all this deep, dark muddiness, and then go back to the car.

"Shall we keep going?" he says.

"I don't know." I straighten up. "Is this a stroll, or is this a walk?"

"Could we continue a bit farther without committing either way?"

"We could."

Ahead of us is a deserted stretch of towpath, scraggy trees and a shrubby fence on one side of us, a brick wall sloping steeply down to the river on the other. The ground is bumpy, half gravel, half soil, with pitty holes where rain has collected. There is the dank, brackish smell of wet clothes and rotting vegetation.

"Did you like your job?" Jack asks suddenly.

"I did. *Do*."

A silence. *Have* I still got a job? Anxiety rises and spills, a dull, murky unease. Terri hasn't rung. Should I ring her? I wasn't needed while the investigation was "ongoing," she said, but she might have had second thoughts. Perhaps she is missing me. Have the ratings dropped? Should I ring her later just to check? Dare I hope?

Jack is looking at me oddly.

"Good bits and bad bits," I say.

"Like?"

I think carefully. This is the sort of information that will go in the profile. I should be cautious. "Bad bits: early starts, being recognized on the street, people thinking they know me—I'm not very good at that, though obviously it's deeply flattering. Good bits: I like meeting people. Sometimes it's just celebrities, but often it's ordinary people with extraordinary stories. Or experts in a particular field. You pick up all sorts of random information that can come in handy."

"Such as?" He raises an enquiring eyebrow.

"The other day when I was at Battersea Police Station, Perivale's boss was there, DCI Fraser, and he was Scottish. We'd had a voice coach from the National Theatre on recently, talking about accents, how the landscape of the area has an effect on how people talk—the tonality of East Anglia is as flat as the Fens, while an accent from Wales lilts up over the hills and down into the valleys. Every accent has a point of tension."

I point to just below my nose. Jack's eyes follow my finger. "Just here," I say, "is the point of tension in an Aberdeen accent. It's because it's bitterly cold up there and everybody wanders around with their mouths shielded against the wind. Anyway, I took a bit of a guess and asked if he was from Aberdeen. I think it played into my hands. I don't think he minded."

"Clever," he says. "What is there to say about mine?"

"Somewhere with hills but a lot of open space. I think the voice coach said the Yorkshire accent was in a major key—ends on a definite note, makes you sound sure of yourself. And of course reliability, trustworthiness—both qualities one associates with the Yorkshire accent. Perfect for a journalist."

"And what about your accent, Ms. Mortimer? Your Somerset burr? Where's your point of tension."

"My Somerset burr?" So he knows I'm from Somerset; he's

done some research. "I've learned to cover that," I say. "I've *long* kicked over the traces."

For a moment, I worry I have revealed too much. The way I drew out *long*. Intimations of guilt and anger. Points of tension. I don't want that going in the profile. A time might come, but I don't want to sound resentful, or angry. I look away.

A man on a bike comes into sight, swerves to avoid a puddle, cycles past.

"Anyway," I say.

Ahead of us, along the bending path, is a solitary boathouse. We are tramping toward it when Jack says, "So, Philip coming back from Singapore anytime soon?"

Another faint alarm bell. My husband's name is public information, but the fact that he's in Singapore? Not many people know that. And then I think, all those hacks, the Mickeys and the Petes, they could have found out, they could have told him.

"I've insisted he stay out there longer," I say lightly. "Philip's work . . . it's on a knife edge." Why "knife edge?" It sounds so dramatic, which it isn't.

"Is he always 'Philip'?"

"He hates the name Phil. I tried at the beginning, but I was banned."

"Ah!"

"And the first Mrs. Hayward?" I say. If he has mentioned my spouse, I can bring up his. "Where does she fit in?"

"Mrs. Hayward," he says. "Mrs. Hayward. She was younger than me. There were cultural differences. She pretended to be something she wasn't—" After a second or two, I realize he isn't in the middle of a sentence, but at the end of it. "Women," he says. I look to check he's joking ("women?" *really*?), but he isn't.

We are at the boathouse. I had thought perhaps there might be activities in play, people to watch, but it's just a flat, shuttered-up building, closed and deserted. The sun has gone down and the path ahead is empty and bleak. There's no one in sight at all.

"Everyone's back at the pub," I say. Somehow I've got new doubts about him now. "Perhaps we should turn round."

I look at Jack. A muscle is going in his jaw. His eyes, under their heavy brows, have darkened, as if their light has also gone behind a cloud.

"I'm not sure," I say again, "whether we shouldn't be turning back."

A breeze rises, ruffling the surface of the Thames like the skin on boiled milk.

He still doesn't say anything. I feel a quiver down my neck. What was it Perivale said? Assume nothing. Believe no one. Check everything. I never got round to confirming Jack was who he said he was. He could be anyone. He's just been here, lurking, following, outside my house, knowing things about me other people don't. All that bluff, all that chat, all that homity pie, it could be an act. He is bending down now. I don't know what he is doing. I think about the flex of the muscles on his arm. I have an instinct to walk quickly away, to run even, back to where there are boats and people and ducks.

His back is to me now. He is searching the ground, kicking it over with his foot, and whatever he is looking for he seems to find because he bends to pick it up. He has got a stone in his hand.

I stand very still. He walks toward me and then veers off down the slipway, bends sideways, and skims the stone across the water. It bounces twice and then sinks. "Lost my knack," he says, coming back. He's smiling again; his eyes, under those strong eyebrows, are all crinkles again. His whole face changes when he smiles. He looks positively boyish.

I was wrong to doubt him. I am all over the place.

"I thought you might hit me with that stone!" I say, trying to sound light.

"What? Why on earth?"

"You looked so cross."

"Sorry. It's the thought of my ex-wife."

"I shouldn't have asked."

"We'll turn round now, shall we? Get back to our bench and try Christa again?"

"That sounds like a plan."

I look to see what his face is doing, and for a split second our eyes lock. I'm not sure if we are still walking or whether we have stopped. I hold my breath. I don't know whether I am scared of him or whether I am scared of myself. Suddenly, two things happen: a moorhen darts from the bushes like an arrow released from a bow, and Jack's phone goes. His ringtone is the slow, insistent peal of an old-fashioned office phone in 1950s New York.

He taps around his body, fumbles to find it. It's not in his top pocket. It's in the back of his jeans. He nearly drops it, taking it out, does one of those comedy oh-oh-oh butterfinger almost-tumbles, and answers breathless. "Jack Hayward," he says. Then, "Yes. Thank you. I did." He widens his eyes at me, mouths, "Christa."

"Yes. I am sorry I did not leave a message. It is complicated."

I smile. He's doing that loud talking-like-a-foreigner thing English people sometimes do when they are talking to a foreigner.

"I am a friend of Ania's employers in Putney. I am organizing a book of remembrance for the children to remember her by. They loved her very much."

He listens for a moment.

"Yes. I know. So please, if it is okay, can I come and visit you to talk about Ania? Is that convenient? Yes?"

When he has slipped the phone back in his pocket, I say, "So we walk back to the car now?"

"Good idea."

"And Christa. She see us tomorrow, yes? The convenience of that is suited to her?"

"Oh, fuck off," he says affectionately.

Searching in my bag for my house key—never in the inner pocket, never where it should be—I am braced for the gate, for footsteps on the path. I'm on edge. The world, on the way home from Putney, seemed full of red cars. I place my bag on the ground and crouch down for a proper rummage. At last. Here they are. I need a bigger fob. I stand, scrabble for the lock, collect my bag, and I'm inside, leaning against the front door, feeling as if I've dodged a bullet.

A package, the size of a paperback book, is lying on the mat. It is the same kind of brown padded envelope that Marta has in her cupboard. I sit on the stairs and open it. Inside the packaging is a DVD. *I've Been Watching You 2: Prom Night*. No note.

The doorbell peals a second later. The noise goes right through me. My bones vibrate.

I look through the peephole.

Perivale is standing there, my keys dangling from his fingers, like dog poo in a bag. I open up. "You left these in the lock," he says.

A pause before I take them. "Thank you. I must have . . . I would have realized in a second."

He has terrible posture, so tall he's hunched. He is not a man comfortable in his own skin. His eyes move toward me, but when he speaks, his jaw seems half locked. "You might not have noticed until you looked for them tomorrow. Anyone could have taken them. You were in too much of a hurry. I've told you to be careful."

Did I just walk past his car without noticing? Has he been here all day?

"I was searching in my bag. I couldn't find them." I breathe in deeply, scanning the street for a silver Mondeo, a red Renault. "I never can. Is that a female thing? Men tend to have them wearing holes in their back pockets."

He taps his thigh. "Front pocket."

"I'll be more careful." My voice catches.

"You all right?" Perivale asks. He actually sounds genuinely concerned.

"Look." I pick the DVD off the floor where I hurled it. "This was waiting for me just now, inside this envelope."

He takes them from me. "I'll make sure the officer in charge of the case gets them fingerprinted," he says.

"Marta, my daughter's nanny . . . I know you've talked to her, but . . . she's got the same sort of envelope in her cupboard. Quite a few of them."

"I'll bear that in mind," he says, with a patronizing dip of his head. "I'll fingerprint Rose, the PA down at the station while I'm about it. She's partial to a padded envelope."

I decide to ignore this jab. "And someone followed me this morning, in a red Renault. Was it one of yours?"

He shakes his head. "No."

"Well, now you know," I say. "Anyway, I'll leave that with you, and if that's all . . ." I hold the door, as if I'm about to close it on him. "I've learned my lesson from last week. I'm not going to speak to you without my lawyer present. So—"

He puts his hand out. "Just one thing. Quickly."

"No, seriously."

I mustn't do this. I mustn't let him draw me in.

"Off the record, nothing formal, as you're . . . we find ourselves here. And it's not about you, but your mother . . ."

"My mother?" The hall walls close in very slightly.

"Did a background CRB check. Mortimer, G.: Avon and Somerset Constabulary, Yeovil Brympton beat. Nothing."

"That's because I've never been in trouble with the law. There is nothing to find, in any police constabulary, anywhere. You know that."

"Mortimer, J., on the other hand. Quite a record."

"Hardly," I say. My voice sounds as if it is being squeezed out of a tight place.

"Public-offense cautions, drunk and disorderly—October two years ago and again February last year—a conviction for drunk driving." His eyes watch me, not with mistrust, but sympathy.

"Yes," I manage to say. "You've done your homework."

"Tough growing up with a mother like that."

"What doesn't kill you makes you stronger."

"Nietzsche."

"Is it?" I say, conversationally. "I thought it was Kelly Clarkson."

He laughs, a quick burst of warmth. "Take care, now," he says.

The evening is empty and long. My limbs are heavy, dull with inactivity. My head aches. I'm scared: Perivale did that. But also, low in my stomach is a damp, curdling dread, of things that should have been done and haven't. I retreat to my bedroom. The rest of the house is too empty of Philip and Millie, too consumed with ghosts and shadows, the walls echoing with normal life.

I can't sleep. The bed is uncomfortable and too full of *me*—my heat, my smell, my toast crumbs from earlier. I turn the pillow over, seeking freshness. I've closed the door to the landing, but I'm not secure. I plan my escape—open the window, throw out a bunch of pillows, and jump. Or the bathroom? The rear extension. Less far to fall.

Time passes. I think about Millie, asleep in Robin's farmhouse. I hope she is asleep. I hope she isn't scared. Or having a nightmare. Will she get into bed with Robin if she does? Will Robin mind? I wish she were with me, now, her limbs curled around mine. I close my eyes, imagine her face; my fists clench. She *could* be here—the reporters have gone; I'm not working—but . . . then . . . she's safer where she is, isn't she? It's dangerous here. I'm right about that.

At midnight, I switch the light back on and I try to read. I didn't ring Terri earlier, I felt too insecure and unnerved. I should have done. If I could concentrate on work, this would be easier. I'd have a rhythm to my days, perspective, other people—Stan!—to spar with. I'd feel less trapped. How many more days until they will let me back? Two? Three? Shall I go in, see her face-to-face, and beg? What if she turns me down? That would be worse. Better to hope. Better not to know . . .

There are noises in the street. Shouts and cries. The sound of pounding steps. Shrieks. Teenagers.

If I lie here any longer, I'll go mad. Madder than I already am. I had a missed call from Clara, but she didn't answer when I rang back. It's too late to speak to Millie. Philip? No.

Jack.

His number is on the flyleaf of my book. I wrote it down when he rang all those days ago.

"I'm sorry. Had you gone to bed?"

His voice is low. "No." He yawns. "I was working."

"What on? Me?"

He laughs, a sleepy laugh. "A book review for the *Mail on Sunday*." He mentions a middle-aged thriller writer, but I'm not really listening.

"I'm sorry to ring," I say. "Feeling a bit . . . I don't know . . . on edge. I've had an anonymous package from my stalker." I try to sound casual, but my heart is thumping. "A horror DVD. *I've Been Watching You 2: Prom Night*."

"*I've Been Watching You 2*?"

"Yes."

"*Prom Night*?"

"It's horrid."

"That's actually quite funny. The idea of trying to scare someone with a sequel. The first *I've Been Watching You* must have been out of stock. Imagine how annoyed they felt, trawling the aisles, trying to find a DVD that worked. Wonder what they rejected? *The Killing*? Too classy. *Night of the Living Dead?* Hmm . . . too schlocky."

I half laugh, half sob. "They've never done anything so threatening before, though."

"It's just a silly prank. Put it out of your mind."

"The envelope was the same kind we found in Marta's cupboard."

"Could be a coincidence, but tell the police."

"I have. Perivale was here. I gave it to him."

"Well done. Marta in the house?"

"No."

"Probably at the post office."

"Exactly!"

"We'll talk tomorrow. You should get some sleep."

"I know. Night then."

"Night. I'll see you in the morning."

"A book review," I say quickly. "So you *are* a journalist? You're not lying to me?"

He is quiet. I think he might have gone. "It's not exactly something to be proud of," he says. "As if I'd lie about that."

MONDAY

Christa lives in Roehampton, in a tall, square tower block on stilts. It's one of five or six slabs, at a slant to the landscape, which march across it, heading for Richmond Park. You can see them on the horizon from the Isabella Plantation—Philip's mother likes to be taken every year to see the azaleas—but I've never been this close.

No one has followed me, I think. I *hope*. I took a convoluted route, double-backing on myself in Earlsfield. I checked the mirror every few seconds, like you do on your driver's test. I didn't feel calm, or in control. If I'd seen a red Renault, I think I'd have stopped the car and screamed.

I find a parking space right outside and wait. The flats are rather wonderful actually—1950s, Bauhaus or Le Corbusier, *unité d'habitation* or something. Should look it up. You can see how much thought was put into the landscaping. An expanse of cropped grass and tall pine trees. A sense of space, of nature—jackdaws chattering, pigeons pecking—not too far away.

I've been awake since 4:00 AM. Two hours before Philip called—he knows I wake up early. He'd just had lunch, a few sakes, too, just enough to take the edge off. "All well?" he said, "Coping?"

I fell backward on the bed. "Yes," I said.

"Well, I won't keep you," he said. "Anything fun lined up today?"

"No," I said. "What about you?"

"Busy afternoon ahead," he said. "Tonight—Chinese-style banquet at the Mandarin."

I clutched my scalp, screamed silently. "That's good."

"I'll ring you later."

Jack texts to find out where I'm parked, and a few minutes later, on the bend in the road up to the apartment complex, I see him emerge from behind a delivery van.

I wind down my window. He leans in, faintly flushed, as if he has been hurrying. He is freshly shaved—I catch the soapy tang of foam—and wearing a newly ironed white shirt. I can tell immediately, by the way his fingers drum against his thigh, jingling coins, that he has put last night's call out of his mind. His mood has shifted. He is distracted. No joke, no greeting, no concern, no pastry crumbs.

"Sorry I'm late," he says. "An editor rang. I've got an assignment today. Let's do this and then I'd better get off."

"Oh, okay," I say, swallowing disappointment. What was I expecting? Kindness? A husband's concern? At the very least, a bit more English foreign-speak. I am wrong-footed, like the one person at a black-tie do in casual dress. "No biggie," I say, trying to sound offhand.

"You all right?" he says. "Did you sleep in the end?"

"Like a log."

I am to wait in the car while he sees Christa, ready for a debrief when he comes out. I watch him galumph across the sloping sheet of grass. The pigeons by the bins scatter. I see him tilt into the shadows, his face turning as he talks. He consults his watch, a swift, irritated flick of the wrist.

I wait. On the fourth floor of Christa's building, a man with a shaved head is leaning on the balustrades staring down. The delivery van slams shut and rattles by. A burst of music: "Don't you want me, baby?" The van passes. The man with the shaved head goes into his flat.

Jack treads back up the grass toward the road. Christa is with him. He is being careful not to look in my direction.

Even from inside the car, I can tell she is a striking woman, pointy-featured with a chestnut bob and bangs. It's a chilly day, but she is wearing a summer dress with wedge sandals. The final wind of rope on the wedge has come unraveled. It snaps at her ankle as she walks.

I don't think about it and the moment I am out of the car it is too late. I intercept them on the path. Jack looks alarmed. He begins to introduce us, flustered, but she interrupts.

"Gaby Mortimer," she says. "You are Gaby Mortimer from *Mornin' All*."

"Yes."

"You found Ania. You found my friend."

I nod. *My friend.* The two women were friends. I curl my toes tightly to stop myself from swaying. I think about them on the phone, chatting, out together, arm in arm, laughing.

"And you know each other?" She looks from Jack to me. He opens his mouth and closes it; he is still trying to pull himself together.

"Yes, we do," I say, moving my feet farther apart. "And I wanted to meet you. I'm sorry. We should have said at first. I should have been more open."

"Gaby's helping with my book of rememb—"

She cuts across him. "But the police, they took you in?" she says. "They question you about my friend?"

"It was a mistake," I say. "I tried to help. Poor Ania. I just got caught up . . ." But there is a look in her eyes, so helpless, so sad, I stop explaining and put my arms around her. I feel the narrowness of her bones, the point of her chin, her breath on my neck. "I'm so sorry," I say. "I am so, so sorry about Ania. It must be very difficult for you, to lose a friend. I can't imagine." I pull away. I catch Jack's expression. He is startled. He hadn't thought of this.

She bites her top lip and nods. Her eyes are green, diamond-flecked with hazel. Her complexion is pale. When she lets go of her lip, color floods into her cheeks. She looks back at me. "You are so kind. Thank you." She rests her hand on my arm, and I am aware of something dull and heavy diminishing. She believes me.

Jack interrupts now and explains that Christa's husband, Pawel, is sleeping—he works nights as a security guard—and the plan was to walk to a café. He widens his eyes to remind me he is in a hurry to get to his other assignment.

"Well, it's always lovely to go to a café. Not that I'm hungry. What about you, Jack?" I'm coaxing, as if to a child. "I've only just had breakfast."

We are walking back down the hill toward the main road, through velvety shadows and squares of light. Lopsided buses congregate at the bottom, reverberating throatily. It's a narrow sidewalk, and Jack walks a few feet behind. I ask Christa if she has spoken to the police, and she says yes, once, but had nothing to tell them. She was in Poland on her honeymoon when Ania . . . died.

A car pulls up. Miniature Union Jacks fly from the rear windows. Rihanna blares and abruptly dies. A young man with tattooed forearms emerges, clutching a helium balloon in the shape of a three. Christa nods at him.

"I had been home to Kraków, to get married," she says after he has gone. "A big wedding with all my family. Ania came. It was the week before . . . the last time I saw her."

"Did you have a nice wedding?" I ask gently.

"Yes. Big. My mother was very busy. She was very bossy." She gives a rueful smile, and I ask if she wore a lovely dress and she spends the rest of the walk describing it—the layers of tulle skirt and the lace bodice and the decorative beading. I mention a frock I saw in a magazine, which had a flower at one hip, fashioned out of the fabric of the skirting, and Christa, animated, says, "Yes, yes, exactly. My dress was like that."

"How beautiful," I say. "You're so lucky. Mine was some cheap old thing."

"Have you just had your wedding?"

"No!" I laugh. "My wedding was a very long time ago."

"And your mother, was she bossy?"

"Not so much," I say, smiling.

She rubs her eyes with the back of her knuckles. Goose bumps speckle her chest.

"Are you freezing?" I ask.

She laughs, rubs her arms." My coat is in the room where Pawel is sleeping."

The café is at the far end of a stretch of shops, between a posh florist and a Greggs bakery. It smells of bacon and fresh coffee and cheese toasties. A table has just come free in the window, and Jack leaps to secure it. Two middle-aged women clock me—I see something complicated cross their eyes—and an old man reading a newspaper glances at me and then away too quickly. It makes me feel both restless and exhausted. But Christa and I are at the front of the queue now and I'm ordering lots of tarts, because she looks like she needs feeding up, and a pot of tea and a cappuccino and—after calling over to Jack—a double espresso.

He leans forward the moment we sit down and clears his throat. He hasn't spoken for a while. "About this remembrance book," he begins.

"Yes." Christa sits down. "I do not know quite what you mean, remembrance book?"

"It's a scrapbook," he explains.

"A scrapbook?" She takes a scoop of froth with a spoon and swallows it.

"Yes. A book in which you stick pictures and memories of a person."

"No it isn't," I say.

They both look at me.

"I mean, it *is,* but that's not why we're here. Jack is a really good journalist and he wants to write a piece for a newspaper about Ania, what she was like, and what might have happened. It was an accident me finding her, Christa. It could have been anyone. But because it was me, I feel entangled, responsible somehow. I don't know if that makes sense. But I want to find out how she died and bring her killer to justice."

"She was very, very kind. She wouldn't . . . what do you say? She wouldn't kill a fly."

Jack looks from me to her. "So you don't mind talking to me about her?"

"You are kind people. Whether it is for a book or the newspaper, I know you tell the truth." She picks up one of the custard tarts with long, tapered fingers and takes a small bite.

"The truth is always best," I say, looking at Jack.

He gives a sheepish smile.

"The people she worked for said she used to bring the kids to Richmond Park," he says.

"Yes." She puts her hand over her mouth while she swallows. "Excuse me. She loved the park. When she lived with me, we used to go in every day last summer. She took the children to the pond, and afterward, we met here for tea and cake—Ania and Molly and little Alfie."

"Did he bite you?" I say.

Jack makes a noise that is a bit like a laugh.

Christa says, "Oh, yes. I know Ania said he could be a very

naughty boy, but with her he was very good. All children are very good with Ania. *Were,*" she adds. She pulls in the corner of her lower lip.

What if I had employed Ania, if she had been our nanny? If she moved in with us, would it still have happened? My chest feels tight. The pain of missing Millie and the pain of Ania's death seem to get mixed up for a minute. I can't entangle one from the other. It's the cat dream all over again, a powerful need to keep something safe, the desperate fear of failure.

Jack continues to ask questions. How long had Ania lived with her? (Six months.) How long had they known each other before that? (Since childhood.) He helps himself to a tart—pops it in his mouth whole. He swallows it with a look of alarm—there is more of it than he thought—and afterward wipes his mouth with a paper napkin. "Was it expensive, the flat she found?" he asks.

She shrugs. "She had many jobs, and she was hoping to get work as a teacher in a good school, good paid job, when she was trained. But it is a very small flat, so maybe not so expensive. She has a cupboard here with some of her things—books, papers, her old diaries—that she didn't need. I suppose"—she breaks off, looks slightly lost for a moment—"I should send them to her parents in Lodz."

Her *parents*. Her poor parents. It's just unbearable. I need to get back to work, pick up my normal life, forget all this. I should have stayed in the car.

But Jack looks at her intently. "Can we see them? The diaries, I mean?"

"Maybe." She sounds doubtful. I wonder if he is pushing too hard.

"Her boyfriend?" I ask, forcing myself to focus. "Was he a good thing?"

"Yes. No." She is biting her bottom lip again. "A good thing? I don't know."

"A bad thing?" Jack interjects.

"Tolek, he loved Ania very, very much." She smoothes invisible crumbs from the knee of her dress. "*Too* much."

"What do you mean?" Jack says sharply.

She studies me as if she's thinking hard. Finally, she says quickly, "He wanted to marry Ania soon, but she was always talking about a career, her teaching. Tolek, he is good with his hands, a kind man. He wanted to have a wife who loved him like he loved her. It was difficult."

"Was he excited about the baby?" I ask.

"Oh, yes," she says vaguely. "So worried Ania was, with the baby scare. Blood spotting. Big relief for Ania and the baby father when the scan say it was okay."

I see Jack start. He catches my eye. He noticed it, too. *"The baby father."*

"Do you have a number for Tolek?" Jack says. "We would like to speak to him very much."

"His English is not good. He was in Poland when she died. He is very angry, and so guilty."

"And you're sure he was in Poland?" Jack asks.

She makes a little movement in her seat, a squirm. "Yes. He is very angry with the police, asking and asking questions."

"Angry?" Jack says. "Even though he is innocent? What do you mean, angry?"

"He is a plumber, a hardworking man," she says enigmatically. She runs her hands up each forearm, as if pushing up invisible sleeves, a gesture that says she wants to get going. She is rattled. She is looking anywhere but at us.

The old man at the next table has got to his feet, and I nudge my chair forward so he can get past. Christa is staring at the newspaper he has left on the table. In the bottom right-hand corner, there is tiny postage-stamp photograph of me.

Christa looks up and catches my eye. She stands. She wants to go out into the fresh air, but Jack clings to his empty cup. He has another question. "Had Ania come into any money recently? Her employers thought she had started living more expensively: new clothes, underwear, jewelery."

"Ania worked hard," she says. "Very single-minded. She always wanted the best."

"Tolek?"

"He earn good money," she says emphatically. "People in South London"—she waves vaguely in the direction of Wandsworth—"always want new bathrooms."

We walk Christa back up the hill and say good-bye to her at the entrance to her flat. I hug her again. "When you find out," she says, "you tell me." Her mouth straightens into a fierce line. Her head is nodding; she is trying not to cry. "I promise," I say. I nod, too, and at that moment I would love to bring back an answer, for Christa, Ania's friend, if no one else.

Jack is fussing with his phone. He is checking something and fiddling. I don't say anything. I just walk away, back up over the grass to where the car is parked. I'm trying not to cry.

I sit down in the driver's seat and take the old man's newspaper out of my bag where I stuffed it. It's one of the Sunday tabloids—yesterday's paper. The postage stamp photo is a teaser for an article inside. I turn to page six.

Mornin' All Presenter Chucks It All In

Troubled Gaby Mortimer has resigned from the TV show that made her name.

"I'd rather not do the program at all," the forty-two-year-old presenter told close friends. "It's the wrong type of publicity."

> Colleagues say she has been behaving in an increasingly erratic manner since she stumbled on the dead body of Polish nanny Ania Dudek on Wandsworth Common a fortnight ago.
>
> "Yes, we do feel left in the lurch," says a representative at *Mornin' All,* "but Gaby knows we are here if she needs us."

Pictures of me on my doorstep and of that bruise, of Stan the Man—head on one side, handsome and concerned. I haven't seen that photograph before. It's newly taken: vain bastard. A head shot of India, "my replacement." An old one, from *Spotlight* probably.

I hear the clunk of the car door and the scrunch of someone getting into the passenger seat. My head is on the steering wheel. He puts his hand on my shoulder.

I lean back. He takes his arm away quickly before I squash it.

"Did you know?" I say. "Yesterday? Had you read the papers? Is it in all of them?"

He nods.

"Why didn't you *say*?"

"I was waiting for you to mention it, or to tell me you'd resigned. Then, when it became apparent that you didn't know anything about it, and you hadn't even seen the papers, that you were stuffing them under the sofa, well, it didn't seem up to me. I thought somebody else would have told you."

Did Philip know? Was that behind his forced jollity? Was he feigning ignorance as a defense mechanism, in case I burst into tears and made him come home? Or perhaps he didn't know. Perhaps he is just in his own bubble, hedge-funded in, not reading the UK papers, or watching TV, or even opening texts. But Clara's missed call—she was probably ringing about this. And Robin knew. The solicitude in her voice, the talk of yums, the way she tried to urge me to come and stay. And those people in the pub yesterday: the way they looked at me.

"It's all lies," I say. "I haven't resigned. They've taken my words out of context. I told Stan I'd rather not do the program at all if it meant using Ania. And 'wrong type of publicity,' I meant *me. I* was giving the *show* the wrong kind of publicity."

"I'm sure."

"Is this their way of firing me?"

"I don't know. I'm sorry." He puts his hand on mine. It's obviously one of those things he does.

We sit for a minute. "Do you still want the interview?" I ask after a bit.

"Yeah! The rehabilitation of Gaby Mortimer. I like a challenge."

"Thank you," I say dubiously.

He looks at his watch. "Look, I'm on a bit of a tight schedule. Is there anyone you can be with today? I ought to get on. We need to talk more about this. And Christa . . . Lots to say there. But later, yeah? Or tomorrow?"

"Of course. Do you want a lift?" I turn the key in the ignition. "Where do you need to get to?"

"Tottenham."

"Oh. Not sure . . ."

"Any Tube station will do."

I drive. I put my foot on the clutch and the car into gear. I click on the radio and check the mirror and keep my eye out for cars and for lights. But all the time I'm thinking, they've stitched me up. They've fed the papers all this stuff. How *could* they. After everything I've given them, all those years of soap stars and EC regulations and bloody bent bananas. Stan, the big cheeses, ambitious India: I don't care about them. But *Terri*. I thought she was my friend.

Jack is talking, but I'm not listening. He's trying to take my mind off things. He's saying something about today's commission, how he's hoping the piece will make the magazine cover.

I pause at the lights. "What did you say it's about again?" I manage to ask, to show I'm grateful.

"The father of the teenage boy from Tottenham killed in that hotel bomb a few months ago on the Red Sea. Do you remember? There's an appeal: British families are awarded compensation if loved ones are lost in terrorist attacks on home ground, but not abroad. He wants to change things."

"Poor man," I say, chastened—what's a job to this? "Losing a child, the worst thing." Ania's parents in Lodz. "Unimaginable."

"Bit of a tough assignment," he says, with a little edge of self-importance.

"I always feel—*felt*—guilty interviewing people who have suffered appalling trauma. They want to talk—that's why they've agreed; it's a sort of therapy, I suppose. As a journalist, though, you know you should get the quotes, the story . . ."

"You have to disassociate," he says shortly. "Be who you need to be. Play a kind of game. Chop a bit of yourself off."

"Poor you. Poor him." I check my mirror and turn left onto the A3, speeding into the middle lane of the highway.

A police car is parked up some way ahead at an angle, with its lights turning. Two policemen are standing next it, one of them holding out his arm. I slow down. A white van almost jackknifes across the lanes in front of me and skids to a halt on the hard shoulder.

I drive past slowly. In the rearview mirror, I see the policeman approach the van. I close my eyes, fleetingly, shake my head. It takes a few minutes for my nerves to steady. Are the police going to spook me now for the rest of my life?

At the roundabout ahead, Jack lets out a laugh. "You are a terrible driver. I hope you don't mind me saying, but you really are."

"What?"

"An extraordinary combination: simultaneously bullish and insecure."

"Am I? I'm not. I am not a terrible driver! Am I?"

"You are. The way you cut up that Chrysler just then, pulled in front of them and then slowed right down." He's having another playful go at me, trying this out as a means of distraction.

I turn onto West Hill. "I'm not sure I will take you to a Tube station now. I'll just dump you here, and it's a very long walk."

"Sorry. I won't say another word. In fact, I'll close my eyes."

And he does close his eyes. He actually does. He makes himself comfortable and leans back in the seat. *This* is distracting. He has pushed the hair away from his face, and I can tell by the slight movement of his head that he is listening to the radio. The song is one Philip doesn't like, catchy with rude lyrics—Millie hums it all the time. If Philip were here, he would have changed the station and I would have felt a tiny bit judged. It is shocking how on edge I have been with Philip recently, how I have imagined every gesture held up against some distant ideal and found wanting. How much easier it is to have been, temporarily, cut loose from that.

I have reached the Tube and pull into the bus lane to stop.

"Have a nice day, then," I say, imagining for a moment I am a Somerset housewife—the one, if things had been different, I might have turned into—dropping her husband at a rural station, before going home to an armful of kids.

Jack opens his eyes and looks at me. His mouth moves softly. "Don't worry about your job," he says. "It'll be fine. It's just a blip, a misunderstanding. You're too valuable to them. You'll sort it."

He steps out, bag over his shoulder, and gives the roof a little double bang.

• • •

I scoop the newspapers out from under the sofa when I get home, yesterday's and today's: I read the lot. The broadsheets are the worst: their prurient disapproval, like a high-court judge sneaking a peek under a lavatory door. They use the passive voice like tweezers. "Sources close to the troubled presenter . . . ," "Doubts have been raised . . ." Am I really that interesting? If I were a producer of a midmorning current affairs show, would I put myself forward as a subject? I suppose I would. Murder and celebrity: it's a delicious cocktail.

One of today's tabloids has a photograph of me in the pub, "enjoying a drink with a mystery male companion." Someone clever took it with their phone. I didn't even notice. More dangers of the modern world. You're never alone with a Samsung Galaxy.

I can't put it off any longer. I know I shouldn't. It's like going down into the basement. There'll be a madwoman with a knife. But the compulsion is too strong. I go into the kitchen. If I hadn't found the remote control, I'd have put the television on with my teeth.

Sky Plus. Thursday, Friday, and today's episodes are lined up neatly in the series link. I choose today's.

At first, I think it'll all be okay: I'll survive. When he does his introductory blurb to camera—a group interview with the cast of *Made in Chelsea,* an item on the rise of eyebrow threading—Stan looks diminished. A bad shirt, too short in the sleeve. Too much body hair. He needs ballast. He needs *me.* It's our relationship that gives him his youthful edge. I'm Mrs. Robinson to his Benjamin Braddock, Francesca Annis to his Ralph Fiennes. Without me, well, he looks sordid, grubby, a bit old. As for India? She's nervous. She's perching on the sofa, her hands wildly gesticulating, in the way they always tell you not to. She's got a habit, too, of swallowing in the middle of a sentence, almost a gulp, as if she's got so much to ask, so much to tell me—*me,* the viewer—she can't get the words out.

I'm not sure when it dawns. It's like a thought I can't quite pinpoint, fluttering lightly like a moth in my mind. They've got a catchphrase going. Stan says, "Top news . . . top views . . ." and India finishes with, "Top gossip." It's a first, he's giving *her* the punch line. Stan, legs crossed, is subdued, avuncular, oddly sweet, and India is slightly leaning into him. Her hair has been pulled back. No, chopped. I detect Annie's magic touch, the kind of shocking, deliciously flattering cut that will set a trend. Binky from *Made in Chelsea* can't take her eyes off it.

The Tory backbencher doing Pick of the Papers is so charmed by India's girlishness he slips up. He refers to the prime minister as "an Eton mess." It will have been Tweeted. It'll already have been propagated by *The World at One*. Perfect publicity. That's all Terri ever wants: to get people talking. Stan shakes his head at the MP, more in sorrow than anger. "Top news . . . top views . . ." he says, and India says, "Top gossip."

I know what it is. It's chemistry. It's what Stan is always banging on about.

I switch off the television, groan into the silence of the kitchen. A terrifying realization. This isn't about publicity, good or bad. Accusations, true or false. This is no blip, no *misunderstanding*. This is the opportunity they've been waiting for. This is their way of nudging me out. I'll never get back now, whatever happens with this case. Not after this. India's triumph. I'm old news, past it. If I'm honest with myself, I know they've been trying to get rid of me for months.

"Good bits and bad bits," I told Jack. I think about them. And it's Steve, my driver, who comes into my head. Steve's face, his chatter, his tact, the updates on his wife and daughter. If this is the end, I won't find out what happened about the polyp. The *polyps*! Or whether Sammy got an interview. And it's thinking about Steve that finally makes me cry.

Upstairs in the bathroom, I splash water on my face. It is a face that has seen too much and done too much. It's a face that's been around too long. Frown lines and smile lines, and a little crack across one of my front teeth. Secret hairs that need plucking, violet shadows that need more concealer by the day. I'm costing them too much in Touche Éclat. My hair, too: ridiculous. Nail scissors poke out of the toothbrush pot, and I start hacking at it angrily, watch the coils spiral into the basin, clog up the drainage holes. I keep going. Once, my mother, in one of her spurts of exuberant extravagance, decided to prune our patch of garden. She came back from the shops with clippers, loppers, and pruning shears, and I watched from the house as, arms scratched and flailing, she slashed at the hedge of rambling roses, tugged and swore. She didn't seem to know when to stop. She just kept cutting and cutting until the beautiful bushes were reduced to a few black stubby branches.

Afterward, I study the hair in the sink. It looks like a dead animal. I study my face again. All those comments, I believed them, but I don't look like Ania, not without makeup. It was just the hair, the same length of reddish hair, nothing more. People have no imagination. Christa, who knew her well, who saw the expressions of her face shift and change, didn't even notice.

I bundle the hair into a bag and take it downstairs. For a moment, as I hold it above the bin, I wonder if I could sell it. We live beyond our means—school fees, holidays, tennis club, a ridiculous mortgage. And if I have lost my job, and if Philip is planning . . . well, I'm not going to think about that now. Disassociation: Jack is right. Images flock and throng if you let them; better to lay them flat like photographs, let them fade, slip them into dark, undisturbed corners, into books and under stones.

Life will be different, I tell myself, when this is over. I start by ringing up the Harbor Club to cancel our membership. I can feel the sneer of their surprise. Philip will be furious. I don't care! And then I collect a roll of black bin bags from the drawer in the kitchen and go through my wardrobe. It's a purge. Three identical brown

V-necked sweaters, four wrap dresses, several pairs of heels that weren't to be trusted on the slippery studio floor, silk scarves, silk shirts, kitten-heeled boots, and smart black trousers with crease marks down the legs: they all get bagged up. Then I start on clothes I *do* wear and bag up most of them too.

Nora comes in while I am in the middle of this. I make her a cup of tea and tell her to take what she wants. "Oh, okay," she says happily. She decides on the trousers—Agnès B. and Joseph—and all the scarves and dresses. She tries on the heels, which are far too big, and shows interest in a pair of Juicy Couture tracksuit bottoms, which have lost their elastic. I mend them for her—doing that trick with a safety pin, when you pin it to the end of the elastic and wrinkle it through the seam.

She lives in Burgess Hill, she tells me, with two friends. "Long, long way." Her little girl, back home in Manila, is twelve.

I screw up my courage and ring Jude. Nice, interesting Jude, who could have been my friend, who still could be. But friendships don't come free, you have to work at them—take the plunge, even when you're scared. She might be away, or she might be free for a coffee one of these days, but I won't know unless I try.

"Oh," she says. "Hi. Yes. Gaby. How are you?"

"Oh God, Don't ask," I say. "It's been a nightmare."

"I've heard. You've left your job."

"It's not what it seems. If you've read the papers you'll think—"

"Listen," she interrupts, "I'm glad you've rung. I've been meaning to get in touch. Well, it's just this PTA quiz night. You'd probably forgotten it. But just to say Polly's husband, an auctioneer at Christie's, says he'll do it. I'm sure it's the last thing you feel like doing at the moment on top of . . . everything."

"No, I—"

"So basically, you're off the hook!"

I don't want to be off the hook. I want to be *on* the hook. I want to be hanging from the scruff of my neck from a school peg.

"I can still do it!" I say. "I've been looking forward to it. You know, perching with the PTA squaddies!"

"Another time maybe. I've sort of told him he could now."

There is a cool tone in her voice. I don't know whether it is the police investigation, or the person the papers are making me out to be, or just the simple fact that I haven't been straight with her, but it feels like a door is closing.

"Oh. Are you sure?"

"Yeah. Best, probably. Anyway, have a good holiday. I'll see you."

"Yes. See you."

The friendship that never was.

Clara is leaving her last class when I ring. She is so pleased to hear my voice. She has been so worried. Am I all right? Am I really? All that stuff . . . Lies, of course.

I tell her I'm actually relieved, that I hadn't been enjoying work. "Change is good," I say.

I'm trying to stop her from worrying, but there is truth in my words.

"I've cut off all my hair," I tell her.

"Oh, my rising stars. *Bold*. Some posh Mayfair salon?"

"No. Bathroom basin. Did it myself."

"Are you on your own?" The anxiety in her voice has gone up a notch.

"I miss Millie," I say, caving inside, now I've got Clara in my ear. "Got that horrible feeling when you think you are never going to see your child again."

"At least you know she's in safe hands."

"No one's hands are safer than Robin's."

"Exactly. Yes."

I've been pacing a bit, and I'm looking out of the sitting room window now, pressing my nose to the glass, so as not to be distracted by my own reflection.

Clara is offering to come down to see me, or meet me in town, but I can tell it wouldn't be that easy. Her voice is cautious with piano practice and physics homework and project marking—a hundred visions and revisions.

I tell her I'm fine, that actually I have a mountain of things to do—"you know, admin et cetera. Later in the week would suit me better." I don't want her to worry, or put her out. I say I have a friend coming round in a minute. "You know, Jude, that woman from the school gates? A local friend. I'm working on it."

A movement catches my eye beyond the olive trees.

Clara is relieved. "Lovely. Better go. Staff meeting."

A shadow shifts. Branches move.

I burst out of the front door. I am filled with fury—Stan, the producers, the tabloids, the opportunistic drinker in the pub—it's for them all, my mad, enraged dash. The body, the man, darts out from behind the railings, charges across the road. He turns at the alleyway. I see his face, short hair, squat pugnacious features. I shout at him—a hot stream of temper and outrage—but it's too late. He's turned into the alley, and by the time I've got to the end of it, he has disappeared.

I'm out of breath when I get home. My fingers are shaking. I have to tell Perivale. This is as close as I've got to catching anyone. It's vindication. If he's doubted me before, he'll believe me now.

I am about to hang up when he answers. I tell him a man was outside my house, lurking. I describe him. Perivale might be driving. His voice sounds blurred, as if he's talking loudly at a distance. Same man as yesterday? The one from the red Renault? I tell him

I don't know. I can't be sure. I think so. His voice is reassuring. He'll look into it, he says. I'm to leave it with him. And for the first time, I wonder whether he knows something I don't, that he isn't watching me, but guarding me.

"Have you eaten?"

I take a deep breath. I've been lying in my bedroom with the shutters closed. "No, not yet."

"Can I take you out for a slap-up meal?"

"You're back from Tottenham, then."

"Yes, and you sound like you are in need of cheering. It was a bit traumatic."

"Even with chopping bits of yourself off?"

"Even with the chopping."

I stand up. My legs are wobbly. I peer through the slats, holding the phone with my chin. The evening is strangely lit. Violet over the rooftops. No one in the street.

Jack is suggesting a new place nearby, one of those bistros/bars/cafés that does sharing plates and *demi-plats* or demi-pliés, or Demi-Moores, or something. In my ear, he is talking goat's curd and razor clams and rhubarb sorbet.

"Seasonal produce," I say, trying to sound normal. "Simply cooked."

"Tantamount to a moral code," he says. "You coming? Are you morally up to it?"

I don't answer. I would have to put clothes on, and shoes, and go out again through the front door. I would have to assume I wasn't hated and despised by everyone in the world, forget the short squat man, and Jude, and the women with their buggies who glared at me on the common. I would have to pretend I was morally up to it. I make a noise. I'm not sure if it is a yes or a no.

"Great," he says, deciphering for us both. "See you there."

. . .

I'm going to walk. I scour the street when I open the front door.
A yellow parking-suspension sign has gone up on a lamppost. An
Asda shopping bag skits between the wheels of cars.

My mobile rings.

"Gabs, Gabs," says Philip's voice, "I miss you, doll. Move closer,"
he sings. His words are slurred. "Move your body real close until it
feels, feels like I'm reallyIdon'tknow."

"You're up late," I say. "Hello."

It's the middle of the night in Singapore, or the early hours of
the morning.

"Where's my little girl? Can I talk to her? My Mills, my baby."

"She's in Suffolk with Robin, Philip. Just for a few days, until . . ."

"My lovely Millie. My Gabs. 'Member that time we went skin-
ny-dipping in Cornwall? So cold, wasn't it?"

"It was really cold."

"Brrrrrr. It was so cold. Do you remember how cold we were?"

"I do. We were really, really cold."

"Do you miss me?" I can hear music in the background, shouts,
laughter, singing. A Chinese-style banquet. Karaoke and shots of
sake. Lots of shots of sake.

I close the front door with a quiet click behind me. My phone is
cupped under my chin. "Yup." I open the gate and turn left toward
the common. Tears are pricking the corners of my eyes. "When are
you coming home?"

"Endoftheweek. Promise, if I can. Soonermaybe." I turn out of
the alley and into the trees. Why does he have to ring, with this,
now? It feels like too late. The common stretches out, empty, green.
A cathedral of trees, of dark corners and empty places.

"Love you. Promiseseeyousoon. Bye. Bye." His voice goes as if
someone has pulled him away.

I feel the phone, heavy in my pocket, knocking against my thigh as I crunch along the gravel path. I want to turn round. All the way across the common, I have to force myself not to. I put one step in front of the other. I pull my shoulders back. I don't turn round.

The bistro/bar/café is all dark wood and steel, Ercol chairs and vintage Anglepoise in alcoves.

Jack is nibbling on some olives and what look like toenail clippings.

I pause a minute at the door to collect myself, to pull my face into the right expression. And then I stand up straight and walk over, as if we were old friends and life was just normal. "You couldn't wait?" I say behind him.

He looks up, outraged. "I haven't eaten all day."

"Not since you put away your body weight in custard tarts this morning."

"Oh, yes. Forgot you were there."

"Charming." I slip off my coat and hang it on the back of my chair. It's busy. A mixed crowd—singles straight from work, couples on a night out, women plying small children with cold chips. (Round here, even in late-night bars called Doom and Inferno, you find women plying small children with cold chips.) Nobody notices me, but I sit down quickly, shield my face.

Jack has a trendy French carafe of red wine in front of him. We do a swift mime of him offering and me accepting and I lean back and take a big gulp. I can feel it bypassing my veins and going straight to my head. I close my eyes briefly, give the alcohol a few minutes to work away the phone call from Philip.

When I open them, Jack is looking at me, with a slight frown. "New hair?"

"Cut it all off."

"Makes you look younger."

"Thank you. I . . ."

He sweeps his hands through his own. "So glad you came. I know we've got things to talk about, but first, God, this afternoon, this bloke . . ."

That's it about the hair then. He starts talking about the father of the dead boy and how, when the bomb had exploded, he had run down to reception, scoured the wreckage, hoisted masonry, sifted through body parts, demanded answers from police, officials, hospitals, plastered the resort with posters. Then finally, after a week of desperate searching, had driven five hours across the desert to a morgue in a different part of Egypt, where the body of his son lay.

Jack carefully rolls up the sleeves of his white shirt, one fold after the other, when he gets to this bit. It's not an easy movement. It's controlled, but his hands are shaking. "Meanwhile, he and his wife and his two other sons had been relocated to a different hotel— much posher than the one they'd booked—and when they weren't searching, they were sitting by the pool. Can you imagine that? They didn't know what else to do."

"It's the banality of tragedy, isn't it?" I shake my head. "The fact that life just goes on—kids demanding another Coke. They were probably hand-washing knickers in the hotel bathroom."

"They ran out of suntan lotion. They had to buy more from the hotel shop." He takes a swig of his wine.

"Bloody hell."

"I didn't see his wife—she didn't want to meet me—but I could hear her, through the walls. She was washing up the whole time."

"God. Losing a child, and in such terrible circumstances."

I sigh deeply. The horror, the finality of death, it's more than I can bear. I feel intense sorrow for this mother and father welling and growing, and then very slightly stagnating. Everybody is somebody's child. Ania. Alfie, the biter. *Millie*. I feel I am dying just to think of it.

"He wanted to tell me every detail."

"Maybe he thought if he kept telling the story, it would have a different outcome, that he would have some control over the ending."

"Yes perhaps. And now he's fighting to change the compensation law, but it's not really what he wants. He just wants his son back."

"Poor guy." I'm wondering if it is too early to change the subject. We've run out of things to say, but we can't launch straight into me. Even the man outside my house. It would be heartless. I sigh again. "My problems seem so pathetic after—"

Jack smiles at me, as if I am someone he has known all his life. He slaps his thigh. "Listen," he interrupts. "We are going to clear your name. Get you back to work."

"I don't know if I even want to." I tell him how good India was and how hopeless I've been recently, how my career is probably over, but I don't know what else to do.

"First things first," Jack says. "Let's at least finish what we've started. Once there's a lovely piece out there, proclaiming your innocence, you'll feel differently. I've had time to snoop about a bit today, by the way."

The waiter arrives, and I leave the ordering to Jack. He continues.

"This afternoon, when I got back from Tottenham, I found myself 'passing' Battersea police station. Got a tip from Mickey Smith at the *Mirror*, that Hannah Morrow—the PC—had a few more things to say off the record about the investigation."

"And?" I am watching him carefully. This has surprised me.

"She sneaked out for a cup of tea and a 'millionaire's shortbread' in the café round the corner. I think she's playing a clever game—sees a chance to undermine Perivale, which is not to say that she doesn't believe what she's saying. She implied he has been prejudiced against you from the beginning of the investigation. Pursuing you, proving to his superiors that he won't be cowed by a person's fame or reputation, a way of showing he's made of strong stuff, worthy of promotion. Personally"—he smiles—"I think he fancies you and has quite an interesting way of showing it."

I look down at my glass, swill the contents, because I think I've blushed.

"Hannah doesn't understand why he hasn't followed up properly on Marta," Jack continues.

"Hannah already?"

"*Hannah*—it's amazing how intimate you can get over a shared shortbread slice—also thinks it's worth looking at the possibility Ania had been seeing another man, or men."

"Did she have any idea who?"

"No. But I think Christa knows. She was cagey this morning, wasn't she? She referred to 'the baby's father.' Not Tolek. Did you notice how she kept talking about Tolek being angry? Odd adjective for someone who has just lost his girlfriend."

"Not necessarily—"

"I'm going to get back to Christa. Deploy my famous charm. Try and meet him."

"Be careful," I say. "It's not a game."

The food arrives. It is delicious—such ordinary offerings as beetroot and hard-boiled eggs with exotic extrusions from places like Santiago de Compostela. I realize, as we eat, that I don't want to think any more about Ania's death. For the first time, I think perhaps we should drop it. We are getting out of our depth. If Christa has things to hide, we should leave that to PC Morrow. It is beginning to feel dangerous.

"There was a man outside my house today," I tell Jack. "Just lurking. I don't think we should pursue Tolek, or Christa. You know. There's a killer out there. How close do we want to get?"

He laughs, as if I have made a joke. His focus has shifted, now that the food is here. He peers at things before he eats them, flips a slice of beetroot over with his fork, and investigates its underbelly like a botanist.

"So let's leave it and talk about other things," I say, refilling our glasses. "A new subject, something different. Let's pretend we are two normal people having supper. Cheer me up. Tell me about your family."

He smiles, as if this is a nice thought, something he wouldn't mind doing at all, and starts telling me about his sisters: the eldest is in marketing, based in Leeds; the second is a GP; the third lives with her family out in the country near his dad. Jack was "spoiled rotten" as a child, the longed-for son. His mother died three years ago—cancer— though his father found a new "fancy woman" within six months.

"Men usually do. We had a grief counselor on *Mornin' All*. Widows, on average, take ten years to remarry. Men often remarry within the year."

"Your father remarried?"

I think hard. Do I really want this in the finished article? "Off the record?"

"Off the record."

"Dead."

"That's a bugger."

I laugh. "Yes, it is a bugger."

"What happened?"

I haven't talked about this in years. I feel uneasy putting the two words *my* and *father* together; there is no relationship to refer to. I've never come clean in the press before, and is now really the time? Do I want to open this all up with Jack? Is it the kind of material I want him to collect, or use, or even idly mull over at the back of his mind? Will I start to cry? I take another glug of wine. "There isn't much to say. He was a manic-depressive, and one wet November night he drove straight into a tree."

"Accident, or . . . ?"

"My mother never used the word *suicide* but . . ."

I used to talk about my dead father late at night with boys when I was a teenager. I used to feel guilty then, too. It was like a trick I could play, a way to get close. Now, I have the disturbing sensation of something similar unfurling. I hadn't meant this confession to be an invitation for intimacy. I should have been more careful.

"Tough on your mother, though, with a small child."

"It was hard on her. She was the sort of woman who needed a man. Her life was full of tragic failures in that regard—a long line of them. Only one relationship lasted. With the booze."

"Oh God, sorry."

"Don't be. It was her tragedy, not mine. I was always self-sufficient. Mature for my age, my teachers used to say. Some of them looked after me a bit. Friends' parents, too."

"Took you under their wing?"

"Made sure I applied to university and things. And actually, to her credit, during my childhood my mother did keep it together. It was only after I left that things went a bit . . . pear-shaped. But listen, I hate . . . I don't normally . . . you know, people's childhood! Old hat!"

"Brothers and sisters?"

"Nope. Used to long for a big family, but no. Just me. Typical only child."

He says gently, "Simultaneously bullish and insecure?"

"Ah," I say. "Direct line between alcoholic mother and 'erratic driving.' I get it now."

"I think," he says, his eyes crinkling. "I think I got you wrong." He stares at me, the smile still there. I feel a shock in the air, a tiny moment of possibility. Perhaps it's the wine, but it hasn't been what I thought, all this: not a guilty disclosure but a release.

One of the women with the small children has looked across

at us twice. Her brow is furrowed, as if she is trying to study the picture above Jack's head. Jack notices and makes a face. He pays the bill—holding it stiffly away from me like a tour guide's flag above his head—and, before the woman can nudge any of her companions, we are out in the night.

The sky is clear, dotted with stars. Shouts float down from a party in an upstairs flat. A car cruises past with its music throbbing. Jack says he will walk me home. I am quietly grateful. We wander slowly up the road, past bikes and bins and litter-entangled front railings, houses where accountants and lawyers and teachers are sleeping, children in bunk beds, starfished babies in cots, families and young marrieds and students. A run of normalcy.

We don't talk much. The wine has hit my head, the world is full of liquid movement. A sliver of moon slides low above a quivering skyline of trees. I shiver, but Jack doesn't notice. He put his hand on the small of my back as we ran across the road, and I can still feel the shape of it.

We walk, hands in pockets, and after a few minutes, I say, "So, come on, tell me about your ex-wife. What did she do to make you so angry?"

He tips his head back and looks up at the sky. The wind ruffles the loose curls of his hair. He takes his hand out of his pocket to smooth it down. Still gazing up, he says, "Married at thirty-five, separated at thirty-nine. I wanted children. Lots of children. She didn't. I thought fidelity was an important component of our union. She disagreed."

"Can see how that might have created tension," I say lightly, thinking how nice and refreshing to meet a man who wants lots of children.

"Then, of course, she got pregnant within six months of meeting someone else."

"Typical."

He makes a *hmp* noise, a laugh or a clearing of his throat. "So I've got a question for you. You don't have to answer."

"Okay."

"You said you always longed for siblings, for a big family. So why didn't you have more kids yourself? Why just one, why just Mills?"

I actually don't answer at first. I'm registering the fact that he called Millie Mills, as if he knows her. He must *feel* as if he knows her. I continue along the path. When he catches up, I say, "I wanted more. I thought we would have lots of children. Three or four at least. And animals. Cats and dogs. Chickens." I am waving my arms. "But life doesn't always work out the way you want."

"True, but . . . ?"

"My job—Philip felt it wouldn't be fair, with us both working, that we would be spreading ourselves too thin." I'm chanting all this. "That was how he put it," I add. "And I love, *loved,* my job. Other priorities seemed important at just the wrong time. But I'm lucky: I've got Millie. *Mills.*"

"No dog? No cat?"

"Philip's allergic."

He laughs, and I do, too. "He's allergic to all sorts of things," I say. "Domestic animals, shellfish, pollen . . ." And life with me, I think, though I am not sure I say that out loud. Or maybe I do. It doesn't matter anymore. I've told him so much now. He's got his exposé, and maybe that's fine.

We wander the last bit of the path without talking. Two figures, teenage boys, are hovering by the bench just ahead of us. They sidle away as we get close, seem to melt into the bushes. Only two glowing lights—the ends of their cigarettes, moving like fireflies—show they are still there.

We put them behind us and reach the alley. Jack touches the metal post that bars it from cyclists, hangs sideways from it, and says, "Don't walk this late at night across the common on your own, will you?"

I shake my head.

"And you do lock up and everything?"

I nod, trying to sidle past the post, heading for my road. "Aye, aye, Cap'n."

"Whoever did it . . . I mean, as you say, they haven't been apprehended."

"No one is going to kill me," I say. He's caught up with me. "'Hodge shall not be shot.'" Dr. Johnson said it about his cat. It's one of those obscure references Philip and I quote now and then."

"Dr. Johnson?" Jack says. "A fine cat. A very fine cat."

I stop and turn. It's as if he sneaked into my mind and poked around. I laugh. "A familiarity with Boswell's *Life of Johnson*? Jack Hayward, you are a man of many, many surprises."

We have reached the end of the alley. I'm aware Jack has stopped, a dark shape against the ivy wall.

"Gaby?" he says.

The sky spins a little. I have that feeling you get when you look down into a puddle and see clouds moving and you don't know what's real and what isn't.

"Gaby?" He moves an inch. Green tendrils catch in his hair. The throb of an engine: a police car, cruising, light spinning, slowing down when it passes my house. And before he says anything else, I run across the road toward the safety of home.

My eyes open.

Something has woken me. A shape by the bedroom door. An animal? A crouched body? No. My head sinks into the pillow. Relief. Nothing, just a black bin bag full of clothes.

And then the sound again. An abrupt bang, a rattle. I know what it is, this sound. It is the front door pushing against the security chain.

Could it be Philip, or did I leave the key in the lock again?

My legs are shaky, my head thick, my mouth dry. I stumble downstairs. The front door is open a crack. A hand is reaching through the gap, trying to reach the hook of the chain.

"Who is it?" I yell.

The door slowly closes. I shout, "Who is it? Who's out there?"

A pause and then, a small voice, "It's me. Marta."

"Oh God." I think about Jack, telling me to be careful. And for a second I consider not letting her in, but only for a second, because I know I can't leave her out there, in the dark. I open the door. "You scared me half to death," I say, tightening my dressing gown. "At this time of night! Come on, then."

"Sorry. I was out at that bar. I needed to come back."

Her hair is pulled tight in a high ponytail, and she is wearing a startling amount of makeup: black eyeliner and heavy foundation. She is taller than usual, too, in tight jeans and clumpy heels.

I look at my watch. It's 1:15 AM. "So you've been out on the razzle?"

"The what?"

"Have you been somewhere nice?"

"Yes. To that bar you told me about, Doom."

"Oh, yes. Was it jolly?" Oh Lord. I'm doing that thing again.

I go into the kitchen and I am surprised to hear her follow me. I put on the kettle. I am ragingly awake now. When Millie is older, will she and I meet in the kitchen for cups of tea late at night? Will I be the sort of mother she can confide in?

Marta has sat down somewhat unsteadily at the table.

"You okay?" I ask her carefully. "Do you need something to eat? There isn't much, it just being me." I open the fridge. "Some eggs. A lot of carrots."

She shakes her head. "No. I'm not hungry."

I make tea, trying to feel calm. I wasn't expecting her back. I sit down at the table, clutching mugs and milk. Should I ask her about the post office receipts? Would this be a good moment or a very bad one? Should I wait until we aren't alone? "So you had an enjoyable time?"

She shrugs. "My friend, she is a silly girl."

"Oh dear."

"Yes. She talked to some boys who were not nice and I tell her we have to go, and when she wouldn't come, I leave her there."

"Oh dear," I say again. "You mean you left her on her own in the bar?"

"Yes."

"Do you think she'll be all right?"

"I don't care. And if she's not, it's her fault."

"Oh. Okay. Gosh."

"So I walk home."

"Marta, you must be careful. I told you that. Someone could have followed you."

"I kept to the main road. My friend she find her own way back to Colliers Wood. I never see her again."

"Well, good thing you came back," I say after I have let this sunk in. "I've been meaning to speak to you about something."

She turns to me. In the light from the side lamp, her face is full of shadows. "Yes?"

I sigh. I am not sure whether it's because I think I should have the conversation, or because I think I shouldn't, or whether it's just for the long, dull sleepless night that lies ahead.

"It's a bit awkward."

"Yes?" she says quickly. Her eyes look heavy. She is scared. She thinks I'm going to fire her. I feel a caving, a little internal subsidence, which I register as pity.

"Actually, it's nothing really," I say. "Time for bed."

TUESDAY

I was wrong. The sleep I sink into is so catatonically self-effacing it wipes, for the first few moments of waking, everything before it.

It's the phone that rouses me. What's that? Where am I? Who am I? Twenty seconds of confusion.

"Did I wake you?" Jack says.

"Yes," I say.

"Sorry. Did you sleep well?" A note in his voice I'm not quite sure of: tenderness or reproach.

"I did, actually. Probably the wine."

"God, yes. I had a skinful last night—those French carafes, deceptive. Can hardly remember getting home."

He's letting us off the hook. "Me, too," I say. "All a bit of a blur."

He takes a deep breath. "Can you meet me?"

He names a place: Spencer Park, a triangle of private houses backing onto four acres of communal garden not far from my house. I have never been in, though we were once invited to a party there by some hedge-fund contact of Philip's. Rumor has it there are tennis courts, and a rose garden, a walk lined with rhododendrons. Maybe even a swimming pool surrounded by figs, though that might just be talk.

"Why there?" I ask, tentatively.

"That would be telling."

He's keeping it back like a treat, like Millie with the toffee layer in a Twix.

"I don't know, Jack," I say. "You know, what I said last night. I meant it. I'm not sure we should carry on with this. We've met Christa, and I feel better that we've done that. But PC Morrow has got it in hand. We're just playing detectives. It's too dangerous."

"You don't understand! I've got Tolek!" He punches his name out like a clenched fist. "Christa has just rung. I was wrong about her. She *has* cleared the way. And it's because of you. She said she liked you and you are swept up in 'a miscarriage of justice': I think she got that phrase off the telly. She wants to help. Tolek has been working at Spencer Park for the last few months, on a house refit. She'll translate. He's hanging around today, waiting for a crane, has time to kill. This is what we wanted, isn't it?"

What's wrong with him? He's not listening to me. "I'm not sure . . ."

"What's the matter?"

"I'm scared of what it might lead to."

He laughs. Clearly, nothing I say will make any difference. "Spencer Park. The house with the Dumpster. I'll meet you in fifteen minutes."

He is sitting on the front wall of a Victorian mansion, a polystyrene cup precariously balanced next to him, nibbling something out of a paper bag. "Hm. You should taste this," he says. "Raspberry financier from Gail's on Northcote Road. A tiny, almondy morsel of deliciousness."

I raise my eyebrows. "Do you never stop eating?"

"I ran here," he says. "Built up an appetite." He points with a comic expression to the trainers on his feet. (Asics. As I told Perivale, *everybody* wears Asics.)

"Go on—try." He brandishes a few crumbs in my direction, and I have the hysterical thought that I only have to open my mouth like a bird and he will feed me; his fingers would touch my lips. Instead, I hold out my hand. The crumbs disintegrate further—ground almonds, a red smear of raspberry across my palm.

"Utterly delicious," I say, licking it away quickly. He is wearing baggy khaki shorts. I can see the muscles on the back of calves, a madeleine of brown skin. "Where's this Tolek then?"

He gestures farther down the street to a white stucco mansion, crenellated in the style of a castle. It has a sweep of in/out drive, which is crammed with pipes and beams of wood, like the building blocks for a Tudor hanging. Two men are crawling on the roof. Music is blasting—Tinie Tempah; Millie likes that one, but I bet it annoys the neighbors.

A battered Audi, with chalky scratches along one side, parks up across the street from us, and Christa gets out. I cross the road, and we kiss on both cheeks. She holds me at arm's length. "Your hair!" she says, "Hm!" She is wearing the same floral dress as yesterday, with a cardie and flatter shoes. New polish sparkles on her fingernails, a shell pink.

"Thank you for this," I say. "It's so kind. I can't imagine Tolek really wants to see us. We won't take up much of his time."

"For you, I feel sorry," she says. "You are kind, and I can tell you are innocent. I want to help you. You find information and you give to the police and they let you alone."

I nod. "And Ania," I say. "We're doing it for Ania."

"Okay. But I hurry. I have not long. I have an appointment in Chelsea. On Battersea Bridge sometimes, the traffic can be very heavy."

"An appointment?"

"My own mobile beauty business." She hands me her card. South London Beauty Services. "Manicure, pedicure, Brazilian, massage. I come to the house." She pats my hand. "I do you a cheap deal. Now I go to find Tolek."

"Mobile beauty business," Jack says when she has disappeared behind a Dumpster. "Wasn't expecting that."

"And she talks about Battersea Bridge as if she crosses it all the time," I say. "I deduce from that a regular Chelsea clientele."

"You and me," he says. "Proper detectives, we are."

We smile at each other and then, as if by mutual agreement, look away.

"This is Tolek," Christa says. "He has five minutes."

A slight, lithe man with a wispy blond beard and short-cropped hair nods at us. He looks vaguely familiar. Tanned shoulders extend from a sleeveless vest; a complicated eagle is inked on his bulging bicep. He's clutching his lunch to his chest—a Greggs sausage roll, an apple, and some crisps. He has been at work, Christa explains, since 6:00 AM.

We cross to the common and sit down awkwardly under a tree in a damp circle. Above us, a wood pigeon alights, with a panicked flapping and disarrangement of branches. The grass looks greener than it has for months, as if it's been painted grass color overnight. I try to think of a word for the color it was before—khaki or jaundice.

Tolek squeezes a can of Red Bull out of the pocket of his track-suit bottoms and opens it with a cheerless fizz. He downs it in one. The sinews in his hands flex; the backs are coated in a spray of white paint. He eats his sausage roll, chewing almost too regularly, his jaw working hard. I wonder why he has agreed to come, and how well he knows Christa. She is talking to him rapidly in a stream of Polish.

He wipes his mouth with the tips of his fingers and says something in response. His voice is unexpectedly high, a silver stud in the center of his tongue.

"Okay," she says to us. "Tolek is worried because of the police, because of the money in cash that he earns. He has spoken to them enough. For you, he will talk, but no quoting in the newspaper. Start your questions."

"Background really," Jack says. "How long had they been together? Where did they meet? That sort of thing."

Christa and Tolek confer in Polish, and then Christa tells us that Ania and Tolek met at school, that their parents live in the same village.

"How long had they both been in London?" Jack asks. "Did they come here together?"

Christa looks at him. She doesn't bother to translate. "Ania came two years ago," she says. "Tolek, he arrive last spring."

"That was always the plan was it?" Jack asks. "I mean, Ania had *wanted* him to come?"

Again Christa studies him hard, as if she is considering whether to translate this or not. When she speaks to Tolek, he answers at length and then looks away.

"Yes," Christa says. "It was the plan. Tolek, he needed to earn the money to come. And Ania was waiting for him. They were getting married. They loved each other."

Tolek takes a large bite out of his apple. It's an unnaturally glossy Granny Smith.

"I'm sorry to ask about money," Jack says. "But Ania's employers said he had sent her lavish flowers and that over the last six months she had started dressing more expensively. Can you ask him if he can explain that?"

Christa and Tolek speak in Polish for a bit.

"This job," she says, jutting her chin toward the white stucco mansion, "it is big money for Tolek. He work very long hours."

Tolek throws his apple core toward some pigeons, who scatter and regroup. He looks away again, his eyes following the cars streaming along Trinity Road. For some reason I am reminded of the man in the vest who looked at me from a balcony on Christa's building. It crosses my mind that this might be the same person. Am I paranoid?

"Tell him how sorry we are," I say quickly, "that we are so sorry for his loss."

She translates, and Tolek looks at me, impassively, for the first time. His pale blue eyes are red rimmed, as if he is very tired or has been crying. Deep grooves are carved into the sides of his mouth. I look at his hands and his arms, snaked with violet veins. I try to imagine them round Ania Dudek's pale neck.

He says something in Polish.

"Thank you," Christa translates.

"Did he know anybody who wanted to harm Ania?" I say. "Had she had an argument with anyone, a friend or . . . an ex-boyfriend—?"

"Or could she have been seeing another man," Jack interrupts, "when he was away in Poland, or even after . . ."

Christa purses her mouth. A muscle twitches in her jaw. She says something in Polish, and Tolek makes a movement with his arm—like someone beginning to answer a question in class and then abruptly changing their mind. He gets to his feet, balling up the Greggs paper bag. For a minute, I think he is going to kick the Red Bull can into one of our faces. A stream of words—invective?—pours from his mouth.

Jack stands up, too. The two men face each other. Tolek is slighter, but there is a set to his jaw; you wouldn't want to get on the wrong side of him. He raises his hand again, slicing upward this time like a blade. Jack steps back an inch, and Tolek scowls and tramps off back toward the stuccoed house. Jack runs after him. I make a face at Christa after they have gone, pulling out the corners of my mouth.

"Tolek is a good man, but a sad man," she says. "He needs to go back to Poland to be with his family, and Ania's. It would be better for him." She gets to her feet. "And now I must go. I will be late for work."

I pick up the Red Bull can, and scramble up, too. "Thank you for meeting us," I say quickly. "I really appreciate it. I don't want you to think . . . Christa?" She looks at me. "I'm doing this for Ania, You know that, don't you? No other reason."

She nods. She stares at me and I think she might be about to say something. But then Jack, who is on the other side of the road, shouts "Tolek!"

Christa begins to walk toward her car.

I run after her. "Do you know something, Christa?" I ask when I have caught up. "Is there anything you're not telling us about Ania?"

She has reached her car. She has her key in her hand and she is fiddling with it in the door. Her hand is shaking slightly. "No."

"Please. Christa. I am begging you. Think about Ania. Think about the baby."

She turns, her eyes dark. "I am thinking about Ania. And the poor baby. It's because of Ania and the baby that . . ."

"Was she in love with someone else? That's what it's beginning to look like. And I think the baby wasn't Tolek's. Am I right, Christa? Are you protecting someone?"

She leans against the car for support.

"The police will find out the truth," I say.

"I don't want to speak to the police," she says.

"I can shield you from them. If you tell me."

She stares at me considering. "I promised Ania," she says, taking a deep breath.

"What did you promise?"

"I owe that to her and to her parents. They are grieving. They love Tolek . . ."

"So she *was* seeing someone else?"

A long silence.

"Please, Christa," I say.

And then she nods. It is slight, but it is still a nod.

"Who is he, the other man? Who are you protecting?"

"I'm not protecting anyone. I . . ." She gives her head an irritated shake, as if she has had enough. "I never see him. He was British, a kind man, Ania said. But he didn't kill her, I know that, or I would have told the police. He adored her. He treated her like a princess." She looks across the road. Jack is running back toward us. "Don't tell him!" she says, pointing with her chin. "So charming, men like him. I don't trust him. Promise me. *Gaby*."

"I . . . promise."

Jack, breathing heavily, reaches the car. "What did Tolek say before he ran off?"

Christa has got into her car.

"Christa?" he says, holding her door so she can't close it.

Her eyes flash in my direction. "No," she says. "He knew of no one who would hurt his Ania."

I can't wait to get away so I can think clearly, but Jack doesn't seem to want to move. He crosses the road again and watches as Tolek hauls the components of a discarded bathroom into the Dumpster, hurling slices of plasterboard and pieces of jagged porcelain as thick as human limbs as easily as if they were autumn leaves.

"Someone is lying," Jack says. "One of them is hiding something."

"I wish we spoke Polish."

"It would be a help," he replies seriously.

"I think I've seen him before," I say. "Do you?"

He shakes his head. "Nope."

I don't know what to do. The natural thing is to tell him what Christa told me, of course it is. But her car is still in the road—she is doing a three-point turn—I couldn't tell him immediately. I would have at least to wait a little while. She made me promise not to; and I can't help but wonder why.

"Come on, let's go. Get a coffee." I pull on his arm. He yields, and we walk round the bend until the house is out of sight.

"That temper," Jack says. "He just saw red. He exploded. If she was seeing someone else, got pregnant by him, I could imagine Tolek losing it in a jealous rage. If Perivale hasn't bothered to follow up on Marta, maybe he hasn't even checked to see if Tolek really was in Poland?"

"It's a possibility,"

"The money," Jack adds, "the new underwear . . . Does Tolek look like the Agent Provocateur type?"

"I don't know, Jack. Who is the Agent Provocateur type?"

He starts thrashing through ideas. "Maybe she was making financial demands, pushing him into working harder and harder to satisfy her expensive tastes. And then he found out she'd had a one-night stand and it wasn't even his baby."

"Possible."

"They do soup at Gail's," he says thoughtfully. "Chickpea and spinach, I think I noticed. As long as it's quite chunky. I like a chunky soup."

It occurs to me that perhaps Jack isn't always as absorbed by the next meal as he pretends to be, that maybe he talks about food when he is actually thinking quite hard about something else.

"If she was seeing another man," I add tentatively, "perhaps that man killed her."

He looks at me, then. There's a question in his eye, a flickering of doubt.

I am about to tell him. We are in the shade of spreading sycamores in fresh full leaf, bark peeling. A whiff of carbon dioxide. The repetitive howl of a train passing on the tracks beyond the road. But then I begin to imagine what he might do next—tear back to confront Tolek, chase after Christa, entangle us both more? Now she has told me, now I *know,* I want to let go. It's an instinct, a sense of self-preservation or something. Or perhaps I will tell him, but later, when I have thought through what to do next—take it to the police even—and when he has had a chance to calm down.

"Jack," I say. "It isn't feeling right, us talking about it, wondering about it. We should drop it, leave it to people who know what they are doing."

"I don't understand."

"It's what I was trying to say last night and earlier . . . on the phone."

He throws out his arms. "What the fuck?"

"I mean it."

"You started it, Gaby!" His face contorts. "You drew me into this."

We have reached the main road. Opposite us squats the black granite memorial to the victims of the Clapham Junction rail crash. Behind it is the railway, the same line that leads to the part of the common where I found Ania Dudek's body.

"I think I made a mistake."

He stares as if I have slapped him. "Who would have thought?" he says. "Is TV's Gaby Mortimer by any chance behaving erratically?"

All sorts of things are wrong. The meanness of his tone, and "TV's Gaby Mortimer." A low blow. I look at him. Perhaps Christa's right not to trust him. His eyes meet mine. I can't read his expression. He runs a finger and thumb through one eyebrow.

"Only teasing," he adds after a beat.

• • •

I leave Jack standing on the corner, on his own. "No soup?" he calls after me.

"No soup," I say, without turning round.

I walk very quickly, legs like scissors. I have an almost obsessive need to get home, to hunker down, to feel safe. I cut through the posh modern apartment building that abuts Fitzhugh Grove and cross the cricket pitch only feet away from where Ania's body lay. A movement in the bushes. A person? No, just a dog. I've been suppressing it, trying to, but the image of her battered neck, the superficially incised curvilinear abrasions, as Perivale called them, is suddenly so immediate I think I might be sick. I can't whistle, but I hum, throat vibrating, to chase the ghosts away. A man, a British man, Christa said, but she didn't know who. Does Tolek know? The trees close in. I start to run.

The café and its courtyard when I reach them are a bustle of mothers and nannies and small children, a bramble patch of bikes and scooters and dropped bread sticks.

The sky is a cerulean blue. Children dance. Spring has sprung without her.

No red-and-white police tape, not even a torn remnant ribboned in a branch. Nothing to show it happened here at all.

Perivale is sitting at the kitchen table, talking to Marta, when I get home. Fear presses into my chest. I should tell him what Christa told me. For God's sake, he should already know. It's on the tip of my tongue. All I have to do is open my mouth and let the words out. I would be free of this. But I promised Christa, and it's here, the information, inside me. I can use it anytime, when I need to, just perhaps not now. So instead, I do what I always do when I'm in a state. I become arch, study the situation over my shoulder, hold any real emotion at bay. "Ah. DI Perivale," I say. "Déjà vu."

He stands. I move forward as if to kiss him, once on each cheek, as if this were a social call. I pull myself back just in time. Marta, barefoot in leggings, slips past me at the door. Has he interrogated her properly?

"Sorry to intrude," he says. He is unshaven, white tips to his stubble. His jowls have aged faster than his scalp. "We have had a minor—" He breaks off. "You've had a haircut."

"Yes." I put my hand up to touch the new blunt ends. "Do you like it?" I don't know why I ask. It's just the question that came next.

"Certainly different."

"I will take that," I say, painfully coy, "as a compliment."

He gives a mock-courtly bow.

"Yes, as I was saying, we have had a minor development. I wondered whether you would mind coming down to the station."

It's not a question, it's a statement. A command. Could I say I *did* mind? Could I lie down on the floor, right here, and bang my head and scream until he went away?

"What sort of minor development?" I say. "Minor development like having found the killer?"

"Not in the Ania Dudek case, though things"—he tucks his polo shirt into the droopy waistband of his jeans, each stab conveying a certain self-satisfaction—"are progressing. Gone back to the flat, had another dig about. Most illuminating. More evidence in the pipeline."

"In the pipeline?" I say. "Didn't you look there first time round?"

"Very funny, I don't think," he says. "No, the minor development I refer to is in relation to your stalker. Another resident, a neighbor of yours, reported a person behaving oddly at around eleven AM, and one of my officers was dispatched in time to apprehend the alleged perpetrator. So if you're not *doing anything,* perhaps you could come down to the station for a look at the VIPER. I've got the car outside."

"The viper?" I say, surprised. It is an odd use of language. "As in 'viper in the nest'?"

"Video Identification Parade Electronic Recording system." Each word is like a poke in my side. "It's the database we use these days instead of the old-style ID parades."

"Who knew?" I say.

PC Morrow—*Hannah*—is at the front desk when we arrive. She waves at me, a little trill of her fingers, and calls, "Hiya!" I wonder if Perivale has any idea how disloyal she is, how much she's been spilling down at the café.

"Caroline Fletcher anywhere handy?" I ask Perivale as we parade the corridors.

"You don't need Caroline Fletcher," he says. "As you are the victim in this case, and not the suspect." He stops dead outside a room, peers in through a small square window. "Unless you insist."

"No, of course not. You're right. Why would I need Caroline Fletcher?" His hand is gripping my elbow in a manner that is not reassuring. Just being here brings it all back, the terror and the claustrophobia. My legs feel sodden with dread.

He pushes the door open. It's another of those small white cells, only this one has a desk, three chairs, and a computer. We sit down, and he fiddles about for a while. The red light above the CCTV camera on the wall blinks.

The door opens and PC Morrow scurries in, slinking into the third chair and mouthing, "Sorry, oops," over Perivale's head.

"Okay." Perivale has got the information he needs up, though the screen is murky and PC Morrow has to lean over and show him where the brightness button is before we can see clearly.

"Right," Perivale says, with a little extra pomposity to cover this blip in his technological prowess. "What you are about to be shown is a series of twelve short videos, each of a different person, face on and side view, matching the description you gave us of your stalker. Please study each video carefully and indicate to myself or PC Morrow if you see the man you recognize. This session is being filmed"—he points to the CCTV camera—"and voice recorded"—he points to a table in the corner—"to ensure neither myself nor PC Morrow influence your decision in any way."

"No coughing or nudging," I tell PC Morrow. "Got it?"

He sets the program in motion and I watch face after face shudder and spin across the screen. Short hair, squat features, wide faces. Millions of pixels. I wonder about the third. I am almost convinced by the fifth. I am losing confidence in my own memory by the eighth, but the ninth . . . "That's him," I cry. "That's definitely him."

"Percentage certitude?"

"Hundred percent," I say. My eyes bore into the screen. The stocky stance, the narrow forehead, the bellicose set of the eyes. I shudder. "Yes, hundred percent. It's the man who was outside my house, the man in the red Renault." Perivale clicks off the machine and stands up.

I ask him if I was right, but he tells me he doesn't know, that it isn't his case. He couldn't be in the room with me if it was. He will inform PC Evans, the officer in charge of this file, and someone will be in touch.

A spasm of unease. "So you don't know if there were any fingerprints on the DVD?"

"I can find out."

"And that man, do you know if he is in custody or—"

He winces. "He'll have been video recorded, possibly cautioned, and released."

"So. Yes. Okay."

I push my chair back and join him at the door. "I don't understand—if it's not your case, why did you come and get me? Why did you sit with me just now?"

Perivale pulls down on his speckled jowls. "Come on," he says. "Do you really imagine I would miss an opportunity to spend time with you?"

PC Morrow giggles nervously. I don't know what to say. All the jokes I've made, the "no coughing or nudging," is this what they have led to? This cringing stab at flirtation. Have I let him think he knows me? Or was Jack right? Is it just a sign of how misjudged this whole investigation is?

I'm so riled, I can hardly speak. "I wish I could say the feeling's mutual," I reply eventually.

Marta is back in the kitchen, standing at the island counter. Clara once said, in her experience (years of staff room coffee breaks), that people divide into two types: drains and radiators. Clara herself is a radiator: no question. Robin is a radiator. Marta is definitely a drain. I ask her if she saw anyone suspicious poking around this morning, and she shakes her head. "No. I see no one." She has been eating cereal and she puts her bowl in the dishwasher and the milk back in the fridge.

I watch her as she shifts around the kitchen, small, careful movements. She sits back down at the table, her eyes scanning a magazine. I decide, this time, to skip the preamble. "I was spring cleaning this week," I say, trying to smile, "and I had a little dust round your room."

Little dust. I can't even talk to her about this without making myself cringe.

She looks up, her eyes heavy.

"Found my jeans! They must have been put away there by mistake . . ."

She has flushed. She doesn't actually have to say anything, and I can see the struggle in her face. Finally, she says, "I'm sorry. I borrow them. I just see if they look good."

My heart softens slightly. "And did they?"

She looks down at the magazine. "No."

"Well, that's one mystery cleared up. The other thing, I couldn't help noticing all the envelopes and the box of receipts under your bed."

Her fingers spread a fraction on her mug. She is wearing black nail polish, with a diamanté star in the center of each nail, the sort of manicure that demands a nail bar or a beautician. The world seems to be shrinking to a few people, tight points on a graph.

"It's just, I wondered . . ." She is waiting tensely to hear what I am going to say. "I don't want you spending your own money on things like that," I conclude. "Sending things home or whatever. You know, let me pay."

Her face is rigid. "No," she says. "Don't pay. It's fine."

"But all those presents home."

"Not presents. They are not presents home. I sell." She puts down her mug, pulls the ends of her ponytail to tighten it. "I sell on eBay."

"On eBay?" I can feel myself getting closer. "What do you sell?"

"Just things."

I watch her carefully. "Things?"

"Things I find . . . things I buy cheap."

A haze clears. The screen brightens. You just have to find the right button. It is as clear as it is shocking. She has been taking my clothes, siphoning off the odd item here and there, stealing them.

It's a relief to sit down. My legs are leaden. "Did you sell anything to Ania Dudek?"

Her face closes. Her hands rest on the table, flat. "No."

Is she lying? "Do you know," I continue carefully, "I've got a big bag of clothes upstairs you could have. They're just going to charity otherwise. Keep the proceeds. You'd be doing me a favor."

She rubs under her eyes. "But . . ." she begins.

I am a little gratified to see the traces of mortification, a different sort of blush, higher on the cheeks. I should probably be outraged, but I am aware of a grudging respect. Was it so bad? I get sent so much. Some of those clothes still had their labels. I didn't even notice them gone.

"Did you tell the police about your eBay business?"

"No."

"Did they ask if they could see you again? Did Perivale ask you any questions earlier today?"

"No."

I lean back. "I'm baffled. All the evidence they have about Ania Dudek's murder is tied not to me but to *this house*. It could be anyone. Today, Perivale said he had dug up something *else,* though I've no idea what that is. It might not be connected. The peculiarity for me is, why aren't the police questioning you as much as me?"

She shrugs. "Perivale tell me. He know I am not the murder."

I find it harder than I imagine to put what I want to ask into words. "How do you know?" I say eventually.

"How do *I* know I am not the murder?"

I let out an involuntary laugh. "How do *you* know that *he* knows that you are not the murderer, yes."

"I know because I could not have done it. I was with another person the whole time."

"Do you mind me asking who?"

She starts telling me a story, and to begin with, I can't work out where it is going. It's about Millie and a bad dream and how the night Ania was murdered "Millie was frightened and came into my bed." Details land in my brain—Marta sang to Millie and told her stories about a chicken—but I don't know what to do with them. I don't hear how the story ends.

"Sorry? What did you say?"

"I said so I told the police I could not kill Ania Dudek, because I was with Millie all night."

But I'm still not really listening, or concentrating, because I don't care about that. I don't care who killed Ania Dudek. Or whose alibi Perivale has followed up and whose he hasn't. All I can think is that when Millie had a nightmare she went not to me, her mother, but to Marta; she curled into her back, tangled her limbs with hers. This woman, who may be complicated and a little bit deceitful, who may borrow my jeans and use my perfume, sung to my daughter the night Ania died and hugged her and kept her safe.

And for a moment that's all that matters.

When my mobile rings, I almost don't answer. I have been lying on my bed in semidarkness. Marta has gone to her evening class. Creaks and groans and rasping come from the walls. Traffic on Trinity Road is heavy tonight, or the wind is in the wrong direction. Every now and then, the house shudders. My thoughts have returned to turmoil, rationality subsumed by indecision and fear.

"Hi," Jack says. "I'm ringing to say I'm sorry."

I try to sound unconcerned. "What are you sorry about?"

"I'm sorry I was rude and insensitive."

"That's okay."

"Well, it's not, is it? I should never have called you 'TV's Gaby Mortimer.' You're not TV's Gaby Mortimer."

"Well, that's nice!"

"You know what I mean. You're more than just TV's anything."

"Thank you."

"I was being a cock."

"A cock?"

He laughs. "Do we not use the word *cock*?"

I smile. "Not if we can help it."

"Okay. I was being an arsehole."

I raise my eyebrows. "An arsehole?"

"Is that banned, too?"

"I don't know. Maybe."

"A tosser?"

"You can probably get away with tosser."

"It's just . . . I don't know . . ."

"What?"

"Well. You know. You're funny and sweet, and you are in trouble, and we seem to get on quite well, but one minute you want my help, and the next minute you don't."

Funny and sweet: the words are like daisies. I could reach down and pick them, turn them into a chain and hang them round my neck. It's such a long time since anyone has called me funny, or sweet. They seem like cheats, words from somewhere in the past. "I am sorry if I keep putting you in a bad mood," I say eventually.

"I was probably just hungry."

I smile. "Well, it had been at least ten minutes since you'd had something to eat."

"I wasn't that keen about the whole thing at first. To be honest, I thought I'd play along just to get you to give me the interview, but now . . . now I've got to know you, I want to sort your problems out. I really do. So I wish you'd let me." His voice is scratchily deep, as if he has a bad chest, or has just had a cigarette, a nice voice, the kind of voice a nice girl should fall for.

I caterpillar my head off the pillow so it is flat on the duvet. My feet dangle off the end. A small black dot comes into focus on the ceiling. It might be a tiny spider, or a fly, or it might just be a black smudge. Is it moving? Is the space between the black spot and the chandelier increasing or staying constant?

"Thank you," I say after a bit.

"You know, I was thinking. Christa knows something. I'm sure of it. We need to ask her if we can see Ania's diaries, Gaby, don't we? See if we can find out what was going on, dig up anything that might take the focus off you."

I should tell him now what Christa said about Ania's other man. But it has been a long day. I am ridiculously tired, too tired, even, to keep trying to clear my own name. What does it even matter anymore? And I'm liking this conversation now, as it is. Here is a man who knows I am in trouble and is desperate to help—unlike Philip. And maybe it's awful of me—I think fleetingly of that woman we had on the program once, who was recovering from Munchausen syndrome and had made up illness after illness in search of the sympathy and attention she had never had as a child. This is probably a sort of Munchausen's, keeping the information back for a bit, letting the warmth of Jack's concern lap over me. I wish I could say I don't tell him because I am keeping my word to Christa, battling with my conscience, but it's not that. It's wanting the focus, the solicitude on me, just for now. So no, not honorable. My motives are altogether more dubious.

"You okay?" he says.

"Yes." My voice is a squeak. "It's just the beginnings of a cold."

"Gaby, something is up. What is it?"

The black dot on the ceiling hasn't moved. It's not an alive thing at all. It's just a black dot, a smudge of dirt.

I give in to temptation—let him feel even more sorry for me than he already is. "The police have got new evidence. I don't know what it is. Perivale told me today when I . . . when I was down at the station."

"You were down at the station? Why were you down at the station?"

I let out a sigh. "A man was caught poking about outside my house this morning—the same one as yesterday. The police took him in, but they've released him."

"Have you locked all the doors?"

"Yes."

"Are you on your own?"

"Marta is at her evening class."

"I'm coming round."

A car engine idles outside the window. I let myself wonder when Philip last made me feel *looked after* like this. Ambition and drive: they can leave ordinary kindness behind. In the last few days, I have felt stripped down to something bare and ordinary, and Jack wants to take care of that ordinary, bare person. It stirs up doubts I don't know what to do with.

Jack says, "Do you want me to come round?"

There is a tone in his voice, in the seriousness of it, that makes me think about his hands, the span of them, the blunt shape of his fingers. I think about his face and how his moods flicker across it in such a simple, uncomplicated way. I reflect with impartiality on his body and how heavy it might be if he lay across me, the soft texture of his hair entangled in my fingers.

"I'm not doing anything," he says. "Stuck here on my own. Highlight of my evening was going to be a glass of cheap plonk and a takeaway pizza."

A glass of cheap plonk and a takeaway pizza. A flat above a launderette, bunk beds full of kids. If I hadn't met Philip, perhaps Jack is the sort of man I would have married. Perhaps he's even the sort of man Philip might have been, with a few more knockbacks, a little less success. Could Jack be my alternative ending?

WEDNESDAY

The bottom sheet is wrinkled and bunched; the duvet half across me, half off. My clothes lie twisted in a trail across the floorboards: my T-shirt and my bra, my everyday M&S pants inside my jeans. My armpits bear the salty dampness of fresh sweat.

The loo flushes, and he stands in the door to the bathroom, naked, his face ruddily tanned, his body lily white. He smiles and flops face forward across the bed. The mattress exhales.

"Hello," he says.

"Hello."

Extending his arm along my upper back, he rolls me over so we're spooned. His chin rasps against my neck; his mouth and nose nudge my naked nape. "I do like it short," he says. "I really approve."

"Well, I am glad," I say. "Your approval is obviously paramount."

He came directly from the airport, straight to the house, not the office. I can't remember when he last did that. The door, the thump of his bag, the cry of my name, and he was in the kitchen. I was eating cereal, and the spoon catapulted muesli and milk onto the table. There was no time to swallow my shock. He was just there, arms outstretched, an outpouring of anguish and emotion—half drunk, half jet-lagged; I don't know. A tide of hyped-up sentiment.

He decided to surprise me. As soon as his meetings were done and dusted, he had wanted to get home. It was all he cared about. There had been a boat trip planned—he had been keen to go, but . . . My mouth was squeezed into his shoulder, my whole body crushed. When I laughed, taken off guard, it came out like hiccups.

"I've got to see Millie," he said, pulling back.

"She's in Suffolk with Robin and Ian. I told you."

He arm-lengthed me for inspection. "Your hair!" he said. And then, careering straight into a speech I imagined him planning on the flight, the queue for passports, the taxi: "I'm sorry for everything, Gaby. I know you've been through hell. It's all going to be different. We'll start again. We'll do anything, go anywhere you want."

"Okay."

"What's happening with the police? Have they . . . ?"

"They haven't charged anyone yet."

"Have they left you alone?"

"Sort of."

"Thank God. And work? They gave you some time off?"

Did he really not know?

"Sort of," I repeated.

"Gabs. I'm so sorry about everything. Not just with . . . what's been happening to you, but with how I have been . . . I can't believe . . . Come here."

He pulled me to him. It was like a full-body massage. He wasn't himself. He was trying too hard. Marta was coming into the kitchen, and we exchanged a look of alarm. She backed up the stairs and disappeared. I heard her door shut and floorboards creak overhead.

"Do you not have to go to the office?" I asked.

"No. They can give me a bloody day off."

"Have you been drinking?"

"Just those minibottles of rioja on the plane."

"Have you slept?"

"Gaby, I am in full control of my faculties."

He sat on the edge of the table, his trousers wrinkled from travel, the same handsome, youthful Philip. But I just looked at him. It was peculiar. I felt detached. I didn't even feel angry anymore. It had calcified into something duller. I couldn't put my finger on it. This was everything I had longed for, but it felt wrong, off-key, *too late*. I had got through all this on my own, without him, and it had changed something. I didn't know if I could change it back. Was all this outpouring of emotion about *me,* or was it actually more about *him*? And a "boat trip?" That was worth *mentioning*? He kept talking, a stream of words: "I buggered off to the other side of the world, despite your trauma. I wasn't here to support you when the police were badgering you . . ."

"Arresting me, in fact."

"You kept it together, as you always do."

"I spent a night in a cell. Philip. In a cell!"

"Oh my God. They kept you in? Overnight?"

"Yes." Surely he knew this? "A whole night."

He takes a sharp intake of breath. "Was it awful?"

"Actually," I decide to say "it was fine. I survived."

"You poor darling. I don't deserve you." I noticed a vein in the delicate skin under one of his eyes. "I'm a worthless piece of shit."

"Be careful with the self-flagellation," I said, "or it might start being about you again."

He turned his head a fraction and pressed his fingers between his eyes, pushing down on the bridge of his nose.

The familiarity of the gesture stirred something in me. Philip always does this, grip his nose, when he is tired—as if he thinks he can squeeze the tiredness out. I moved toward him and kissed him full on the mouth, which is a place that had felt out of bounds for a while. I was trying it out for size. He spread his palm across the back of my head. I could feel the pressure of his teeth against my lips. Then he took my hand and pulled me out of the kitchen, past Marta's closed door, and up the stairs to our room.

His body is as familiar to me as my own. I know where the bones protrude and the skin has begun to wrinkle, where a mole has grown and where muscles have firmed. I was shy at first—the mortification of sex after a period without, the *embarrassment*—but it was not like Brighton. A part of me looked down, imagining the conversation I might have with Clara. Words like *engaged, attentive, considerate.* I could feel the force of Philip's emotion. It wasn't passion precisely; it was something different.

I turn, a dolphin flipping, to study his face. His stubble is white-tipped, paler on the chin than above his mouth, a bit like Perivale's, though that's a thought I wish I hadn't had. Skin flaking on the side of his nose, the odd hair that needs plucking. An age spot blooms on his temple—is that new? The smell of peppermint.

"You've brushed your teeth," I say. "Cheat."

"I was in the bathroom and I saw my advantage!" He looks at me seriously. "I'm going to make an effort, Gaby."

"Starting with teeth."

"Starting with teeth."

I consider him for a moment.

Philip sneezes suddenly, as if the attention is too intense. "Sorry. Hay fever."

He sneezes again, and this time makes the conductor thing with the invisible baton. Something tweaks in my heart, when he does that, deep in the muscle.

I prop myself up on my elbow. "We have become very distant," I say.

"I know." He slips down next to me, folds a pillow into a bolster behind his shoulders, gazes into my eyes. "So while I was away, tell me everything that happened. Go through everything. So the police kept you in, the bastards, and then decided to leave you alone, thank God. What else?"

I open my mouth to speak, but I close it again. I don't know where to start. I should want to tell him everything, shouldn't I? It should all come gushing out, and I should cry and he should comfort me and beat himself up again for not having been here. He'll be horrified when he hears the details—how intimidating the police were, how sinister Perivale's obsession, how menacing the stalker, how bloody lonely a custody cell is at night. I fantasized about this moment at the beginning, imagined the guilt Philip would feel, how perhaps he might love me a tiny bit more. But something fundamental has changed. I don't know where to begin. I feel as if I am treading water in a storm.

Eventually, I say, "Work hasn't been great actually."

"I thought they had given you a few days off to recover?"

He seems genuinely not to know. Perhaps I have maligned him. I half laugh. "Not sure that's quite how I would put it."

I start to explain about Terri's awkwardness on the phone, the leaks to the press, the fact no one will return my calls, the conviction I have that they have pushed me out. I'm aware as I am talking that this isn't what really matters, but it seems easier somehow, for now, than telling him about anything else.

"They can't do that," he says.

"Everyone's expendable, Philip."

"We'll fight, don't you worry. I'll get on to Steven at Witherspoons. If they won't have you back, it'll be unfair dismissal, plus defamation of character. They don't stand a chance against Steven. He'll have Terri fired within the week."

Here it is. Philip back and fighting for me. Why don't I feel better? Also I don't want Terri *fired*. As a response, it's so bullish, so lacking in empathy, so *him*.

He strokes my hair. I have to fight the instinct to pull away.

"Tell me about your trip," I say.

He leans back, fiddles with the pillow to make himself more comfortable. He talks about going long and going short and the importance in the current market of being trade orientated, of meetings with CEOs and optic companies, and the effect of fraud and the tanking of shares. It is a bit like his lovemaking. He continues to deploy engagement and consideration. He is attentive in the retelling.

"Meet any interesting people?" I ask. "Eat any good food?"

"Few posh restaurants, lot of wining and dining, mainly international." He shrugs, and for a moment I think about how Jack would have answered—some forensic description of a bean curd mee goreng probably.

"My poor darling," he says.

My poor darling.

Philip yawns, shakes his head as if clearing his ears. He slips down. His eyes half close. He is not going to ask any more, I realize, about my ordeal. His hand is stroking my leg. I'm wondering whether to tell him now about the stalker, *I've Been Watching You 2,* the VIPER at the police station, when my mobile rings. It's in the pocket of my jeans, and they vibrate against the floor as if harboring a creature.

"Leave it," Philip says.

"It might be Millie."

I lean over, dig my hand into the pocket, and bring the phone to my ear just in time.

"Gaby!"

"Oh, hello." I should have left it. I don't want to speak to Jack now.

"I need to meet you," he says. "Can I come round? Something big has happened."

I am already half over the bed, the mattress pressing into my stomach, and I slither a tiny bit farther, dig my elbow into the floor for balance. "It's not ideal timing," I say brightly. "My husband has just returned from a business trip. Can it wait?"

"He's back? Philip is back? No. It can't. It's really urgent."

"Urgent? Really?" I turn and ham disbelief at Philip, who rolls his eyes.

"Okay. Look, I'll tell you quickly. I've just been back to Christa's flat. I begged to see Ania's journals. She was cagey, but I got to the bottom of it. She's basically not paying any tax, petrified of being deported. I had to go on a full-out charm offensive, telling her I'd sort it out with HM Revenue and Customs for her while vaguely threatening to inform on her if she didn't play ball. Not pretty, but needs must."

"That sounds a bit brutal."

"Thing is, Gaby, it worked. She agreed to show me, though they are in Polish, so it's not that much of a help. Anyway, the point is—"

"Yes. I'm not sure any of those times is convenient," I say.

Philip has started kissing my toes.

"Gotcha. Listen, I did get Christa to check. Last year—the thirteenth of August, two thirty PM. Your name, your address. It's in her diary, Gaby. She *did* come for an interview. It's down there. You might have forgotten, but you did see her, Gaby. It's written in her diary. She came to your house."

As soon as I can, I throw on some clothes and go downstairs to make tea. I tell Philip I will brew it properly—warm the pot and let it steep. "None of your dipping in and out, your squeezing against the side," I say, "your casual, callous treatment of a tea bag."

"Steep away," he says lazily. "I'm going to have a shower, try and wake myself up. Got to keep going or I'll never sleep tonight."

I stand in the kitchen and look about me. I'm getting my bearings. I mustn't panic. I mustn't hurry. My cereal bowl has been cleared from the table. The J-cloth hangs in a wet rectangle over the arch of the tap. The kettle is hot to the touch. Marta is obviously still in the house, though I can't hear any sounds.

I put the kettle on and start searching. Last year's household diary: it was a pale blue Smythson with gold-crinkled silk pages—a present from the big cheeses at work. I can visualize it, almost reach it in my mind. Did I give it to the police? No, they never asked about it.

It isn't in the pile of books by the TV and it isn't on the shelves in the sitting room, or nestling among Millie's grade two piano music.

The pump for the hot water emits its whistling metallic crank; the pipes in the wall begin to hum.

I start spinning from surface to surface. I'm not so calm now. Has it been recycled? Did we throw it away? Could it be in the bedroom? Have I time, while he is in the shower, to run back upstairs and look?

Then an image, a visual memory: Jack picking up a book and putting it back, running his fingers along the spines. And yes, there it is—not hidden, not buried, but on display, lined up neatly alongside the shiny cookbooks Philip's mother gives me in hope, every Christmas, just sitting there between *Jamie at Home* and Claudia Roden's *The Food of Spain*.

A spider is curled on the upper spine. I blow it off. The leather cover smells of dust and cooking grease. The pages are soft as butter.

I find the page: Saturday 13 August. The date is filled with scrawls. Millie had a gym competition in Dagenham—"Warm-up 8:30 AM. Main event 9:15 AM Izzie's mother taking"—and a party in the afternoon—"Harriet Pugh's 8th: Sammy Duder Pottery, Webb's Road, 4–6 PM." I've scribbled, "<u>BUY PRESENT!!!!</u>" in underlined capitals across the space, too, so it's not surprising this other thing got missed. No writing, just the vague dent of pencil marks long erased. You have to hold the book up to catch the light to make them out. No name, no details, just a shape "2:30 PM: AD"—hidden in all these other hieroglyphics.

I stare at it. It comes in and out of focus. I flick the pages back. The previous week is full of neat, firmly penciled numbers and letters. On Monday is written "6:30 PM: CS. 7 PM: PT." The Armenian from Croydon and the off-to-uni-any-minute student. On Tuesday, it says, "7 PM: NM. 7:30 PM: NS. 8 PM: PB." The nondriver, the male South African, and the lovely Portuguese with no English. Then on Wednesday, "5:30 PM: MB." Marta Biely, a competent, well-rounded Polish nanny with excellent references.

I had spoken to Robin on the way to the hospital to see my mother. I remember that. I asked her to call off my appointments for the week, reschedule a dinner and a trip to the dentist. She said she would sort it. I could leave it in her hands. She was preoccupied with the wedding, though—some last-minute hitch: the chairs in the marquee were too wide. Had she tried to get through to Ania and then failed? Had she never got to even that? Had Ania come all the same?

I slide the diary back in between the cookbooks. This is everything and nothing. It is not *proof*. Explanations: they're just out there, waiting to be plucked.

I think about the week my mother died. Those last few months were a fresh kind of hell. Police. Doctors. Interventions. Vodka decanted into vases. Miniatures in the medicine cabinet. Inappropriate men passed out on the sofa. Philip, who had found my mother "such a character," was nauseated by the raw savagery of it. I didn't make him do anything he didn't want to do. I went to the hospital that last time on my own. Her skin was jaundiced, the whites of her eyes like yolks. Her bloated fingers shuffled invisible cards. She had picked at the sores on her arms and the scabs on the backs of her hands until they bled. Her abdomen was distended beneath the sheet. When she vomited into the kidney-shaped bowl I held, blood ran from her nose like snot.

She told the nurses I had set upon her, pulled her hair, beaten her black and blue. "An unnatural daughter," she spat. I stroked her back until she slept. When she woke, she vomited black clots.

Philip wasn't with me when she died. "My darling," he said on the phone the following day, "my poor darling." He sent flowers, a neat posy of carnations and alstroemeria. He was late for the funeral, came straight to the crematorium from "a work thing," tiptoed in.

The kettle clicks off and I jump. The hot-water pump jolts and quiets. I hear the overflow hissing down the pipes in the wall.

I have started pouring water into the teapot when the phone rings. The cradle on the side table in the snug corner of the kitchen is empty—the receiver is by the bed upstairs—but the spare one is buried in the sofa cushions. When I press the button to answer, I think I hear a distant click.

"Hello, Mum! We're at a service station. I'm having lunch and it's not even lunchtime. Sausages, and what do you think is nicest: chips, sauté or buttery mash? I'm going for chips because Robin says they probably don't use real butter."

"More like I Can't Believe It's Not Buttery Mash," I say. I had forgotten. Millie and Robin. It's Wednesday. Ob-gyn. Millie is on her way home. I'm about to see Millie. "Or. Margariney Spread Mash."

"Really disgusting anyway. Have you recorded *House of Anubis*? Robin and Ian don't have Nickelodeon and I have to find out what happened. I *need* to, Mum."

"Mills?"

"Hang on. Robin wants to talk to you."

"Millie. Can I ask you something?"

"Okay."

I walk with the phone to the window. "Can you remember

back to last summer, the weekend I was with Granny in hospital, the weekend before you were a bridesmaid at Robin's wedding?"

"Ye-es," she says doubtfully.

Most of the garden is in shadow, but the camellia is still out. "You had a gym competition in the morning and Harriet Pugh's decorate-your-own-pottery party in the afternoon."

"The one where they spelled my name wrong on the back of the plate I made and we weren't allowed to do penguins. I really wanted to do a penguin, with a bow tie. They were so cute."

"In between those things, do you remember a tall pretty woman with long red hair coming for an interview to be your nanny?"

Movement in the hornbeams.

"Yes," Millie says.

A squirrel trapezes to the bird feeder under the apple tree. "Yes?"

"Yes. She was really nice. She said she could do a cartwheel, but she was tricking. Daddy made her a coffee with the new Nespresso machine and he burned the milk."

I sit down heavily on the bench. A dog in a distant garden barks.

I speak to Robin on autopilot. They are aiming to arrive at some time or another. They are expecting something. Robin has to be somewhere at some point.

If Ania came and Philip saw her, made her coffee, why did he keep quiet?

Robin is still speaking and I must have responded in the way that's expected, because she has said good-bye and hung up.

I dial Jack. It doesn't ring but goes straight to voicemail.

I put the phone down and groan out loud.

"What's up?"

Philip is standing in the doorway in my dressing gown, his hair wetly slicked back from his face, his cheeks pinkly shaved. Damp prints darken the steps behind him. "You okay?"

I try and smile. He turns his back and starts opening cupboards, finding frying pans and cutlery. "I met Marta on the stairs," he says over his shoulder. "I gave her thirty quid and sent her out for the day so we can have the house to ourselves. I'm going to make my wife breakfast." He has his face in the fridge, arms out to each side, as if he is stretching out a leg muscle. "Not that there's much here: eggs, manky cheese, one onion, carrots . . . An omelet *à la* Philippe."

As he removes the items one by one, he makes a face at me, sort of "tra la la, aren't I clever?" I manage to say, "Aren't you clever?" I join him at the counter, and while he melts butter and sautés the onion and beats eggs, I take a frozen loaf of Hovis out of the freezer and chip away two slices to make toast. I find the Nespresso capsules and fill the back of the machine with water and scrub away the scorched deposits in the base of the milk frother. I'm trying hard to think, but my brain is racing, spinning, the wheels not touching the ground.

Over on the table, my phone rings and vibrates.

"Don't answer it," Philip says. "Ring them back later. Look." He shows me his empty hands, the empty pocket of my dressing gown. "BlackBerry-free!"

"You've actually left it upstairs?"

"Well, not exactly. It's in the hall, just about in earshot, but I'm not holding it, not clasping it to my bosom. Small steps, Gabs, small steps."

It's the old, self-mocking Philip.

"Okay."

I sit and eat my eggs, conscious of the scraping of my fork on the china, trying to behave normally. I tell him about Millie and Robin, how they will be here in the next couple of hours. I watch his face. Did he pick up the phone upstairs and already know this? He covers it well if so. He looks delighted—his expression brightens and expands. I think of balloons filling with air, the paper sea horse Millie got for her birthday that grew to ten times its own size in water. "My little girl," he says.

"Is it possible Ania Dudek came for an interview here last summer?" I say suddenly. "The dead girl. Are you sure you haven't forgotten some small thing, her coming here by mistake, you know . . . ?

"No. No, of course not. Why?"

"Oh, nothing. Just something Millie said."

He would remember if he made coffee and if she did, or didn't do, a cartwheel.

When, at last, his BlackBerry chirps in the hallway, he looks at me, with his head on one side, his mouth twitching. I nod. I pretend to be reluctant. "Go on," I say. "You know you want to." He moves to the sink, plops his plate in, reties the belt of the dressing gown, and disappears out of the room.

"Clive," I hear him say, his voice getting closer again. "Yup . . . Yup . . . okay. Yes." He is back in the kitchen. "Okay. Run it past me."

I twist the top of the plastic Hovis bag and return the loaf to the freezer, rearranging the frozen peas to make room. I slide my hands into Marta's "satin touch" latex gloves to wash out the frying pan.

Philip is trying to catch my eye. "Twenty minutes," he mouths. I nod.

"So who else are you showing it to?" He leaves the kitchen, but he doesn't go downstairs. I hear the sitting room door open and close.

I listen for a while to Philip's voice coming in and out of earshot as he paces the sitting room, churning out those mathematical calculations that come to him so easily, that drown out everything else. And after a few minutes, when I am sure he is absorbed, I slip down to the basement.

His drawers are a foreign country. Files, in his neat writing, labeled TAX AND VAT AND DIVIDENDS. A sheaf of clippings from newspapers—articles on optic multinationals. Pens, staplers, loops of white wire, bluntly ending in USB connections, headphones in a tangle, spare chargers. A sudden sharp pain in my thumb: a loose staple piercing.

Last drawer down: passports, old and new, driver's licenses, a boxed file of photographic negatives, a plastic folder of muddled receipts and guarantees. The manual for the fridge, Philip's Nikon, a "present" to himself from his last trip, hardly used.

As I search, I think about Philip and the kind of person he is, the kind of person who is vigilant with his possessions, who, unlike me, files away all documentation, keeps it safe in case the item breaks or doesn't fit, holds on to every guarantee in the event of electrical fire, or flooding, or something going wrong. He's careful and meticulous, not wild or impassioned. This is what I am thinking when a small piece of white paper, shuffled between the receipt for the Krups titanium Nespresso machine and the Weber 5-Burner gas barbecue, slips into my fingers. It is a long, curled-up receipt, figure totted upon figure, dated last December. Agent Provocateur.

Love. That's the range. A Love bra and a Love thong, a Love basque and a Love slip. A whole lot of Love. It's all about love in the end.

I force myself to breathe. Sometimes the intensity of an emotion can be so overpowering you can hardly move.

I throw it back into the file and I stuff that file back into the drawer. The moment the receipt isn't in my hand, I'm not sure anymore. Those undies he bought me? For my birthday or was it Christmas? They were from Myla, weren't they, from the shop round the corner from his office? Quick dash at lunchtime. Maybe even by his secretary. Or have I got that wrong? Were they Agent Provocateur? A trek across town. A labor of love. Maybe they were. Can I explain it all away?

I have put the other files back in the drawer on top, and I try now to push it closed, but it won't go all the way; something is stuck behind. I put my hand in, at the back, squeeze it down behind the drawer and bring it out again. A gold chain dangles from my fingers. It's tarnished, and a link is broken—I think I snapped it myself. A small round pendant nestles in the palm of my hand: St. Christopher shouldering his infant burden. A fugitive thought: do saints go out of fashion? They're so rarely worn these days. Except, of course, Ania wore one.

I take an enormous breath. It's more like a shudder. Then, with abnormal calm, I shut the drawer and stand up. I cross the room quietly on the balls of my feet and pause at the bottom of the stairs. His voice is getting closer. Is he on his way down here? I duck into the gym. Nautilus machines hulk across the room. I listen hard. He isn't on the stairs, or near them. He's turned back. He's still talking on the phone—wandering from room to room. I lean on the running machine to think. I can see the window from here, crisscrossed by iron grating, a patch of sky, a crown of tree.

I make a decision. I am going to go upstairs as if nothing has happened, and get out of the house as quickly as I can. But I am still holding the St. Christopher. There's a hole at the bottom of the running machine where a pair of rectangular rods lead from each footrest into deep hollows—it's dark in there; in any other circumstances, you wouldn't want to risk your fingers. I stuff the necklace into the space and then leave the room and run back into the kitchen. Philip is in the sitting room, still on the phone, barking commands. By the sound of it, he's sitting on the piano stool. Our plates and coffee cups are still by the sink. They could go in the dishwasher, but I need something to do with my hands. Plunging them into scalding water is a start.

Philip must hear the taps running. I hear him padding down the steps and then he is in the room. He makes a face and a winding-up gesture with his free hand and then he pins the BlackBerry to his shoulder with his chin and comes up behind me and puts his arms round my waist. "So their position again?" he says.

My own hands are in the water. I am scrubbing and scraping at the pattern on his plate.

"Yup," he says. "We'll go with that. We'll decide when to sell later. Bye."

He hangs up, slips the phone into the dressing gown pocket, and rest his chin on the top of my head. A pointed weight. If he leaned any harder, my vertebrae would crumble, my head would be forced into my neck. I am not sure that I can move, but I manage to bring my soapy hands out of the suds.

"Things will change," he says slowly.

"Do you mean that, Philip?" I peel off the latex gloves and wriggle so I can turn to face him. "Five-year plan and all that? Are you talking Suffolk? Bees and blackberry jam and village schools?"

A beat. A pause. Two seconds of betrayal. He has no intention of moving to Suffolk.

"We'll talk about it," he says.

If only he'd been honest.

I can't keep it in. "Are you absolutely certain Ania Dudek didn't come here? Such a small thing to forget, in our busy old lives?"

"I told you. No. She didn't. For fuck's sake." He steps back, takes the phone out of the dressing gown pocket, and slams it on the counter.

I turn to the sink again and take out the plug. The water circles and disappears. I wipe my hands on a tea towel, the same one I threw to Jack. For some reason, I think about DNA, and whether this tea towel is steeped in his. "I'm going to nip to the supermarket, buy milk and food," I say curtly. "I've got nothing to give Robin or Millie. Any requests?"

He is rubbing his eyes now. "Can you get some antihistamines? Pollen count seems high."

"Of course."

"Gaby?"

"What?"

He is looking at me with a peculiar expression on his face. "Nothing."

I grab my purse, force my feet into shoes, and leave the house.

The silver Mondeo is parked on the other side of the road. I cross right by it to reach my car. Perivale is hunkered down in there today, just sitting. I should feel reassured, but I don't. I know I should knock on the window and climb inside, but I'm not ready. Instead, I walk by quickly, his eyes on my back, and get into my own car. I have the urge to drive and drive, to put my foot down, to get far away from here. I make the short trip to Waitrose. I park the car and walk the aisles in a daze. At the checkout, I pay for items I don't even remember picking up: a chicken, a bag of salad, two liters of milk, a bunch of purple alliums, a bar of chocolate, a couple of packets of Benadryl.

In the parking lot, I sit with my forehead resting on the steering wheel and my eyes closed. I'm being so calm. It's extraordinary. I almost want to laugh. Who knew?

I am holding Christa's card—South London Beauty Services—and I dial the number.

There's a long silence after I tell her who I am. "I thought you might call," she says eventually.

"So Jack came to see you this morning," I say.

"Yes. He bought me flowers and more cakes from that café. I . . ."

"I thought you didn't trust him, thought he was too charming."

"He tell me he wants to make things right for you, and he will help me with the tax office."

"But you promised Ania—"

"As Jack said, she is dead. You are alive. And the police they want to put you in prison. Jack told me you had a little girl and . . ."

"So you translated a bit of her diary?"

"He says it was just to clear your name. And I didn't want him to let it be taken away. She has written personal stuff . . ."

"I can understand that."

"But he was so persuasive, Gaby. He made me feel so bad. He said I could be prosecuted for interfering with police enquiries, for withholding information."

The parking lot is filling. "I don't understand. You mean, you *did* give Jack the diary? He has it now?"

"I didn't know what to do."

"Did you tell him about Ania's lover?"

"No . . ."

"But it will be in the diary. And if Jack takes it to the police, which he will, her parents will find out, you realize that?"

She sounds tired. "I do my best for Ania. I don't know what is right."

"Okay," I say. "Thank you, Christa. As long as you are sure."

"You are a good woman," she says. "Kind. You care about Ania."

Vibrations. A woman in a 4x4 has pulled up next to me and rolled down her window. She taps on mine. "You leaving?" she shouts.

"Not quite yet," I mouth.

The woman tuts, rolls her eyes, annoyed.

I have three missed calls from Jack. "Where are you?" he says, when I get through. "Can you meet me?" His voice is low, full of import.

I interrupt before he can say anything else and tell him that Ania did come for an interview at the house but that she didn't see me. She saw Philip, but he doesn't "remember."

"That's very odd, Gaby—"

I need to tell him what I have found out as calmly as I can. Now. Before he says anything, before I scream. "There's more. Christa confirms that Ania was seeing another man and that he had got her pregnant, not Tolek."

"I know. Gaby—"

I keep going. "I've found an Agent Provocateur receipt in Philip's drawer, and the St. Christopher, the one the police are looking for. He had it. She gave it to him, or he took it. He'd hidden it at the back of his drawer. The St. Christopher. The missing St. Christopher." I sound hysterical. "The other man. It's Philip. Philip is the other man."

"Where are you?"

"I'm at Waitrose."

"You're at *Waitrose*?"

"It all makes sense, Jack. If Philip was having an affair with Ania, nipping round there all the time—the Asics mud-shavings from our front garden, the pizza receipt. He'd have picked up my card without thinking . . ." I break off. My PIN: 2503. Our wedding anniversary.

"And the newspaper clippings—she'll have had an obvious interest in you if she was having an affair with your husband."

"The clothes." My voice cracks. Not bought in Fara, not sold to her by Marta. Presents from Philip. I imagine him flicking through my wardrobe for little garments that might suit.

"I'm ten minutes away," he says. "I am coming to find you, now. We'll go to the police together. We'll take Christa's diary. Get someone to translate it."

"No, don't . . ."

"We have to. If Philip is the killer . . ."

"We don't know that. I'm trying to work it out in my head. He could have been Ania's lover without *murdering* her. I mean, couldn't he? I can't imagine it. It's not possible. I know Philip better than I know myself. He's not a killer."

"So if he was just her lover . . ."

"'Just' her lover." I laugh again. It's not my best laugh.

"If he was 'just' her lover, why didn't he come forward, Gaby, when you were arrested? An innocent man would have done that. I'm sorry, I don't like it. I'm coming to find you."

"I just can't believe he killed her. *Why??*"

"Maybe she was threatening to tell you."

"His alibi. He's got an alibi."

"Alibi or no alibi, of course he killed her. It's the obvious explanation. I mean, how cast-iron is an alibi that crosses a whole night—that gets passed like a baton among secretary and colleague and waiter? I've heard about his statement. He used the gym in the office basement, supper at Nobu, drinks at the Dorchester. In that city crowd, who notices who's there, who isn't?"

I close my eyes. Philip's Parlee Z2: how proud he is of its streamlined speed. Office to home in less than fifteen minutes. A jiffy. A flash. Two shakes of a lamb's tail.

"It could still be Tolek," I say. "He could have been lying about Poland. I mean, it could still be him. In a jealous rage. I mean . . . I'm not going to go to the police until I know more. They don't need to know anything unless Philip killed her. I don't want Millie being put through hell otherwise. The press outside the house again. She's coming back today. She'll be home any minute."

"Gaby, come on." His voice is patient. "It's evidence. I'm sorry. The police have to know one way or another. And if Philip did do it, you're not safe. For Christ's sake, he might even have tried to frame you."

"Perivale mentioned new evidence. I wonder what that is."

"I'll get on to Morrow, see if I can put the screws on her."

"Do anything to find out. Sleep with her if necessary."

"Steady on," he says.

We both laugh. Or I think I laugh. Perhaps I cry.

"Give me a few hours. There must be some other explanation." I'm begging now. "I have to hear it with my own ears. Trust me, Jack. Please."

. . .

The house is empty. No sound at all. As quiet as the grave. The sort of stillness that settles about your ears like muffs.

I move to the foot of the stairs to listen for a voice, a creak. An envelope with my name on it lies on the bottom step. Philip's writing. He has left me a letter.

The back of the envelope isn't sealed, or even tucked in. The shiny strip of glue is unused. Two folded sheets of paper inside. I sit down and open them.

> Dear Gaby,
> I thought I could carry on without telling you the truth, but I can't. I have to tell you everything or it is all worthless. Nothing means anything. Is it cowardice to write this in a letter? Well, I am a coward.
> Ania did come to the house for an interview. I should have told you, but it was the weekend your mother died. And it turned out you had given the job to Marta anyway. And it went out of my mind. It didn't seem important.
> I bumped into her on the common a couple of days later. I was on my way home from work on my bike and I nearly knocked her over, just beyond the bridge, where the cycle path ends. I felt guilty because I had never got back to her about the job and I ended up buying her a cup of coffee. I walked her home.
> We started an affair. There, I've written it down. I can't unwrite it.
> We didn't mean to fall in love. I should lie and say I didn't love her, but I did. I have to be honest. I owe her that. When she told me she was pregnant, I didn't know what I thought or felt. I never intended to leave you and

Millie. This was something of a bonus. Lots of men at work see people on the side. I played for time. I told her I needed to find the right moment to tell you. I didn't know what to do. When she thought she'd lost the baby, I think I was almost glad, as if the decision was being made for me.

I felt sick, Gaby, torn in half. I was tortured by the thought of you finding out.

This is not the place to write about her death, her murder, the horror of which I am sure I am responsible for in some way. She was a woman who inspired great passion. And if—

The rest of this sentence is crossed out.

Gaby, I didn't kill her. I promise you that on my life. I don't know how to make you believe me, but I did not kill her. I could never have killed her.

I turn to the second page. His tears have fallen on the paper and in places the ink has smudged. He used a fountain pen, and proper stationery—watermarked Basildon Bond and a Montblanc nib for letters of condolence and adulterous confessions.

The grain on the second page is thicker—he's used the wrong side of the paper—and the writing is spikier. There are only a few lines left:

I can't go on lying anymore. It is a terrible thing I have done, and I don't know what else to do or say. I am so sorry, my darling. I only hope that in time you will forgive me.

Philip

I fold the two sheets of paper and return them to the envelope. Then I lay the envelope down next to me on the bottom stair. A window is open somewhere. A cold draft brushes my neck.

The Waitrose bag is still at my feet and I pick it up. The plastic handles dig into my fingers as I take it into the kitchen and place it on the counter. I put the food away, arrange the alliums in a vase. Philip's medicine I leave on the counter.

The phone goes and I answer it, unthinking. It's someone calling themselves PC Evans. I vaguely recognize the name. "I have some bad news, I'm afraid," he says. "DI Perivale asked me to bring you up to speed with the case."

"The case?"

"Unfortunately, the DVD you supplied had no recoverable prints apart from your own. As for the suspect you identified on VIPER, he is a news reporter with the *Sunday Mirror*. We've had a word with him, told him not to be such a silly bugger. They're all scum, I'm afraid. Not much else we can do."

"Okay," I say.

Then I walk slowly upstairs.

Philip is scrunched up on our bed, his face entombed in the pillow. He is wearing new shoes. The price tag is still stuck to one of the soles.

For a fraction of a second, I think he is dead. I stand in the doorway, considering him. Then I kneel down and say his name, and he turns his face to me, blotched and red and tear stained, eyes squeezed by swollen skin, a ruin of a face.

"Philip," I say again, and like a desperate child conceding need, he pulls himself up and buries his head in my chest and sobs. His hands claw at my top. Is it grief for the girl, or anguish at his actions, or guilt, or fear at what I might say? I don't know. All and nothing. His body is racked. A creature, not a man. I can't quite bear it at first—*we didn't mean to fall in love*—but after a few minutes, I touch him. First his hair and then his shoulders. The strokes are light, then firm, like a massage. I knead the anguish out of him. Pity like a small caged bird beats inside me.

Time passes. His shudders slow and then stop.

When he raises his head, he shields his eyes with his hand so I can't look at him. Gingerly, I lift his hand away.

"I've made your shirt all wet," he says in a small voice.

"Budge up."

He moves over, and I lie next to him. We stare at each other.

"I'm so sorry, Gaby. I'm so sorry for everything."

He says sorry again and again.

I interrupt: "Why didn't you tell me?"

"It was an *affair*. I thought you didn't need to find out. Everyone at work has affairs. I just thought . . ."

"You just thought?"

"I thought I could get away with it." He groans. "Pete Anderson once told me a little extramarital is something extra, a treat for working so hard, a perk of the job."

My stomach turns. "But you were in love with her?"

He lets out a noise, a strangulated moan. "I don't know. I wasn't going to leave you. I would never have left you and Millie. I got in out of my depth." He has stopped crying, taken control of himself now. "She reminded me of you. As you were when we first met, so fiercely independent, so determined to put the past behind you and make something of yourself."

He is gazing at me with tenderness.

"She even bit the corner of her lip the same way you used to—half confident, half desperately insecure. The day she was in the kitchen, when your mother was ill, she was so sweet with Millie. I . . ."

"When I asked why you didn't tell me, I meant when she *died*, Philip. How could you not have told me then? How could you have kept it to yourself? I just don't understand."

He closes his eyes. "I was terrified. Gaby? Please. Listen to me. I didn't know that the dead woman, the body you—*my wife*—had found was Ania until the police came to my office. I thought it was a teenager. You told me it was a teenager."

"I didn't. I said 'a girl.' You misunderstood."

"I almost passed out when the policewoman told me her name. I had been worried about her. She hadn't been answering her phone. I hadn't seen much of her for a week or two. She'd been in Poland for a wedding. I was supposed to have gone to her flat, but then you threw that date night at me. I'd been trying to ring her, I had been round there . . . I never imagined . . . I got through the police interview—it was you they were worried about, not me, they had no idea. I could see the policewoman giving me funny looks—I was sweating; I told her I had eaten something dodgy. They took my alibis and they went away. I was sick in the loo, Gabs, really, I just couldn't . . . And then I just got on my bike and cycled. I didn't know where. I spoke to you from the middle of Hyde Park, told you I was still at the office. I was in shock. I didn't know what to do with myself. I waited until I knew you'd be asleep before I came home."

"I saw you that night downstairs, at your desk. You looked as if you were working."

"I was dying."

"So you lied to me, and you lied to the police? You didn't think either of those things mattered? All this evidence that linked *her* to *this* house—the soil from our front garden; the Tesco receipt, the clothes? Even when they suspected *me,* even when they arrested me, took me to a police station, put me in a cell, and kept me there overnight." I have raised my voice. I can't stop myself. "You didn't come back and sort it out. You let them think *I* did it."

He begins to bite his hand. I pull it away from his mouth. He has started weeping again. "I couldn't," he says. "I couldn't tell the police." The words are only just decipherable.

"Why?"

He shakes his head.

"You need to tell me," I say.

A long silence and then finally: "I was there." His hands cover his face. "The night she died. I was there."

"Tell me," I say again. Gently, I take his hands away.

He puts them on his head, presses them down hard. "I did use the gym. I did go to Nobu and for a nightcap at the Dorchester. I was with people most of the time. But there's a window, a forty-minute gap, when I wasn't with anyone. Bob thought I was on a call, but I wasn't. I left Nobu and cycled to her flat. She hadn't been answering her phone, and I was worried."

"And you fancied a quickie?"

"No. Gaby. Don't." He turns to me, his face anguished. "She wasn't in, and I didn't want to come home so I cycled back. I thought I would have to come clean. I thought the police would find out, but no one seemed to have noticed I was gone for a bit. I'd got away with it. And no one knew, you see. I'd used a pay-as-you-go phone, and I destroyed it. We always met in secret. I hadn't told anyone. Not even Pete. I was scared. It didn't look good, Gaby. My girlfriend—dead—and me outside her flat the night she died. I wouldn't stand a chance."

"So you thought life could go on as if nothing had happened?"

"No. I tried. God, that weekend in Brighton, the hell of trying to pretend. I cooked up that work trip, just to get away. I needed time to think."

"To grieve?"

"I suppose. Yes. I only had one meeting. I could have been back in thirty-six hours. I sat for hour upon hour in my hotel room, or random bars, drinking myself into oblivion, trying to pull myself to-gether, trying to work out what to do. The strain of those phone calls, pretending everything was fine, making up boat trips and karaoke."

We stare at each other until at last I say, "So who killed her, Philip, if it wasn't you?"

He lets out a bellow, like childbirth. "I don't know. An old boyfriend. Tolek? His jealousy drove her mad. Or someone she met? There was another English bloke before me. Everywhere she went, men fell for her. She wasn't that pretty, but you couldn't take your eyes off her. She just had something, you know." He lets out another terrible sob. "Or some nutter? I don't want to . . . But not me, Gaby. I promise you, not me. Please believe me."

"Ssh."

"She pulled me in, Gaby, enchanted me. It was like a dream. I wasn't thinking straight."

I stroke his hair. I wish he wasn't saying this, trying to absolve himself. It grates.

"It's okay," I say.

His limbs loosen a little. He nestles into the pillow. A corner of the duvet is free of our bodies, and he subtly nudges it so it covers his shoulder.

"You sent her flowers and bought her expensive presents— Agent Provocateur. You gave her my clothes."

He puts his hand over his face. I can't quite hear what he says.

I don't pull the hand off this time. I just say, "Did you really love her?"

"I did, but it was more—"

"More of a physical thing?"

I'm feeding him his lines. He nods.

"Even with that tattoo? Tasteful as those cherries were. I don't think of you as a tattoo man."

"She was different. It was all different. I was a different person when I was with her."

He is removing himself from the equation, shucking off responsibilty. It wasn't him. It was "a different person."

He puts his hand on my face now, cups a whole cheek. "I'm sorry, Gaby. I never wanted to hurt you."

"Well . . ." I breathe in soap and coffee and the salty lemon scent of his body. Then I can't think of anything else.

A pause. "I should go to the police," he says.

I put my hand over his to keep it where it is. My tears are catching in his fingers. "Millie will be here any minute," I say into his skin. "Go later. Maybe even tomorrow. What's a few more hours? Let's have our day."

He releases a sigh like a shudder. He looks at me with hope and trust. I hold his life, the beating heart of it, in my hands. "Where would I be without you?" he says.

We lie for a little while longer. I don't know how long. I lose track of time. Maybe it is only minutes when noises erupt below our window. Car doors, laughter, voices, the clattering of gates.

I leave Philip in the bedroom and go downstairs and open the front door wide, and there is Millie, in shorts and bare feet, her face rosy with country walks and fresh air and home cooking. And coming up behind her is dear Robin, cheerful and no-nonsense, holding a handful of muddy rhubarb.

We hug and shriek a little. Millie jumps up and down and makes a cross face at my hair and Robin makes a dash to the loo because her pelvic floor is shot to shreds. I hold the rhubarb and wonder what I'm supposed to do with it. Then Philip is on the stairs, his cheeks silvery with cold water, and Millie gives a yelp when she sees him, and he comes down and picks her up and swings her round and kisses and hugs her, a noise in the back of his throat like a growl. Then Robin emerges from the loo, still zipping up her jeans, and says something about a family reunited, and for a moment I forget about it all and think everything will be all right.

• • •

We have our day. We roast chicken, which Millie is too full of sausages and chips to eat, and we play Racing Demon, a holiday treat. We go for a walk, over to the playground, and Philip sits next to me on the bench, his fingers coiled in mine, protection from the nudges and the stares. They don't know me, these people. They think they do, but they don't. You have to make more of an effort when you're not on the telly, when you're no one in particular. As soon as this is over, I'm going to work harder at things like this.

Later, at home, I find a recipe, in the shiny cookbooks, for a cake with rhubarb, and we curl up on the sofa, the three of us, and eat it watching *House of Anubis*. Philip tries to stay awake. Millie taps him when his head lolls. His eyes seep. His nose runs. Hay fever, or jet lag, or grief. I'm watching him dissolve.

When his BlackBerry chirrups, he doesn't notice, or perhaps he doesn't care.

My phone doesn't stop: Philip's parents back from their cruise, with tales of the Ancient World and Modern Plumbing. Can they come at the weekend? Is that okay? Their heads are full of Sparta and Byzantium, the lovely couple they met from West Byfleet. I want to tell them everything that has happened while they've been out of contact, but I don't. A neighbor will tell them, or one of their friends. It can wait. Texts and missed calls from Jack I don't read or return. My voicemail fills and overflows. Everything turns to liquid.

Robin gets back at 5:00 PM, flushed, her curly hair wild. The sky has darkened; thick clouds have chased her from the station. I tell her she's an allegorical representation of health and fecundity. "I'm certainly that," she says. "Doc says I'm tickety-boo down under." She gulps down a cup of tea and a slice of cake, but she's bushed, her boobs are bursting, and she's bloody desperate to get back to her baby. "What about you, little lady?" she says to Millie. "Do you really want to come back with me?"

"I want to stay with Mum and Dad," Millie says. "But I also want to go to Roxanne's party."

"We'll come and get you at the weekend," I say.

Robin heaves herself to her feet. "Are we going to do this, or are we going to do this?"

I carry Millie to the car. I feel her hot arms on my neck, her legs at my waist, her small, muscular body wrapped around mine. I belt her up and kiss her forehead and her chin and both cheeks. Philip kisses her and bends to say good-bye.

We stand and wave. I chase the car up the street, shouting, "See you in two days!" Drops of rain polka-dot the pavement. When I turn round, Philip has returned to the house. The brickwork, wet now, has darkened. He has left the front door open, and I close it behind me.

It's murky in the hall. Philip has gone upstairs. It's gloomier in the kitchen than it should be. It's not raining heavily—you need to concentrate hard on the dark patches of shrub to tell it's raining at all. A square of halogen stares down above the apple tree. I still haven't ordered blinds.

I have my finger on the light switch when Philip says, "I don't understand one thing."

"God!" I put my hand to my heart. "You gave me a shock."

He is sitting on the sofa in the shadows.

"The tattoo. How did you know about that?"

I switch on the light. The empty cushion beside him holds the shape of Millie.

"What tattoo?"

"Ania's tattoo, the one of a cherry."

I put the cups and plates in the dishwasher. I open the cupboard for the dustpan and brush to sweep cake crumbs from the floor. "I saw it, on the body. Her top was rucked up. My top"—I give him a pointed look—"which you weirdly gave her, along with all those other things. Though, actually"—I pause in my sweeping and reflect—"maybe I didn't see it. Maybe the police told me and I imagine that I saw it. In all those hours of questioning, it might have come up."

"God. Hours of questioning. I am so sorry."

"I thought they would never release me. But—hurrah—they did! And now I'm going to run you a bath."

"I'm so tired, Gabs."

"I know you are."

"I need to go to the police."

I kiss the top of his head. "Later," I say. "There will be time enough for that."

I climb the stairs to our bathroom and turn on the taps, dribbling in a capful of my precious Deep Relax. You don't need much.

He wanders in. He's so drowsy he can hardly speak. He pulls off his clothes with his back to me, his movements clumsy, eases himself into the water. "That's nice," he says.

"How about a whiskey?"

"Even better."

When he's settled, a large tumbler in his hand, I put on my tracksuit bottoms. I wish I had my Asics. My Dunlops are too jolting. I chuck them back into the cupboard and lace on Philip's Asics instead.

I stand in the doorway of the bathroom. I gaze at the face I loved. His eyelids are closing. The fatigue, and the stress, the grief: for once, he looks older than me. "I'm going for a run, my darling," I tell him.

And I leave the house.

I prefer running in the evening to the morning. It helps me sleep. I'm not good at letting the turmoil of the day rest. Not always. The rain has stopped, or perhaps it never really got started. The clouds threatened more than they delivered.

I take the path round the pond. It's wet, tacky underfoot. Even with extra socks, Philip's Asics are too big. The mud doesn't help. I can't get up any speed. I need that to run it out. We all have coping mechanisms. The slap and pound of rubber compound on tarmac and gravel and grass, that's mine.

Small flies swarm above my head. I bat them away. It can be idyllic, Wandsworth Common, in certain seasons, certain lights—a patchwork of rich greens, the pale mist of hawthorn, autumn in its bright regalia. This evening, it feels dull and flat. A supermarket cart is upended in the weeds. There's a gathering of bored geese.

I leave the pond and join the central path. A black scarf—cashmere, perhaps, though that might be the effect of raindrops on wool—hangs on a railing. A child's broken scooter sticks out of the bushes. Pieces of people. Dropped. Forgotten. Abandoned.

I keep my eye out for that bracelet. I always do.

Breathing is harder when I'm upset. It catches and tangles in my throat.

The real hell of life, someone once said, is that everyone has their reasons.

Running: I couldn't have got through this without that. The fake smiles, the brave face, the pretend family jollity, hoping it would go away. Birthday teas. Pub lunches. Date nights. Running helped release the anger. It massaged out the pain, the acid. Perhaps it would all have been different if I had been honest, confronted him at the very start, but dissimulation is my natural response, my childhood training. All those hours at the kitchen table—the life cycle of the frog, the origins of the Second World War—blocking out the drunken jags. The life lessons given by an alcoholic mother. Keep laughing and carry on.

I turn the corner. Another runner passes, elbows like knives. At the playground, two teenage girls dangle on the swings. I stop, lean forward on my knees. I try and inhale. I am not sure I can run this evening after all. I can't do it right. I can't do *anything* right. My head is throbbing, churning, my heart is beating, too fast. Is this panic? Or is my body giving out? I lean against the playground railings, try to recover.

Did he really think I didn't know? Of course I knew. Oh not at first, not when I was burying my mother, when I couldn't see for grief and guilt. It was a week or two later, when that had settled into something lower and duller, that I suspected. My husband the secret philanderer: not so much. And what gave the great lover away? A yawn. In September, a Sunday night after a weekend when Millie and I had been in Yeovil packing up my mother's flat, "shoveling shit" as Robin put it. What had he been up to, I asked, how had he spent the days? He began to answer—"I, er . . ." and then paused to open his mouth, force it out: a slow, fake yawn that played for time. "Bit of bike," he said. "Bit of work." Not lipstick on the collar. Not a blush or a long, blond hair. Philip slipped up with casual exhaustion.

I watched him carefully. Erratic in his behavior—overly loving one minute, distant the next. He disappeared at peculiar hours. His phone went straight to voicemail. He smelt odd, not of perfume, nothing so romantic, but of fried food and washing aired on radiators. One Saturday, when I didn't go to Yeovil as I had planned, he was edgy, irritable with Millie. He took a phone call in the garden.

Later he fiddled with his bike, said it needed parts.

The girls at the swings look across at me. I straighten up, run on as far as the entrance to the closed-up café.

He didn't even take the car. How stupid did he think I was? He crossed onto the common and I followed him. They met not far from here. I saw them walk toward each other and not kiss, not touch, just meet. They wandered toward the cricket pitch. The accidental brushing of their fingers. Over by the tennis courts, protected by the trees, I watched him turn, walk backward, pull her into his chest with both hands. They were a patchwork of color in the wilderness. Stillness and movement. A rearrangement of clothes.

There is a picnic table outside the café and I sit down on the bench, put my head between my knees. I fight the nausea in the back of my throat. I didn't know, until today, how they first met. So she came for an interview. To be my daughter—our *daughter's*—nanny. She has been in my house. She met Millie. The betrayal just goes on and on. Sexual jealousy is agony, but this is the real pain, so sharp you don't know what to do with it. Philip was my best friend. He knew my every secret. And yet he conspired against me in a way no one ever had. My mother let me down, but she was in the grasp of something bigger than her, an illness. But Philip did this to me of his own free will. He knew what he was doing. It was—*is*—unbearable. I rock back and forth. I trusted him, and he betrayed me. No one is really who you think they are. Everybody has different sides. Nobody cares enough to keep you safe.

I bring my head up, lean back against the wooden struts. I watch the car lights glide along Trinity Road, then across the cricket pitch, the silver-gray buttresses of Wandsworth Prison beyond.

I force myself to my feet and start running, properly now, try to pound it all out, along the bowling green, up the steps, past the tennis court hut. I want to clear my head, but I can't. I've stirred the pool.

I was pitiful, wasn't I, back then? Waiting, watching, pathetically hoping if I were kind and loving and cheerful, it would go away. I told myself a scene would make things worse. Under siege, Philip becomes entrenched. When I wanted another child, and he didn't, the more I wept, the firmer he became. In this crisis, I kept quiet. In my head, I took sanctuary in cliché: "a fling," "a bit on the side": phrases pert with insignificance and brevity. I would have done anything to keep him. The thought of life without him was unimaginable. It had to go away. But it didn't—it went on and on. At Christmas, he took long walks to "clear his head." We needed milk at funny hours. Once or twice I followed, hovered outside her grotty flat, feeling sordid, grubby, ruined by it.

I have to think it through. I have to keep going, to be sure. The week of Millie's birthday. I don't know whether he went to see Ania, or whether he was just distracted by the thought of her, but he forgot. He didn't come home. Millie blew her candles out without him. Marta and I sang and she opened her presents and I pretended everything was fine—"Busy old Dad." Our wedding anniversary. At the back of my mind, I kept thinking, "we just need time away, the two of us." Not just sex, but companionship, breakfast in bed, ordinary Sunday chat. I booked the hotel, sorted the lingerie, planned the date night to discuss it. He wouldn't come. "Take a rain check, Gabs," he said, so casual, so dismissive, as if he had stopped noticing me at all.

Despair, then. I feel it even now. Thinking about him and worrying about him for so many months, losing touch with what's real and what isn't. Blaming myself. If only I did things differently. If only . . . I was worn down by the fear of him leaving. I didn't know who I would be without him. I presented this front—this capable working mother. What a lie. I'm laughing now, into the bushes, the net of trees; the sound echoes over the railway cutting to the path on the other side. I stop abruptly. I'm going mad. I've already gone mad.

That night. Images I have buried, black and murky, rise to the surface.

I had screwed up my courage, practiced in my head. I tried out phases, fought cliché (what he "owed" me; what I was "worth"). I would be calm and gentle. I wouldn't rage. I waited. I cried. I put on his gray hoodie for the smell of him against my skin. I tried to remember what it was like when we were close. I had forgotten to be natural, how to be myself. I fantasized about him collapsing in remorse, tears, and love. I had a drink. And another. I waited. When he rang from Nobu, I was rolled tight with tension; one blow and I would break.

He wasn't coming home. All for nothing. I ran out of the house. I tore along here that night, battering the path, arms tilted and askew, my head hot. I hammered on her door, stood there, crazed and out of breath. Why did I go? To beg? To fight? I can't remember. Every time I try, I can't. All I can remember is the sight of her, standing there, with her tatty fingernails and her dyed hair, her cheap little Topshop trousers. She looked a bit like me, it's true. Not a sinister resemblance, a deeply banal one. She was just his "type." She said I "looked upset" and made me tea. I couldn't even touch it. She didn't taunt. She was sweetly apologetic, the natural condescension of the young. She told me she was sorry, but that it was too late. Phil was going to give up his job, move away, start afresh.

Phil.

"Philip doesn't like the country," I told her. "He won't go."

"He doesn't care where he is," she said, with a shake of her head. "As long as we're together. Phil wants to start a family."

"Philip doesn't need to start a family. He's already got one."

She smiled secretively. "And a baby on the way."

A baby. Another baby.

"Philip doesn't want another baby," I said. I was speaking too fast, shouting. "He doesn't want to spread himself too thin." His words in my mouth; what had I been reduced to?

"He wants this one," she said. She smoothed her hands over her flat belly. "Come! Look what he bought."

I followed her into the bedroom. It was hot in there. I couldn't breathe, and I was fighting not to cry, not in front of her. I was standing in the doorway, in my running gear, thinking about the baby, fiddling with my heat-tech top, fiddling and fiddling. It was rising in my chest, the sobbing. I was sort of panting, twisting one foot behind my leg, gasping for air, fiddling with the string in the hood of Philip's top, knotting and unknotting, and she bent to pick something up from her bed. A triangle of thong above her trousers. And when she turned, I saw she was caressing her face with a stuffed rabbit.

It was like Millie's pink rabbit, only newer.

Her expression—childlike, trusting, a woman who has always been nurtured and loved—bored into my head. And the inanity of Philip giving his mistress the same stuffed toy as his daughter. And in that moment the drawstring came loose, one side unknotted, and I had slipped it out before I even realized. It was in my hands in a single stroke, and I had moved forward and it was wound round her neck. Her fingers clutched at her own throat, grappling and digging, but I just stood there. She flailed, twisted, thrashed, and writhed. It seemed to make it worse. I held her off her feet. How light some women are. The dying, as I told Clara, are more frightening than the dead. It didn't take long—only a few minutes before her body went still and I laid her down on the pink laced duvet.

I catch my foot on a stump of root and almost fall, face forward, arms flailing. I steady just in time. I'm sobbing now. I didn't mean to kill her. I am not a bad person, though I know I have become one: I do see that. I have killed a woman. It was a chain of events. I just wanted a family of my own. It's all I ever wanted. Does that sound self-pitying? I'm sorry.

I'm muttering now. "I'm sorry. I'm sorry. I'm sorry."

Afterward, when I realized what I had done, I didn't know what to do. I howled and paced the flat. I kept going back to the body in case I was wrong, in case she was alive. I dug my nails into my hands. I scratched my own arms—Perivale noticed that. I had this feeling that I could stop time, put back the clock, that it wasn't real, and then it kept dawning over and over again that it had happened, there was nothing I could do. Even now, sometimes, I wake in the morning and there's a moment before the reality of what I have done hits me. I'll have that forever, I suppose. I hope I do. That moment of innocence is the sweetest part of my day.

I should have rung the police. I was going to. I took out my phone. And then I put it back. I thought about Millie, and a different sort of adrenaline took over. I started thinking, my thoughts racing. Would it look like a break-in, a robbery gone wrong? I paced the flat again. Was there anything to place me here? I hadn't drunk the tea: good. Had I touched anything else? Perhaps her neck. I went to the kitchen and used a tea towel to open the cupboard. I found the bleach and sprayed her with it. I tried not to look at her face, the bulge of her eyes and tongue. A glass of water, spilt. Her necklace was lying on the floor. It must have broken in the struggle. I put it in my pocket, along with the drawstring from the hoodie, sticky from her neck. I wanted to sit down, but I didn't dare. I had to act fast. I had to keep moving.

What else? What else? An hour went by, or two, or three: I lost track. All I could think of was DNA; had pictures in my head from *CSI Miami,* microscopic close-ups of the double helix. I must have left something, a fragment of skin, a drop of saliva. I wish I had known more about it: how long it survives, what it survives on. Would it matter if I had? My DNA wasn't on record, but once they found out about Philip—because they would, he would come forward as soon as he heard—once the affair was in the open, I would be a suspect. And then if my DNA was on the body . . . ?

And then suddenly an idea grew to move her out onto the common, where I could "find" her myself. That would explain my DNA. And it was better: a random mugging or a psychopathic murder. I had to hurry. I made myself look at her body again. I wasn't sure I could touch it, let alone lift it. She was light, slim, a few cells growing inside her, not a baby, not a baby, no, not a baby. I tried hoisting her over my shoulder, but a body . . . they don't talk about a dead weight for nothing. I lay her back down, her T-shirt caught under her armpit. I caught sight of the cherry tattoo on her lower back.

I thought hard, scanned the flat. If there was a pram or a buggy or a . . . and then my eyes fell on the wardrobe. Something on top of it: a hold-all, an enormous squishy suitcase on wheels. I pulled it down, and zipped it open. I picked her body up off the bed again, cradled her, and then forced her in, her arms folded, her knees bent back. I threw the bottle of bleach in there, too. I could close it almost, but not to the top. A bit of her hair got caught in the zip.

It was a quiet night, light drizzle, some big match on the television. I took the narrow chestnut path from the flats to the common; a two-hundred-meter dash, the suitcase bumping, scraping. I sobbed the whole way. It's a path people avoid at night, too dark, too spooky. And no one was out: luck, serendipity: so much of this has been about that. It must have taken three minutes to get there, the longest three minutes of my life. When I got to the trees, I had meant to lie her down gently, but in the end, in my haste, after I had torn loose the strands in the zip, I yanked her out of the case by her hair. I just left her there, on the ground, under some saplings, only a few feet from where I had seen them kiss.

I shiver and run on, past the wooded copse, back to the bowling green. I've run round this part three times this evening now. I'm stuck, entangled. I don't seem to be able to get free. I reach the little cabin where the skanky black and white cat used to live. I sit on the step. I'm still sobbing. I wish I could stop. I'm crying for her, and a bit for him, but mainly—and I'm sorry, I know it's wrong—for me.

You think you know about these things from detective books and TV dramas. It is both easier and harder. The line between living and dying, in contemplation, such an unimaginable cavern, infinite in its width and depth, is just a delicate thread in the end. It snaps like cotton. The knotting is harder. You make it up as you go. It's the little things that catch you out.

I blow my nose on the corner of my top and try to think clearly. I've made mistakes, I know. I'm close to being caught. I have been all along. I go through it again. I do it all the time. I need to be cautious, but caution slips into paranoia before you know it. Her phone: I threw its components—the battery and the casing and the SIM card, along with the bottle of bleach—into separate Dumpsters. (That's this area for you: two "refits" on every street.) For the suitcase, I chose a Dumpster piled so high with rubble, it would have been taken away the next day. The chain, I took home; I don't know why. Murderers often collect keepsakes. I've read about that. I'm just following type. But I hid it well. A house has a hundred hiding places when it comes down to it, toothcomb or no tooth-comb (how self-aggrandizing, the clichés of the job). A bag of fro-zen peas early on, and then later in the back of Philip's drawer—I liked the idea of him crushing it a little more every time he opened it—but the running machine is better. No prints—I wore Marta's latex gloves; they will just think it was Philip who wiped it clean. The Nautilus was clever. It's the sort of place men would choose, the sort of place men would look. It's easier to find there, and they will—tonight, or tomorrow morning.

A train rattles along the railway in the cutting down behind the shrubs. It vibrates up my vertebrae, under my skin.

I still had the drawstring from the hoodie, *the murder weapon,* when I got home. I scrunched it in my hands, tried to make it go away. I thought of flushing it down the loo. In the end, my hands shaking so hard I stabbed myself a million tiny times, I rethreaded it back into the hoodie. I knotted it onto a safety pin and inched it along, and then when it was all the way through I undid the knots and stretched out the neck so the drawstring disappeared into the seam. I put both his hoodie and the running trousers I had been wearing in the laundry. My own matching running top was already in there. Marta would wash and iron them by the following lunchtime—I knew that. It was a risk, but to wash them sooner would alert suspicion.

Philip came home and got into bed and I made sure our bodies didn't touch. I had to force my limbs not to twitch, my mouth not to howl, my eyes not to open. I waited until it was nearly light, and then I took my running gear and Philip's hoodie out of the dirty clothes basket, got dressed, and left the house.

The shock of seeing her again, lying in the copse where I had left her, was beyond words. The savagery of my own actions, the finality of it, the sickening spectacle of her body; it was physical, my horror. I think a part of me thought she wouldn't be there, that I had dreamed it, that it was some nauseating fantasy in my head. But I had to check, and there she was, lifeless. I had done this. She was barefoot. Her bra had come unpinged—the bra Philip gave her, though I didn't know that then. She looked so vulnerable. I forgot she was Philip's lover for a moment. She was just a young girl, someone's daughter, with the rest of her life brutally cut off.

The police came, Morrow and Perivale. Let's face it, I'm an actress by trade, not a journalist, but the shock, the desperate sadness, it wasn't faked. I managed to ask the questions I thought I should ask and the ones to which I wanted answers (the rash on her face). I went to work, got through the day. It was when Perivale came later that I began to make mistakes. I panicked. I gave him my running top, not Philip's, the one I had been wearing, in case they found the string, but it bothered me. What if the fabric was slightly different? I knew I'd touched the body, but in my terror I couldn't remember *what* I had done. Or what the right thing to *say* was. I overthought it for a moment, tried to think what a woman, a witness, in my position would remember, what she would say. The seconds ticked and it became too late to say anything.

I got the words out later, "unburied" the memory. It shouldn't have mattered, but something in the delay triggered Perivale's suspicion, a tiny thing, a mishandling of information, with exponential consequences. Or was it me? Was it my manner? I have tried so hard all along to react appropriately in every circumstance, funneling the dread and foreboding I felt so much of the time, the blind fear, into the sort of shock and outrage an innocent person might project. All that evidence he trotted out, the photographs laid out like trophies. How hard my brain had to work. The soil: I should have swept Ania's floor, that was stupid. The cuttings: how peculiar of Ania to have squirreled them away—keepsakes of her own. The clothes: I was baffled by them. It didn't occur to me that Philip would have rifled so creepily through my wardrobe. The secondhand shop, Marta, and her eBay: both seemed plausible explanations. Reminders of her pregnancy were like a blow to the head. And then Perivale produced the credit card receipt. Philip had used mine by mistake: that was obvious. But what possible explanation could I come up with? Did Perivale see the agony in my eyes, behind the flippant comments, the off-key jokes? Was that what it was?

Damp from the step has seeped into my tracksuit bottoms. I shift along the bench. I feel like lying facedown. Other people's emotion, other people's suffering, it's gotten to be too much. Christa's sadness, Tolek's anger. Someone dies and it isn't over. The misery goes on and on.

The weekend he couldn't get hold of her, when I knew she was dead, and he didn't, how twitchy he was, how desperate. The lunch with his parents: I might have been in hell, but I kept it together, just as I kept smiling, kept my face on, at work. I loathed him for ignoring his father, his self-indulgence. I remember thinking, I'm glad she's dead. The day he found out was different, the phone conversation in which he could hardly speak. When I saw him in his office that night, staring blankly at his screen, the anger went, consumed by remorse and pity. I had to force myself just to stand there, not to wrap him in my arms.

I expected Philip to go to the police. I watched him out of the corner of my eye, waiting, but he didn't. I was tense with anticipation. When he stayed quiet, I had to adjust, think ahead, keep my brain turning. And once I was arrested, Philip *had* to keep away. I longed for him with every nerve in my body, but I had to play it down or there was a danger he would rush back. He would come armed with lawyers and injunctions—but it was too risky. He would have told the police everything, perhaps even suspected me himself. Singapore played into my hands. As long as he was out of the picture, I didn't have a motive.

I manage to get to my feet and immediately duck down. A man is hovering by the café, peering across. Has he heard me scream or sob? Has he seen me? I try and stay still, but my whole body shudders. I cover my eyes.

Imaginary voices, creaking boards. The police, the hacks, I could cope with them, but the feeling of being spied on, followed, the pranks played by guilt to keep itself diverted, is driving me insane. My stalker didn't exist. He was a cry for help, a failed bid for sympathy at the height of Philip's affair. Philip hardly noticed. I brought him out again last week, one last flight of terror, the DVD purchased with the Polos in the corner shop in Putney, to divert attention, try and convince Perivale someone was out to get me. All those suspects I kept finding, throwing them in my path like meat before a dog: Marta, Tolek, the man in the red Renault. All of them innocent. The police kept on coming.

A sudden movement in the bushes—a bird rises, squawking. My heart pounds. The thing is, Perivale *is* out to get me.

A vibration in my pocket. My phone.

Jack.

I switch it to silent. I stand and scan the area. No sign of the man by the café. He seems to have gone. I've got to pull myself together. I've got to keep going. I can't give up. I haven't got much time.

I used Jack at first—a despairing response to the trap I was in. Was he using me, or not? I needed to investigate and I couldn't do it alone. A sympathetic write-up was an extra bonus. Ania had friends, people she might have talked to, employees; I had to find out if anyone knew about Philip. Choosing Jack was random. I wanted him to help me, but I didn't want him to be too clever, too good at his job. I watched and listened, considered everything he said and did, adjusted my opinion by a million daily calibrations. I had to be in control. It was fine at first—he seemed a little lackluster in his interest, had other work to follow through. But there were difficult moments. He was both more sentimental and sharper than I realized. He remembered names—Caroline Fletcher's, Millie's, and Clara's—too promptly for my comfort. He knew Philip was in Singapore. There was even a moment down by the river, when I thought he'd guessed.

I liked Jack. I *like* him. He is gentle and funny and straightforward. And the heart-rending thing is, he likes me. He knows things, too. I told him. In the restaurant, I drank too much. I opened my mouth, let him see into the dark morass of my soul. Here's the odd thing: it drew him closer, made him more interested. And perhaps I began to fall for him, with all the loss of control and dignity that that implies.

Shifts and adjustments; they've been needed all along. As soon I discovered Christa knew Ania had another man, "the baby father," I tried to head Jack off. I couldn't risk him getting any closer to the truth. But he was out of control. He'd gone rogue, passionate in his determination to prove my innocence, meeting Tolek, Hannah Morrow, and her loose lips. And then whatever he did to get the diary from Christa—charm and threats. The diary is the clincher. Philip will be named in there. Down in black and white. Even if he doesn't go to the police himself, the truth is out.

This is the end. And the ironic thing is: Jack did it for me. He ruined my life out of kindness. It's all gone wrong. You make it up as you go along. You have to make the best of what you have.

I'm calmer now. Altogether calm. I have to think. I have to act.

I start walking in the direction of the house. I must pace myself. It's busier out now, a couple of dog walkers on their evening constitutional, a gaggle of kids horsing about on the parallel bars.

We used to come out here, Philip and I, when we first moved in, stroll out over the common when we got back from work. We would link arms and talk about our days, my hopes, his ambition. We would do the house up, when we had the money, dig out the basement. "Fill it with children," I remember saying.

On bright evenings, we would sit by the bowling green, coax out the skanky cat.

Philip's hair curled about his collar. I remember watching his hands as he stroked the cat's white throat. Once from his pocket, he produced a piece of ham, saved from lunch.

I lean against a tree. I can't remember this now. It's a snapshot from another world. It's all too late. Philip isn't that person anymore. He has changed too much. That person has gone. I have to wrench my mind away. I must get this straight. I mustn't get this wrong. No more mistakes.

Think. *Sort*.

Alibi. He cycled down here. He was outside her flat. His alibi has holes.

Motive. She was pregnant, threatening to tell me. Or seeing another man—Tolek? Or blackmailing him? Several possible motives.

Evidence. My DNA can be explained. I found the body. It is my contamination. The clothes, the credit card receipt, the mud: they link to the house—to Philip—as I have said all along. The police will have the diary now. One last niggle, one last obstacle that might trip me up. The most recent evidence from the flat: what is it?

I take out my phone and call Jack. He wants to know if I'm all right. There is alarm in his voice. "I am," I say. "I'm fine. It's going to be okay." I tell him I will ring him back when I know what's happening. "No, I'm not in any danger. I promise."

He has given the diary to Morrow, he tells me; she's finding a translator. And the new evidence, I ask, from Ania's flat: did he ask her what it was?

"Nothing interesting," he says, almost conversationally. "She said it was a bracelet. Some old broken bracelet."

A bracelet. My bracelet. It snapped when I killed her, slipped into the folds of the sheet, or down behind the mattress. My DNA is on it, but so is Philip's. I think about his bent head as he leaned to fasten the clasp. A man who would steal his wife's clothes to give to his mistress. What's one bracelet more? I can deal with the bracelet. I'd been dreading a tissue, dropped from my sleeve. There would have been no explanation for that.

So the police have the diary. There's no going back from that.

Jack is still talking. He says something about he wishes I'd rung earlier, how he's been out of his mind with worry.

"I've been out of my mind, too," I say.

I lean against the wall, just outside the alley. I look up at the trees. Do people change? I think they do. Philip is not the same person. It makes it easier to think that. And I have changed, too. I must get home. I don't have long.

Philip is still in the bath. He's in the gaping depths of sleep—the jet lag, the Deep Relax, the packet of antihistamines dissolved in his whiskey. The tumbler glints under the bath. It will have fallen from his hand. On the mat, a single ice cube melts. I hope he drank every drop. When we talked earlier it would have been better if he had been less selfish, thought more about poor Ania. I didn't like all those excuses, that shifting of blame. He was lucky to have her. I know that now. She deserved more. We both did. But I don't want it to hurt. I don't want him to feel pain.

I'm wearing gloves. My hands are shaking so hard I can hardly hold the blade. A vertical line, I know that from Dr. Janey on *Mornin' All*. I grip one wrist to stop the tremor, and it helps. It isn't hard once I've made the first cut. There's barely a splash on the floor at all.

A suicide. PC Morrow had said, "You get a lot of them in this job."

I curl up on the bathroom floor, clutching my knees. I cry as silently as I can. I feel the blood pumping in my own veins. This is worse, so much worse than I imagined. I'd have done anything to keep him, and I did. But nothing was enough. I'll take off his Asics in a minute. The St. Christopher is waiting for the police in the running machine. The murder weapon? I have pulled the ends back through the seam of the hoddie and knotted them, so they dangle back where they should. And the suicide note: he wrote his own—the confession letter. So neatly divided, page one from page two. So easy to lose page one, and leave page two sitting on the bed. It's all there. Words, phrases, stories, lies. How many mistakes have I made? Are there more to come? All I can do is hope.

I will wait a little while, here in the bathroom, until the horror passes. My face is pressed into my hand; I can feel the imprint of my fingers on my cheek. Soon I will take my hand away and I will scream.

ACKNOWLEDGMENTS

For sharing their knowledge and experience, thank you to Matt and Vanya Nunn, Ben Smith, Hilary Kirkbride, Diana Eden, Emma Smith, and Jill Mellor. For guidance and advice: Francesca Dow, Derry Clinch, Lucy Akrill, Lucy Horton, and Gill Hornby. Much gratitude is due to Judith Murray at Greene & Heaton; Grainne Fox at Fletcher & Co; Ruth Tross at Hodder; and to Emily Bestler and Kate Cetrulo at Simon & Schuster—all of whom made this possible. Most of all, thank you to Giles Smith, who helped in everything.

Read an excerpt from

REMEMBER ME THIS WAY

SABINE DURRANT

Available in hardcover from Emily Bestler Books/Atria

Zach

I stood on the common and watched her up in the school library. The lights were on and she passed by the window several times. The third time, she leaned her elbows on the sill and looked out. She seemed to stare straight at me, though I knew I was hidden, my back pressed against the tree, my face concealed behind a web of branches. I had it in mind to step forward when a man came into view behind her and, as she turned, I saw her laugh, a chink of white throat. I imagined his lips then in the dip of her neck, where the vein throbs, her eyes closing, his hands on the swell of her breasts.

If I know for sure that she's moved on, that she's forgotten what we had, I'll kill her.

She has no one to blame but herself.

CHAPTER ONE

Lizzie

February half-term, 2013

A deep breath. Petrol, manure, the mineral tang of salt. I'm not that far from the sea, even here. My face is damp from the drizzle and the spray of tires on wet road. I'm gripping the flowers in both hands now, like a bride. I chose hyacinths, though I wasn't sure—blue ones only. Zach told me you should only ever have one color in a bunch. I've wrapped the stems in wet paper towels and secured them in a small freezer bag. Either I made the paper too wet or there's a small hole in the bag, because water is seeping out. It's dripping down to my elbow.

Over the road, I can see a slope of grass, a copse of blunt trees, the shadow of a hill behind. Above that, sky the color of dirty sheep, darker patches, a dribble of falling sun in the distance as the cold afternoon closes in. I am concentrating hard on all these things, because I know that somewhere in the corner of my vision, across the carriageway and away to the left, is the spot. But I'm not going to look. Not yet.

It is Valentine's Day, exactly a year since my husband's car crash, and I am two hundred miles from home beside an A-road in the middle of Cornwall. This trip is an ending or a beginning—I'm not quite sure which. It's time to move on. People tell me that all the time. I'm trying to believe them.

I pick my moment between the streaming cars and run. When I reach the far side, I look back at the lay-by where my Nissan Micra sits, rocking in the backdraft of the passing lorries. My dog watches me from the side window. I've had a feeling since I parked that I'm being shadowed. It's probably just the remoteness of the place; so many people driving past, no one else stopping. Or it's guilt—guilt about all sorts of things, but mostly that I should have come sooner.

It's conventional to visit the scene of a fatal accident, to leave flowers: all those lampposts decked with cellophane where poor cyclists have been killed. It's less usual to leave it this long. The night it happened, when PC Morrow came to the door, she would have brought me here straightaway. The patrol car was waiting. My sister Peggy stopped me. She told Morrow I needed to go home with her, not drive five hours to a wet, windswept Cornish roadside, to smoke and wreckage. It would be insane, she said. I could go another time. Zach was gone. There was nothing I could do.

And it wasn't as if I didn't know what happened. Morrow, fresh from her Family Liaison training, went over it again and again. I understood about the lethal combination: the sea fog and the wet road, the sharp bend, the soft-top roof, the bottles of his favorite distillery-only whiskey on the passenger seat, the oil paints, the solvent-soaked rags in the boot, the thick trunk of the tree—the disastrously placed tree.

I kept putting it off. People understood. Cornwall was Zach's favorite place. He had a house down there that would need sorting out; they assumed I would get to it in my own time. But then, in the days and weeks that followed, I began to dread it—seeing the emptiness of his bungalow, feeling the loss of him all over again.

I feel a shiver up my back. The clouds are thickening. A gust whips my coat. I must hurry up, get this done, return to the car before it gets any darker. A motorbike, overtaking a lorry, howls. I step back. This thing that had seemed so necessary when I was two hundred miles away has started to feel mad, reckless.

I pick my way along the narrow crumbling shoulder between the white line and the barrier. One foot in front of the other. That's how you get through—everyone tells you that. One step at a time. I focus as hard as I can on the littered ground: a hamburger wrapper, smeared with ketchup; a used condom, oddly bright in the polluted grass. A polystyrene cup, lodged in the barrier, flips and flaps every time a car passes. As I near the bend, a horn blares—in anxious warning maybe, or perhaps in astonishment at the madwoman in the road with her hands full of flowers.

When I get there, I'll put the hyacinths down flat at the base. Is that right? Or do they need to be higher? Perhaps I should have thought more about it, brought Scotch tape. Zach would know— though he'd hate me for coming. He would take it as an insult, not a tribute. He hated sentimentality. He didn't even like anniversaries. He'd think I was giving in to cliché, or to the advice of others. "Who've you been listening to, Lizzie Carter?"

I can sense the tree's form now, its arms veined against the gray sky. I reach the frayed slash in the hedgerow. Pale green shoots on the tip of each twig. It's callous, the way this hawthorn has regenerated, the way it has bounced back. I glance behind once more and then I hoist myself over the crash barrier, and there it is: the tree, an oak, oddly dignified despite the deep gash in its gnarled bark.

Zach's tree. I reach out to touch it, to feel the rough grooves of the bark with my fingers. I rest my head against it. My eyes fill.

My friend Jane didn't think I should have come on my own today. I made her laugh to prove I could cope. I put on a funny voice and talked about my "ceremonial visit," my "ritual deposit of floral tribute"—phrases from the self-help book my sister gave me. I didn't tell her the whole truth—how complicated my grief is, how murky, how, more than anything, this is about laying ghosts.

Is all grief so confused, or is it just my particular misshapen form of it? There are days I accept his death and I move through the world as if underwater. Ordinary tasks, like filling the dishwasher, or sending off bills, feel brutal and empty. I resent the pigeons nesting outside the bedroom window, the schoolkids at the start of the term in their new uniform. I can be sideswiped by the smallest of things. I saw a white bike helmet on the head of a man cycling down Northcote Road last week and a wave hit me with such strength, my knees buckled. I had to crouch for a bit on the pavement outside Capstick Sports. Other days, I forget. I am almost carefree, relieved, and then I am overcome by feelings of such intense shame I don't know where to put myself. I succumb to lethargy and depression. I put things off.

Standing here, I feel close to him in a pure way. This was the point of coming. His death feels real for the first time. I must let him go, hard as it is, because, despite everything, he was the love of my life. Peggy is right. He was the man I have spent most of my life loving—the most minutes, the most hours, the most days, the most time. I close my eyes, blink my tears away, and wonder if I can now let my restless thoughts lie.

Something crackles beneath my foot, and I look down.

Propped against the roots is a bouquet of flowers. Casablanca lilies, formally wrapped in cellophane, secured with a large purple ribbon.

I step back. Another accident in the same place: that's my first thought. A black spot. The curve of the road, and the unfortunate lay of the land. Another night of fog, perhaps. More rain.

I'm disconcerted. I don't know where to put my hyacinths. The lilies look so professional and important. I stand there, wondering what to do. I'm not sure Zach, despite his contempt, would want to share. So it's a moment before I even see the note. It's white. Someone has drawn a large heart with a name—I tilt my head sideways: *XENIA*—spelled out around it. And at the top, in big black letters, it reads: FOR ZACH.

And for a moment, honestly, I think: what a coincidence. Someone else called Zach has crashed and died here. Did they, to use PC Morrow's verb, "fireball" too?

And then, as the truth settles, I lay the flowers down meekly, on the ground. I rise and, in a trance, pass again through the gap in the hedge, over the crash barrier, and I'm heading along the road the way I came, empty-handed, head down. It's only when I look up that I see another car—a silver SUV, right up close behind the Micra, tight against its bumper.

A knot begins to press at the top of my spine. I try to run back across the road, but my legs feel weighted, drugged. Cars are coming from behind. A horn blares. My skirt is flapping, trails of scarf whip around my face. Brakes squeal, another horn sounds. A rush of air and spray.

I fumble at the car door, hurl myself into the seat, greeted by the dog, his wiry lurcher body, licking and wriggling and trying to get away from me all at the same time. In the rearview mirror I watch the SUV pull out, catch the hunched form of the driver wrestling the wheel. He must have stopped to check directions, or take a call. Mustn't he?

Seen in the mirror, my eyes are red-rimmed. A scratch has appeared across my cheek. I rub the top of Howard's head, roll my fingers under his collar and dig them into the folds around his neck. I am trying not to cry.

A hand-drawn heart. Xenia. He never mentioned a Xenia.

I feel a sharp ache of jealousy, mixed with the old longing, but I am aware also for the first time of its opposite: a slipping of responsibility. Someone else loved him. I have a taste at the back of my throat, clean and metallic, and, despite everything, I realize it's relief.

. . .

The Internet played Cupid. I like to be up front about that. My sister Peggy, who cares more about appearances than I do, decided early on that we shouldn't. Pretend it began with a chance encounter at the supermarket. "Tell people you bumped into each other by the fresh fruit," she said, "reaching for the same Fairtrade pineapple or what have you."

"Or at the ready-made meals for one," I said.

"Picking over the Mr. Brains Pork Fingers," said Zach. "Or what have you."

I was wary at first. I couldn't think what he saw in me. But at that moment, in Peggy's kitchen, watching him charm my sister, the "what have you" already a private joke between us, I let myself fall in love.

Jane, happily married to her childhood sweetheart, had encouraged me to sign up. Since we first met at sixth form college, apart from a brief period in my twenties she had never known me not single. We worked at the same school—it was Jane who put me forward for the job in the library—and she nagged every break time. "It's not like it used to be," she said. "No stigma. You just need to pick a website attached to a broadsheet newspaper. You'll get the right kind of person there. You know"—she made a rolling gesture with her hands, spinning delicacy from snobbery—"educated." Jane went to university and sometimes forgets that I didn't.

For my profile, I wanted to write: dowdy librarian, few qualifications, main carer for parent with dementia, very little romantic experience. Jane had other ideas. My friends describe me as an outgoing and fun-loving world traveler, she wrote, batting me away from the screen. Equally comfortable in jeans and a little black dress.

"I don't even own a black dress."

She tutted dismissively. "Who cares?"

Zach was my sixth date. An artist, he lived in Brighton, way beyond my prescribed five-mile radius, so I almost didn't meet him. On the phone, he suggested a walk. They tell you to avoid that sort of interaction; better to meet in a public place. He had already showed himself a rule breaker. The others had engaged in a series of emails in which personality-revealing issues were debated—country life versus town, sexual excitement versus companionship. He just asked if he could ring me. Plus he used his real name right away, not "Lookin'forluv_007," say, but Zach Hopkins.

In his photograph he wasn't skiing, or braced in front of a vintage car. He didn't have his arms around a German shepherd. His picture was black-and-white, out of focus, shot at a low speed, taken from above, his mouth half open, a slight frown, the puzzled concentration of a person deciphering a crossword. The picture looked artless, picked at random, though as I would find out, nothing was ever artless or random with Zach.

I said yes to the walk. I don't think I hesitated. His low, steady voice; his air, very slightly ironic, of cutting to the chase. Already I was enthralled, knocked off course by his certainty.

He caught the train from Brighton to Clapham Junction, and I waited for him nervously outside the new entrance at the top. It was November, overcast, with a light chill in the air—but it wasn't cold. He was wearing a Russian fur hat and a heavy coat over a baggy linen suit. As we set off toward the common, me tugging at Howard to stop him from leaping up at the hat, he told me it had taken a long time to choose his outfit. "I wanted to impress you with my natural sophistication. You are, after all, a world traveler." He gave a small bow. "I was also pursuing a note of eccentricity, an oddity about which we could reminisce. I wanted us to be able to look back and say, 'Remember that fur hat you wore on our first date. What were you thinking?' With the added advantage"—he paused to strike a pose—"I thought the trench made me appear more muscular."

I found it hard to talk because I was so overwhelmed by how handsome he was. The breadth of his shoulders, the blue intensity of his eyes, the stooped height of him. Halfway through my previous date, a coffee in Starbucks with Mr.NiceGuy, a telecoms engineer from Crystal Palace, I had caught sight of the two of us in a mirror. Our rounded shoulders, our bland and yet vulnerable expressions. We looked like two turtles without their shells. I couldn't think what Zach was doing here. Or why he would waste any time with me. The way he spoke, too, the self-conscious theatricality and the slight nervousness behind it, the accelerated intimacy that might have been ironic or might not. He was the opposite of shell-less turtle, the opposite of bland.

"You seem quite muscular to me," I said eventually.

We hadn't even walked as far as the traffic lights across the South Circular when he reached for my hand, stuffing it inside his pocket along with his own.

I remember that more than anything—the rough warmth of his fingers, the dryness I was to discover came from oil paint and white spirit, the cracks across his palm. I remember that more than his volubility, or the heavy overcoat, or the ridiculous hat. He didn't told my hand stiffly, either. He rubbed it as we walked, massaging it back and forth with his thumb, as if testing the flesh.

Later, when I knew more about him, when he'd explained about his childhood, the problems he had with trust, when he had gazed so deeply into my eyes I felt as if my insides were melting, he told me it wasn't loneliness that had led him to the Internet. In the normal run of things, he met single women all the time. He was in search of a new beginning, that was all. He just wanted to start again.

. . .

I turn the key in the ignition and pull out. The traffic is heavy. It's the dull end of a Saturday afternoon, locals are heading away from a soccer match. Dusk is beginning to roll out across the fields. I still have twenty miles to drive from here and I promised Jane, who knows how much I am dreading opening the door to Zach's holiday house, that I would reach it before dark.

I keep going the long way—the Bodmin bypass and the main road into Wadebridge; two sides of a triangle. It's the route Zach used to take to Gulls before he discovered the shortcut. A year ago, according to Morrow's analysis, Zach missed the junction and turned round at the next roundabout. Morrow said he'd probably been drinking. He would definitely have been tired, out late the night before with an art dealer in Exeter, a bad night in a B and B, and then a long day with his paints on the moors.

I think, before I can stop myself, about the last time I saw him—the morning before he died. We were in our small kitchen in Wandsworth. The radio was on, broadcasting the results of a by-election in Hampshire. I was late for work, wary of him, shrugging on my coat, finding a lead for the dog, stuffing on my hat. But as I passed by the door, he reached out and grabbed my sleeve. His pupils were smaller, the irises a lighter blue. His mood had changed. "I love you," he said intensely, tugging me closer. "You do know, don't you?"

"I do," I said. I never doubted that.

"Because I do," he said. "I do love you."

He kissed me full on the mouth. I tasted coffee, and mint, and last night's whiskey. I felt myself sink, yielding, as I always had. My stomach clenched. Tears began to prick. If he had moved his lips to brush the hollow of my neck, I'd have gone upstairs with him, however late I was for school, however scared I was.

I said: "I'm sorry the chicken had mushrooms in it."

His voice was soft. "It's just I thought you knew."

I said: "I should have remembered. And I'm sorry I was late home. Peggy was in a state about the baby."

"She's got you round her little finger," he said.

Howard came up then and nudged my elbow. I scratched behind his ears. He hadn't been well and I put my hand to his chest, checking.

Zach looked away. "You love that dog more than me."

"I don't."

He rearranged the coffeepot and his coffee cup on the table so the handles faced the same way. He aligned the teaspoon on the saucer. "Do you promise?"

I'd been kneeling and I stood up, forcing myself to laugh. I had already decided to leave. I had written the letter and posted it. It would be waiting for him in Cornwall. I'd sent it there because I thought it would be better if he were a long way away when he read it. I was hoping this last breakfast would be normal. But my voice sounded too high, strangulated, the words squeezed dry on my tongue. "I promise I don't love the dog more than you."

I spoke to him twice more before he died—once on the phone that night and once late the following afternoon. I wanted to hear his voice one more time. He was still on Dartmoor when I rang, at a point called Cosdon, painting a run of ancient stone tors. Bleak and funereal, he said, stretching into the distance like unmarked graves. He was after a dying light. He would reach the bungalow after dark. I told him to be careful on the last unlit stretch of road. It was the last time I spoke to him.

I pull off the dual carriageway, slow down, head over the bridge. The road narrows to a single lane. I put my lights on. I stay under the speed limit. I always do. Zach said I drive like an old woman. It's the sort of thing I try to remember, his fondness for a casual insult, the way his jokes could tip into something nastier. I hope it will make me miss him less.

It doesn't work.

You can love and hate someone at the same time. You can so pity them it's like a fist in your stomach, be so resentful you want to hit them. They can be the best thing that ever happened to you, and the worst. You can have thoughts of leaving them, and yet the memory of their skin, the pads of their fingers across your rib cage . . . these can take your breath away, even after a year.

The letter will still be there at the house. It has sat unopened for a whole year. I imagine it buried under the pizza flyers and the TV license reminders, the Electoral Roll brown envelopes.

Thank God he died before he read it. That's one thing to be grateful for. He never learned of my betrayal.

When I get there I am going to burn it.

I change gears for the hill. The car jerks. Howard, curled next to me, doesn't lift his head from his paws.

I have driven past the holiday park, and caught, through a hedge-row, my first velvet glimpse of sea, when I see headlights glaring in my rearview mirror. Undipped, right up close. I am on a slight incline and I accelerate until the lights have receded. Stupid idiot, I think, but then the lights are back. Dazzling, flashing. The car is on my bumper. Its horn is sounding. I think of the silver SUV in the lay-by. Is this an SUV? I can't see anything else, not the sea, not the banks, not the road, just these insistent, blazing lights, and I've started driving faster and faster, hurtling down the hill toward the village until I reach the farm shop. I skid into the entrance and screech to a halt.

The car zooms past and is gone. I wait for a moment. Howard has got to his feet and is nosing at the window. It is dark out, the vegetable racks loom like gallows, and suddenly everything is very still.

The self-help books with their formal stages of grief, they expect a standard trajectory: shock, disbelief, bargaining, anger, depression, final acceptance. I think I've got jammed. The one Peggy gave me,

The Flowering of Your Passing, had a chapter on "pathological grief." It's when a bereaved person finds it impossible to move on. I think pathological grief might be what I've got.

No one is out to get me. It's pathological. Survivor's guilt. Leaver's guilt. Unfinished business.

If I had stolen the lilies, I could have them with me now. I would touch them, rub their dusty satin between my fingers, breathe their sickly scent and know that I hadn't made them up.

It's a short drive from here, along a web of rough roads that follow the contour of the hill. Gulls is on the outside of this network, close to the edge of the cliff where the properties begin to run out. I put on the radio and rattle the last pockmarked stretch of journey, singing thinly to Taylor Swift.